Just as she reached the porch steps, her grandfather came out of the house.

'What the hell's going on out here?' He frowned when he saw Eden.

She shook off his questions. 'You've got to get a doctor, an ambulance. He's been shot—'

'Who's been shot? Vince?' He bulled his way past her and headed straight for the truck.

'It isn't Vince.' Eden ran after him, reaching him as he opened the passenger door and peered in, the dome light clearly illuminating Jeff's deathly pale face and the darkening blood stains all over the front of his shirt.

'He's bleeding bad,' Eden said when he bent over him. 'I tried to stop it, but . . .'

Her grandfather turned, a stunned and hopeless look on his face. 'He's dead.'

'No.' Numbly, Eden shook her head, needing to deny it. 'You're wrong. You've got to be wrong. He's alive. I tell you, he's alive!'

Frantic, she tried to push past him into the cab, but her grandfather caught her back and turned her away from it.

'He's dead, Eden,' he repeated.

'No.' Her voice broke into a sob.

Also by Janet Dailey

Notorious

Janet Dailey

WARNER BOOKS

A *Warner* Book

Published by arrangement with HarperCollins Publishers, Inc.
New York, New York USA

First published in Great Britain in 1996
by Little, Brown and Company
This edition published by Warner Books 1997

Copyright © Janet Dailey 1997

The moral right of the author has been asserted.

A CIP catalogue record for this book
is available from the British Library.

ISBN 0 7515 1734 8

Typeset in Palatino by
Palimpsest Book Production Limited,
Polmont, Stirlingshire
Printed and bound in Great Britain by
Clays Ltd, St Ives plc.

Warner Books
A division of
Little, Brown and Company (UK)
Brettenham House
Lancaster Place
London WC2E 7EN

Notorious

1

The town of Friendly, Nevada, shimmered in the heat haze of an August afternoon. The distorting waves were kind to the time-ravaged buildings that flanked the main road through town, wrapping them in a veil that hid the crumbling and peeling of age. A battered, bullet-scarred sign on the town's outskirts claimed a population of seventy-two, but the number of boarded-up storefronts and abandoned buildings made that number suspect.

A lone pickup truck with Texas tags limped into a combination service station, garage, and welding shop. Road dust caked the truck's black exterior and steam hissed from beneath its hood.

Inside the station, the clunky *ding-ding* from the gas hose bell roused Hoague Miller from his contemplation of a calendar photograph picturing a mountain lake reflecting snow-capped peaks. He rocked forward in his torn office chair to look out, indifferent to the squeals of protest the chair made at the shifting of his nearly three hundred pounds.

A stranger stepped out of the truck, tall and trimly muscled. A straw cowboy hat shaded a face that was all lean planes, hard angles, and that had the beginnings of a five o'clock shadow. The stranger paused in the furnace-like temperature of late midday, then moved to the front of his truck with the slow, rolling gait of a cowboy.

Strangers were rare in Friendly. It was too far off the beaten path, accessible only by a graveled road that the highway department remembered to oil every few years. Most of the new maps didn't even bother to list the town anymore.

Impelled by curiosity, Hoague Miller maneuvered his considerable bulk out of the chair and headed out to the pumps, bypassing the scattered innards of an ancient Jeep that waited to be put back together. Only a fool or a cowboy worked in this heat, and Hoague Miller was neither.

The tall stranger had the hood of his pickup raised. More steam bellowed out. If he noticed Hoague Miller waddling toward him, jowls swaying, he gave no sign as he swiveled to idly survey the town.

A dustdevil came out of the sage flats, kicked up an empty beer can, and sent it clattering down the town's main street. The stranger observed it and murmured just loud enough for Hoague to hear, '"Thus the whirligig of time brings in his revenges."'

Hoague frowned in puzzlement and cocked his head. 'What's that you say?'

The man turned back and gave him a lazy, sleepy-eyed look that almost concealed the hard, cold blue of his eyes. 'Just quoting a line from Shakespeare,' he replied, a shoulder lifting to shrug off the remark.

'Shakespeare?' Hoague grunted and took a closer look at the stranger. 'Are you one of those poem-writing cowboys?'

On the wrong side of thirty, the stranger had a rider's narrow hips and wide shoulders. The bridge of his nose showed a small break, and the pale track of an old cut was visible on his right temple. His hair was the tawny color of a mountain cat, and the man looked just about as dangerous as one – until he smiled with an indolence that had Hoague relaxing.

'I can't say that I am,' the stranger said and stepped forward to check under the pickup's hood.

'Thought maybe you was, knowing Shakespeare and all.' Hoague pulled a kerchief from his pocket and mopped at the perspiration flowing free down his face. 'A bunch of them cowboy poets gather in Elko every January and recite poems they wrote. Folks come for miles to listen.'

'So I've heard.' Using a wadded-up handkerchief for protection, the stranger unscrewed the loosened radiator cap, then picked up the grimy, green plastic pitcher next to the gas pumps and poured water into the radiator. There was an immediate sizzle and hiss and a fresh rush of steam.

Hoague Miller peered under the hood. 'Looks like you got a busted radiator hose.'

'Yeah.' The stranger nodded. 'How long will it take you to fix it?'

'Well . . .' Hoague scratched his jaw and thought about that. 'It'll take an hour or so for your truck to cool down, and I got a couple other jobs ahead of you. Be two or three hours, I'd say.'

He watched the stranger's reaction, gauging how long he could stall him. *Hurry* wasn't a word in Hoague Miller's vocabulary.

'There's no rush,' the stranger said and turned to again survey the town. A half-dozen vehicles were parked along the street, but the sidewalks were empty. Nothing stirred. Nothing moved.

He shifted his gaze to the high desert country that surrounded the town. Here was the West of legend, subtle in its grandeur and awesome in its vastness, a land of broad, undulating valleys clumped with sagebrush, riven with dry arroyos, and walled by jagged, saw-toothed mountains.

He looked to the southwest, across the leagues of rolling sage and rough soil. Granite mountains, treeless and rugged, lay vague behind the layers of hot air that swam like liquid glass. In the valley between, a sullen banner of dust boiled up and swept forward like smoke from a grass fire. It was the only stirring of life to be seen for miles. The stranger watched the dust cloud a few seconds, then faced his truck again.

'Where can a man get something to eat here?'

'The Lucky Starr, just down the street.' Hoague motioned toward a two-story building on the corner. 'The beer's cold, the food's hot, and the coffee's strong.'

'Sounds good.' With a parting nod, the stranger moved off in the direction of the corner building, angling across the street.

There were no clouds overhead to break the strong, hard blue of the sky or to filter the streaming white light of the sun. He narrowed his eyes against its brilliance and pulled the brim of his straw Resistol lower on his brow.

The sun-bleached sign above the corner building identified the establishment as the Lucky Starr Hotel and Casino. A second smaller sign announced it was 'Always Open.' An old planked sidewalk wrapped the structure on two adjacent sides, and the roof shaded the walk.

A scant four feet separated him from the promised relief of that shade. Sweat rolled down his neck. His shirt was damp and sticky with it when he finally stepped onto the planked walk. He paused and swept his gaze over the town again. Somewhere an air-conditioning unit rumbled and rattled, laboring mightily against the hot temperature. The smell of sun-scorched earth and alkali dust was strong in the air.

An old yellow dog lay sprawled along the edge of the road, panting in the full glare of the sun. It rose briefly on its front legs, then fell back, too uncomfortable to stay in the sun and too tired or too lazy to move out of it.

Across the way, a woman walked out of a dual post office and grocery, capturing the stranger's attention instantly.

Long-legged and slim, she stopped and looked first in one direction then the other with an impatient swing of her shoulders. She wore a man's white shirt open at the throat and a pair of faded denims that hugged the rounded curves of her hips. A flat-brimmed hat sat low and square on her head, and her hair was the dark, rich shade of expensive Swiss chocolate, its length bound behind her neck to fall in a gleaming tassel halfway down her back. She tapped the riding quirt she carried against her leg in a further show of impatience.

There were restlessness and turbulence in the gesture, and beneath them, the impression of a pride that wouldn't bend. Watching her, the stranger felt the first stirrings of interest and immediately killed them. Even as he swung toward the corner entrance to the hotel casino, the dark-haired woman pivoted and moved off in the opposite direction.

Cool air whispered over him when the stranger walked inside. The place reeked with the sour odor of stale tobacco smoke and spilled liquor. He stood for an instant with his back to the door and ran his gaze over the half darkness.

To his left a set of steps led to a landing then angled sharply to climb the rest of the way to the second floor. Next to the steps stood an old wooden registration desk, blackened by decades of oil and grime. An arched opening on his right led into a lounge and casino area. He moved toward it.

The front window panes were painted green to keep out the sunlight, and a row of slot machines were racked up in front of them to further block the outside light. In the near corner a set of drums sat amid an array of amplifiers and microphone stands on a raised platform. The space in front of it had been cleared to form a small dance floor. The far corner was taken up with a couple of blackjack tables, a roulette wheel, and some poker tables. Scattered in between was a collection of scarred bar tables and chairs.

A once-impressive mahogany bar anchored one entire side of the long room. A woman in skin-snug white leggings and a teal silk blouse sat on a bar stool, counting bills from the cash drawer in front of her. Her shoulder-length hair was the soft blonde color that came from a bottle. When he walked in, she looked around, her almond-shaped eyes making a slow and thorough study of him.

'Come on in and take a load off, cowboy. As you can see, you got the place to yourself.' Her voice had the low, raspy quality of a purring cat. It matched the exotic, feline look of her features – wide, slashing cheekbones and a jawline that came to a sharp point at her chin.

'Thanks.' He touched a finger to his hat and headed for the bar.

With a slight lift of her head, she called out, 'Hey, Roy! You have a customer out front.'

A portrait in an ornately gilded frame hung in the space between the shelves of the back bar. It showed a sultry blonde in a slinky gold dress crooning into a microphone, a much younger and softer version of the woman on the bar stool.

'That's me – Starr Davis,' her smoky voice confirmed, drawing his glance back to her. 'The portrait was done during my days as a singer when I played the lounges in Reno and Tahoe.'

'The clubs in Reno are a long way from this place – in more ways than just miles,' the stranger observed with dry humor.

Her smile echoed his sentiments. 'You've got that right, cowboy.' Starr Davis gathered up a stack of bills and slipped them in an envelope. 'But it's the old story. I found myself with a kid to raise and no father. Show business is not the most stable career choice. So, I looked around for something else and found this.' The gold bracelets on her arm jingled as she waved a hand at their surroundings. 'I got it for a song.'

His glance made a slow sweep of the empty tables and came back to her. 'Bad song, I'd say.'

She laughed in her throat, taking no offense. 'At the time there was talk they were going to put a highway through here straight north to Oregon. But it turned out to be just talk.' She turned and called out again, 'Roy!'

A withered, bone-thin man pushed his way through the set of doors at the far end of the bar, accompanied by the sound of Waylon Jennings singing about goodhearted women. The smell of grease and old kitchen odors rushed into the room with him. The doors swung back and forth on their hinges behind him in an ever-slowing beat.

The man slipped behind the mahogany bar and advanced toward the stranger, an expression of utter indifference on his face. 'I suppose you want something to drink.'

'A gallon of water and a cup of coffee.'

Roy set a pitcher of water with three lonely ice cubes floating in it on the counter, which was quickly followed by a scratched and cloudy glass and a cup of thick, black coffee. Roy watched in silence while the stranger drank down the first glass of water, then poured a second.

'I suppose you want something to eat, too,' Roy grumbled.

'What do you have?'

In answer, the man slapped a plastic-covered menu on the counter. 'That says we got breakfast anytime, but we ain't. I shut the griddle off three hours ago, and I ain't turning it back on.'

The stranger ordered a T-bone steak with all the trimmings. Roy grunted an acknowledgment and disappeared into the kitchen, the swinging doors slapping the air in his wake.

'Roy has a real sunny disposition, doesn't he?' the stranger remarked with a faint smile.

'Draws customers for miles.' Starr Davis's full lips curved in a small, answering smile as she slid off the stool, picked up the money drawer, and carried it behind the bar to return it to the cash register.

The stranger drank down the second glass of water, filled it again, then carried it and the coffee to one of the bar tables. He kicked back a chair and settled his long frame into it, removing his hat and hooking it on a chair back.

The kitchen doors slapped open again and Roy came out, an arm wrapped around a collection of bottles. He made straight for the stranger's table.

Silverware clattered onto its liquid-stained surface, followed in quick succession by a set of salt and pepper shakers, a bottle of Tabasco sauce, one of ketchup, and one of steak sauce. Relieved of his burden, Roy wandered over to the row of slot machines strung along the green-painted front windows. At a place where the paint had peeled away from a corner pane, he stopped to look out.

Behind the bar, Starr Davis poured herself a cup of coffee and eyed the stranger over her shoulder. 'You're new in town, aren't you?'

'Just drove in,' he confirmed and rubbed at eyes gritty from lack of sleep.

'I thought so.' When she walked out from behind the bar with the cup, the stranger pushed back a second chair at his table, inviting her to join him. 'I've always been good at faces. I would have remembered yours if you had been in before.'

His wasn't a face a woman would forget. He wasn't handsome exactly, but he had the kind of tough, go-to-hell good looks that challenged women and broke hearts.

At forty, Starr had lost all her illusions about life and men. She had learned that you got out of life what you took, and she had become a taker. Yet, looking at this man, she found herself wishing she had met him fifteen years ago. That made him dangerous.

'Where are you from?' She studied him over the rim of her cup.

He shrugged. 'You name it, I've been there.'

Roy half turned from the window. 'He's driving a pickup with Texas plates.'

When no comment was forthcoming from the stranger, Roy headed back to the kitchen. Starr waited a beat then asked, 'What brings you to a forgotten corner of Nevada like Friendly?'

'A busted radiator hose.' Again he didn't elaborate. Roy came out of the kitchen carrying a plate of greasy home fries and a T-bone steak that hung over the sides of its platter. 'The town's pretty quiet.'

'And pretty apt to stay that way.' Roy shoved the food in front of him. Traces of blood oozed from the seared sides of the steak. Medium rare, just the way the stranger had ordered it.

'The Lucky Starr is about the only life there is in this town,' Starr declared. 'The place really gets to roaring on Friday and Saturday nights. We have a little four-piece band that comes and plays. People can dance, drink, gamble, whatever they like. You should stick around and check it out.'

'Do you sing with the band?' he asked between chews.

'I've been known to take a turn or two at the microphone.'

'In that case, maybe I will.' He smiled, his eyes making a slow, assessing sweep of her figure.

Starr wasn't offended by it. As far as she was concerned, there wasn't a straight man born who didn't look to see what a woman had to offer without engaging in a few lusting thoughts, however fleeting they might be. It was inherent in the male animal, married or single. And the woman in her reacted to his glance, wisely or not.

'Are there many ranches around here?' he asked.

'The Diamond D is the biggest in the area, maybe in the whole state. Are you looking for work?'

'Right now I'm not looking beyond this steak, a hot shower, and a month's worth of sleep.' A smile edged the corners of his mouth and brought a glint of humor to his eyes.

As he sliced off another chunk of steak, the cuff of his left sleeve rode back exposing a reddened and recent scar. Noticing it, Starr remarked, 'That looks like a fresh cut. What happened to you?'

The stranger glanced at it and unconsciously flexed his grip on the steak knife as if testing the mobility of his fingers. 'I got thrown from a bronc about a month ago and broke my wrist. It took a surgeon who was good at jigsaw puzzles to piece it back together.'

'You must have been laid up for a while.'

'A while.' He nodded and continued to eat.

When the stranger finished his meal, Roy came out with the coffee pot and refilled his cup. The stranger kicked back in his chair and lit a long, slim cigar. The cigar was half-smoked when the muffled beginnings of a racket came from outside, a kind of low clatter and rumble that grew slowly and steadily louder. The stranger brought the chair down on all four legs and lifted his head in a listening attitude.

Starr was halfway to the kitchen with the stranger's dirty plate and silverware. 'Roy, go see what that is.' She issued the directive over her shoulder.

Roy walked over to the pane of glass with the paint scraped off a corner and peered outside. 'The Diamond D's moving cattle,' he said. 'Now the whole damned town's going to stink of shit for a week.'

The stranger stood up. 'Think I'll go have a look.' With the cigar clamped between his teeth, he dug loose bills out of his pocket, counted out enough to pay for the meal, and tossed it on the table, then he scooped up his hat and headed for the door at an unhurried gait.

Outside the heat hit him first, then the choking dust churned up by the stream of bawling, fretful cattle that came out of the desert and filed down the middle of town. The stranger moved to the edge of the planked walk and leaned a shoulder against a post to watch.

An outrider on a bald-faced roan horse positioned himself at the intersection on the hotel's side of the street. Two other riders covered the opposite side. One was a gawky kid, barely in his teens, all gangly arms and legs. But it was the tall, big-shouldered man on the steel-gray horse next to the kid who drew the stranger's interest. There was an indefinable air of authority about the man that said he was the boss of the outfit – if not the owner, then definitely the foreman. In his hand he carried a bull whip, the length of it uncurled to trail to the ground.

The dust haze grew thicker and the clatter of lumbering hooves grew louder as the main body of the herd entered town, accompanied by more riders slapping coiled ropes to keep the cattle moving at a steady trot. The stranger wasn't the only spectator on the scene. Several others had ventured out of air-cooled buildings to watch as well. The ones across the street from the stranger were obscured by the dust fog that hung over the herd, but the tall brunette coming down the street toward the stranger wasn't. She was the same slim, well-built woman he had seen earlier.

She walked with a smooth, swinging step and a small sway of her hips that was easy to watch. She stopped at the corner directly across from him and paused there, her head turned, her attention on something or someone on the other side of the herd. The stranger followed the direction of her gaze. It seemed to point straight to the big man on the gray horse, the one the stranger had mentally singled out as the boss of the Diamond D.

For an instant there was something challenging, almost defiant, in her stance, then she stepped off the curb and angled across the dirt road, taking a diagonal course toward a small, false-fronted building separated from the hotel casino by a narrow alley.

A sound, sharp and explosive, cracked across the backs of the cattle. The stranger turned toward it with a jerk of his head. There was another harsh *pop* and an arm motion by the man on the gray horse, the kind of movement that made a whip talk.

The river of beef bent in the middle, veering away from the snapping whip. In that same pitched-off instant, the stranger saw that the near cowboy on the roan horse was out of position. The dirt road to the north lay open.

Pressed from behind by riders and from the side by the veering herd, a dozen cows swung their noses toward the open road and immediately bolted for it. The rest followed.

Not ten feet away was the woman. She was nearly to the middle of the road, still walking, her back to the street, completely unaware of the cattle rushing toward her.

'Look out!' the stranger shouted.

As the brunette glanced back, he took a step toward her, but his path was already blocked with brown hides. There was no way he could reach her on foot.

She started to break for the corner building, then saw she wouldn't make it. Stopping, she turned and faced the onrushing cattle, tall and slim and straight. She lifted the quirt in her left hand and brought it smartly down on the nose of the nearest steer. It swerved, creating a wedge of space. Wielding the quirt like a slashing sword, she forced the cattle to flow around her, carving out an island of safety with a coolness the stranger would have applauded if there had been time.

But time was the enemy. Any second the crush of cattle could overwhelm her. The stranger recognized it even if the woman didn't.

He looked around for help. The closest rider was the cowboy on the roan horse, but his back was to the woman, oblivious to her plight. In a flash, the stranger was off the porch and catching at the horse's reins. Before the cowboy could offer a protest, the stranger grabbed a handful of shirt and pulled him out of the saddle. Catching hold of the saddle horn, the stranger swung on board, pulled the hard-mouthed roan around, and aimed it for the woman. Cursing his lack of spurs, he dug his heels into the horse's belly, and pushed it into the traveling tide of beef.

For an instant he lost sight of the brunette. Then he saw her amid the boiling dust on his right, still valiantly lashing out to defend her ever-diminishing space.

The roan needed little urging to plunge into the opening she had created. Bending low in the saddle, the stranger hooked an arm around her middle and swept her up, ignoring her shriek of rage.

She immediately struck out at him with her quirt. 'You bastard, let me go!'

Fighting to control his rearing mount, the stranger spared her one glance, enough to see the blaze in her dark eyes before he had to dodge the slashing quirt. 'Hang on, dammit!'

She went motionless for an instant, then grabbed hold. He dragged her fully onto the saddle. The roan came down on all fours and stumbled, nearly going to its knees. The stranger hauled back on the reins and winced at the pain that shot through his left wrist and arm. He blocked it out and guided the roan to the side of the road.

Fewer cattle trotted past. At the intersection, a rider was once again in position, turning back the rest of the herd. A pair of cowboys galloped past, spurring their horses to catch up with the fleeing cattle.

Satisfied the danger was over, the stranger lowered the brunette to the ground, then swung out of the saddle himself and caught up the horse's reins. He turned to check on the woman and saw at once she wasn't as tall as he had first thought. It was an illusion created by the way she held her head, the way she carried her shoulders, and the soldier-straight line of her back.

Her face was away from him, and her hat hung down her back, caught by the throat-string around her neck. A heavy powdering of dust coated her clothes and skin, but she seemed otherwise unharmed.

'Are you all right?' he asked.

She turned on him, her eyes flashing fire and fury. 'Don't you dare pretend to be concerned! Those cattle were deliberately turned on me. I heard that whip cracking and it wasn't to stop them. If this is some new scare tactic, it didn't work. Do you hear? It didn't work!'

She was trembling. Whether with anger or leftover fear, he couldn't tell. But her face was alive and beautiful in its rage. There was a look of breeding about her, an innate pride in her features and a strength the stranger couldn't clearly define. He studied her, feeling the edge of sexual awareness kick through him like the explosive heat of excellent whiskey.

'"O tiger's heart wrapped in a woman's hide,"' he murmured the apt quote from *Henry VI*.

'What?' She frowned, then shook off her momentary confusion and his comment. 'Get on your horse and go tell DePard he failed.'

His eyebrow shot up in idle curiosity. 'Who is DePard?'

That stopped her. She glanced at the roan horse with the Diamond D brand on its hip, then back at him, her expression wary and guarded. 'You don't work for DePard?'

'Is that who owns the horse? I never took the time to ask when I borrowed it.' Turning, he looped the reins over the roan's neck, then gave it a slap on the rump, sending it trotting off.

'You must be new here.' Her eyes narrowed on him in sharpened study.

'I landed in town about an hour ago.'

He watched her breathe in, then slowly nod. 'That explains it then.' She looked away, then immediately stiffened when a trio of riders pulled up, led by the big-shouldered man on the steel-gray horse.

The young kid was on the man's right, his boy-soft features streaked with dust and sweat. He glared at the brunette, trying to look as stern and forbidding as the big man he was obviously attempting to emulate.

The second rider had a purpling birthmark that covered most of his left cheek. He sat with the loose ease of a man who had spent a lifetime in the saddle.

He had not the size of the big man, but the impression was still one of lean toughness and sharp cunning. His attention stayed on the stranger, sizing him up with eyes that were narrow with suspicion and cold with warning.

But it was the man on the gray who dominated the group. He sat wide and heavy in the saddle and had a muscular swell to his chest and neck that was as impressive as his big shoulders. Past middle age and showing gray hairs below his hat brim, the man had all the earmarks of a large cattle owner about him, with such a man's accustomed sense of power and unchallenged authority. He had broad features and a thick mustache sprinkled with gray.

The glitter of hatred in his eyes was almost tangible, and all of it was directed at the brunette. 'You're a damned lucky woman.' He dragged out each word, venom coating his voice.

'That galls you, doesn't it, DePard?' she shot right back, fearless and defiant. 'If you want to get rid of me, you'll have to come up with something better than trying to run me down with a bunch of hot, weary cattle.'

The second rider surged forward. 'You smart-mouthed little bitch—'

Even as the stranger stepped forward to intercept the threat, the man called DePard raised a hand and issued a low-voiced order that silenced the rider, who with seething reluctance sawed at his reins and backed his horse a few steps, agate green eyes flashing a look at the stranger and marking him in his memory.

'You're smart to keep Sheehan on a short leash, DePard,' the brunette said.

'Shut up,' DePard snapped, then threw his glare at the stranger. 'You're the one who took Jenkins's horse.'

'It seemed the thing to do at the time.' The stranger

pushed his hat to the back of his head and looked up at the man with calculated indifference.

'You must be new here.'

'Does it matter?' Amusement edged the corners of his mouth.

'Not much. It just means you don't know what you're sticking your nose into.'

'I thought I was sticking it into your face.' This time the stranger didn't smile. In his face there was nothing but cold, hard challenge.

The suddenness of it took DePard by surprise, momentarily shocking him into silence. The young kid immediately took up the cudgel. 'You better watch what you say, mister. You're talking to Duke DePard. He owns the Diamond D and half this town.'

'Is that a fact?' the stranger drawled, unimpressed. 'I don't know about the Diamond D, but from what I've seen of this town, it isn't something I'd brag about owning.'

'Then clear out and move on!' DePard roared the warning and dug his spurs into the gray, hauling back on the reins and spinning the gelding around. As one, the trio rode back toward the main herd.

The stranger watched them a moment, then turned back to find himself under the brunette's close scrutiny. She was examining him with new interest.

'You just made yourself an enemy,' she warned. 'DePard isn't going to forget this. And, believe me, he has a long memory.'

'So do I.'

A hint of frown briefly marred the smoothness of her forehead. 'Who are you?'

'The name's Kincade,' he said after an instant's hesitation.

'Are you looking for work?'

He grinned and shook his head. 'I'm not broke yet.'

She gave him a rueful look and nodded. 'When you are, try the Spur Ranch, north of town about thirty miles.'

'Who should I ask for?' Kincade suddenly wanted a name to go with her face. Maybe because he had rescued her, or because he admired her courage – or maybe because he was only now remembering how she had felt in his arms, the lightness of her body, the hardness and the softness of it.

Watching her Kincade had the feeling she could read his thoughts, then dismissed the fanciful notion. She knew she was a beautiful woman; her assurance said as much. Other men had looked at her with hungry eyes; her manner said that, too. And he was a man like other men, driven by the same ancient needs.

A hint of annoyance showed in her face. 'You can ask for the boss.'

'Is that you or your husband?' He didn't see a wedding band on her finger, but that didn't mean she wasn't married.

'I don't have a husband.'

Women ranchers weren't uncommon, but the majority took over the role following the death of their husband. Automatically assuming she was a widow, Kincade said, 'I'm sorry.'

'I'm not.' The answer was firm and very definite. Without another word, she turned and walked off, again bound for the false-fronted building just down from the hotel casino.

He watched her a moment, curious and not wanting to be. Turning, he saw Starr Davis outside the corner entrance to the Lucky Starr. She met his gaze, her expression faintly amused and wholly cynical. He had the impression she had been standing there for some time. Unhurried, Kincade wandered back to join her.

'That was not a smart move,' Starr remarked, yet

there was a glint of admiration in the look she gave him.

'I gathered that.' He nodded and glanced after the brunette. 'Who is she?'

Starr glanced down the street in time to see the woman enter the boot and saddlery shop. 'She is trouble, in capital letters, for anyone fool enough to side with her against DePard.'

'Why? What did she do?'

Her lips curled in a smile that was pure feline amusement. 'She killed his brother.'

'What?' His gaze whipped back to her, a frown creasing his forehead. 'Was it an accident?'

'It was no accident. It was a deliberate act. DePard is convinced she shot Jeff in cold blood. Naturally she claimed self-defense.'

'Which was it?'

Starr laughed, a low and throaty chuckle. 'You never struck me as a fool. Maybe you'd better take another look around. This town survives solely on the business DePard throws it. You know the old saying the customer is always right. Well, believe me, cowboy, when that customer is your biggest and best, you don't disagree with a single thing he says. Whatever comes out of his mouth is gospel. If you're smart, you'll even swear to it.'

His mouth quirked, wryness tugging at a corner. 'Something tells me you are a very smart lady.'

'Smart enough to lick the hand that feeds me, not bite it.'

His glance shifted to her lips, lushly full and ripe, the things erotic dreams were made of. 'DePard must enjoy the hell out of it when you do the licking.'

'I make sure he does,' she replied in a sultry voice that briefly fired his own imagination.

'Are you his woman?'

Starr released another throaty laugh, rich with amusement. 'He may think so, but I wear no man's brand, cowboy.'

It was the second time within a handful of minutes that a woman had disavowed any kind of tie. Kincade thought of the brunette again, and that intriguing blend of beauty and bravery, pride and strength. He had known few women who possessed both class and courage. It was a combination that could ignite a man's imagination – and his interest. Kincade acknowledged the flaring of his own.

He briefly wondered what the real story was behind the death of DePard's brother. Had he been guilty of assault? Had it been a case of the brunette being 'more sinned against than sinning,' as Shakespeare once wrote? He tended to believe that.

It was an opinion shaped, no doubt, by the recent past.

2

A whip cracked. Kincade faced the street again as DePard rode by on his big gray horse, pushing the last of the herd through the intersection. The young kid rode beside him. He lifted a hand and flicked it in Starr's direction in a small, self-conscious wave. She waved back, then tucked her fingers in the hip pockets of her slacks and gazed after the boy, her eyes soft, that cynical edge gone from her expression.

'That's my son, Rick,' she said to Kincade. 'Right now he's into the dust and sweat and hard work of being a cowboy. He thinks it's a great way to live.'

'It could be worse.' He shrugged. 'He could be into the bulls and blood, the spills and the mud of rodeo.'

She shuddered. 'I don't even want to think about that.'

The herd moved out of town and the bawl of cattle grew fainter, but the dust continued to hang in the air. A long and lanky cowboy crossed the street and stepped onto the planked sidewalk. He touched his hat to Starr, then looked at Kincade, a grin splitting his thickly freckled face.

'Looks like I pulled into town just in time to catch all the excitement. That was some piece of work you did getting that gal out of the path of those cattle—'

'Thanks.' Kincade cut short the praise and pushed out a hand. 'The name's Kincade.'

After an instant's hesitation, the cowboy recovered and shook hands. 'Mine's Smith, but most folks call me Rusty.'

'For obvious reason,' Kincade said, glancing at the brick-red color of the cowboy's hair, which was visible below his hat brim. Then he swung to include Starr. 'Meet Starr Davis. She's the owner and namesake of the Lucky Starr Hotel and Casino.'

'Now I am really pleased to meet you, ma'am. The air-conditioning in my truck quit on me about three hundred miles back, and as you can see' – Rusty Smith cast a disparaging glance at his sweat-ringed shirt – 'I have a powerful need for a hot shower and a cold beer. If you've got an empty room in that hotel, I'll take it.'

'They're all empty,' she told him. 'You can have your pick.'

'Just show me where to sign in,' he declared.

'I think I'll take one of those rooms as well,' Kincade spoke up.

'In that case, you can both follow me.' Starr turned and led the way to the door.

Kincade cast one last glance at the false-fronted building, aware that the brunette had yet to emerge from it. Nothing stirred.

An oscillating fan whirred from its corner perch on the counter, blowing around air that smelled of new leather and old polish. Eden Rossiter turned her face to the fan, savoring the rush of air and the illusion of coolness it produced.

A new, hand-tooled and hand-stamped saddle sat atop a wooden rack near the counter. More saddles, mostly used, hung from ropes fastened to the ceiling. An array of tack lined one short wall of the shop. On the opposite wall, shelves of repaired boots and shoes shared space with hooks holding leather chaps, vests, rifle scabbards, and saddlebags. Brightly colored saddle blankets and thick pads were piled on a ladder-backed chair in the far corner.

The counter's glass display case held necklaces, earrings, and buckles made of leather. More filled the small cardboard box on top of it while a larger box on the floor contained an assortment of belts in various sizes and colors.

Dust motes shimmered and danced in the sunlight that poured through the shop windows. Eden glanced at the dirt street beyond the grimy panes. Her mind flashed instantly to that moment on the road when the cattle boiled around her, tightening her small circle of safety.

If that stranger Kincade hadn't reached her when he did—

Eden shuddered in recognition of the very real danger she had been in. She took a deep, steadying breath to quell the sudden, nauseous churning of her stomach and concentrated on her rescuer.

She remembered his hard, beard-shadowed face and the deep bronzing of his skin. His hands had had the kind of calluses that a rope made, and he had handled the horse with the skill of someone born in the saddle. His boots carried the telltale black marks that indicated a habitual use of spurs.

The stranger Kincade had cowboy written all over him, a member of that restless, wandering breed who jumped from ranch to ranch and payroll to payroll, following the drifter's circuit that laced northern Nevada and eastern Oregon and twisted into parts of Arizona, Montana, and Wyoming.

Eden knew his kind well. Yet the feeling lingered that he was a cut above the others. DePard certainly hadn't intimidated him. In fact, Kincade hadn't appeared to give a damn who the man was, deflecting all of DePard's verbal thrust with a lazy mockery that had dealt a greater blow to the big man's ego than harsh words ever could have done.

She was about to decide he didn't give a damn about anything. Then she remembered the way he had looked at her with eyes that were level and too direct, disturbing in their intensity. Men had looked at her with woman-hungry eyes before. But this time she had felt a slow heat radiate through her, a heat that she had thought she had become immune to long ago. She was annoyed to discover she hadn't.

The sound of approaching footsteps came from the back room. Eden turned back to the counter as a stocky, middle-aged woman of Basque ancestry came through the curtained doorway carrying a pair of old boots, resoled and polished to a high shine.

'It was just as I thought. Your boots were still in back, but they are finished.' Rosa Winters set the boots atop the crowded counter. 'I'll fetch your bridle and you'll be all set.' She took a step toward the wall shelves, then saw the flood of sunlight through the front windows and changed directions, shaking her head and clicking her tongue. 'That sun, it turns this place into an oven in the afternoon.'

'It is hot in here,' Eden acknowledged.

'And dusty.' Rosa Winters reached up and pulled down a dark green window shade, then crossed to the other window to do the same. 'That DePard, he didn't have to drive his cattle through town. He could have taken his herd around it, but he wants everyone to know how big he is and how much he has.' She unrolled the last blind with a snap, throwing the shop into deep shadow. Then she turned, her dark eyes fastening their gaze on Eden. 'I saw what happened out there. The man who rescued you, who was he?'

'Some stranger named Kincade.'

'I knew it couldn't have been one of DePard's men, not if he wanted to keep his job.' The woman retraced her steps to the wall shelves and took down a bridle with a new leather throat-strap. 'You were lucky the stranger was in town.'

'I know.' Too well.

'I am ashamed to say that none of the rest of us would have dared to help you.' Rosa laid the bridle on the counter next to the boots, then gave a long sigh, heavy with despair. 'Hatred is an evil sickness. Like a cancer, it begins as a small thing that spreads slowly over time. It has been almost fourteen years since Jeff died, and I have watched DePard's hatred for you grow year by year until he is eaten up with it. He will never rest until you are punished for Jeff's death.' She lifted a hand toward Eden in a beseeching gesture. 'Leave, Eden. Sell your ranch and go from here before he destroys you.'

'I will not sell.' The very idea was unthinkable. Spur had been the Rossiter home for four generations. The house she lived in had been built by her great-grandmother. Her roots were anchored deep in the desert soil. She would never willingly give up the ranch.

'You are a fool, Eden Rossiter.' Rosa shook her head at her. 'DePard is too big, his reach is too great, his friends are too powerful. No one can stand against him for long.'

'People have been predicting my downfall for years. I'm still here.'

After her grandfather's death seven years ago, everyone had been certain Eden would sell out and leave the area. When she hadn't, people had shaken their heads and declared that she wouldn't be able to keep the ranch going. Not a woman. Especially not one so young. But she had. So far that is.

'How much do I owe you?' Eden dug some folded bills out of her jeans pocket.

'Twelve-fifty.' Rosa rested both hands on the counter, palms flat, her expression grim with disapproval. 'You know it was DePard who made sure your permit wasn't renewed to graze cattle on government land, don't you?'

'I guessed it.' Eden laid thirteen dollars on the counter and waited for her change.

'Now you have more cattle on your range than your land can support, and you can't find a shipper to haul them to market.'

'I haven't so far.'

'And you won't. DePard has made certain of that. He has told all the local companies that if they haul any of your cattle, they will never haul for him again.'

'I suspected something like that might have happened.' But that didn't lessen the surge of anger Eden struggled to control.

'They don't want to lose his business and most of them don't think you will make it much longer anyway.'

'They're wrong.'

Rosa slipped the money into the cashbox under the counter. 'Now there is talk DePard has put the word out no one is to work for you. Without ranch hands, you won't be able to keep the place going.' She gave Eden two quarters in change.

'If I can't hire help, then I'll pare the operation down until I can manage it by myself. There are hundreds of small ranches run that way.'

'Next DePard will order everyone to stop selling to you,' she warned. 'He has thrown a noose around you, and he's going to keep pulling it tighter and tighter until he squeezes you out.'

'He can try.' Eden reached for the bridle and boots.

'People are saying that if you can't get your cattle to

market, the grass on your land will be grazed to the roots within two months.'

'They forgot to factor in my hay surplus.' With it and subtracting the amount she'd need to feed the cattle she would normally market in the fall, Eden had calculated she had about three months, give or take a week. After that . . . Tension, a kind of desperation, clawed at the back of her throat. She fought it off, telling herself she would find a solution before that deadline arrived.

Rosa stole a glance over her shoulder. A young man in a wheelchair sat in the backroom facing a low-built workbench. His sweat-drenched T-shirt outlined every bulge of thick muscles in his shoulders and arms, a contrast to his stick-thin legs. Satisfied that he was paying no attention to them, Rosa turned back and leaned closer to Eden.

'I know someone who might haul your cattle,' she said in a low voice.

'Who?'

'My sister Anna has a brother-in-law who hauls live-stock for the ranches across the border in Oregon. I will see him tomorrow when I deliver these orders to the shops in Winnemucca.' Rosa gestured at the cardboard boxes packed with belts and leather jewelry, items she made and sold to tourist shops along the interstate from Winnemucca to Reno. 'He's bringing a load of sheep to a herder east of town. Anna is going to ride along with him and meet me for lunch. I could speak to him for you.'

'Do you think he would agree to haul my cattle to the stockyards?'

'I know he needs the money.'

Eden thought out loud, 'DePard has to know that sooner or later I'll start looking for a stock hauler outside the area. Does he know about your sister's brother-in-law?'

'I doubt it. Jerry is just getting started so not many people know about him.' Rosa hesitated, her expression sharpening in concern. 'You can't tell anyone how you found out about Jerry. If DePard ever learned that I helped you—'

Rosa's eyes sprang to Eden's face. 'He must know nothing of this. He can't. You must swear to tell no one that I had anything to do with this. DePard owns this building – and most of the equipment.'

'This will be strictly between you and me,' Eden promised. 'When you see your brother-in-law tomorrow, tell him I'll pay the standard rate, and the sooner he can get here, the better. I'll have the cattle penned and ready to load on whatever day you tell me.'

'I'll call Friday morning and let you know what he says.'

Eden left the shop and headed straight for the truck parked on the town's main street. As she passed the Lucky Starr, Eden saw the stranger, Kincade, lift a duffel bag out of the back end of a dusty black pickup.

The sight of him instantly reminded her of the hard pressure of his arm around her. He had held her so close she could feel every shift of his body, every ripple of lean muscle. The smell of tobacco smoke had clung to his shirt, and the stubble of his whiskers had been only scant inches from her face.

She hadn't been held that close by a man in years. She hadn't wanted to be.

Blocking out the remembered sensations, Eden threw her boots and the bridle into the front seat of the ranch pickup, then climbed in and started up the truck.

The dirt road leading north from town ran straight for a distance, then swerved to angle across the undulating sage flats toward a gap in the craggy mountains to the west. Eden followed it, slowing her speed when the road narrowed and roughened.

The windows of her truck were rolled down. A hot wind tunneled into the cab, spiced with the scent of sage. Typically, Eden met no other vehicle, and passed none. The road was one of many backroads in Nevada that never appeared on highway maps, roads that linked remote ranches and isolated mining camps with the main routes or followed the march of power lines across the vast emptiness of the high desert country. Out here, there were no emergency services. Help was invariably hours, rather than minutes away. A fact Eden knew only too well.

Her eye was drawn to the rutted track that branched away from the dirt road and ran like a long scar through the silvery green sagebrush, before it clawed its way up a mountain slope. Halfway to the top, it disappeared onto a wide volcanic bench stippled with green. Hidden from view was a hot spring that bubbled to the surface and collected in a series of small rock pools. The site was well known by the locals and a favorite haunt of teenagers out to chug-a-lug a few beers with friends or score with their steadies.

As Eden passed the spot where the track joined the dirt road, she tightened her grip on the steering wheel, her knuckles turning white from the pressure. From this point, it was exactly seven miles to the ranch, and more than twenty to town. The distances were forever etched in her memory.

If only she hadn't snuck out of the house on that long ago night fourteen years ago . . . If only she hadn't agreed to meet Jeff DePard . . . If only she had gone to town instead of the ranch . . . maybe everything would have been different.

If only . . .

She drove as fast as she dared over the rough road, her breath coming in panicked sobs. Her leg shook with the effort to keep her foot pressed on the gas pedal. Her hands, wet with blood, were slick on the steering wheel.

There was more blood staining the front of her blouse, more on the seat. Jeff DePard lay beside her, sprawled at an awkward angle, one leg folded up against the passenger door, the other hanging over the edge of the seat. Blood soaked both the front of his shirt and the compression bandage she had tied over the ugly bullet hole in his chest. With each breath she drew, her stomach churned anew with the nauseating, oddly sweet smell of blood.

'Where's the turnoff to the ranch?' Her whispered words held a silent plea. Shaking all over and terrified out of her mind, Eden scanned the road ahead, probing the darkness beyond the reach of the truck's headlights. No night had ever seemed blacker. 'Dear God, don't let me miss it.'

A sob broke from her and tears momentarily blurred her vision. She wiped them away with the back of her hand and pushed harder on the accelerator. Immediately the pickup lunged forward in answer, hit a chuckhole, and careened sideways, nearly wrenching the steering wheel from her hands.

Jeff's limp body pitched forward, and Eden grabbed for him with one hand, frantic little sounds coming from her throat as she fought to regain control of the truck. Somehow she managed to get it aimed straight again and keep Jeff on the seat.

She spared a worried glance at him. In the dim and eerie light from the dashboard, his face looked gray, his eyes were closed, and no sound came from his lips. Gulping back a frightened sob, Eden searched the road.

The ranch. She had to get to the ranch. There was a phone there. And help. She refused to think about facing her grandfather and telling him what happened. She clung to the one thought that he would know what to do for a gunshot wound.

Tears filled her eyes again. She looked down at Jeff, whispering tightly, 'You can't die. Damn you, you can't.'

*   *   *

But he had.

And before that night was over, she had been arrested and charged with first-degree murder. DePard had made certain of that.

In his eyes, she had caused the death of the brother he had raised like a son and for that she deserved to be punished. Harshly.

During the three years of legal wrangling that preceded her trial, DePard spread the vicious story that she had killed his brother in a jealous rage after she caught him with another woman. Some had believed him. Some hadn't, although few had ever said so to his face.

When a jury in faraway Tonopah returned a verdict of not guilty, DePard was outraged over what he saw as a blatant miscarriage of justice. Eden had thought he would eventually come to terms with the verdict. Instead he had brooded over it, and the grief and bitterness he felt festered over time into full-blown hatred and a need for vengeance that had become a raging thirst.

Where would it all end, Eden wondered as she drove into the homeyard of Spur Ranch.

Desert hills rose behind the site, forming a natural break against keening winter winds. A spring-fed stream meandered through it on its way to the sage prairie beyond. Summer heat had reduced its flow to a trickle, but no Rossiter had ever seen it go dry, a rare thing in desert country where a constant water supply was a valuable commodity.

Bypassing the corrals and low outbuildings, Eden headed straight for the hacienda-style house, a two-story affair roofed with corrugated iron now rusted a deep reddish brown and shaded by century-old cottonwood trees. Against the green of the trees, the thick adobe walls had the look of old parchment, faded and grainy with time. Wooden verandahs stretched across the front of the house on both levels and the dun of the desert ran all the way to its front step.

In size, the house was neither grand nor imposing; it was simple and solid, built to last. For Eden, the house was the heart of Spur. And like it, her roots were anchored just as deeply in the soil. She could not imagine ever leaving this place. Not willingly.

An old stock dog, an aging Blue Heeler named Cassius, emerged from the verandah's shade and trotted out to meet the truck when Eden pulled up in front of the house. Tail wagging, he waited by the driver's side for her to climb out, his mouth split in a welcoming grin. His marled coat carried the scars from fights with coyotes and other varmints that dared to invade his territory. In size, the dog wasn't much, weighing a scant fifty pounds and standing only eighteen inches tall at the shoulder, but he had the heart of David, ready to take on any Goliath.

'Hey, Cash, how are you doing?' Eden stepped out of the truck and reached back for the boots and bridle. 'Did you have a busy day holding down the fort?'

The dog replied with an excited whine, then froze in a stance of alertness and pointed its erect ears at the screen door. It sprang open at the shove of a hand as Eden's older brother Vince charged out of the house, a look of concern etched in the handsome cast of his features.

'Damn, am I glad to see you. Are you all right?' He caught her arms and held her still while he made a worried and hasty inspection of her.

'I'm fine—' she began, but Vince had already come to the same conclusion.

'Do you know how close you came to getting trampled by those cattle?' he demanded, angry now. 'My God, you could have been killed.'

'How did you find out about that?'

'I got a phone call a few minutes ago telling me all

about it.' He let go of her and stepped back, sweeping off his hat and running a hand through his thick dark hair. 'Dammit, I've been worried sick. How the hell could you have let something like that happen?'

'*I* didn't. It was all DePard's doing.' Eden made that clear, then conceded, 'I probably should have been more alert, but I had other things on my mind. The part for the generator still hasn't come in and I don't know how much longer we can keep it running without it. I never dreamed DePard would try something like that in broad daylight.'

'He's out to get you, Eden,' Vince muttered, 'and he isn't going to stop until he does. When are you going to wake up to that?'

'What is it you think I should do?' Eden demanded in exasperation. 'Shake in my boots or grovel at his feet and beg for mercy?'

'No. I want you to get the hell out of here while you're still in one piece!'

'I will never give up Spur.'

'There is no reasoning with you.' He turned on his heel and stalked off.

Eden recognized the rashness of his temper, and suspicion surfaced. 'Vince, where are you going?'

'To check the tank at Flat Rock.' He fired the answer over his shoulder.

'You were supposed to do that right after lunch.'

He yanked open the door to his truck, a new and shiny blue pickup, then stopped to answer her. 'The baler broke down and I had to play mechanic. I got it running again, but who knows for how long?'

Eden threw a quick look at the wide yellow strip of hayfield located just beyond the loading pens in an area they called the Basin. Square bales were scattered over it in a haphazard line. The grumble and clatter of an aging hay baler came from the far end of the field, the sound confirming that the machine was still running, scooping up the windrowed hay and compacting it into tight bales.

Vince's pickup blocked Eden's view of the field as he reversed it away from the house. The stock tank at the section of range known as Flat Rock was due east, beyond the sage flats. Vince turned onto the rutted track that would lead him to it.

But the uneasiness Eden felt didn't go away.

This argument about selling the ranch and leaving was an old one, one they had every time Vince showed up. Eden knew better than most that if control of Spur had passed to Vince following their grandfather's death, he would have sold it on the spot. Vince had never felt her attachment to the ranch. To him, it had never been more than a source of cash, one he was eager to exploit.

Suppressing a sigh, Eden headed for the house.

The thick adobe walls kept the temperature inside several degrees cooler. Eden left the bridle by the front door and set the boots on the staircase to the second floor, then crossed the wood floor and entered the main room.

Overhead, the blades of a ceiling fan rotated slowly, circulating the air. The odor of old smoke drifted from the arched fireplace, wide enough to roast a whole steer in. Fat easy chairs filled the space in front of it, their cushions threadbare and faded. The marks left by spurs scarred the room's hardwood floor, and the area rug had a path worn into its design. It was the living room of a working ranch and made no pretense to be otherwise. Yet for all its signs of use and abuse, the room had a definite sense of comfort and ease that touched all who entered it.

Unconsciously Eden responded to it and slipped off her hat to let it swing from her fingers by the throatstrap, some of the tension leaving her. She ignored the silent invitation of the big easy chairs and went instead to the old rolltop desk in the corner alcove that served as the ranch office.

The day's mail sat in a neat stack amid the clutter. Eden picked it up and leaned a hip against the edge of the desk while she sifted through the half-dozen envelopes, a mix of bills and flyers. Finding nothing urgent, she laid them back on the desk.

As she turned to leave, her glance strayed to the oval-framed picture on the wall. Its antique bubble glass protected an old photograph of a woman in her forties, dressed in a long split riding skirt, a wool jacket, a flat-crowned hat, and dusty boots. She wore a holstered gun belted around her slim hips and held the reins to a tall, rangy horse. Her face had that tanned and leathered look that came from years of exposure to the sun and the wind. There was a hint of fineness about her features that suggested she might have appeared beautiful if the impression of strength and determination had been less dominant.

In the background stood the adobe walls and wooden verandah of Spur's main house.

Eden studied the photograph of her ancestor Kate Rossiter, the woman who came West as a bride of fifteen and eventually built Spur into a successful ranch with little help from her often-absent husband.

'I guess Vince takes after your Daniel, always chasing the dream of hitting it big,' Eden murmured, a weary resignation in her voice.

Gold, silver, copper, it hadn't mattered to Daniel Rossiter. With each new rumor of a strike, he had taken off to track it down. He had been gone months, sometimes years, at a time, leaving Kate to run the place.

Vince was back, but like Kate, Eden didn't fool herself into believing he would stay. She was on her own against DePard.

3

A Ford Bronco led a small convoy of pickup trucks with stock trailers in tow over a graveled road. The vehicle slowed as it approached one of the entrances to the Diamond D Ranch, and the trucks behind it followed suit. In the stock trailers, saddled horses stood with legs braced against the changing movement, the sweat of a day's work slowly drying on their bodies.

Duke DePard sat in the Bronco's passenger seat, his gaze directed out the side window in a sightless stare. Forty-year-old Matt Sheehan, the cowboss at the Diamond D for the last fifteen years and second in power only to the man beside him, was behind the wheel.

Rick Davis, who was thirteen going on fourteen, rode in back, tired and sweaty, every muscle aching, unaccustomed to long hours in the saddle moving cattle from one section of range to another. Yet at the same time he was filled with a kind of exhilaration that made any physical discomfort seem trivial.

Rick kept reliving the experience, forgetting the heat and the dust and the tedium, dwelling only on those moments of high action – like the time a young steer bolted for the open country and he chased after it, whipping his horse into a full gallop, leaping over sagebrush and plunging into gullies, hooves pounding beneath him, disaster only a misstep away, his heart in his throat – and the lingering adrenaline charge he'd felt even after he had driven the steer back into the herd. Or the time a sagehen exploded from a bush right under his horse's nose, and the horse nearly jumped out from under him, then started bucking like a rodeo bronc, but he had stayed on, and never even lost a stirrup.

Rick was fairly bursting to recount every exciting moment. Only the fear that he might sound to DePard like some dumb town kid held him silent. Duke DePard's opinion of him mattered more than anything else to Rick. Duke DePard was the biggest man around, the richest and the smartest, too.

When the Ford Bronco swung between the twin pillars of stacked rock that marked the ranch's entrance, Duke DePard finally broke the silence that had lasted for miles.

'Call ahead and let them know we're on our way in. If there are any messages, tell Harve to take them to the house.'

'Right.' Sheehan picked up the radio mike and relayed the message.

Watching him, Rick thought about the string of strategically placed communication towers that linked the farthest reaches of the Diamond D headquarters. It was quite an accomplishment considering the Diamond D Ranch stretched across 2.5 million acres, a checkerboard of private holdings, government grazing and leased railroad land.

It was that kind of forward thinking that made Rick look up to him. Duke DePard was quick to embrace modern technology and new methods that would improve efficiency and ultimately increase profits. Computers gave him weekly reports on the weight gain of the cattle in his feedlot program and tracked the ranch's income and expenses. Airplanes and helicopters reduced the number of man hours spent in the saddle during spring and fall roundups and enabled him to make cursory checks of range and water conditions. Satellite dishes kept him up to date on market trends and allowed him to participate in livestock tele-auctions without ever leaving the ranch.

At the same time, DePard lived by a set of Old West codes. He demanded absolute loyalty from those around him, and gave it, too. When DePard gave a man his word, he lived up to it, and he expected others to do the same. Once a man went back on his word, DePard had nothing more to do with him. And he believed a man's family and his good name were to be protected and defended against the smallest slight. Rick admired that about him, although it wasn't something he would admit to his friends.

The dirt road they traveled led directly to a thick cluster of buildings and corrals located at the base of a low mesa. This was the headquarters of the Diamond D Ranch, the well-kept barns, sheds, storehouses, mess hall, and employee living quarters of a vast and prosperous ranch.

Beyond the buildings another road cut a diagonal line across the face of the mesa and curved to the top. Sheehan took it while the rest of the vehicles peeled away toward the barns. The road split at the top, one branching off toward the airstrip with its metal hangar and helipad, and the other swinging to the main house, a long, low, rambling structure, built of wood, glass, and rock, galleried on three sides. Sheehan turned the Bronco toward the house and braked to a stop even with the flagstoned front walk.

Rick was a step slow climbing out of the vehicle, the sore muscles in his buttocks and thighs screaming in protest. DePard gave him a knowing look when Rick finally joined him.

'A little stiff, are you?' DePard observed, the line of his mouth tightening in a smile of dry amusement.

'It's nothing.' Rick feigned a shrug of macho indifference and did his damnedest to walk naturally when DePard and Sheehan headed for the front door.

'You did a good job today.' DePard made the remark almost as an afterthought, the way one might absently pat a dog's head.

As praise went, it was scant, but Rick Davis flushed with pleasure just the same. Fatherless, he ached for a man's approval, and none meant more to him than Duke DePard's. He happily followed the two men inside.

The thud of their boots and the jingle of their spurs echoed throughout the spacious interior as DePard led the way past the sunken living room to the corner den from which he directed the ranch's entire operations. He walked in and went directly to the built-in bar next to the stone fireplace.

'How about a Coke, son?' He opened a small refrigerator behind it.

'Coke will be fine, sir.'

DePard set a cold can of Coke on the bar counter, then took down two glasses from a back shelf and filled them with ice. Matt Sheehan leaned on the bar and ignored the kid when Rick picked up the Coke can, popped the top, and took a long deep swig from it, then wandered back to the room's center. Out of the corner of his eye, Sheehan saw him pause before a grouping of photographs on the wall.

All showed the brash, handsome face of Duke DePard's long-dead brother Jeff. The tribal stamp of a DePard was evident in his strong, square jaw and broad features. His eyes had a wild and wicked glint to them and his smile was reckless, irresistible. There was no doubt that Jeff

DePard had been a hell-raiser and a charmer as well as a star athlete and straight-A student. Talk had been that Duke was grooming his little brother for a career in politics. Some people had even started making bets that Jeff DePard would one day be Nevada's youngest governor.

Idly, Sheehan studied the photos on the wall. It had been years since he had been inside a church, but he couldn't shake the feeling that he was looking at a religious shrine. Only the prayer candles were missing.

Ice clinked against the sides of the glass Duke DePard offered to Sheehan. He held a second one, filled with whiskey and water. Sheehan lifted the whiskey drink in a silent toast, then took a short sip, feeling the liquor trickle down his throat like fingers of fire.

'That cuts the dust,' Sheehan stated.

'I thought it would.' DePard moved out from behind the bar carrying his drink.

The kid turned from the photo collection with a guilty little start, then tried to cover it by downing a quick swallow of pop. Sheehan turned a speculating glance on him.

For years there had been talk that he was really Jeff DePard's bastard son. The rumor had been fueled by the interest Duke had taken in both the boy and his mother, Starr Davis.

There could also be a simpler explanation for DePard's interest in her – after all, DePard was a bachelor and Starr Davis was a good-looking woman with the wiles of Eve. Still, she was close-mouthed about the boy's father, never saying who he was or where he came from. Sheehan wondered if even the boy knew.

He looked for, but couldn't find a physical resemblance to the DePards. The boy had his mother's angular features and pointy chin. Which didn't mean he wasn't Jeff's illegitimate offspring.

DePard placed a hand on the kid's shoulder. 'I have some things I want to go over with Sheehan. Why don't you go shower and change clothes? Starr won't like it if I bring you back looking like that.'

'I guess not.' The kid managed a quick grin, but it was with obvious reluctance, Coke can in hand, that he left the room.

DePard watched him go. 'Rick handled himself well today,' he remarked once the boy was out of hearing.

Sheehan knew he was referring directly to that moment in the street when the kid leapt to his defense during the confrontation with the Rossiter woman and her rescuer.

'Too bad that stranger showed up,' Sheehan observed. 'If he hadn't butted in, you might have been rid of that Rossiter woman for good.'

'I know.' Bitterness and repressed anger tightened the corners of DePard's mouth.

'You let that stranger off easy, Mr DePard.' Sheehan always put a handle on his name. It was the way Duke DePard wanted it. After all these years, Sheehan knew his boss inside and out, and took care never to offend his tremendous sense of pride. If DePard wanted to rule the region, then Sheehan wanted him to rule it. As DePard's second-in-command, he got his power from him, and Sheehan liked having it.

'Half the town was looking on. There wasn't much choice.' DePard tossed down a swallow of whiskey as if ridding his mouth of a bad taste.

'Seeing you back off like that might give some people the idea they could get away with helping that Rossiter woman.' Sheehan met the cold, black look DePard turned on him. 'Be a shame for that to happen just when it looks like you got her right where you want her.'

'By God, it better not!' DePard let the full blast of his temper thunder out. 'Any man who tries to help, I swear will regret it.'

Sheehan nodded and took another short sip of his drink, letting DePard's anger boil. 'Seems to me you've got to keep them afraid. You've been crowding people for a while now, and you can't crowd a man and expect him to like it. Sooner or later he'll want to crowd back. Part of my job is to make sure they stay humble. The Diamond D is too big and too heavy-handed to have any friends around here. People don't forget. It strikes me, this is when you should increase the pressure.'

'I intend to,' DePard stated, 'when and where it is wise. This is not the time to make a foolish move. It could prove costly in the long run.'

'You know best.' Sheehan didn't completely agree, but he had offered his advice on the matter. DePard had listened to it and made his decision. Sheehan accepted it and shifted the conversation to a discussion of the next day's work.

Steam from the shower clung to the outer edges of the bathroom mirror and condensed into little beads of water that slipped and slid their way down the slick surface. Rick Davis stepped up to the mirror and gazed for a minute at the face it reflected, scrubbed clean of the day's dust and sweat, the reddening of a sunburn on the nose and cheeks. He ran a hand along his jaw, searching for the first soft fuzz of a beard. He found none and sighed his disappointment, then picked up a comb and ran it through his wet hair, combing it into order.

Finished, he started to lay the comb down, then changed his mind and held it above his mouth to see what he would look like if he grew a mustache. Even with his imagination, it was a stretch. He shrugged and caught the movement of his shoulders reflected in the mirror. Giving in to another impulse, he pushed the sleeve of his clean T-shirt back and raised his arm, making a fist of his hand and flexing his muscles. The bicep popped up with high definition, but it didn't have a man's bulk to it. It didn't have Duke DePard's.

Not yet, Rick told himself as he turned from the mirror.

His dirty clothes lay in a heap on the tiled floor. Rick gathered them up, rather proud of the rank smell of hard work that issued from them. He carried them into the guest room he always used on the occasions when he stayed overnight at the ranch. He liked to think of it as *his* room.

It had always been a secret fantasy of his that his mother would marry Duke DePard and they would live here all the time. But it didn't look like that was ever going to happen. Yet it was a hope he continued to cherish each time he saw them together.

Rick had stopped asking questions about his natural father years ago. No matter how many times he asked, he never got a straight answer from his mother. He knew nothing about his father, not even his name.

He had heard the whispered talk that he was Jeff DePard's bastard. But he was afraid to ask about it – afraid to find out it wasn't true. He wanted to be a DePard. This way he could believe he might be.

He shoved his dirty clothes inside the canvas bag with the rest of his things, then zipped it shut and set it beside the door. All cleaned up and ready to go, Rick went to see whether Duke was still busy with the foreman.

He was halfway down the hall when the doorbell rang, pushed by an insistent hand. Below its strident sound came the familiar slip-slap of the housekeeper's thongs as she hurried across the foyer's Saltillo tiles to answer it.

The heavy mahogany-stained front door swung inward

under the pull of the stout housekeeper's hand. Rick's eyes rounded, staring in surprise when Vince Rossiter charged past the housekeeper, angrily demanding, 'Where the hell's DePard? I want to talk to him.'

Without waiting for an answer, Vince Rossiter made straight for the den. Rick moved closer, more out of curiosity than concern. He knew Duke could handle Eden Rossiter's brother. And Sheehan was still with him; Rick had a glimpse of him moving to intercept Vince. People claimed Sheehan had a mean streak and Rick believed it. Just the sight of the big, ugly birthmark on the foreman's face was enough to give Rick the willies.

Vince Rossiter ignored the foreman's presence and confronted DePard face to face, his body rigid with anger. 'You've gone too far, DePard,' he declared. 'My sister nearly got killed this afternoon because of you.'

'I don't know what you're talking about.' Duke DePard appeared cool, almost amused.

'The hell you don't!' Vince Rossiter thundered. 'I'm warning you, Duke, if you so much as hurt my sister, you better start looking over your shoulder, because I'll be hunting you.'

At a signal from Duke, the foreman walked over and closed the door to the den. Rick could no longer hear what was being said, only the murmur of voices punctuated by the sound of Vince Rossiter's raised in anger. Soon there wasn't even that.

What was going on?

4

Revitalized by a three-hour nap, a hot shower, and a change of clothes, Kincade came down the steps, his room key in his pocket. At the bottom of the stairs, he turned and headed into the casino lounge.

The television set on the back bar was tuned to a rerun of an old Andy Griffith show, its picture grainy with age and poor reception. None of the Lucky Starr's half-dozen patrons were watching the show. A few glanced up when Kincade walked in, then just as quickly looked away and displayed a sudden, rapt interest in their previous occupation.

Only Starr Davis smiled when she saw him. She wore a simple, body-hugging dress in a black floral print that flared about her legs as she walked toward him with a smooth sinuous grace, her smile holding welcome and pleasure.

'I was beginning to think you were going to spend the entire evening in your room . . . alone,' she said in greeting.

'Not hardly,' Kincade responded with a near smile that lightly mocked, his glance drifting down to the vee neckline and the succession of buttons and loops that ran down the front of her dress.

'You shaved.' Starr touched him because she wanted

to, trailing her fingers across the smoothness of his cheek. His skin was warm to the touch and scented with some fragrance that was earthy and all male.

'I needed it.' Along with a shower and a nap, Kincade could have added but didn't. 'I intended to see if my truck was fixed, but I saw from my window there was a closed sign hanging on the door.'

'I'm not surprised. Hoague usually locks up around five. You might as well sit down and have a drink,' she told him as she turned, hooking an arm through his to lead him to an empty table. 'Hoague will be in later. He always is.'

'Is it permitted to ask the owner to have a drink with me?' He pulled out a chair in invitation and waited, an eyebrow cocked.

'Always,' Starr replied with a pleased and husky laugh. 'But tonight I have other commitments.'

'A pity,' he said.

'It is.' The flicker of regret in her eyes was genuine. 'What can I get you to drink?'

'A beer.' Kincade sat down facing the doorway.

When Starr returned with his beer, the red-haired cowboy, Rusty Smith, strolled into the lounge, spotted Kincade, and wandered over.

'Care if I join you?'

'Not at all.' Kincade nodded at an empty chair.

'Thanks. I think I'll have me a beer,' he said to Starr, then pulled out the chair and sat down. 'I went for a walk around town. It sure didn't take very long. I got the feeling people aren't used to strangers showing up. They sure aren't very talkative.'

'People in small towns tend to be fairly close-mouthed – especially if someone starts asking direct questions.'

'Close-mouthed?' Rusty scoffed at the term. 'More like springing a steel trap, if you ask me. They'll give you the time of day and that's about it.'

The remark didn't require a response, and Kincade offered none, simply nodding. But Rusty Smith was a talker. He kept up a steady run of chatter that lasted through the first beer and into the second. Kincade listened with half an ear, relaxed and loose in his chair. Yet there was an alertness to his eyes, a kind of casual vigilance as he observed the comings and goings of customers through the front door.

When a cowboy sauntered into the lounge, Kincade's attention centered on him briefly. He wore a flat-brimmed hat with the front snapped down. A large square of white silk was knotted behind his neck and hung down the front of his shirt. Buckled over a pair of crisp new Levi's was a pair of short chaps called chinks. He had big Mexican rowels on his spurs with jinglebobs that chinged musically with each stride.

'That's what I call a genuine buckaroo,' Kincade remarked, using the vernacular for a term derived from the Spanish word *vaquero* and one that predated *cowboy* in common usage. At one time the word had been used to describe a man who adopted a different style of dress and used different gear and different methods to do essentially the same work as a cowboy. But over time there had been a gradual melding of dress, equipment, and method until a distinction could no longer be made between a cowboy and a buckaroo, and the terms became interchangeable.

Rusty Smith looked the man over, a sparkle of devilment in his eyes. 'I hope he don't forget himself and squat with his spurs on.'

'A point well taken,' Kincade replied with dry humor, a smile tucking in the corners of his mouth.

Rusty chortled.

'Audie Hayes, you slim-hipped little devil,' Starr Davis declared when she spotted the new arrival. 'This isn't Saturday night. What are you doing in town?'

'Well now, I'll tell you how it is.' He stopped in front of her and pushed his hat to the back of his head, showing a face drawn in serious lines. 'I was in Winnemucca last month and saw a camper with Iowa plates. It had a bumper sticker on the back that read: "Have you hugged your kids today?" I got to thinking about that. The more I thought, the more I realized just how long it's been since I was hugged. So I came to town to get me a cold beer and a warm hug.'

He grinned and opened his arms to her. Starr looked at them and shook her head, clearly amused at the ploy. 'The cold beer I can handle,' she told him and signaled to Roy to draw the man a draft. 'But as for the other, you're on your own.'

A ripple of low laughter traveled through the listening customers as they exchanged glances and nods that said Starr's response was precisely the kind they had expected her to make.

'You know, that woman could have her pick of any man in this town,' Rusty observed with a touch of wistfulness.

Kincade recalled his earlier conversation with Starr after his run-in with DePard. 'I think she's already done her picking.'

'Figures,' Rusty said and downed another swallow of beer as Starr approached their table.

'How are your drinks holding out?' Her glance went to their nearly empty glasses. 'Ready to order another round?'

'Not me.' Rusty tipped back in his chair and rubbed a hand over his stomach. 'I need to put some food in this stomach of mine before I pour another beer into it.'

'The same goes for me,' Kincade said.

'In that case . . .' She half turned toward the bar. 'Roy, bring these gentlemen some menus.' She directed a quick smile at Kincade and moved away from the table, trailing a hand across the back of his shoulder as she passed him.

Roy came out from behind the bar and crossed to their table, toting a pair of plastic menus, grumbling under his breath the whole way. He tossed them on the table without ceremony. 'We still ain't got breakfast,' he announced and walked off.

'Jolly fellow,' Kincade murmured, then looked up when the front door opened and Hoague Miller steered his ponderous bulk through the opening and propelled it into the lounge. The smile on his face fled the instant he noticed Kincade.

'Did you get the radiator hose fixed on my truck?'

'Yeah, it's fixed.' Hoague's expression was cold and shuttered. 'But the station's closed for the day, and I won't be opening up till around seven in the morning. You can come by then and settle up what you owe. Then you can have your truck.'

Something in the man's body language suggested that he expected an argument from Kincade, but Kincade didn't give him one, replying dryly, 'I wouldn't want you to put yourself out. I'll come by in the morning around seven.'

There was a hint of swagger to his lumbrous gait when Hoague Miller proceeded to the bar, joining the handful of his cronies gathered there. All smiled their approval at the way Hoague had handled the stranger, and sent smirking, sidelong glances in Kincade's direction. Totally indifferent to them, Kincade picked up his menu.

An hour later, finished with his meal, Kincade settled back in his chair and drew another long, slim cigar from his shirt pocket. He lit it with a match and shook out the flame before tossing the dead match into the plastic ashtray on the table.

The clump of booted feet accompanied the opening of

the front door, heralding the arrival of more customers. Again Kincade's attention swung to inspect the trio, centering first on the teen-aged boy who quickly distanced himself from the others.

'Hey, Mom, I'm back,' he said to Starr Davis as she came forward to welcome the group.

'It's about time, too.' She looked at her son with a mother's pride and adoration. Well on his way to becoming a strapping young man, he topped her by a good two inches. Starr reached up and brushed an imaginary strand of hair off his temple, needing an excuse to touch him. This was her child. The one good thing in her life. She wanted the best for him, no matter the cost. 'I was beginning to wonder where you were.'

'Well . . .' He looked back at the other two men, then faced her again. He was bursting with a hundred things he wanted to tell her about the day's happenings even as he struggled to project a manly indifference to it all. 'We would have been here sooner, but we were pretty dirty by the end of the day. Duke thought we should clean up first.'

'So I see.' Starr smiled her approval of the result, then directed that smile at Duke DePard when he joined them.

In a western-cut suit, with his darkly silver hair tamed into order beneath a black hat, Duke DePard looked every inch a range lord. 'Your son has worked up a man's appetite, Starr.'

'Have *you*?' The smoke in her voice and the smolder in her eyes injected a whole new meaning to the phrase.

DePard released a low chuckle, pleased by her calculated attempt to arouse his sexual interest. Around her, he always felt as virile as any young stud despite the advance of years. 'I don't recall a time when my appetite hasn't been healthy,' he declared with a trace of smugness.

'Good.' Starr's smile lengthened in silent promise before she turned back to her son. 'Why don't you run your things up to your room, Rick?' She waved a hand at the duffel bag he carried. 'Then join us at the table when you come down.'

'Sure.' But it was with reluctance that he moved away from them and headed for the stairs. Once there his pace quickened, taking him up the steps two at a time.

'Come on.' Starr hooked an arm around DePard's and clutched it with both hands the way a lover would. 'I have our table all set.'

Starr deliberately didn't include, either by look or gesture, the foreman of the Diamond D, who hovered nearby like some malevolent shadow. DePard however showed no such inclination as he glanced back at the man.

'You'll join us, Sheehan,' he stated, giving no one an option.

But Sheehan had spotted the stranger. He pointed Kincade out to DePard with a nod of his head, a look of malice in his eyes. DePard turned. Recognition flashed through his expression and hardened it. He flicked a censorious glance at Starr.

'You should be more particular about whom you serve.'

She made a quick, nervous attempt to soothe him. 'Now, Duke,' she began.

But he pulled his arm free of her and walked straight to the stranger's table. An instant silence gripped the room as other eyes swung to watch with a kind of tense expectancy.

'How come you're still in town?' DePard challenged.

Unmoved, Kincade lifted his head and released a puff of cigar smoke into the air. 'My pickup had a busted radiator hose. I had to get it fixed.' He gave DePard an amused stare. 'It should be ready in the morning.'

DePard swung about. Before his searching gaze located Hoague Miller, Hoague was on his feet and hustling forward with surprising quickness for a fat man. He darted an anxious glance at DePard and pawed in the side pocket of his coveralls.

'Fixed that hose this afternoon, Mr DePard. Got his keys right here.' He produced them from his pocket and pushed them onto the bar table in front of Kincade. 'Your truck's parked in front of the garage. Pick it up any time.'

DePard fixed another hostile look on Kincade. 'There. Now you have no more reason to stay.'

With amusement still tugging at the corners of his mouth, Kincade picked up the ring of keys and jingled them in his hand. 'I've already paid for a night's lodging here. I think I'll use it.'

The room hummed with shocked murmurs. No one defied DePard that way. It surprised DePard as much as it angered him. It was an affront to his authority, something that could not be tolerated. Conscious of his audience, DePard showed only a rigid composure.

'I wouldn't stay where I wasn't welcome,' DePard warned.

'No, you probably wouldn't,' Kincade agreed in a lazy drawl that drew even more wide-eyed looks.

DePard's temper flared, hot and bitter. It took every ounce of his will to check it. He was losing ground every time he opened his mouth and he knew it. Needing to regain it, DePard fired a glance at the red-haired cowboy sitting at the stranger's table.

'Are you with him?'

Rusty pulled back with a startled look. 'Me?'

'Rusty here had the misfortune of arriving in town about the same time I did,' Kincade inserted. 'I guess you could say we're two strangers passing the evening hours away with a few beers and some idle talk.'

Starr came up and laid a soothing hand on DePard's

arm, feeling the rigid contraction of his muscles as she cast a quick glance at Kincade, cautioning him not to bait DePard further. She knew better than most how hot and deep DePard's pride ran. It was the kind of pride that could not stand injury.

'Misfortune is the perfect word to describe all of this, Duke,' she said, keeping her voice husky and warm, and trying to inject a lightness into the moment. 'Kincade had barely been in town an hour when you drove your cattle through. He couldn't know the true situation.'

To her relief, DePard listened. 'I suppose ignorance is an excuse of sorts.'

'Of sorts,' Starr agreed, her lips curving in a smile that both teased and praised.

'That's real big of you,' Kincade murmured with mock sincerity and raised the cigar to his lips, holding it there between his teeth.

DePard studied him with sharpening eyes. 'You don't look like a fool, Kincade. But you talk like one. For now I'll overlook it.' DePard shifted slightly, in control and sure of himself again. 'If you're looking for work, come out to the Diamond D tomorrow and we'll hire you on.'

Kincade lowered the cigar. 'Isn't that curious? Do you know that is the second job offer I've had today. I never guessed there would be such a shortage of help in this part of Nevada.'

'What outfit offered you work?' DePard frowned in anger, already guessing the answer.

'Spur,' Kincade replied with a faint, slow smile.

'You'll work for the Diamond D, or you'll work for no one,' DePard snapped the threat. 'Make no mistake about that.'

'I hear you talking.' Kincade tapped the build-up of ash from his cigar.

DePard looked at him for a long, measuring second, then nodded. 'You will,' he stated and walked off.

Starr flashed a half-irritated, half-worried glance at
Kincade, then moved quickly after DePard. The foreman
Sheehan trailed more slowly, ambling past Kincade, his
eyes small and mean with promise.

'So that's the he-bull of the woods,' Rusty said in a soft
undertone once they were all out of earshot.

'That's him.' Kincade smiled crookedly. 'He does a lot
of pawing and snorting and shaking his horns, doesn't
he?'

'I got the feeling he's big enough to back it up.' Rusty
glanced at Kincade and gave a troubled shake of his
head. 'It might not have been smart to prod him the
way you did.'

Kincade's smile turned reckless. 'It's that streak of
Irish in me, I guess. Nothing gets my back up quicker
than a man telling me what I can and can't do.'

'A man can borrow a lot of trouble that way,' Rusty
declared and pushed his chair back. 'I think I'll go see
if that jukebox works. This place could stand some
livening up.'

'You might want to take your beer with you and find
somewhere else to sit,' Kincade suggested. 'Nobody will
have anything to do with you if you keep hanging
around me.'

Rusty looked around the room, then shrugged. 'I
figure they've already got me branded with the same
iron. I'll probably be back.' But he took his beer with
him when he sauntered over to the jukebox.

DePard walked straight to the table he always occupied, acknowledging no one along the way, and no one
attempted to attract his notice with a nod or a greeting.
The locals, always sensitive to his moods, left it to Starr
to deal with him, to placate or cajole – whichever the
occasion required.

Starr waited until DePard was seated, then asked,

all smiles, 'What can I bring you from the bar, Duke? Whiskey—'

'Coffee,' he answered, dry and distant, then flicked a glance at his trailing foreman. 'Matt, what do you want to drink?'

Starr swung about, her expression carefully schooled to conceal her dislike of the man. Her eyes went first to the large birthmark that stained his cheek, but it wasn't the birthmark that repelled her; it was the latent streak of cruelty she sensed in him. He had long arms and he carried his fists closed as though always prepared to hit at something.

'I'll take a beer,' Sheehan said, then continued without a break, 'How well do you know this fellow Kincade?'

'I don't know him well at all,' she replied. 'Why do you ask?'

'It struck me you were awfully quick to defend him. I thought maybe you might have known him back in Reno.' Sheehan looked at her with a slanting contempt.

She smiled her disdain at his suggestion. 'I never saw the man before today. As for defending him,' her smile turned smugly righteous, 'you know I don't allow any trouble in my place, regardless of who starts it . . . or why.' Smoothly Starr swung her attention back to DePard. 'By the way, I have a special treat for you tonight, Duke. The old sheepherder Winston Charlie came by with a big mess of trout. I knew how much you like it, so we're having it for dinner.'

'Sounds good.' He gave an absent nod of approval.

'I'll be right back with your drinks.' Starr touched his shoulder and moved off toward the bar.

DePard watched her, then let his glance sift through the scattering of local patrons, all of whom were studiously avoiding his eyes. There was a subtle change in the room's atmosphere. The tension was no longer electric, yet there remained a kind of taut expectancy.

Twice now, the stranger Kincade had stood up to him with people looking on. DePard recognized that – just as he recognized that everyone was waiting to see what he was going to do about it.

Sheehan pulled out the chair next to him, sat down, and lit a cigarette. He puffed on it a few times then held it near his lips. 'You want me to do something about that stranger's smart mouth, Mr DePard?' His voice was couched low, his hand concealing the slight movement of his lips.

Everything inside DePard said, No, let him be. What was the point? The man was unimportant, a stranger, a nobody, a nothing. By tomorrow, he would be long gone.

But DePard pulled in the impulse and thought back to Sheehan's earlier remarks at the ranch. If he failed to come down hard on the stranger for this small show of defiance, would the locals see it as a sign of weakness? Could it give one of them the idea he could act against DePard's wishes with impunity? A few were fool enough to think that way. If one did, DePard would have no choice but to deal harshly with that individual. Which would only create ill will among the rest over an injury to one of their own.

However, if he made an example of the stranger Kincade, the reaction would likely be a general nodding of heads and an 'I could have told him something like that was going to happen' attitude.

After weighing his options, DePard chose the logical one. 'Kincade needs to learn the error of his ways.' He glanced sideways at his foreman, considering him more carefully than before. Sheehan had his faults, all on the side of violence. 'Rough him up some, but make sure he's still able to travel. I want him out of town by morning. And do it outside,' DePard added. 'Not in here.'

'I may need a couple of the boys.' Sheehan studied

the stranger through the trail of smoke spiraling from his cigarette.

'Use your own judgment,' DePard stated, as always leaving the details of a job to Sheehan.

'Right.' He got up from the table with an expression of surly pleasure and headed for the back hall where the restrooms and public telephone were located.

At the bar, Starr filled a cup with coffee and set it on the serving tray, her mother's ear turned to the sound of her son bounding down the steps. The instant he reached the lounge, Rick concealed his haste and entered at a casual saunter. Starr fought back a smile at this obvious simulation of a cowboy's gait as she tipped a glass mug under the beer tap.

Three strides into the lounge, Rick's wandering gaze fell on Kincade. He did a slight doubletake, shot a concerned glance at DePard, and immediately altered his course, angling toward the bar.

'Mom, isn't that the guy—' he began in a low tone that reeked of accusation.

'Yes. I'm taking drinks to the table. What would you like?' She capped the beer with a head of foam and placed it on the tray with the coffee.

'What? Oh, a Coke, I guess. Has Duke seen him?'

'He has.'

Rick drew his head back in surprise, her answer clearly not the one he had expected. Starr saw it, but chose not to tell Rick of the confrontation between Duke and Kincade – or the role she had played in it. She was irritated with herself now for stepping in. It had been a foolish move. Even then she had known that.

As she turned to fetch Rick's Coke, her glance strayed to the far table where DePard and Sheehan were seated, conversing in low tones. At that moment Sheehan stood up and threw a half-smirking look at Kincade before his long legs carried him off toward the rear hallway.

Suddenly uneasy, Starr kept an eye on him. Sheehan didn't go into the men's room; he went straight to the pay phone. Something told her Sheehan's phone call had to do with Kincade. DePard wasn't finished with him; he was going to make trouble for him. What kind of trouble Starr didn't know, but she knew it was coming.

She crushed all thought of warning Kincade to watch his step tonight. She had foolishly come to his defense once on the pretext of keeping peace in her establishment. She wasn't about to jeopardize her position or her plans by interfering again. While it was true she was attracted to Kincade, he wasn't worth what it might cost her. No man was.

Hardened by the thought, Starr picked up the drink tray and balanced it on one hand, then flashed an indulgent smile at her son. 'Let's go join Duke.'

Rick's frown lifted as he swung away from the bar with undisguised eagerness, the stranger forgotten. 'I forgot to ask what we're having for dinner tonight.'

'Fresh trout.'

'Trout?'

Starr laughed at his less than enthusiastic response. 'Don't worry. I told Roy to throw a steak on the grill for you.'

He grinned his gratitude, which was more than sufficient thanks for Starr. When they reached the table, Rick pulled out the chair Sheehan had recently vacated and sat down next to Duke. Starr set the drinks around, then took a seat on the other side of Duke.

'I heard on the radio that the weather bureau is forecasting a seventy percent chance of rain by the end of the week.' Starr opened the conversation with a safe topic. 'You may have moved your cattle prematurely.'

'I doubt it,' DePard replied. 'In this dry country, I believe rain forecasts when I see the drops coming out of the sky – especially at this time of the year.'

'Yeah,' Rick chimed in. 'The Sierras usually grab all the moisture from any clouds long before they get here.'

'True,' DePard agreed, then glanced up when Sheehan returned to the table.

Their eyes locked briefly and Sheehan gave a slight nod of his head as if in answer to his question. Starr witnessed the silent exchange and sensed immediately that some plan had been put in motion. She had no doubt Kincade was the target.

He sat alone at the table, his back to her, blue-gray smoke from his cigar rising above the crown of his hat. The red-haired Rusty was at the jukebox, punching up song selections. A George Strait tune came over the side speakers, its swing tempo and lighthearted lyrics injecting a false note of conviviality into the undercurrents of tension that swam through the room.

Looking at Kincade, Starr felt a twinge of longing and immediately rejected it. DePard had made him a marked man. She couldn't help him. More than that, she wouldn't try.

Around nine o'clock, two Diamond D ranch hands wandered into the Lucky Starr, hesitated, and looked around until they spotted the foreman. Starr pretended not to notice them or the movement of Sheehan's head that directed them to an empty stretch along the mahogany bar. Once both men had claimed a section of the brass footrail, Sheehan pushed his chair back.

'Jenkins and Foster just came in,' he told DePard. 'I'll be over with them if you want me.'

DePard responded with a nod, then deliberately turned his attention to Rick, catching him in the middle of a yawn. Rick tried vainly to smother it, a redness creeping into his face.

'Tired, aren't you?' DePard observed.

'Kinda,' Rick said sheepishly. 'It's been a long day.'

'And a hard one,' DePard agreed, then included Starr with a glance. 'You should have seen your son today riding hell-bent-for-leather after a steer that bolted from the herd.'

'You saw that?' Rick said, surprised and pleased by the discovery.

'I did.' DePard's expression turned thoughtful. 'In fact, I know of only one other man who rode with such abandon.' He didn't identify the man by name, but it was obvious to Starr that he was referring to his late brother, Jeff DePard. His comment was just the sort of comparison she wanted Duke to make, the kind she encouraged at every opportunity.

'Have you told your mother about that incident?' he asked.

'Not yet.' Rick hesitated, then launched into a second-by-second account of it.

Starr tried to concentrate on his words, but she was distracted by the scene unfolding before her. Sheehan had joined the other two Diamond D riders. All three leaned idly on the bar, striking poses that were too nonchalant to be natural. They conversed in low tones, with Sheehan doing most of the talking. Every now and then one of them would steal a look at Kincade.

After a time Sheehan moved off, taking his beer, and wandering down to the other end of the bar where the buckaroo Audie Hayes was bending Roy's ears with his tall tales. One look from Sheehan, and Roy found something else to do. When Audie started to leave as well, Sheehan said something to him and the man turned back. A discussion followed, but not about the weather. Finally Audie checked his watch and nodded. Sheehan lifted his beer mug in acknowledgment, then downed the contents and shoved the empty glass onto the bar top.

Before he pushed back from the bar, he looked at the

two Diamond D hands. Some invisible signal passed between them. The two made a noisy show of paying for their beers and taking their leave. Only Starr noticed when Sheehan slipped into the kitchen where a back door would take him outside.

The jukebox came to life again as Rusty Smith fed more quarters into it. After he made his song choices, he ambled back to Kincade's table.

'I was right,' he said, pulling out a chair and slumping onto it. 'Every time I try to strike up a conversation with a local, I get the cold shoulder. They figure I'm with you, so I figured I might as well be.'

'Be my guest,' Kincade said with a near smile.

'Thanks. The place is pretty quiet on a week night, isn't it?'

'It's a small town.'

Rusty snorted at that. 'Full of small-minded people.'

'I'll drink to that.' Kincade raised his glass.

'Good idea.' Rusty followed suit and gulped down the two swallows of beer left in his mug. Finishing it, he released a gusty sigh of pleasure and placed his empty glass on the table. 'I think I'll have me another one. How about you?'

Kincade shook his head. 'I'll nurse the one I've got a while longer. But since you're here, I'll take a walk back to the men's room. Make sure Roy doesn't take my beer while I'm gone.'

'Will do.' When Kincade left the table, Rusty tried to catch the bartender's eye, without success. 'Hey, Roy,' he finally yelled. 'Bring me another beer, will ya?'

But Roy continued to ignore him. In the end it was Starr who brought him a beer. She set it down in front of him, her expression all apologetic and warm.

'This is real nice, but I sure never meant to bother you.' Rusty dug into his pocket to pay for the beer.

'No problem at all. I like my customers to be happy,'

Starr replied in a rather loud voice, then held out her hand for the money and added in a quick, low tone, 'Don't say anything. Just listen. Tell Kincade to watch himself. Sheehan is laying for him.' She took the bills from his unresisting fingers and said, again quite loudly, 'Thanks.'

Rusty gave her a startled look, then recovered and offered a distracted 'Thank you' as she stepped away.

Kincade came out of the men's room in time to see Starr take her seat again at DePard's table. In the next moment his view of her was blocked by the approaching Audie Hayes. Kincade moved to one side of the narrow hall to let the man pass, but the buckaroo stepped into his path, stopping him.

'Are you the one who calls himself Kincade?'

'I am,' Kincade admitted with a slight frown.

'There's a guy wants to see you. Privately. He's waiting outside. He doesn't want to be seen talking to you.'

'What does he want?'

'Hey, I'm just the message boy,' the cowboy declared with a careless grin and went past Kincade into the men's room.

Kincade paused and scanned the room. All eyes were turned away from him, yet there was something in the air. A faint chill fiddled through his nerves. It was the way a sense of trouble always came to him. But curiosity got the better of him. He struck out, aiming for the front door.

'Where are you going?' Rusty called out when he passed his table.

'I'll be back.' Kincade threw the words over his shoulder and continued on.

Once outside, a sense of caution checked him and he stopped and swept his gaze over the town's main street. The staggered pattern of streetlights spilled pools of light all the way up and down the street.

Here and there a light glowed from a storefront window. The rest of the town's buildings were darkened. A few vehicles were parked farther up the street, but most were crowded around the Lucky Starr, strips of their chrome reflecting a pale silvery sheen. In every area not illuminated by the town's lights, the shadows lay black and velvet-thick.

Beyond, night closed around the town, swallowing the roads that led out of it, linking the isolated community to the outer world. The air had a cool nip to it, the setting of the sun bringing a rapid drop of temperature at this elevation. A breeze drifted softly out of the high desert, carrying the smell of sage, baked earth, and a trace of wildness.

There was a waiting stillness to the town. Nothing stirred. Nothing moved.

'Kincade. Over here.' The furtive whisper came from his right.

Turning, Kincade studied the solid darkness beneath the roofed walk where no light reached. 'Step out where I can see you.'

A board plank creaked. Kincade zeroed in on the sound as the silhouette of a man in a rolled-brim hat emerged from the shadows to show itself against the pale track of the town's north road.

'I'm over here.' It was the same voice, still pitched in a low whisper.

Unable to see the man's face or recognize his voice, Kincade hesitated. 'Who are you?'

'Not so loud,' the man hissed and motioned for him to come closer even as the man retreated to blend again with the black shadows.

More curious now than wary, Kincade followed the man. 'What did you want to see me about?'

The words were barely out of his mouth when two figures sprang at him from the darkness. Kincade tried to spin to meet them, but he was a split second slow. They were on him in an instant, seizing his arms and yanking him back around. Before he could shake loose, a fist slammed into his midsection doubling him over.

Again and again blows hammered his face, ribs, and stomach. Some he managed to absorb; the rest he reeled from, but the imprisoning hands always pulled him back for more, allowing no escape. There was a roaring in his ears as pain dulled his senses. At last his legs buckled and he sank to his knees.

'Stand him up,' a voice said.

The hands hauled him upright again and shoved him against the wall of the building, holding him there. Numbly Kincade tried to brace himself for the next blow. When it failed to come, he forced his eyes to open and stared at the hazy figure directly in front of him.

'You're not such a tough guy anymore, are you?'

Half-groggy from the beating he had taken, Kincade was slow to recognize the jeering voice. DePard's foreman. The one with the large birthmark on his face.

The man loomed closer, his features still shadowy and indistinct in the darkness. 'Stay away from the Rossiter woman – do you hear?'

'Rossiter?' Kincade repeated the name, grabbing at it and struggling now to concentrate. 'Is that—'

His jaw and chin were seized in a talon-grip that cracked his head back against the building. Color exploded behind his eyes.

'Don't play dumb with me, Kincade. It won't work,' the foreman snarled. 'Now hear me and hear me good. Come morning, you better be long gone from this town—'

Light from an open door suddenly flooded the walkway as a man stepped out of the Lucky Starr. In one glance, he took in the scene and called out a sharp, 'Hey, what's going on there? Let him go.' He rushed forward, the door closing behind him.

The foreman released Kincade's chin and swung to block the red-haired cowboy's advance. 'You're reading this all wrong, mister,' he taunted smoothly. 'Your buddy here must have had too much to drink. He fell and banged himself up pretty good. We were just helping him to his feet, weren't we, boys?'

The two ranch hands backed up his claim.

'That's right.'

'Yeah, we sure were.'

'Yeah, and coyotes guard sheep, too,' Rusty scoffed in a reckless temper. 'I think you've *helped* him enough. I'll take over now.'

'You heard him, boys,' Sheehan said, smiling his contempt. 'Give him his friend.'

Hands tightened their grip. With a hard yank, they jerked Kincade away from the wall and pushed him straight at Rusty. Rusty staggered back under his weight, but managed to keep them both upright. Sheehan laughed softly and strolled on by, followed by his snickering cohorts.

With his legs solidly under him again, Kincade recovered his balance and straightened away from Rusty, but Rusty kept a steadying hand on him. Punch-drunk and dazed, Kincade shook his head to clear it, then tried to take a deep, cleansing breath. His battered ribs made an instant protest, drawing a grunt of pain from him.

'You okay?' Rusty peered at him.

'I've been hurt worse,' he answered in a voice that was low and hoarse. 'Just get me inside.'

5

By the time Kincade reentered the Lucky Starr, the numbness had begun to wear off. Pain jabbed him in a dozen different areas. There was a throbbing along his cheekbone and a savage pounding in his head. He walked slightly hunched forward, one arm cradling his badly bruised midsection and the other hand clamped on Rusty's shoulder for support. Each step jarred.

The chatter of voices and clink of glasses ceased the instant he came into view, then erupted again in a fresh rush. Intent on reaching the staircase to his room, Kincade never saw where Starr came from. One moment there was nothing between him and the stairs, and in the next, she was in his path.

She made a quick visual inspection of him, her lips tightening their line, her only outward reaction to the sight of him. 'I don't need to ask what happened,' she said briskly.

Kincade tried to smile and winced, discovering a cut along the inside of his mouth. He saw movement with his peripheral vision. Kincade swung his head toward the movement, fighting his head's heaviness. A handful of bar patrons had gravitated closer for a better look. Starr's son Rick was among them, staring at Kincade with shocked fascination. DePard was in the forefront, coldly satisfied with what he saw.

Kincade looked for and found the Diamond D foreman a discreet distance behind DePard. 'You might hear two different stories. If you did,' he said to Starr in a voice that still lacked its former strength, 'DePard's man would tell you I had too much to drink and fell.'

'Did you?' The deadly soft challenge came from DePard.

Kincade opened his mouth to reply to that, but it required too much effort. He swayed a little. Starr saw it and intervened.

'It doesn't matter.' She moved aside and motioned to Rusty. 'Take him up to his room.' Starr pivoted, her skirt flaring, her voice lifting. 'Roy, bring me the first-aid kit from behind the bar. The rest of you, go on back to your drinks. The excitement's over.'

With outspread arms, Starr herded the small group back into the lounge, all except DePard, who remained where he was. She treated him to a cool, critical look.

'Was that necessary?'

'It was,' he stated as Roy arrived with the first-aid kit. 'Make certain he's fit to travel.'

'I will.' With the kit in hand, she crossed to the stairs.

Rick intercepted her at the bottom. 'Will you be okay, Mom? Maybe I should go with you?'

Smiling, Starr cupped a loving hand to his cheek. 'I'll be fine. Stay here and keep Duke company.'

Reluctantly Rick stood back and watched her climb the steps.

The second-floor room measured a scant eight-by-ten with most of that space taken up by an old iron bed. The first-aid kit lay open on top of a massive pine dresser too big for the small room. Kincade sat on the edge of the bed, his muscles slack and his head tipped down while Starr examined the egg-sized knot on the back of his head.

'The skin isn't broken,' she said, drawing back.

Kincade reached up to check it himself and sucked in a wincing breath when he touched a tender spot. Rusty saw it and grimaced in empathy.

'They didn't waste any time banging you around,' he said. 'You couldn't have been gone more than a couple of minutes.'

'He mentioned a name,' Kincade said. 'It sounded like Rossiter.'

'Rossiter?' Rusty echoed.

'Eden Rossiter.' Starr supplied the rest of the name. 'She's the woman you foolishly rescued today.'

'The notorious owner of Spur, the one who killed DePard's brother,' Kincade recalled in a dead-flat voice.

'Killed his brother?' Rusty repeated. 'You're kidding, aren't you?'

'Not hardly.' Starr gave him an amused look. 'She shot Jeff out of jealousy when she learned he was seeing someone else.'

'You make it sound like she killed DePard's brother in cold blood.' Rusty frowned. 'If she murdered him, how come she's still walking around free? Why isn't she in prison?'

'Her grandfather, Jed Rossiter, gets the credit or the blame for that, depending on your point of view. He was the first to learn about the shooting. Before the sheriff got there, he hit her, ripped her clothes, and staged it to look like Jeff had assaulted her. Then he hired one of the best criminal lawyers in Nevada to defend her. Her lawyer not only managed to stall the trial for three years, he also convinced the judge that it would be impossible to get a fair and impartial jury here. The trial was moved to Tonopah. By then she had her story down pat. I've been told she gave a remarkable performance when she took the witness stand.'

'There were no witnesses to the shooting?' Kincade asked, his curiosity rising.

'None,' Starr replied with a small shake of her head. 'As so often happens with a jury, the fact that the DePards owned easily one of the largest ranches in Nevada and that Jeff was a star athlete, extremely handsome and popular, went against him. The jury preferred to believe the worst about someone who – as the old saying goes – had everything. It didn't matter to them that Jeff could have had his pick of women, he didn't have to force himself on someone. Their verdict was not guilty by reason of self-defense. You can imagine how that decision went over around here. There was outrage, to say the least.'

'It sure wouldn't win her any friends,' Rusty concluded.

'Where's her grandfather now?' Kincade wondered.

'He died a few years back and left control of the ranch to Eden.' Starr reached into the first-aid kit again. 'That cut on your cheek could use a bandage.'

'It's okay.' Kincade waved off the suggestion and started to shift his position on the bed. The movement drew an instant protest from his badly bruised ribs, stopping him. 'If you have anything in that kit for pain, I'll take some of it.'

'Whiskey is the best pain-killer I have on hand,' Starr said with a smile and turned to Rusty. 'Go downstairs and get a bottle. Tell Roy I sent you.'

'Be back in a jig's tail,' Rusty promised and went out the door.

When the latch clicked shut behind him, Starr took an antiseptic wipe from the kit and moved back to Kincade's side. 'If you don't want a bandage, at least let me clean the dried blood from your cheek.'

She curved a finger under his chin to tilt his head up. Kincade obeyed the pressure, his gaze coming up to examine her face.

'Why are you doing this?' he asked. 'DePard isn't going to like it that you're up here tending to my wounds.'

The line of her mouth lengthened in a long, ironic smile as she dabbed gently at the trickle of dried blood on his cheek. 'I hope you aren't laboring under the impression that I have a heart of gold,' she mocked. 'Believe me, if I had one, I would have sold it for twice what it was worth a long time ago.'

Kincade smiled back, liking her candor. 'If you aren't here out of the goodness of your heart, then why?'

'Maybe DePard sent me.'

'To make sure his message was hammered home, I suppose,' Kincade guessed. 'That makes sense.'

'And was his message hammered home?'

'It came through loud and clear,' he replied in a dry voice.

Starr wiped the last of the blood from his cheek and straightened, her expression turning serious. 'He had to make an example of you, Kincade, to keep the others in line. You stood up to him. He couldn't allow that.'

'You're telling me it wasn't personal,' he mocked.

'It wasn't.'

'You can tell him for me to go to hell. Nothing personal.'

Starr smiled and tossed the soiled antiseptic wipe into the metal wastebasket beside the dresser, then turned back to again inspect the damage to his face – the small cut along his high, hard cheekbone, the puffy flesh around it, and the beginnings of a bruise on his jaw. 'You're lucky he didn't have Sheehan mark you up worse.'

'He would have, if Rusty hadn't shown up when he did.'

As if on cue, Rusty returned, a whiskey bottle tucked in the crook of his arm and his fingers clutching a trio of glasses. 'I figured we could all use a dose of this.' He plunked the glasses on the dresser, uncapped the whiskey bottle, and poured a measure into each glass, then passed them out. He lifted his glass to Kincade. 'Look out bruises, look out pains, this'll wash you right down the drain.'

'Hear, hear.' A smile briefly twisted Kincade's mouth before he downed a healthy swallow of whiskey, welcoming the lava-burn in his throat. Without waiting for the fire to numb him, he cradled a supporting arm around his bruised middle and inched his way closer to the head of the iron bed. He fortified himself with another drink of whiskey, then set the glass on the pine commode and lay back against the pillows, his teeth gritted against the pain.

'How do you feel?' Rusty studied him with quiet concern.

Kincade released a short breath, the closest he could come to a laugh. 'Like some bull did a Mexican hat dance on my stomach.'

'What about your ribs? Are any of them broken?'

Kincade took a silent inventory, listening inwardly for the grate of bone against bone. Hearing none and feeling no hot-centered stab of pain, he gave a quick shake of his head. 'No, they're just bruised.' He focused on Starr. 'DePard will be wondering what's keeping you. You better go make your report.'

'What do I tell him?' Despite the lazy smile on her lips, her eyes were sharp and watchful.

'Tell him I got his message, that come morning I'll be checking out and looking at Friendly in my rearview mirror.'

Starr weighed his words, then nodded in apparent satisfaction. 'I'll tell him.' She set her untouched drink on the dresser. 'I'm almost sorry you'll be leaving, but it's best all the way around.' Her eyes softened. 'Take care of yourself, Kincade.'

'I will.'

Rusty opened the door for her. Starr walked out, leaving a trace of her cologne in the air. As soon as she left, Rusty turned an amused look on Kincade.

'So you're leaving in the morning, are you?' Rusty said, not buying a word of it.

'First thing.' Kincade nodded, a smile forming. 'Eden Rossiter has a job waiting for me at Spur.'

Dust motes danced and sparkled in the stream of morning sunlight that flowed through the second-floor window. In the street below, the revving of a pickup broke the town's early morning quiet. Starr wandered over to the window and leaned a silk-clad shoulder against the frame; her fingers were laced around a cup of coffee.

The pickup reversed away from the Lucky Starr, backing into the street. From her angle, Starr couldn't see the driver, but she recognized the truck. It belonged to the stranger, Kincade.

He was leaving. The knowledge registered with a mixture of regret and longing that Starr crushed before it could take root. But she stayed at the window, watching as Kincade's pickup approached the intersection, slowed, and made a *right* turn, taking the north road out of town. The road to the Rossiter place.

The fool, Starr thought, but she smiled the smallest of smiles.

'Did I hear a truck?' DePard came out of the bathroom, freshly showered and fully clothed. 'Who was it? Did you see?' he asked in idle curiosity.

'It was Kincade.' Starr pushed away from the window and wandered over to him, the silk of her short wrap whispering with her movements.

A coffee service sat on a glass-topped table in the bedroom's sitting area. DePard walked over to it and refilled his cup. 'I take it he was leaving town?'

'What other choice did he have?' Starr deliberately avoided a direct answer. It was rare for DePard to stay the night, and she wasn't about to have their time together end on a sour note.

'None,' DePard stated in a self-satisfied voice.

Starr didn't argue with that. 'Have you decided what you want for breakfast?'

Dirt boiled around the speeding pickup and fanned out behind it in a long tan plume. In all directions there was nothing but miles and miles of wide-open emptiness, dotted with clumps of sagebrush and carpeted with tough grasses. Iron-gaunt hills showed on the horizon and high above, a hawk rode a morning thermal.

The dirt road ran straight, hugging the dips and swells of the high desert country. For the last twenty minutes Kincade hadn't seen another vehicle or any sign of human habitation except for the powerlines racing alongside his pickup and the occasional cross-fences and cattle guards that marked boundaries between ranches.

He glanced at the odometer. He should be coming to the ranch turn-off any time now. There had been a small wooden sign on the last cross-fence with faded lettering that read: Spur Ranch, J. Rossiter.

He was watching for the turn-off, and still almost missed it as the power poles raced on and only a telephone line made the swing up a low hillock on his right. The lane was little more than a pair of ruts that ran more or less parallel. Braking, Kincade swung the wheel and the pickup bounced onto the track, the tires sliding into the twin ruts.

When he topped the knoll, the track faded to a faint trail, partially overgrown with grass. He bumped another three miles, wincing now and then at the jolting his battered ribs were taking despite the Ace bandage that girdled them.

The road snaked in and around a succession of foot-hills, then made a final swing into a wide and shallow canyon, walled on three sides by long, gentle slopes. A stand of cottonwood trees made a splash of green at the head of the canyon.

Off to the left, Kincade saw a cluster of low buildings tucked among gray boulders. A half-dozen horses stood in a corral and more grazed in a fenced pasture, their tails busy swishing away flies. Several lifted their heads when he drove into the ranch yard.

Kincade bypassed the collection of outbuildings and headed straight for the two-story adobe house nestled among the cottonwood trees. A roofed porch ran the entire length of its front. An old cowdog bounded from the shade to intercept the pickup, hackles raised as it barked an alarm.

Kincade slowed to a stop in front of the house and climbed out of the cab. The dog immediately planted itself between Kincade and the house, growling a warning. Kincade noticed the scars on its coat and chose not to test the old dog's mettle.

'Hello! Anyone home?' he called to the house.

There was no answer, and no one came to the door. Kincade wasn't surprised. At this hour of the morning, it was likely everyone was about their jobs.

The chugging rumble of a tractor starting up came from somewhere in the near distance. The old Blue Heeler swung its head toward the east, then faced

Kincade again, whining anxiously in its throat and baring its long, yellowed teeth.

'Is that where they are, fella?' Kincade turned, as the dog had, to locate the tractor.

A rough track curved away from the house toward a set of holding pens with a loading chute. Beyond the pens, the gold of a hayfield gleamed in the morning sunlight, half-hidden by the footslope of the canyon that walled the ranchyard. An old tractor chugged into view, pulling a flat rack loaded with a dozen square bales.

Kincade crawled back into his truck and headed for the hayfield. The old cowdog followed. Ahead, the tractor slowed and two men hopped off the wagon and began tossing hay bales onto it for a third person to stack. Kincade parked at the edge of the field and stepped out of the truck to wait for the tractor and hay rack to draw level with him. The sun was in his face and the smell of cured hay mingled with the odor of dust and sage.

The driver of the tractor saw Kincade first and hollered something to the others, his exact words lost under the growling rumble of the tractor. A figure appeared from behind the rack's growing stack of bales. It was Eden Rossiter.

Again Kincade was struck by the illusion of height she projected with the stiff squaring of her shoulders and the proud tilt of her head. She stood with legs braced against the bounce of the flat rack, a hay hook gripped in each gloved hand. She had on a black tank top that bared her arms and showed the ripeness of her figure, which the man's white shirt she wore yesterday had only hinted at. A hat shaded her eyes, but Kincade knew the instant she saw him. It was like a leap of something electric between them.

The connection was broken when she turned and signaled to the driver to stop, then issued an order to one of the men tossing bales. He nodded, pushed a bale onto the wagon bed, and climbed after it. She passed the hay hooks to him, then jumped to the ground and proceeded toward Kincade, cutting a straight line across the hay stubble.

Kincade met her halfway. She stopped, keeping a good yard of ground between them. There was a sheen of perspiration on her skin. His glance drifted to the small rivulet of sweat that ran down the front of her, disappearing under the black tank top. When he looked up, Eden Rossiter regarded him with cool censure.

He touched a finger to his hat brim, feeling an edge of sexual awareness kick through him. 'I'm looking for the boss.'

'You found me.' She inspected his bruised jaw, the cut on his cheekbone, and the discolored flesh around it. 'I see you did some brawling last night. I trust you landed a few punches of your own,' she remarked as she stripped off her leather work gloves.

'Not a one.' Kincade smiled when her eyes narrowed on him, sharp with surprise and question. 'It's hard to hit back when two men are holding you.'

'DePard,' she guessed with sudden grimness.

'His foreman.'

'Same thing.' She shrugged off the minor discrepancy.

'Is that job offer of yours still open?'

'Why would you want it now?'

'Because DePard ordered me not to work for Spur. Naturally, that's just what I want to do. Call it a character flaw.' It was Kincade's turn to shrug. 'Do I have the job?'

'You're hired.' Eden stepped forward to shake on it. His callused hand engulfed hers, rough and strong and warm. She felt a little involuntary jolt of something she would neither name nor acknowledge. She looked up to his face, catching the slow smile that moved over it, the angles shifting, the shadows playing. Morning sunlight touched his hair, burnishing the ends of it. It was the tawny color of a mountain cat. The word *dangerous* came to her mind.

Eden pulled her hand free of his grip and thumbed it toward the field. 'Go start pitching bales.'

She turned and headed back to the hay wagon, with Kincade walking stride for stride with her. Eden didn't regret her decision. With haying season, she would have hired anything that walked on two legs. In some ways, it was an added bonus that this stranger Kincade had already shown he would stand up to DePard. She considered herself lucky to have him, but that didn't mean she was comfortable with him, or with the disturbing feelings that drifted through her like smoke.

Rejoining the hay crew, Eden wasted no time on introductions and put Kincade to work on the ground, picking up bales and throwing them onto the wagon. She reclaimed her former position on the rack and went straight to the business of stacking the bales.

Tossing thirty- and forty-pound bales onto the flat rack awakened every sore muscle Kincade had. When a halt was called at noon time, he was ready for a break. He climbed onto the rack and rode it as far as his pickup.

When he jumped to the ground, Eden Rossiter motioned to one of the other ranch hands. 'Go with Kincade, Al. Show him where to bunk.'

A short, stocky cowboy who had passed his prime several years ago hopped off the wagon to join him. A tired smile rearranged the deep lines in his ruddy face.

'Your truck is bound to offer a smoother ride for these old bones of mine than that hay rack,' the aging cowboy declared.

'I hear you,' Kincade replied and struggled to ignore his own aches as he pulled himself into his truck.

The cowboy crawled in the passenger side and settled onto the cushioned seat with a contented sigh. 'I remember the time when I could work from dawn to dusk with never a break. Now, they can't come often enough. It's hell gettin' old,' he said with a faint grimace, then glanced at Kincade. 'The name's Al Bender.'

'Mine's Kincade.' He started up the truck and pulled in behind the hay wagon to follow it to the ranchyard. 'You worked here long?'

'About seven or eight months this time. Off and on through the years,' Al replied and ran an inspecting eye over him. 'You ain't worked around these parts before, have you, Kincade?'

'First time.'

'I thought so.' When the tractor-drawn hay wagon swung toward the barn, Al motioned for Kincade to continue straight ahead. 'The bunkhouse is that way.'

Kincade parked the pickup in front and climbed out. Like the main house, it was built of adobe, bleached pale by the sun. Its thick walls promised coolness inside and relief from the sun's glare. Kincade retrieved his gear from the back of the truck and headed for the door, where Al Bender waited for him.

The aging cowboy shot a glance at the duffel bag he carried. 'Is that it?'

Kincade nodded. 'I'll need the loan of a saddle.'

'Got short of cash and had to sell yours, huh?' Al guessed and Kincade didn't dispute. 'There's extras in the barn. A couple of double-rigged saddles and one center-fire.' He glanced at the pickup's Texas license plates. 'I expect you'll want the double-rigged.'

'I will.'

Al nodded and opened the door. Kincade followed him inside, then paused to look around. The common room smelled of stale air, unwashed bodies, and old woodsmoke. An ancient iron stove sat in one corner, providing the sole source of heat during the cold winters of northern Nevada. A table and a collection of mismatched chairs stood in the center of the room, a worn deck of cards spread out in an abandoned game of solitaire. There was an old, overstuffed chair in another corner, its armrests torn and its seat cushion hollowed with heavy usage. The pictures hanging on the walls were yellowed with nicotine and age, and the lone calendar was three years out of date.

'No television?' Kincade observed.

'Not much point in having one unless you got a satellite dish – which the boss don't. And we're too far away to pull in the signals from the television stations. Hell, half the time you can't get anything on the radio but static.' Al shrugged. 'You aren't going to have the frills that you probably had in Texas. All you get is the bare bones in this part of the country.'

'So I can see.'

'The sleeping rooms are that way.' Al nodded at the hall that ran the length of the building. 'The showers and toilets are at the end.'

With duffel bag in hand, Kincade walked down the hall until he found an unoccupied cubicle. He tossed his bag onto the cot and went to wash up.

Al was waiting for him when he came out. 'Let's go eat. The cook shack is this way.'

Taking the lead, Al left the bunkhouse and headed around the building, striking out across the dirt yard, the dragging heels of his boots raising little puffs of dust with each step.

A shrill whistle pierced the air, followed within seconds by the pounding of hooves. Kincade spotted a tall bay stallion racing along a section of high fence, its nose up, black tail flying. When he paused, Al Bender stopped as well and watched the horse as it plunged to a stop at the fence corner and stood quivering, its ears pricked toward the mountains.

Kincade looked the stallion over. 'He has the look of a Thoroughbred.'

'He is, mostly,' Al confirmed. 'In this country you need a horse with stamina to cover long distances at a strong trot. The boss has a band of broodmares she breeds him to. About half the mares are registered quarter horses. She keeps most of the colts out of 'em to use here on the ranch. The rest she sells. Good ranch geldings are bringing top dollar now.' Al started forward again. 'One thing you can say about this place – you got good horses to ride.'

'What else can you say about it?' Kincade asked curiously.

'The grub's good.' Al nodded in the direction of the ranch kitchen, a small one-story building built of adobe, like the others.

Flies beat at the cook shack's screen door. Inside, a radio blared a Willie Nelson song about Pancho and Lefty. Al pulled open the screen door and walked in. Kincade followed him inside, his stomach rumbling as he inhaled the yeasty aroma of freshly baked bread.

Al walked past the long table flanked by wooden benches straight to the kitchen area in the rear. Over his shoulder, Kincade had a glimpse of an old woman with long and straggly gray hair standing with her back to them. Al walked up to the counter near the woman, reached past her, and turned down the radio. The old woman spun to face him, brandishing a long, serrated bread knife.

'What're you doing sneaking up on a body like that?' came a gravelly-voiced demand, too deeply pitched and rough to come from a woman. Kincade had his first clear look at the cook's profile and the gray stubble of a beard on his face – and immediately revised his first impression. This was a man, not a woman.

'That was a damn fine thing to do,' the cook complained to Al. 'I could have killed you with my knife.'

Undeterred by the threat and the cutting slash of the blade, Al countered, 'If you didn't play that damned radio so loud, you would have heard me come in. I hope you fixed plenty of food. There'll be an extra at the table. The boss hired a new man.' He nodded in Kincade's direction.

The old cook swung around to glare at Kincade, then looked up to the ceiling and lifted his arms in a kind of supplication. 'Hear me, great Spirit. For many moons, my grandfather made war against the blue coats and the pale-faces who stole our land. Many times he led warriors into battle. Many times he sat at their council fire and smoked the pipe of peace—'

'Cut the crap,' Al broke in, then waved a hand at Kincade. 'This is the new man. His name's Kincade. And this character, believe it or not, is the cook here. His real name is Frederick Daniels, but we all call him Wild Jack.'

The man shot a look at Al, then turned back to the loaf of bread he'd been slicing. 'Nobody shows respect for their elders no more. A damn fine shame, that's what it is,' he grumbled loudly.

Al grinned at Kincade. 'He claims his grandfather was a Sioux war chief. There's about as much chance of that as there is of me being related to the Pope.' He walked over to the insulated keg that sat on the counter facing the dining area. 'How about some iced tea?'

'Sounds good.' Kincade nodded, his glance running back to the cook, once again busy slicing bread.

As if sensing his glance, the old cook turned his seamed face toward Kincade, a sly gleam lighting his eyes. 'You bring any whiskey with you, maybe?'

Kincade shook his head. 'Sorry.'

The cook grunted his disappointment. 'All this dust gives me a bad cough,' he said, then proceeded to force a cough to prove his claim. 'You got any cough syrup, maybe?'

'Sorry.'

'Maybe some mouthwash to kill germs?'

'Nope,' Kincade replied, seeing the connection.

'Damn fine shame,' the cook mumbled and shoved his knife onto the counter, turning away.

On bowed and spindly legs, he walked over to a cupboard by the rangetop and opened a door, revealing a store of condiments and spices. Gnarled fingers closed around a tall, narrow bottle of vanilla, almost half full, and took it from the shelf. A quick twist and the lid was off. He carried the bottle to his mouth, tipped his head back and the bottle up. In three long gulps, he drained the bottle. The cook squinched his face up, shuddered, then released a gusty sigh.

'Much better.' He walked over and tossed the empty bottle into a dented metal trash can near Kincade.

Kincade heard the clinking of glass hitting more glass. With curiosity, he peered into the trash can. Along with the one Wild Jack had just thrown in, there were two more empty bottles of vanilla extract. When Al handed him a glass of iced tea, Kincade nodded to the waste bin.

'Your cook is guzzling vanilla.'

Al's gesture seemed to say so what else is new? 'When you're desperate for booze, you'll drink anything, I guess,' he said. 'At least with the vanilla, he can still function. But if Wild Jack gets his hands on a bottle of whiskey, he goes off on a binge that lasts for days.' The cook walked by, carrying a basket mounded with thick slices of homemade bread still warm from the oven. Al snatched a slice and bit into it. 'He's a crazy old coot, but he can cook,' he said between chews.

The screen door opened, its cracking hinges heralding the arrival of the rest of the ranch hands. The youngest of the group, a tall, skinny kid with the beginnings of a mustache on his upper lip and a feedstore cap on his head, spotted Kincade and said, 'The boss said you're to come to the house after you get done eating. She's got some forms you need to fill out if you wanna get paid, so you better not forget.'

'I won't.' Kincade smiled to himself and joined the others, stepping over the long bench to take a seat at the table.

6

A footpath wound through the stand of cottonwoods, linking the outbuildings with the main house. Kincade moved along the path at an unhurried pace, a toothpick between his teeth and his stomach full after a most satisfying meal of country-fried steak swimming in gravy, mashed potatoes, and a corn and green bean concoction that had him revising his opinion of vegetables.

The house was visible ahead of him. A shaft of sunlight flashed off the glass pane of a window, catching his eye. At almost the same moment, Kincade caught the sound of voices coming from the front of the house. Voices raised in anger. He recognized the sound of Eden Rossiter's with no difficulty. But it was the second voice, a man's, that he focused on, his stride lengthening and quickening, a feeling of urgency gripping him.

The footpath stopped at the corner of the wooden verandah. Eden Rossiter stood in the verandah's deep shade, arguing with a man in a bright wine-red shirt. The old cowdog sat at her feet. It growled to warn her of Kincade's approach, but she paid no attention.

'The answer is no,' Eden Rossiter stated in a voice that vibrated with anger. 'It has always been. And it always will be.'

'Don't be a fool,' the man erupted. When she started to turn away and walk back into the house, he grabbed her arm and swung her back to face him. 'You can't win. You—'

Kincade cut him off, 'What's the problem here?' The question was addressed to Eden Rossiter, but Kincade had eyes only for the man in the wine-red shirt.

He was five ten, with wide shoulders that tapered to a slim waist and hips. Dark hair curled from under his hat brim and a dark mole marked his left cheek. He was good-looking in that smooth, pretty-boy way some women liked. But his lips weren't curved in a cocky smile and the dark eyes that turned on Kincade were unstable with a sulky anger.

'This is private. Do you mind?' the man snapped.

'My mother told me I never minded when I was a kid. Seems a bit late to start now,' Kincade replied. His dislike of the man was an instant and instinctual thing. It didn't matter that he'd never seen him before.

Eden started to tell Kincade that his help wasn't required, but the words died on her lips when she saw the look on his face. All expression had been pushed out of it and channeled into his eyes, turning their blue color into something cold and deadly. His cheekbones were flat weights high on his face and he held her brother's eyes as he would have gripped a man's shoulders with his hands.

'I think you better let the lady go.'

'My God.' Nerves had Vince releasing a laugh of disgust, but he released her arm. 'Who is this guy, Eden?'

'He's the new man I hired.'

'Well, tell him to get lost.'

'Why don't you tell me?' The challenge came softly, but it carried no less threat.

Vince drew back, his gaze narrowing to take a closer look at Kincade. 'Have we met somewhere?'

Kincade gave a small shake of his head. 'Maybe I look like somebody you know.'

'Maybe,' Vince conceded, still puzzled. He stared at Kincade an instant longer, then turned abruptly away. 'The hell with it, I'm going to town.'

Eden called after him, 'When will you be back?'

'Later.'

He stalked off, heading straight to a blue-and-white Ford pickup, waxed to a high shine. He hauled himself into the driver's side and slammed the door. A second later, the engine roared to life and the tires spun.

When the pickup pulled away from the house, the tension that had bunched Kincade's muscles slowly began to drain away. He sensed Eden's gaze on him and turned to meet it. Her eyes were direct as they explored him with slow and curious attention.

'Don't tell me that guy works for you?' Kincade absently studied her face, taking note of the mingling of small delicate bones and firm positive muscles, smooth on the surface, taut below, and finely shaped under it all. Without a doubt, she was a beautiful woman.

'Vince?' There was a faint shrug of her shoulders. 'He comes and goes as he pleases.'

'Vince – is that his name?'

'Yes, Vince Rossiter. He's my brother.' Eden saw him draw back in obvious surprise.

Then Kincade flashed her a quick, guilty grin that was potent and disarming. 'It looks like I butted into a family squabble.'

'Yes, you did.' Eden smiled back. She hadn't meant to.

'My mistake.' His glance shifted to her lips, centering on them with a man-to-woman interest.

'It was.' Eden stiffened and erased the smile that had curved her mouth.

'I hope the quarrel wasn't about anything serious.'

Eden glanced at the trail of slowly settling dust left by Vince's truck. 'He wants me to sell the ranch,' she replied, and was instantly irritated with herself for telling Kincade that.

'And you don't want to,' he guessed.

'I don't.'

'Do you and your brother own the ranch together?'

'In a way, yes. But make no mistake, Kincade, I have sole authority over everything here.' With that said, she turned on her heel and headed for the front door. 'Come on inside and fill out those payroll forms.'

Kincade cast a thoughtful glance at the dust trail left by her brother's pickup, then followed Eden into the house. She passed through the entryway without a break in her quick, purposeful stride. A step slower, Kincade took note of the age-darkened stairway that led to the second floor as he trailed after her into the main living area of the adobe-walled house.

A huge stone fireplace dominated the room, its smoke and soot-blackened stones indicating years of use. The furniture grouped in front of it was heavy and utilitarian rather than decorative. The rug on the hardwood floor was Navaho in design and showed the wear of years of traffic.

Eden Rossiter headed straight for an old rolltop desk that sat in a corner alcove. Kincade watched as she crossed the room, sweeping her hat off, then reaching back to pull out the confining rubber band and shaking her hair loose with an automatic toss of her head. Her dark hair fell in glossy waves onto her back. Seeing it, Kincade couldn't help wondering whether it would be as silky to the touch as it looked.

'The payroll forms you need to fill out are over here.' She picked up some papers from the desktop's cluttered surface, then searched through the pigeonholes for a writing pen.

Unhurried, Kincade moved toward the alcove, then stopped halfway across the room when he noticed a chess table with chess pieces arranged on its squares, indicating a game in progress.

'You and your brother play chess, I see,' he remarked, studying the board.

'In the evening, sometimes.'

'Are you white?' He picked up a light-colored pawn that had already been removed from play.

'Yes.'

'In three more moves, you can have his king in check. He'll have to sacrifice his queen to save his king.'

'I know.'

'Does your brother?' Smiling faintly, Kincade threw her a sideways glance.

'I doubt it.' She turned from his gaze and pulled a ballpoint pen from one of the cubbyholes. 'Vince isn't the kind to anticipate his opponent's moves very far in advance – which invariably gets him in trouble.'

There was a note in her voice that had him eyeing her thoughtfully. 'Something tells me you're referring to more than just the game of chess.'

'It's no secret that Vince and trouble have been frequent companions.' She held out the payroll forms, seeking to get back to the business at hand. 'Here you are.'

'Be right there.' But he lingered beside the table, examining the game board, which was made out of alternating dark and light squares of wood inlaid in the table's surface. 'This is a good-looking chess table. I haven't seen many like it.'

'My grandfather made it. He was something of a carpenter and woodworker in his spare time.'

'What about these chess pieces?' He fingered the pawn in his hand. 'They look like they're hand-carved. Did your grandfather do them, too?'

'The black set.'

'Who did the white pieces? Your brother?'

'No, I did.'

'You?' His eyebrow shot up in surprise. 'You're a wood-carver?'

'It's a hobby – one I have very little time for,' she said with impatience and waved the papers in her hand. 'The forms, Mr Kincade.'

'Just Kincade will do.' He set the white pawn back on the table and crossed to the rolltop desk where she stood. 'Sorry if I sounded rude a minute ago, but wood-carving isn't a hobby that's typically associated with women.' A smile curved his mouth, creating deep grooves at the corners.

Again Eden felt the disarming potency of it. And again, she resisted its pull. A man's smile was something she had learned not to trust.

'Your apology is accepted, Kincade,' she said coolly, then pushed the papers at him. 'Now if you would fill out these forms . . .'

He took the pen and papers from her, then walked over to a big easy chair and sat down. After scanning the first sheet, he picked up the thin volume of poetry Eden had left on the coffee table.

'Is it all right if I use this book to write on?' He held it up.

'Of course.' Eden sat down at the desk, intent on dealing with some of the paperwork that somehow managed to multiply anytime she turned her back on it for a few days.

'Robert Frost.' Kincade identified the author of the well-thumbed book. 'He was my sister's favorite poet, too.'

Eden made a noncommittal sound, acknowledging his remark, and immediately began sorting through yesterday's mail. The last thing she wanted was a discussion with Kincade about his sister or the interest they shared in the works of Robert Frost. To her relief, Kincade didn't pursue the subject. Within minutes Eden heard the scratch of his pen on paper.

In short order, Kincade completed the forms and walked back to the desk. 'Here you go,' he said, setting the papers in front of her. In the next breath, he asked, 'Who is the woman in the picture?'

When Eden looked up, she saw his attention was directed at the framed photograph of Kate Rossiter on the wall. Automatically Eden glanced at it as well and experienced a familiar surge of pride and admiration for Kate Rossiter and her achievements. Momentarily she lowered her guard.

'My great-grandmother Kate Rossiter. She built Spur – virtually single-handedly.'

More than the note of pride that crept into her voice, Kincade noticed the warmth. And there was a softness in her expression that he hadn't seen before. It was clear that there was more to Eden Rossiter than the tough, all-business exterior she had previously shown him.

'What about her husband? Or was she a widow?'

'No. Most of the time he was off prospecting somewhere, chasing his dream of a big strike.' There was a telling trace of condemnation in her voice that indicated her disapproval.

'Shakespeare called it "saint-seducing gold,"' Kincade remembered. 'Gold fever definitely claimed many a victim back in the Old West.'

'It still does today – only in different ways.'

Kincade had a strong suspicion she was referring to her brother. 'You're right. Some people can't resist the lure of easy money.' He turned back to the faded photograph of the ranch's matriarch. 'Your great-grandmother wore that gun like she knew how to use it.'

'From all accounts, she did.'

His glance traveled over the woman in the picture. 'It's clear you take after her.'

Eden came to her feet, bristling with challenge. 'Why? Because I shot someone?'

'Actually' – Kincade pushed his hat to the back of his head, a rueful smile edging his mouth – 'I was talking about the physical resemblance – the dark hair and eyes, the hint of fine bones, the proud way you carry yourself.'

Taken aback by his reply, Eden looked away, a touch of color rising in her cheeks. 'My mistake,' she said and once again took her seat. 'I thought you were referring to . . . something else.'

'I heard about the shooting,' Kincade admitted. 'As much as people make of it around here, I'm not surprised it's still a sensitive issue with you – it happened years ago.'

'It doesn't matter.' She picked up his payroll forms and began looking them over.

'I also heard the jury acquitted you of any wrongdoing in the shooting.'

'That's right. They did.' She looked up, her eyes cool with challenge. 'Is that a problem for you?'

'Not a bit.' A suggestion of a smile touched his lips before he swung his glance back to the framed photographs, this time his attention focusing on the second one. It pictured a man in his fifties, with hard features chiseled in stern lines. 'The man in this photo, is he Kate Rossiter's husband?'

'Her son and my grandfather, Jed Rossiter.'

'The one who left control of the ranch to you, instead of your brother?'

'That's right.'

'I take it both your parents are dead.'

'My mother died when I was four. I barely have any memory of her.' Eden focused her eyes on the payroll forms, going through them line by line to make certain all the necessary information had been filled out. 'After her funeral, my father brought Vince and me here to live on the ranch. He had a job that kept him on the road.' She didn't tell Kincade that her father had left and never come back. For a long time Eden had thought that if she was a good girl and minded her grandfather, did everything he said, her father would return. But he didn't. 'He was killed in a car crash somewhere in Nebraska shortly after I turned sixteen.'

'So you were raised by your grandfather?'

Eden nodded, shifting papers to examine the second form. 'He was a good man.'

'He looks a bit on the stern side,' Kincade remarked.

Eden chose not to reply to that, while privately recognizing that, in some respects, her grandfather had been a hard taskmaster, a strong believer in work and discipline – although Vince had suffered more from that side of him than she had. For herself, she had always known that behind his gruffness, her grandfather possessed a loving heart. But that wasn't something she cared to discuss with Kincade. He was a stranger, a hired hand.

She let the silence build between them, conscious of his gaze traveling over her.

'You have beautiful hair,' he murmured unexpectedly.

A breath later his hand traced the length of it, almost touching it. Eden went motionless. A dozen different emotions ripped through her like leaves in a storm, every nerve jumping to life.

'You know, I have never been able to resist a woman with long hair.'

Regaining control, Eden turned a withering look on him. 'Really? Personally I have never found anything about a man that I *couldn't* resist.' To her irritation, he looked more amused than repentant. 'If you are wise,

Kincade, you will remember that I'm the boss – and forget I'm a woman.'

'*That*, Miss Rossiter, would be impossible.' His eyes gleamed in humor.

'Try,' she snapped and turned back to his papers. 'The pay is six hundred a month plus room and board – and a bonus if you're still here after a year.' She seriously doubted he would be; ranch hands seldom were. 'Paydays are the first and fifteenth.' She shuffled through his forms and spotted a section he had failed to fill out. Immediately she called it to his attention. 'I need the name and phone number of a relative to contact in the event of an accident or emergency.'

'I have no family left.'

Eden looked up in surprise. It was as if a shutter had come down, closing all expression from his face except for the cold, guarded look of his eyes. 'Your parents are dead,' she guessed, then remembered: 'You mentioned your sister. What about her? Is she dead, too?'

He nodded. 'Some time ago.'

'What about a friend—'

'I said there's no one. As far as I'm concerned, you can write your own name in there,' he said.

'All right.' A little uncertain, Eden set the forms aside and glanced at the wall clock. 'The boys should be at the barn now, unloading the hay. It's time we joined them.'

Eden pushed her chair back and stood, pausing long enough to collect her hat and work gloves from the desktop. Kincade headed for the front door without waiting for her. Eden caught up with him outside, her hair once again confined at the nape of her neck.

Together they set off along the trail through the trees to the barn. The old cowdog roused himself from the shade of the verandah and trotted alongside Eden.

'Is this all the hay you usually put up?' Kincade asked.

'Yes. I don't winter-feed the cattle unless the weather is particularly severe. For the most part, I try not to run more cattle than the land can support in a bad year.'

'How much land do you have?'

'All in all, about seventy thousand acres.'

'How much of that is federal?'

'None. We lost our grazing permit,' she told him, then added with wry cynicism, 'DePard has low friends in high places.'

Kincade chuckled, finding her sense of humor unexpected. But her assessment of DePard matched his own impression of the man. 'Somehow that doesn't surprise me.'

'It didn't me, either.'

'From the little I saw, I'd say the man is out to get you.' He glanced sideways to study her reaction.

'I know,' she replied calmly.

'Is that why your brother wants you to sell?'

'That's one of his reasons.'

'And the other?' he prompted.

'Money. According to the terms of the will, Vince is entitled to a share of any profits. But I'm not selling.' As they approached the barn, she pulled on her work gloves and began issuing orders to the men gathered around the hay rack. 'Jackson and Hart, start getting those bales unloaded and stacked. Deke, give them a hand with the stacking. Al, as soon as that flat rack's empty, I want you and Kincade to head back to the field with it and start picking up the rest of the bales.'

As soon as the wagon was empty, Al Bender climbed into the tractor seat. Kincade stood beside him, braced against the fender. Al fired the tractor up and headed back to the field.

'One thing you can say about the boss,' Al declared,

talking loud to make himself heard above the engine, 'she works as hard as the next man.'

'I don't think the same can be said for her brother, though.'

Al snorted in disgust. 'You've met Vince, have you?'

'Today. Up at the house.'

'Talk about someone who's worthless as tits on a boar, that's Vince,' Al pronounced.

'What does he do?'

'Not any more than he has to. He only shows up around here when he wants money – which is most of the time.'

'What does he do with his money?'

'Gambles most of it away.'

'At the casinos?'

'Casinos, racetracks, you name it. If the odds are long enough and the pot's big enough, he'll bet on anything.' Al slowed the tractor when the lane roughened. 'Believe me, with Vince for a brother and DePard for an enemy, she hasn't got a chance of making it.'

'If that's the way you feel, how come you're working here?'

'It's a job. At my age, they're hard to come by.' Al gave him a sidelong study. 'How come you hired on?'

Kincade smiled. 'Maybe I wanted to even the odds.'

Al looked at him like he was crazy.

7

When the sun rose Friday morning, a bank of low clouds blackened the sky to the west. It rolled slowly toward Spur, thick and heavy with the promise of drought-breaking rain. By the time the morning chores were finished, clouds had blotted out the sky and the wind picked up in advance of the squall line, stirring up the dust and pockets of dead leaves beneath the cottonwoods.

Eden headed back to the house, the old cowdog trotting at her side. 'It looks like we might get some rain, Cassius,' she said to the dog. 'Let's hope so.'

The dog wagged its tail in seemingly vigorous agreement. Eden laughed. 'Sometimes I think you understand everything I say, Cassius.'

He gave her a panting grin and continued toward the house. She laughed again and shook her head.

When she opened the front door, the dog slipped in ahead of her and went straight to the kitchen, its toenails clicking over the hardwood floors. Once there, he flopped on the rug in front of the sink and watched as Eden walked over to the counter and poured herself a cup of coffee.

She carried the coffee cup to the open window and

studied the rolling mass of dark clouds beyond its mesh screen. The wind died and thunder rumbled through the sudden stillness. In the air was the distinct smell of rain, a fresh and invigorating scent.

Finally the first fat drop pelted the dusty ground. Another fell, and another. Then the clouds released their load and rain poured down, falling in straight crystal filaments.

Relief washed over her. As long as this rain kept up, there would be no outside work. Which meant she wouldn't have to come up with a reason to stay around the house to wait for the phone call from Rosa Winters. Eden sent up a silent prayer that Rosa's brother-in-law would agree to transport her cattle to market.

She glanced at the wall phone, wishing it would ring with the answer. Instead she heard the clumping of Vince coming down the stairs. Eden stiffened, unconsciously lifting her chin to a combative angle, the memory of the angry words they had exchanged again last night rushing back.

He came into the kitchen. 'Is it raining outside?'

'Yes.' She took a sip of her coffee and continued to face the window.

'At least it might cool things off a little,' Vince grumbled. 'Although I don't know which is worse – dust or rain in this godforsaken place.'

Eden chose to ignore his comment. 'There's some coffee in the pot if you want a cup.'

'No thanks. It may be your idea of fun to sit around the kitchen and listen to the patter of rain, but it isn't mine.'

The scorn in his voice set her teeth on edge. Silently counting to ten, she turned from the window. 'I suppose you're going into town again.'

'Well, I'm sure not going to stick around here,' Vince mocked, then hesitated, regret flickering through his expression. 'Look, why don't you come with me? You can't get any work done in this weather anyway. We could drive into Winnemucca, grab a bite of lunch maybe.'

She shook her head. 'This rain may be nothing more than a brief shower. Besides, I have a bunch of bookwork piled up.'

'There's always something, isn't there?' Vince glared, his temper boiling through again. 'Can't you see this damned place has—'

'Stop it, Vince,' Eden broke in, her own temper at a flashpoint. 'I don't want to get into another fight with you. Not this morning. If you're going, go. But don't say another word about selling this ranch. Not one more.'

'You're as mule-headed as the old man. Nobody can reason with you,' he fired back. 'It's a waste of time. You can forget it. I'm out of here.' He started to turn away when the phone rang, the shrill sound freezing Eden for an instant. Rosa, she thought, a sudden tension lacing up her nerves. Vince swung back. 'That's probably for me.' He strode toward the wall phone, triggering Eden into action.

'I'll get it.' Moving quickly, she grabbed the phone first. 'Spur Ranch.' Vince stood before her, his jaws clenched in ill-concealed anger. A man's voice came over the line, and Eden relaxed a little, relieved that she wouldn't have to talk to Rosa in front of Vince. She cupped a hand over the mouthpiece. 'It's Ed from the hardware store. The part for the generator's in. Will you stop by and pick it up for me?'

'Why the hell not,' he muttered in disgust and turned away.

'Vince will come by this morning, Ed,' she said into the phone, her glance following her brother as he stalked out of the kitchen. 'Thanks for calling.' She hung up, the click of the receiver masked by the slamming of the front door. Vince was gone.

Shortly after he left, the phone rang again. This time it was Rosa Winters. 'I spoke to my brother-in-law,' she told Eden, who gripped the phone a little tighter. 'He will haul your cattle. He said he can have his trucks at your place Tuesday morning at nine o'clock, if that is good?'

'It's perfect.'

'I will tell him. Remember— someone has come into the shop. I must go.' The line went dead.

As soon as Eden returned the receiver to its hook, her knees buckled with the relief that washed over her. She sank onto the kitchen chair, laughing and crying softly at the same time. The old cowdog padded over to her and pushed its graying muzzle under her hand.

Laughing, Eden rubbed the top of the dog's head in a rough caress. 'We did it, Cassius,' she declared on a triumphant note. 'We've foxed DePard. He isn't going to get the best of us this time.'

The old dog barked once and slapped the floor with his tail, then jumped up and licked her face. Laughing again, Eden gathered the dog onto her lap and hugged him close until the old cowdog squirmed to be released.

'I'm embarrassing you, aren't I?' But she held onto his warm body a little longer, resting her cheek on the dog's head, needing this contact with another living thing – this *safe* contact. 'You're right, though, Cash. Affection is best in small doses.'

She released her hold on the Blue Heeler, and the dog promptly jumped to the floor and padded back to the rug. He circled once and lay down, fixing her with a look.

'It's time for me to get to work, isn't it?' Eden smiled and headed for the living room and the pile of paperwork waiting on her desk.

*   *   *

It rained off and on for most of the day. After the first heavy shower, the rest were light drizzles, some little more than a heavy mist. Around two o'clock, Eden finished the last of the bookwork.

She was on the enclosed back porch, throwing a load of dirty clothes in the old washing machine, when Vince came back. She returned to the kitchen as he walked in, carrying a cardboard box in his arms and whistling away – with no trace of his sulky temper in evidence. Eden should have been relieved to see him in a better mood, but over the years she had learned to be wary of such sudden changes.

'Hey, Sis. Sounds like you're washing clothes,' he remarked, all smiles as he crossed to the kitchen counter and pushed the box onto its tiled top.

'I am. What's in the box?' Eden walked over to look.

'Lemons.' He lifted one out to show her. 'Some guy pulled into Hoague's with a pickup-load of citrus. As cheap as he was selling them, I figured they came off the back of some produce truck. Anyway, the minute I saw these lemons, I decided to buy some and see if I couldn't talk you into making some of that good Rossiter lemonade.' He grinned at her, the sparkle of warmth and laughter in his eyes. It was a combination difficult to resist. And Vince knew it.

'Sure. Later on,' Eden agreed, fully aware that she was being manipulated.

'That's my girl.' He dropped the lemon back in the box. 'It looks like you got a good amount of rain here. In town they didn't get enough to settle the dust.'

'That's the way it usually goes,' she said, then asked, 'Did you remember to pick up that part for the generator?'

Vince nodded. 'It's out in my truck.'

'Would you go tell either Deke or Hart to switch

the generator parts? Hart might still be in the shed working on the tractor. Deke's in the barn helping the others replace the rotten boards in the stalls and the feed bin.'

'There's no need for them to stop what they're doing. I'll take care of it. It's only fair since you're going to fix that lemonade for me,' he told her and sauntered out of the kitchen.

Eden watched him. She knew what was coming. The subject of selling the ranch would be dropped for now, and Vince would be at his most pleasant and charming; an apology would come later, followed by carefully crafted expressions of concern for her. Eden sighed. Her brother was extremely predictable.

An hour later, Eden rummaged through the pots and pans on the cupboard's lower shelf until she found the one she wanted. She set it on the counter near the pile of hollowed-out lemon halves. A breeze drifted through the opened window above the sink, bringing the lingering scent of rain to mix with the smell of lemons.

Rather than fire up the ancient wood-burning range, Eden pulled the hot-plate away from the wall and plugged it in. The screen door banged shut. The sound was quickly followed by Vince's familiar, two-beat stride.

'How's the generator running?' she asked when he walked in.

'It's purring like a kitten.'

'Good.' She emptied the pitcher of freshly squeezed juice into the pan, measured out some sugar, and stirred it into the juice.

Vince strolled over to watch while she scraped a little zest from a rind into the mixture and added a pinch of salt. 'How's that new man you hired working out?'

He leaned an elbow on the counter, angling his body sideways.

'You mean Kincade? Fine.'

'What do you know about him?'

'That he wanted work.'

'Is that all?'

'That was enough.'

'To be honest, Sis, I don't like the looks of him.'

'And I can't afford to be short-handed right now.' Not when she had three hundred and fifty head of cattle to round up and drive to the gathering pens by nine o'clock Tuesday morning, the time the shipper was scheduled to arrive. But Eden didn't tell Vince that. As far as she was concerned, he could find out in the morning when the others did.

'The man's a stranger,' he pointed out. 'There's something about him that isn't right. I can't put my finger on it, but . . .' Smiling, Vince reached out and gave a lock of her hair a childish tug. 'You're running the show – and doing a helluva job of it, I might add.'

'Thanks.' Eden wasn't charmed by his praise; it was a ploy he had used too often for it to have any effect on her.

Between the heat from the burner and the constant stirring of the spoon, nearly all the sugar had dissolved, turning the juice into a thick and tartly sweet syrup. Vince dipped a finger in it, then stuck it in his mouth, frowning in a show of concentration before he smiled his approval.

'Perfect as always, Sis,' he said with a wink. 'When it cools, I'll fix us a couple of tall glasses, splash in some Jack Daniels, and we'll have us a couple of sundowners.'

'In the meantime, make yourself useful and go fire up the grill. We'll cook outside tonight now that it's quit raining.'

'Your wish is my command.' He sketched her a mock bow and sauntered off, exiting the kitchen through the back door.

In some ways, Vince was as irresponsible as their father had been. The only difference between the two was that Vince always came back. Broke, of course. Or, more often, in debt to some casino and wanting an advance on his share of the ranch profits to pay off his IOUs.

Money was the reason he came back. And money was the reason he wanted to sell the ranch. Plus the fact that he hated it; he had always hated it. Eden knew that.

Bubbles began to form along the liquid's outer edges. Eden switched off the hot-plate and lifted the pan from the burner, setting it aside to cool.

An hour later Vince shouted that the coals were hot, and Eden carried out the pan that held the flank steak and its marinade. On top of it sat a pair of foil-wrapped bundles of vegetables. Within minutes the steak sizzled above charcoal briquettes glowing red-hot and the vegetables sat along the grill's outer ring to steam slowly inside the foil.

Eden settled back in a webbed lawn chair that had seen better days, and sipped at the tall glass of spiked lemonade Vince had fixed for her. A fly buzzed near her face and she absently swatted it away.

It was quiet under the deep shade of the cottonwood, with the sun hovering above the rim of the western horizon. Overhead, a vagrant breeze whispered through the leaves, then all was still again.

It was moments like these Eden liked best – at day's end or day's beginning, when there was time to appreciate and savor the sometimes extravagant and sometimes subtle beauty of land and sky in this desert country. In between, the hours were filled with monotonous, bone-tiring ranch work in conditions that ranged from scorching heat to freezing cold, choking dust and foot-tugging mud.

The simple peace of the moment was shattered by Vince's muffled curse as he slapped at his neck. 'If it isn't the heat driving a man crazy, it's the damn flies.'

'They probably like your cologne,' Eden suggested, catching a whiff of its masculine mix of spice and sandalwood.

'Smells good, doesn't it?' he said with a pleased look.

Eden made a sound of agreement, then nodded at the grill. 'Hadn't you better turn the steak?'

Rising, Vince caught up long-handled tongs and positioned the steak between their gripping teeth, then flipped it over. There was a sizzle and hiss of meat juice striking white embers, then smoke billowed, driving Vince a step back.

'Won't be long now,' he announced, taking his seat again.

Eden acknowledged him by tipping her glass to him before taking another sip of her drink. The horses at the corral crowded close to the rails and lifted their heads to whicker a greeting. An answering neigh came from some point behind her. Eden twisted in her chair to see a rider coming in. The slump-shouldered man sat loose and easy in the saddle, a high-crowned hat with a tipped-down brim on his head.

Sunlight glinted on a pair of round, steel-rimmed glasses. The rider was her cowboss, Bob Waters, a full-blood Paiute and seven-month veteran at the ranch. He spotted Eden under the tree and reined his horse toward her, lifting it into a shuffling trot.

Eden rose to meet him. He swung his mount broadside to her and stopped. The horse blew gustily, then pricked its ears at its companions in the corral.

'The windmill at Flat Rock is busted.' He broke the

news without expression, dust dulling the jet-black of his hair and mixing with sweat to cake his face. 'There's maybe six inches of water in the tank.'

Flat Rock was the ruins of an old mining camp. Years before Eden was born, Jed Rossiter had tapped into its well and used it to water his stock. There was plenty of good forage in the area and the water source made it good grazing ground. More than that, Flat Rock was where she had put the cattle she planned to ship next week.

'Busted?' The single word asked for more specifics.

'Shaft's broken.'

Eden glanced back at Vince, sprawled in his lawn chair. 'You checked that earlier this week, didn't you?'

'I did,' Vince confirmed. 'Everything was fine then.'

Eden turned back, giving the orders she had already intended to issue. 'Tell Wild Jack to stock up the chuck wagon and have Deke wrangle the cavvy. We'll round up the cattle at Flat Rock and drive them back here to the home meadow.' Where the gathering pens were, but she didn't say that. 'We'll leave in the morning at first light.'

'Done.' Waters pulled his hands from their resting place on the saddlehorn, lifted the reins and touched the big rowel of his spur against the horse's belly, sending it forward at a trot.

'Flat Rock is about a mile from Diamond D's west boundary,' Vince remarked when she rejoined him.

'I know.' She studied the cubes in her glass with apparent concentration.

'Are you thinking he might have sabotaged that windmill?'

'I wouldn't put it past him,' Eden replied.

'Neither would I.'

She glanced at the smoking grill. 'The steak looks nearly done.' She pushed out of her chair. 'I'll go finish setting the table.'

*   *   *

When they had finished the meal, Eden automatically gathered up the silverware and dishes. Rising from his chair, Vince picked up their glasses.

'Want a refill?' He crossed to the refrigerator for more ice cubes.

'Just lemonade in mine. No Jack this time.' She carried the plates and silverware to the sink and set them in the square plastic pan she used to conserve water.

'Come on, Sis. A little whiskey isn't going to hurt you.' Ice cubes rattled as he scooped up a handful and dumped them in the glasses. 'Loosen up.'

'I'm as loose as I care to get, thank you,' Eden replied dryly, returning to clear the bread, butter, and condiments from the table.

Vince opened the refrigerator door to retrieve the pitcher of lemonade. Eden stepped in and set the butter and ketchup on to a shelf. As she started to turn away, she felt the light stroke of his hand on her hair and halted.

'Hey.' His voice was soft, warm with affection. He gently ran a finger along the underside of her jaw to the point of her chin and lifted it a fraction. 'Lighten up a little.'

Eden looked up and saw the grin that so many women regarded as sexy. But she knew, too well, how many times he used it to get his way. Yet, she gave in grudgingly and smiled back.

'I'll try.'

'Good.' Pitcher in hand, Vince turned and emptied the lemonade into the two glasses and handed her one. 'Let's drink to that.'

Looking at him, Eden shook her head in a mixture of affection and exasperation. '*You* are incorrigible.'

'I know.' He grinned wickedly and clinked his glass to hers. 'Drink up,' he urged when she failed to raise the glass to her lips. Giving in again, Eden took a quick sip and started to set the drink down. 'What are you doing?' He stopped her.

'I have dirty dishes to wash.'

'They can wait. You don't have to immediately hop up from the table and wash the dishes. Let them sit awhile. Forget about wiping off the table. What's the harm in a few crumbs? They'll give the flies something to feast on instead of us.' Again Vince flashed a smile at her. 'Come on, Sis. Live a little. I dare you.'

It was such a ridiculous thing to say, Eden laughed. His smile widened into a grin. Hooking an arm around her shoulder, he guided her back to the table.

'That's better.' He pulled out a chair for her. 'I haven't heard you laugh in a long time. I was starting to worry that you had forgotten how.'

'I haven't.' Truthfully there hadn't been that much to laugh about lately.

'That's a relief.' He swung a chair around to face her, then straddled it. 'I'm sorry about arguing with you so much over selling the ranch.'

The apology. Eden had known it was coming, but oh, this time he had set her up so well. All the good feelings inside started to die a little.

'I know you are.' She looked at the drink, wishing that – just once – Vince wouldn't be so predictable.

'You're my sister,' he said in the most sincere voice. 'It's only natural that I'm concerned about you. I want you to be happy, Eden.'

'I am happy.'

He eyed her skeptically and asked, 'When was the last time you went to a movie? When was the last time you went out to eat or went shopping just for the fun of it? When was the last time you did anything for no other reason than you wanted to?'

'I've been busy. There's a lot of work to do here at the ranch. Work that can't wait.'

'And I should spend more time here, do more to take some of that load off you,' Vince admitted, then grimaced. 'But I can take this hellhole for only so long, Eden, then I have to get out – get away. I don't know how you stand it day after day, year in and year out.'

'It's easy. This is my home. It's where I want to be. It's the life I want. I like the challenges. Believe it or not, I even enjoy the sweat and grime and bone-aching tiredness at the end of a hard day. There's a kind of satisfaction I get from it.' But she could tell he didn't understand. 'This ranch is the only home I know,' she said. 'I'll never give it up. Not willingly.'

'No, you'll go down fighting,' he agreed, his expression grim with concern. 'That's what bothers me, Sis. DePard is out to break you. You can't win against him, not in the long run. And I don't want to see you lose everything. That's why I want you to sell the ranch. Now. While you can still get some cash out of it.'

'Don't you mean – while *you* can still get some cash out of it?' The bitterness came through, the bitterness of knowing he wanted the money.

Vince wasn't fazed by it. 'I would be lying if I said I didn't want my share out of the deal. You can't condemn me for that,' he said with an easy smile. 'Put yourself in my shoes once. How would you like it if I invested all the money we inherited into some venture you knew was going to lose? You would be riding me about it all the time.'

'Probably,' Eden acknowledged, fighting off the guilt he was trying to lay on her.

'You can't win against DePard. He's too big and too powerful. I don't want to see you break your heart trying.'

Beads of moisture collected along the outside of the

glass. Eden ran her fingers over its cool wetness, a growing tension threading through her nerves. 'I don't see it that way, Vince.'

'That's because you've gone stubborn on me and refuse to listen to reason.' He was amused rather than irritated.

'No, I just refuse to sell the ranch.'

Vince immediately seized on the opening she'd given him. 'Then hear me out.'

'We have been over this—' she began but he cut her off.

'Think of all the things you could do with your share from the sale. From the time Dad dumped us here when we were kids, you haven't been more than a hundred miles from the place except when you went to Tonopah for your trial. With the money from the sale, you could travel, see something of this country. Maybe even find a place you like better than here.'

'I'm not interested.' Eden lifted her glass, sipping from it.

'How do you know when you've never been anywhere to find out?' Vince countered. 'Think about it, Sis. You could start over, make a new life for yourself.'

'I am not going to run away, Vince.' She set the glass down and wrapped both hands around it.

'It isn't running. It's making a fresh start someplace where no one knows you – far from small-minded people with spiteful tongues.'

'Their stories would catch up with me no matter where I went. I have everything I want right here and I'm staying.'

He cocked his head to the side and smiled a little sadly. 'That's your pride talking now. You can't be happy here, not living alone like this, working yourself to exhaustion day after day, worrying about what DePard might try next. That's no kind of life for any woman, and especially not my sister. You deserve better. A woman like you should have a man who'll love you and look after you. Somebody good and decent. You'll never meet a man like that around here.'

She laughed, without humor. 'My God, as if I don't have enough to do, you want me to find some man who will expect me to pick up after him and wash his clothes, have a cold beer and a hot meal waiting when he walks in the door.' She rose from her chair in disgust. 'Thanks but no thanks. I have enough work to do already. I don't need some man to make more for me.'

'That isn't what I meant and you know it.' He swung off his chair to follow her, carrying his drink. 'I'm talking about someone to share the work and the quiet moments, someone you can talk to and—'

'Forget it, Vince.' She stopped at the sink and squeezed some dish soap into the plastic pan of dirty dishes, then turned the water taps on full force.

'Don't be so stubborn, Eden.'

'I'm being sensible,' she stated. 'This land gives me all the satisfaction and grief I need. I don't need a man adding more.'

'The land makes a cold lover, Eden.'

'But a faithful one.'

'Now you're thinking of Dad. Not every man is like him. Or worse, like Jeff.'

'I really don't care,' she said and meant it.

'If you say so.' He leaned a hip against the counter and propped an elbow on top of it, watching her as she turned off the taps. 'You can't blame me for wanting to know there's someone looking out for you when I'm not around. You shouldn't get angry about that.'

'I'm not angry.'

'I'm only thinking of you, Sis.' Again his handsome face assumed a tender look of concern. 'You work too hard and too long. I want to see you enjoy life more, relax, have some fun. That's why I keep pushing you about selling the ranch.'

And he was still pushing.

'Look, Vince, we both know that if I put this ranch on the market, there would only be one buyer – DePard.' Eden plunged her hands into the soapy water.

'You can't be sure of that.'

'Can't I?' she flared. 'Forget that he hates me, and think for a minute. The Diamond D already comes up against our fence to the south and east. And all the water sources in both areas are on our side of the fence. Right now that land is worthless to him, but with our water – who knows how many more cattle he'll be able to run on it? He'll swallow up the ranch the same way he swallowed up the Lazy J and McNally's place.'

'All right, so maybe it would make good business sense for DePard to buy it,' Vince conceded. 'What does it hurt?'

'What does it hurt?' Eden hurled the question back at him. 'You know as well as I do what he would do if he got his hands on this ranch. He'd bulldoze this house to the ground, level every building on it, wipe out any trace that a Rossiter ever lived here. He would destroy it all.'

'As long as he pays what the ranch is worth, what do you care what he does with it afterwards?'

'I can't believe you said that.' Eden glared at him.

'Don't sell it to DePard then. Sell it to somebody else.'

'Who?' she challenged. 'Small ranches aren't the greatest investment anymore. People aren't going to be standing in line to buy it.'

'It depends on how you market,' Vince insisted. 'This ranch is full of history. Hollywood and society types eat that kind of stuff up. Owning a ranch has become a kind of status symbol to them. You could sell it to one of them and they'd turn it into a showplace, complete with swimming pool, tennis court, and a private landing strip.'

Eden shook her head in a touch of hopelessness. 'Vince, what on earth makes you think DePard wouldn't try to block the sale the same way he's blocked everything else?'

'Because he wants you gone from here, and he doesn't give a damn how he accomplishes that. He would prefer to ruin you, see that you walk away with nothing. But if he can't do that, if you put the ranch up for sale, he would have the satisfaction of believing he had forced you out. The way I see it, let him believe what he wants.'

Eden sensed immediately this wasn't idle speculation. Vince spoke with too much authority.

'You've talked to him about this, haven't you?' she accused, her temper flaring.

Vince laughed, but it was a little too forced. 'Whatever put a crazy idea like that in your head?'

Looking at him, Eden felt the hurt become stronger than the anger. 'I can't trust anyone, can I? Not even you.'

'That isn't true,' Vince said, then changed tactics. 'Look, if I did wrong, I'm sorry.'

'You're always sorry.'

'Hey.' His voice was soft and coaxing as he caught her wrists and pulled her hands out of the dishwater. Eden didn't resist when he turned her to face him. 'The other day with DePard and the cattle – that changed things. DePard's started to play rough, Sis. Real rough.' With one hand, he smoothed the hair away from her face, then left it there, cupping the back of her head. 'You are my sister, Eden. You're all the family I've got. I don't want anything to happen to you. If that means talking to DePard or convincing you to swallow your pride and sell the ranch to get you out of danger, then I'll do it. Can you understand that?'

'Yes.' That she understood, and believed. In many ways, Vince was selfish and greedy. But she never doubted that he loved her and would do anything to protect her – even going to DePard.

'Good.' Vince gathered her into his arms and rubbed his chin over the top of her head, then planted a kiss on her hair and pulled back to look at her. 'At least selling is a viable option. That's something we didn't know before. You aren't still angry with me, are you?'

She sighed. It never did any good to stay angry at Vince. 'No.'

'That's my girl.' He gave her nose a tweak, then turned her back to the sink, and administered a playful swat on her behind. 'Stop dawdling around and get those dishes done,' he ordered in a gruff imitation of their late grandfather. 'You have work to do – so get it done.'

8

The first magenta streaks creased the sky as the setting sun unleashed another one of its vivid and dramatic preludes to night so typical of desert country. Kincade paused beneath a cottonwood tree near the ranch house and made a slow survey of the vast landscape before him, the rain-washed air bringing a sharpness and clarity to the scene, intensifying the green of its grasses, the amber-gold of its soil and the purple of its far mountains.

All around him the shadows lengthened and darkened while the cool of a high desert night crept in, stealing some of the day's lingering heat. Kincade leaned a shoulder against the tree trunk, took a cigar from his pocket and lit it.

From the corral came the squeal of a horse and a flurry of hooves as the pecking order was reestablished in the cavvy. Then all was quiet again. Quiet and still.

Kincade took another puff of his cigar and turned his gaze, his eyes narrowing in thoughtful study, toward the house. His attention was centered on Vince Rossiter's blue-and-white pickup, which was parked in front.

The front door opened, and Kincade lifted his head

in instant alertness, then relaxed when he saw a hatless Eden Rossiter walk out. She strolled to the end of the verandah, then wandered beyond it. The old cowdog ranged alongside her, pausing here and there to check out a new scent or to lift its leg over a clump of grass, marking its territory.

Eden halted some thirty feet from where he stood, presenting her profile to him as she looked out across the open country, rather like a monarch surveying her kingdom. Obviously pleased with what she saw, she smiled faintly and reached back to pull off the confining band around her hair. She shook her head, letting her hair fall loose to hang down her back.

Visibly relaxing, she slipped the ends of her fingers inside the back pockets of her jeans and tipped her head up as if inviting the evening breeze to play lover and caress her face. She breathed in deeply, filling her lungs with the rain-freshened air, spiced with sage and pungent with the smells of damp earth. The action drew Kincade's glance to the jutting swell of her breasts, which the man's shirt failed to conceal. It was a sight to arouse lusting thoughts in any man, and Kincade had a few of his own.

He deliberately failed to make his presence known to her, satisfied simply to observe Eden Rossiter when she wasn't wearing the mantle of ranch boss. He suspected that she had allowed few men to see the woman underneath the boss.

But the old cowdog caught Kincade's scent and immediately zeroed in on his location. With hackles raised and his gaze fixed on Kincade, the dog growled the information to its mistress.

'What is it, Cassius?' Eden Rossiter glanced idly at the dog.

In answer, it took a crouching step toward Kincade and growled again. Half-turning, she peered into the

thickening shadows beneath the cottonwood, then stiffened perceptibly.

'Who's there?' she demanded in a voice crisp with
authority.

'Kincade.' He tossed his cigar away and moved out
of the shadows toward her. 'It's beautiful out, isn't it?'

'Yes.' She divided her attention between Kincade and
the dog, concealing a smile when the Blue Heeler, as
expected, darted over to block Kincade's path before
he came too close to her. The dog growled another
warning, this time showing its teeth. Kincade halted,
looking more amused at than afraid of the old dog,
which prompted Eden to issue a quick, 'That's enough,
Cassius.'

'Cassius,' Kincade repeated the dog's name, his attention lifting curiously to her. 'Did you name him after the
Roman general or the boxer Cassius Clay?'

'The boxer,' she admitted, watching as Kincade
crouched down to let the dog smell the back of
his hand.

'You may not be a heavyweight like Muhammad Ali,'
he told the dog. 'But from all the scars you're carrying,
there's no doubt you're a fighter.'

'He'll tackle anything – coyotes, rattlesnakes, or a
full-grown bull. Age has slowed him down, but he still
has the heart of a lion.'

'He looks like a tough old boy,' Kincade said with
a smile and straightened, after the dog had sniffed his
hand and backed two steps away.

To Eden's surprise, the dog didn't plant itself between
herself and Kincade. Instead it trotted off to make its
nightly rounds, which was something the dog never did
unless it had known the person it left behind with her
for a long time. She wasn't sure if the dog's action was
a sign of trust or old age.

Whatever the case, she remained wary as she eyed

Kincade. Sundown's fading light played over the lower half of his face, showing Eden the lazy curve of his mouth and the faint bruise along his cheekbone. The brim of his hat threw a shadow across his eyes, hiding them from her, but she felt their gaze on her. She was unsettled by it. And by him.

'It's starting to cool off already,' he remarked.

'It usually does once the sun goes down.'

He looked to the west where the sun had just slipped below the horizon, leaving behind a bright halo of light. Then his glance traveled over the land to the south, now tinged with the lavender hues of the approaching night. His expression turned thoughtful.

'You know, this isn't the kind of country a person can call beautiful,' he mused. 'In fact, a few days ago I thought it was the most dry and desolate land I had ever seen. But there's something about this big, empty country that stretches your eye and works itself under your skin. It has a power and a vastness that seems to pull you under its spell.'

Eden nodded her understanding. 'I know. To a lot of people, this is the middle of nowhere. But to me, it's the middle of everywhere. I wouldn't want to live anywhere else.'

Kincade studied the animation in her expression, and the glow of pride in her dark eyes, his attention drawn once again to the classic lines of her features with their unique mingling of delicacy and strength.

Even without makeup, Eden Rossiter was beautiful, her brows naturally arched and her eyes outlined by a thick fringe of lashes. In another place and other circumstances, Kincade would have been making a play for her, creating excuses to touch her, to run his hands over her ripe curves and find out if he could unwrap the plain packaging and become intimately acquainted with the woman inside it.

The desire was there to do just that, but Kincade controlled it.

'For anything to survive out here, I imagine it has to sink its roots deep,' he observed.

'I suppose that's true,' she admitted. 'I know mine are.'

'I think that's true of the ranch house as well.' He gestured toward it. 'I was noticing earlier – before you came out – that it looks like it grew here.'

'In a way, it did,' Eden replied, smiling as she gazed back at it.

'How so?' One eyebrow lifted, his curiosity aroused.

'Because all the materials used to build it came from right here on Spur.' The pull of the century-old dwelling was strong, drawing Eden toward it as she went on to explain, 'To make the adobe bricks, Kate Rossiter used dirt excavated from the slope of the ridge behind the house. For straw, she cut down the tall grass that used to grow thick where the hayfield is now. The water, of course, came from the natural spring behind the house, and the timber came from the stand of cottonwoods that grew around it.' She paused at the end of the verandah and ran her hand over an upright timber that time and the elements had worn smooth. 'When I was a little girl, Jed – my grandfather – used to tell me that this house was built of Rossiter wood, Rossiter grass, Rossiter water, and Rossiter soil.'

'There aren't many houses still standing that can make a claim like that.'

Eden listened for it, but she detected no trace of mockery in Kincade's voice, only a quiet approval. Maybe it was that, or the cloaking shadows of twilight, or the whiskey-laced lemonade she'd had earlier that had Eden lowering some of her defenses.

'Most old homes get torn down, or simply deteriorate until they fall down,' Eden said, then smiled as she recalled, 'Jed claimed that this house would never crumble to dust because it was held together with Rossiter blood.'

'You're kidding?' Amusement riddled his voice, but it was the warm, sharing kind.

'I'm not,' she assured him, still smiling. 'According to the family legend, there was an accident while mixing the materials for the adobe. Kate was badly cut and lost a lot of blood. In fact, she supposedly lost so much blood that there was a red cast to that particular batch of adobe. The story goes that Kate ordered her workers to use the bricks from that mix to lay the cornerstones for the house.'

'That's quite a story,' Kincade remarked. 'It's one of those that you want to believe, whether it's true or not.'

'It was definitely my favorite story when I was growing up,' Eden admitted. 'I never got tired of hearing it.'

'Kate Rossiter must have been quite a woman.'

'She was. Jed said there used to be a trellis at this end of the verandah,' she went on, warming to her subject. 'Every year Kate would plant sweet peas and train the vines to climb the latticework. Jed claimed there was no scent more pleasing than the fragrance of sweet peas on a hot summer's evening. I tried planting them once,' Eden recalled idly. 'The ground here was as hard as concrete when I tried to dig it up. I must have been ten or eleven then.'

'You should have asked your brother to help.'

'I did eventually. But I had to threaten to tell Jed that Vince had snuck into town before he agreed. Unfortunately only one spindly little seedling sprouted, and it died a few days later. I never tried planting them again. Maybe some day I will.'

'Did your brother do that a lot? Sneak out?'

'All the time,' Eden admitted, her smile widening then dissolving. 'Jed was always strict with Vince. Probably too strict. I think Jed was afraid Vince would turn out to be as useless and irresponsible as our father, so he came down hard on him, harder maybe than he should have.'

'Your brother doesn't strike me as the type who would respond well to that.'

'He didn't. It just made Vince hate it all the more here – not that he ever really liked it. He was older than me when we came here. It was harder for him to adjust to this life after living outside of Sacramento. There was no television, no *Sesame Street*—'

'No Big Bird?' Kincade inserted in mock dismay.

Seeing his smile, Eden realized it had been years – since long before the shooting – that she had talked this easily to anyone other than her brother. It felt good.

'No Big Bird,' she repeated. 'No neighbor kids to play with, and mostly static on the radio. It was a strange and frightening place to a couple of town kids. Coyotes howling at night and rattlesnakes crawling around in the daytime. There wasn't a school close enough for us to attend, which meant we had to take lessons at home. I was thirteen before I attended a real school. By then, Vince had his driver's license, and he drove us back and forth in the ranch pickup. Naturally Jed had figured out the exact mileage between here and the school. He checked the odometer every night. Poor Vince, there was hell to pay if it registered even a few tenths more than Jed thought it should. Finally one of Vince's friends showed Vince how to roll back the odometer.'

'I'm surprised your brother didn't run away. Most teenagers in his situation would have.'

'He talked about it.' But that would have meant assuming responsibility for himself, something Vince still avoided. More than that, there had been an element of danger and excitement for Vince in sneaking out – in doing something right under his grandfather's nose and not getting caught. Eden suspected it was the thrill of doing the forbidden that had kept Vince at the ranch.

'He wanted me to go with him,' she recalled. 'But by then, I already knew in my heart that this was the place for me. Somewhere along the line I stopped hating it and fell in love with it.' She lifted her face to the darkening twilight air, breathing in its scent and savoring its stillness. 'The noise and congestion of a town is something I can't handle for more than a few hours. I'd rather listen to the murmur of the wind through the grasses than the yammer of a dozen voices talking at once. I like the smell of sage, the sight of juniper-covered hills, and the taste of coffee boiled over a campfire. The serenade of the coyotes is my music. To me, rattlesnakes are nothing more than bothersome pests that go with the territory, like rats and cockroaches in a city.' She paused, then said softly, 'I couldn't sell this ranch. It would be like tearing out my soul.'

The instant the words were out, Eden cast a quick, self-conscious glance at Kincade, angry with herself for telling him anything about her feelings or her life. He was a cowboy, a drifter who would stay a few weeks or a few months, then move on to another job and another ranch.

'It must make it tough when your brother hates this place and wants to sell,' he remarked.

'A little.'

'Is your brother trying to pressure you into it?'

Your brother. The oft-repeated refrain finally clicked. Eden suddenly realized how many times he had mentioned Vince. She swung around to confront him, wary and suspicious.

'Why are you asking so many questions about my brother?'

He took his time answering, a slow smile moving across his mouth. But there wasn't one glimmer of guilt or remorse in his expression.

'Maybe because I knew if I asked questions about you, I wouldn't get any answers.'

That was true, she wouldn't have told him anything. In fact, the conversation wouldn't have lasted past the third question before she would have walked away.

'I should have known you were like every other man I've met,' she stated, her temper rising. 'Tell me, Kincade, what did you hope to find out? What Eden Rossiter is really like, maybe? Did you hope to learn if she was as cold and calculating and ruthless as everyone says? Surely by now you've formed an opinion. I'm curious to know what it is.'

'It's a little early to say, considering I've never met a man-hater before.'

'For your information, I don't hate men. Hate requires strong feelings, and I have none one way or the other.'

That was a lie; she was passionate about many things. That much Kincade had observed about her. 'Maybe you don't hate them,' he conceded. 'But you don't trust men very much.'

'You're wrong. I trust them to come and go when the whim suits them and to make promises they have no intention of keeping. I trust them to be selfish and self-centered, caring only about what they want. And I trust them to be cruel and vindictive.' She paused, her lips curving in a smile that was as coolly challenging as her words were hot. 'I believe this is where you tell me all men aren't like that.'

'Given the right set of circumstances, all men can be like that. And all women, too.' But that wasn't what he was thinking. He was thinking how beautiful she looked, with that black glitter of anger in her eyes. He watched her lips part in surprise at his answer, then come together again.

'I underestimated you,' she murmured. It was a mistake Eden didn't intend to repeat.

'Why? Because I told the truth? Or because you didn't expect me to know it?'

'Does it matter?'

'Not really.'

Eden was watching his face and missed the upward reach of his hand. Then it was there, warm against the side of her neck. Her hands lifted in a purely instinctive reaction and flattened themselves against his chest to maintain a distance as she stiffened. But his mouth was already on her lips, the contact light and curious, non-threatening.

And it was curiosity that prompted Kincade, a curiosity that wanted to know whether she was as indifferent to a man as she claimed. He rubbed his lips over hers, exploring their softness, their stillness, determined to evoke some reaction from her beyond this schoolgirl-stiff pose even if it was revulsion.

Beneath his hand, he felt the disturbed and heavy beat of the pulse in her neck. He pressed for more, delving deeper, seeking something more – and tasting her inexperience. Stunned, Kincade drew back, trying to reconcile this new discovery against the sight of the full-blown woman before him.

Anger snapped in her eyes, as hot and wary as before, but something new had been added to the mixture – something that reminded him suspiciously of fear. Pride kept her head high as she brought the back of her hand to her lips. But he noticed she made no attempt to wipe away the sensation of his kiss. At that moment Kincade knew he could have her. The thought tempted.

'You're right not to trust people very much,' he told her and released her. 'And you shouldn't trust me.'

'I won't.' She swore it, and strode past him into the house.

An hour later Kincade lay in his bunk staring at the ceiling, his head pillowed in his hands, his thoughts still tangled around Eden Rossiter. A cold-blooded killer according to many. Yet he was puzzled by her – and attracted to her.

He had wanted other women in the past. Sometimes those needs had been satisfied, and sometimes they hadn't. Desire came and went, erupting in the heat of the moment and vanishing in the cool of sanity. He knew that.

And he knew it wasn't wise to be distracted by her. He rolled onto his side and closed his eyes. Sleep came, eventually.

Somewhere around midnight, he awoke to a scream. His eyes snapped open and he listened. It came again. A woman's cry, sharp with terror. Kincade threw back the light blanket and rolled out of bed. Clad in jockey shorts, he padded to the opened window and looked toward the ranch house.

All was dark. Then a yellow light filtered through the trees, coming from a second-floor window. There were no more cries, no other movement. Kincade turned and went back to bed.

Hands gripped her shoulders. Eden fought them, only to be shaken harder. 'Eden, wake up.'

She jerked back as if struck and cringed into the pillows, a hand raised in defense. Her eyes were wide with fear as she stared at her brother for a long second.

'It's me, Sis,' Vince murmured softly. 'Everything's okay. It's okay.'

Slowly her eyes lost that glazed look. She nodded, then shuddered uncontrollably. When he took hold of her hand, her fingers tightened around his and held on.

'Are you okay now?' Vince sat on the edge of her bed, clad in a pair of jeans unzipped at the waist, his dark hair tousled from sleep.

'Yes.' But her voice was shaky, and she knew she felt anything but okay.

A cold sweat had turned her skin clammy, and Eden refused to close her eyes; the images and sensations were still too close, too real. She dragged herself into a sitting position and drew her knees up, resting her forehead on them. Nausea rolled her stomach while she pulled in deep, long breaths and fought her way back to reality.

'Want me to get you something? Whiskey? Water?'

'No.' She lifted her head, pushing her hair back with both hands and holding it there, away from her face. 'I'll be all right.'

'When did the nightmares start again?' Vince asked quietly.

'This is the first . . . in a long time.' At least two years, maybe three, Eden wasn't sure. She rubbed her hands over bare arms that were still cool and damp to the touch. 'I thought I was over them.'

'Do you want me to sit with you a while?'

'No.' She shook her head. 'I'm sorry I woke you.'

The mattress shifted when he stood up. Reaching back, he cupped her cheek in his hand. 'You can holler for your big brother anytime. Want me to leave the light on?'

'Please.' Eden managed a wan smile. It died the instant Vince walked from her bedroom.

She gathered up the spare pillow and hugged it tight as she leaned back against the maple headboard, the sick, scared feeling slowly receding. A cool night breeze drifted through the screen at her bedroom window, stirring the ruffled curtains. Eden stared at the darkness beyond the window.

Why had the nightmares started over again after all this time? What had triggered them? She had the uneasy feeling she knew the answer to that. The kiss. She had liked it. The warmth of it. The evocative sensation of it.

She had liked being kissed the other time, too. She had liked it a lot . . . at first. She slid down between the covers and curled into a tight ball, moving gently from side to side, trying to rock herself to sleep just as she had done when she was a little girl.

9

In the gray and shapeless light that precedes the breaking of the sun above the horizon, a rooster crowed and flapped its wings. Pleased with itself, it strutted across the yard, indifferent to the steady stir of activity.

Kincade downed the last swallow of Wild Jack's black and bitter coffee and set the cup on the top of a corral post. A faded yellow bandanna hung loose around his neck and he carried a pair of split cowhide gloves tucked in his belt. A row of conchas ran down the sides of the short leather chaps he wore, faded and scarred from heavy use. The spurs on his boots clinked with each stride as he walked to the corral gate, a halter and rope slung over one shoulder.

The horses to be ridden that morning had been separated from the cavvy last night and now waited to be claimed by their respective riders. The young and slim wrangler Deke shook out his rope when he saw Kincade step to the gate.

'You're riding Tex, right?' Deke asked.

'The big bay with the star.' Kincade didn't know the horse's name.

'That's Tex,' Deke told him, already swinging his hoolihan. 'He'll buck a little for ya.'

Kincade filed the information away without comment and watched as the big loop sailed through the air and settled around the neck of the bay gelding. The horse threw up its head, then snorted and offered no further resistance to the pull of the rope. Kincade walked over and slipped the halter on, then led his mount out of the corral as the next rider came to collect his.

Outside the corral, Kincade tied the gelding and proceeded to clean its hooves with a pick. Afterwards, he gave the horse a cursory brushing and ran a searching glance over the figures moving about in the predawn light. He spotted Eden standing at the head of a team while the Paiute Bob Waters finished hitching them to the chuck wagon.

She had been up and busy when Kincade staggered to the ranch kitchen for a much-needed first cup of coffee. When he came out, a full breakfast heavy on his stomach and a fourth cup of coffee in hand, her horse, a good-looking golden chestnut, was already saddled and tied to a rail.

Kincade passed her on his way to stow his gear in the bed wagon and she had looked right through him. But the memory of the kiss was there between them. Once that step was taken, once that invisible line was crossed between a man and a woman, there was no going back from it and no forgetting it. Every time she looked at him she would remember that kiss, just as he did.

A door banged at the ranch house. Kincade smoothed the saddle blanket in place and glanced toward the trees as Vince walked out of them, lugging a bedroll under his arm. He carried it to the bed wagon and slung it in with the rest. Kincade swung the saddle onto the bay.

'It's plain as hell why they call this the crack of dawn,' Vince declared to no one in particular when he joined the crew in the yard, scowling and heavy-eyed with sleep. 'You've got to be cracked to get up at this hour.'

There were a few smiling nods of acknowledgment but no comment.

'Hey, Deke,' Vince called to the wrangler. 'Throw a rope on Jaws for me while I get my saddle.'

'Right.' Deke left his own horse tied at the rail and gathered up his rope.

Kincade adjusted the saddle on the gelding's back and dropped the cinch on the off side, then hooked the near stirrup on the saddle horn and reached under the horse's belly for the cinch. He threaded it through the ring on the latigo strap and watched the barn.

Deke led a thickly muscled and big-jawed sorrel from the corral as Vince returned with his gear. He dumped it on the ground near Kincade and slipped the halter off his shoulder to fasten it around the sorrel's head.

'I need about a gallon of coffee to wake up,' Vince muttered.

Deke grinned and recoiled his rope. 'What you need is some of Wild Jack's coffee. He boils it down till there's a gallon of caffeine in every cup. I guarantee it'll snap anyone's eyes open.'

'And kill your stomach,' Vince added as Kincade pulled up the slack on the cinch. 'It tastes as bad as that chicory coffee they serve down in New Orleans' French Quarter.' He shook his head, a smile appearing. 'Bourbon Street,' he said and threw the saddle blanket on the sorrel without bothering to brush its back first. 'Now there's a place that's wide open and wild. I need to go back there sometime.' He glanced at Kincade. 'You ever been there?'

'Yup.' Kincade tugged on the cinch and felt the bay blow up. Leaving it, he reached under for the back cinch and buckled it.

'I was there a couple years ago. You talk about a party town, that is the place.' Vince heaved the saddle on the sorrel and rocked it into place. 'Were you there recently?'

'Nope.' Kincade stepped to the horse's head and slipped on the bridle, forcing the bit between the bay's teeth.

'I hear they might legalize gambling. I'll have to go check it out. This winter, I think.'

'Do you always talk so much?' Kincade asked. Somebody snickered and Vince went red, his eyes darkening in anger. Then his glance flicked to the bay horse and the corners of his mouth went up in a nasty curve.

'You're riding Texas today,' he observed. 'Good horse.'

Making no comment, Kincade snugged the cinch up tighter, then caught the reins and led the bay away from the rail.

There was silence all around him and covert glances from the other riders as Kincade stopped in the center of the yard and checked the cinch again before dropping the stirrup.

When he looped the reins over the gelding's neck, the bay rolled an eye and laid back its ears. 'I take it you buck more than a little,' Kincade murmured and almost grinned. 'We'll see.'

He took a short rein and swung aboard. The bay humped its back and immediately ducked its head. Kincade planted his feet firmly in the stirrups. When the horse made its first plunge into the air, Kincade started to raise his right arm, out of habit, then remembered form and style counted for nothing in this ride and brought it down.

After the first twisting jumps and stiff-legged landings, needle-sharp jabs of pain stabbed his left arm with each jerk on the reins. Kincade grabbed them with his right hand and took some of the stress off the newly healed bones in his left arm.

Eden watched with the others as the bay horse sunfished across the yard, showing its heels to the sky. She wanted to go about her business, but the sight of Kincade swaying in the saddle like he was in a rocking chair held her attention. He was good. More than good, she admitted grudgingly.

After last night, she wanted to dislike him, find fault with him. It had been a mistake to tell him anything – about herself or her brother. She knew that.

The bay horse made a few more half-hearted jumps, then came to a stop and blew out a loud breath. Kincade waited a minute, then reined the gelding around and walked him back to the corral fence. He stepped down and checked the cinch again.

'Nice ride,' Deke told him, a little awestruck.

Kincade nodded and reached for the coiled rope on the ground. 'He cranks up pretty good.' But the bay wasn't close to being in the same league with the broncs Kincade had ridden in the past.

'When I make a ride like that, there's never anybody around to see it,' Al Bender complained as he went by.

'You ever rodeo?' Deke asked.

'I've tried my hand at it.' Which was one way of saying he had ridden the professional rodeo circuit, full time, for the last ten years. Kincade fastened the lariat on the off side of the saddle.

'Guess we all do at sometime or other. But rodeo can be like a fever in your blood. I had an uncle that caught the bug,' Deke recalled with a sad shake of his head. 'He could've bought a good-sized ranch with the money he spent on entry fees, gas, and doctor bills. He rodeoed for twenty years or more, and when he was done, all he got out of it was a few buckles, a divorce, and a lot of broken bones.'

'It isn't an easy way to make a living.' Kincade knotted the end of the lariat to the saddle horn and ducked under the bay's neck, then scooped up the trailing rein and stepped into the saddle.

'You got that right,' the wrangler declared and moved off when Eden rode up.

She reined in a few feet from the bay. 'Have you got everything?'

When Kincade looked at her, he automatically glanced at her lips. They instantly came together in a tight, compressed line and he knew she remembered, as he did.

'All set.'

She looked at the rope tied to his saddle horn. 'You're one of those hard and fast Texas riders.'

'That's right. When I rope something, I don't let go.' A smile edged the corners of his mouth, forming deep angles. 'Of course, sometimes I'm not sure whether it's a case of I've got it, or it's got me.'

'Dallying is safer.'

'Probably.' Wrapping the rope around the saddle horn instead of tying it always gave the rider the option of releasing it if anything went wrong. '"Throw away the rope or throw away the ranch," as the old saying goes,' Kincade said. 'But I've never made it a habit to play things safe.'

'You might regret that someday.'

'I might.'

Eden looked around at the others. 'Are we ready?'

'Yeah,' Vince spoke up, sarcasm in his voice. 'We're burning daylight.'

'You surprise me, Vince,' Kincade remarked. 'I never took you to be a student of Shakespeare.'

'Shakespeare?' He frowned. 'I don't know what you're talking about.'

'You just used John Wayne's favorite line from *Romeo and Juliet* – "We burn daylight."'

'You're crazy,' Vince muttered and swung onto his horse.

'That isn't really from Shakespeare, is it?' Deke asked, all wide-eyed and worried.

'It is.' Kincade reined his horse away.

Deke turned to Al Bender. 'He's kidding, isn't he?'

'Beats me,' Al said.

Eden ended the discussion. 'Let's move out.' She whistled to the Blue Heeler, calling the dog to her horse's side.

Within minutes they were on their way. A big orange sun sat atop the horizon, watching them as it spread its rays across the land, heating the morning. The chuck wagon – the cook perched atop an old truck seat, a tall-crowned, Hoss Cartwright-style hat on his head, his long gray hair streaming onto his shoulders – led the procession. The bed wagon followed with a rider named Connors at the reins. The cavvy brought up the rear, Deke riding point ahead of the two bell mares, while Kincade and another rider rode drag to keep the stragglers moving. The rest of the riders ranged between the wagon and the remuda.

Passing the holding pens and loading chute just beyond the ranch headquarters, they set out across the basin, a large saucer-shaped hollow nearly a mile wide, planted with tough range grass. Vince brought his horse alongside Eden's, a dark and brooding look on his face.

'What's the new guy's name again?' he asked after a moment.

'Kincade.' She was uncomfortable with the subject and tried not to show it.

'I don't like him.' His tone was unusually flat and harsh.

'You said that before.' She stared straight ahead, conscious of a slow heat stealing over her, a heat that had nothing to do with the warmth of the sun on her face.

'I know,' Vince muttered and fell silent.

'This is the best stand of grass we've had in the basin in quite a few years,' she said to change the subject.

'You're making a mistake moving the cattle here. You'll need every bit of this graze come winter.'

'They won't be on it long.' A few lengths ahead of them, the chuck wagon started up a gentle incline, making the climb out of the basin.

'You're dreaming, Sis,' Vince said critically. 'DePard has all the shippers around here in his hip pocket. They're never going to agree to haul the cattle to market for you.'

'I know. That's why I contracted with an outfit out of Oregon to haul them.'

'What?' Vince reined in.

'They'll be here Tuesday morning at nine o'clock to start loading.' Eden kept her horse moving forward.

Vince spurred after her, then yanked roughly on the reins, pulling his horse up when he was once again abreast of her. 'When did this happen?'

'Yesterday.'

'Why the hell didn't you tell me last night?' he demanded angrily. 'I had a right to know.'

'It was hard to get a word in edgewise last night,' Eden shot back in a rare show of irritation. 'You were too busy trying to convince me to sell. Remember?'

She swung the chestnut out from behind the bed wagon and sent it into a canter to the top of the low hill. Vince didn't follow her.

It was past noon when they reached the ruins of the old mining camp called Flat Rock. Ore tailings from mine tunnels abandoned decades ago streaked the slopes of the surrounding hills, like old scars still visible despite the desert growth that dotted them.

A few crumbling remains of foundation marked the locations of former structures. Only the front section of an old stone building still stood. A rotting wood frame and a set of rusty hinges marked the opening where a door had once hung. The rest of the walls had long ago collapsed in a tumble of rock, now partially overgrown with brush and weeds.

A windmill stood guard over it all, its blades churning uselessly in the morning wind. A small bunch of cows stood around the metal tank at its base, sucking at the few inches of murky water that covered the bottom.

No time was wasted setting up camp in the ruins. As soon as the horses were unhitched from the chuck wagon, the cook fired up the propane stove, put a pot of coffee on, and started throwing together a midday meal. The cavvy was driven into the permanent trap by the windmill and left to graze. The rope corral was off-loaded from the bed wagon. Then the mess tent was erected next to the chuck wagon and the canvas fly stretched over the tongue of the wagon.

Each rider set up his own individual canvas teepee and stowed his gear inside. Then it was back to the trap with rope and halter to select a fresh horse for the afternoon's work.

Carrying his rope and a whip, Deke drove the cavvy toward the rope corral in the corner. Another rider held one side of the corral open and the horses thundered inside. Deke followed.

As each rider called the name of the horse he wanted, Deke swung his rope and the hoolihan settled around the neck of the chosen animal. When Kincade's turn came, he selected a cream-colored buckskin from his string, a lean and rangy mustang with a jet-black mane and tail and short black stockings.

Vince stood a couple of feet in front of him, taking a slug of tepid water from his canteen. When Kincade stepped forward to claim his horse, he bumped

Rossiter's arm, spilling water down the front of Vince's shirt.

'Hey, watch where you're going!' Vince threw a swift, angry glance at him.

'You watch,' Kincade replied, feeling the glare of the man's eyes on his back and not caring. He walked up to the roped buckskin and slipped the halter on.

Ignoring Vince, he led the buckskin to the small wire corral adjacent to the trap. He turned the horse loose inside, where it could readily be caught later, then headed back to the campsite.

On the way he spotted the cowboss, Bob Waters, behind the crumbling stone wall, busy digging a hole in the ground. Curious, Kincade walked over.

'What are you doing?'

Waters looked up, then tossed another load of the gravelly dirt onto the pile next to the hole. Stopping, he leaned a moment on the shovel and pushed his glasses back onto the bridge of his nose.

'Digging the boss's latrine.' He gripped the shovel handle again and stepped down on the head of it.

'The boss.' Kincade's glance traveled unerringly to the slim, well-shaped woman inspecting the damage to the windmill. 'Is that what you call her?'

'That's what she is.' Waters lifted another shovelful of dirt and looked at Kincade, catching the direction of his glance. 'If you don't want to feel the rough side of her temper, you'll remember that,' he advised and went back to digging.

The noon meal consisted of a beef hash liberally seasoned with onions and chili peppers, accompanied by fresh-baked biscuits and wild honey. The hash concoction tasted better than it looked. But it was the dried apple cobbler, steaming hot from the oven, that had everyone coming back for seconds. Except Kincade.

Instead he refilled his enameled coffee mug and took up a position directly opposite Vince. He puffed on a cigar and watched Vince through the curling smoke. After a moment, his plate scraped clean of cobbler a second time, Vince noticed him.

He bristled instantly. 'What are you looking at?'

'Nothing.' Kincade took the cigar from his mouth and said slowly, 'Absolutely nothing.'

Rossiter's eyes narrowed, not liking the sound of that, but uncertain how to take it. 'Do your looking in some other direction,' he retorted and turned his attention elsewhere. 'Hey, Wild Jack,' he called and raised his cup. 'Pour me some coffee.'

Before the cook could lift the pot from the stove, Kincade suggested, 'Why don't you get your own?'

The mess tent went silent. Not a single utensil scraped a plate despite the attention being concentrated on them. Muscle corded along his jaw as Vince lowered his cup and stared hotly at Kincade.

'You better watch that mouth of yours, mister,' he told Kincade. 'One of these days somebody's going to ram a fist in it.'

Kincade studied the smoldering tip of his cigar, then lifted his glance to Vince, a small smile denting the corners of his mouth. 'That's possible.'

'You're looking for trouble. Why?' Vince demanded.

'Who? Me?' Kincade countered.

'Yes, you.' Vince walked over to the cook's wreck pan and tossed his dishes in, then stalked off. Kincade took another puff on his cigar and watched him.

Eden met Vince on her way to the mess tent. One glimpse at the black look on his face and she knew he was upset.

'What's wrong, Vince?'

He paused long enough to snap, 'I don't like that new man you hired.'

Before she could ask what he meant, Vince was striding toward the corral. Eden hesitated, then walked on,
unsure what kind of trouble to expect. But everything
seemed normal when she reached the tent, shadowed
by the old cowdog.

'Is there any more of that cobbler?' the lean and lanky
Deke asked, going back for thirds.

'Yeah, make some more for supper tonight,' one of
the other riders called out.

Wild Jack grunted an unintelligible reply and slapped
another helping of cobbler on Deke's plate. Eden spotted
Kincade hunkered down by the chuck wagon, sitting on
his heels, his back resting against a tire. She looked away
the instant her glance connected with his, a heat flaring
at even that brief contact.

Moving briskly, she crossed to the wagon and took
the plate the cook had dished up for her. With a cup
of coffee in the other hand, Eden left the tent and took
up her usual perch on the wagon tongue, glad she had
never made a habit of taking her meals with the men.
The dog instantly sought shade under the wagon.

She took a couple of sips of hot coffee, then set the cup
down. She ate while listening to the idle talk of the men,
then became irritated with herself when she realized she
was listening for the low timbre of Kincade's voice.

Finished with her plate, she set it on the ground
and retrieved her cup, drinking down half the coffee.
Leaning forward, she rested elbows on her legs and
held the cup with both hands, turning her head to
gaze at the stark and empty land. It was a sight that
usually soothed her, renewed her. But this time Eden
was struck by the loneliness of it, a loneliness so vast
she almost ached with it.

Hearing a crunch of footsteps on the stony ground,
she squared around and saw a pair of long, male legs
in front of her, partially encased in a snug pair of fringed

leather chinks. A gloved hand gripped the handle of a large enamel coffee pot.

'More coffee?' The voice belonged to Kincade.

Eye-level with his hips, she didn't look higher as she held out her cup. 'Thanks,' she said and deliberately focused her attention on the cut of his short chaps, studying first the buckle that fastened them around his hips, then the curved line that scooped under the bulge in his faded jeans.

'I can't fill it any fuller.'

Eden started to make a furious retort to his suggestive remark. It died a wordless death when she realized he was talking about her coffee cup, not his jeans.

'Right,' she mumbled and jerked the cup back, the coffee nearly sloshing over the side. She took a quick sip to cover her embarrassment.

'It's hot,' he warned.

Eden merely nodded, and silently berated herself for thinking in sexual terms. She was relieved when he finally moved away without further comment.

The afternoon orders were simple ones. Each rider was assigned a section and told to search thoroughly and push all cattle back to the trap.

Alone in the camp, Wild Jack cleaned up the dishes from the noon meal, drank a half a bottle of vanilla extract, and began preparations for supper. Late in the afternoon, with the sun making its slow dive toward the western horizon, he hauled himself onto the old truck seat. From this high perch he scanned the area, watching for the first hint of dust, the first sign of movement that would signal a rider returning to camp. He sat silent and unmoving, a hot breeze rippling the canvas of the mess tent.

Detecting a faint cloud of dust in the far distance, he studied it closely, then grunted and hopped to the ground. Back at the chuck wagon, he drank the rest of the vanilla as a reward for his vigilance, then started putting the finishing touches on the night's meal.

Eden was the third rider in, driving twenty head of cattle into the trap with the help of the cowdog. After the gate had swung shut on them, she rode over to the wire corral and dismounted, as caked with sweat and dust as her horse. Cassius flopped on the ground, panting heavily. She stripped off the saddle and used the sweat-damp blanket to squeegee the worst of the wetness from the animal's back, then turned the horse loose.

With a bone-aching tiredness that always came at the end of a hard day, she started to gather her gear together, then paused when she saw an approaching rider hazing less than a dozen head. She recognized Vince and frowned at the smallness of his gather. She waited until he had driven the bunch into the trap.

'Is that all the cattle you found?' she asked when he rode up.

'That's it.' He looked tired and irritable, preoccupied with something as he rested his rein hand on the saddlehorn and lifted a neck cloth to wipe the sweat from his face.

'But you had Big Meadow in your section,' she said, her frown deepening. 'You should have found three times that number.'

He swung his head toward her, his eyes black with temper. 'Are you saying I don't know how to do my job?'

Tired of the foul mood he'd been in all day, Eden fired back, 'No, I'm saying you should have found more cattle.'

'You know everything. You go look,' he said, sneering.

'Maybe I will.'

For a hot run of seconds, Vince glared at her, then hauled back on the reins. 'To hell with this,' he muttered and started to wheel his horse away from her.

Eden grabbed the reins. 'Where are you going?'

'To town,' he snapped. 'It's Saturday night and I'm going to have a few beers and some laughs at Starr's.'

He dug his spurs into the horse's belly. Eden let go of the reins as it lunged forward. Swinging the romal, Vince whipped the horse into a gallop and struck out across the broad valley, heading southwest toward town.

Deke stood at the wire corral, staring after him with a wistful expression. Turning, he glanced at Eden and said nothing. No one worked at the ranch long without becoming accustomed to Vince's abrupt goings and comings.

A haze of dust hung over the backs of the forty head of cattle Kincade herded toward the trap. As he approached it, he had a glimpse of someone galloping away, but the obscuring dust kept him from identifying the rider.

Scenting water, the cattle trotted through the open gate. Kincade reined in and absently stroked the mustang's neck for an afternoon's work well done. The mustang swung quickly at the touch of the rein, as if eager to go back out.

'End of the day, fella.' Kincade briefly envied the animal's stamina. It had been a long time since he had spent an entire day on a horse and Kincade could feel the soreness in every muscle.

He spotted Eden busying herself with saddle and gear, ignoring him a little too completely when he rode up. His gaze lifted to the dust hanging in the air, the rider already lost from view.

'Who's that?' he asked Deke.

'Rossiter.'

'Rossiter?' Kincade glanced at the rapidly dissipating dust cloud and frowned. 'Where's he headed?'

'To Starr's for a beer.'

'A beer, huh? Where's town from here?'

Deke looked in the general direction of Friendly. 'Ohhh, fifteen or twenty miles southwest.'

Kincade hesitated a moment, then buried his foot back in the stirrup and nudged the buckskin forward.

'Where're you going?' Deke frowned.

'To get a beer,' Kincade called back and pushed the horse into a ground-eating trot.

Deke watched him for a minute, then turned to Eden. 'What do you think, Boss? Should I catch him a horse for tomorrow morning or not?'

She knew what Deke was really asking – did she think Kincade would come back? Or was going for a beer simply another way of saying he had quit? She had been given more ambiguous notices than that.

Struggling against the sudden leadenness she felt at the thought, Eden replied, 'Catch a horse for him.'

He nodded. 'Guess it would be easy enough to turn the horse loose if he don't come back.'

The dust trail kicked up by Rossiter's fast-traveling horse served as a distant beacon to guide Kincade. He lost sight of it when he neared a range of low mountains. He gave the mustang its head and let it choose its own path up the rough slopes. When he topped the ridge, he spotted the dark speck of a horse and rider halfway across the broad alley that stretched below him.

Kincade reined in and let the mustang have a blow while he studied the faraway figure. There was little discernible movement, which indicated to Kincade that Rossiter had brought his horse down to a walk. He checked the setting sun, confirming the heading was still southwest.

He waited a minute more, then pointed the buckskin down the slope. Again, Kincade let the horse pick its trail and set its own pace, neither hurrying it nor holding it back.

The sun went down, streaking the sky with swathes of crimson and fuchsia. Soon twilight purpled the sky and the first evening star glittered overhead. Rossiter's dust trail was no longer visible and Kincade had to trust that Vince hadn't altered his direction.

Night's blackness fell swiftly, swallowing the surrounding land in its void. More stars came out to join the moon and Kincade took his bearings from them. Mile after mile he traveled without seeing so much as a gleam of light from an isolated ranch house. Now and then he would catch a whiff of dust on the cool night air. It was the only assurance he had that Rossiter was still somewhere ahead of him.

Lights glittered in the far distance. For a long time Kincade thought he was looking at a cluster of stars low on the horizon. Then he realized it was the light of town. He lifted the mustang out of its tireless trot and into a lope.

10

Vince rode up to the Lucky Starr. His weary horse stumbled to a halt near a corner post supporting the overhang. The muted din of rowdy voices came from inside the building. Smiling at the sound, Vince swung out of the saddle and hastily tied the reins to the post.

He stepped onto the walk and swept off his hat to slap the dust from it and his clothes. Quickly he ran combing fingers through his hair, pushed his hat back on, and headed for the front door, spurs jingling with each jaunty stride.

Starr Davis was at the big mahogany bar when he walked in. She saw him, hesitated fractionally, then fixed a big purring smile on her face and went to meet him.

'If it isn't the proverbial bad penny back again,' she mocked.

Vince laughed. 'You know I can never stay away for long.'

'Unfortunately.' Her smile was long and warm, but her eyes were cool and cautious. 'What's it going to cost me this time?'

'That's no way to talk,' Vince chided with a grin. 'You know I always make things right.'

'You usually do.' She nodded. 'One way or another.'

'That's all that counts, isn't it?' Vince countered. 'So, how about it? Are you going to buy this bad penny a drink?'

'Don't I always?' Starr took his arm and led him to the bar. 'Roy.' She rapped a hand on the counter. Expressionless, the bartender nodded, shoved a pair of beers at his waiting customers, snatched their money off the counter, then shifted down to their end of the bar. 'Give this man a drink – on me.'

'Draw me a cold one, Roy.' Vince pulled a crumpled twenty-dollar bill from his pocket. 'And keep them coming until I tell you to stop.' He pushed the money at Roy, then turned to face Starr. 'So, tell me – how's my lucky Starr these days?'

'Better than ever,' she replied and ran an assessing eye over him. 'The same can't be said for you. You look like you've been rode hard and put up wet.'

'That is a fact.' He picked up the frosty mug Roy set in front of him. Lifting it, Vince saluted Starr. 'Here's to generous women.' He drank down half of it in one long guzzle, then lowered the mug and called to Roy. 'Throw the thickest, juiciest steak you've got on the grill for me, will you?'

'Burn one,' Roy hollered into the kitchen.

'You're in for a treat tonight, Vince,' Starr told him. 'I hired a new cook—'

'Is she good-looking?' he asked, eyes twinkling.

'*She* is a *he*.'

'Just my luck,' he declared with a wry twist of his mouth, then raised his glass and downed the rest of the beer.

Roy had another beer waiting for him when Vince set the empty mug down. He took a quick sip of it, then rested an elbow on the bar and turned sideways to survey the crowded room.

'Where's the kid? I don't see him around.'

'At a friend's house watching a bunch of horror movies they rented.'

'That wouldn't be my idea of fun,' Vince declared.

'He isn't like you. Thankfully,' Starr murmured.

'That's good. I'd hate to think of anybody getting the kind of luck I've been having lately. It's been running against me for too long. It's time it turned around. Starting tonight, I hope.' He studied the crowd. 'It looks like you've been invaded by the Diamond D. Is DePard around, too?'

'Over in the corner playing poker.' With a backward nod of her blonde head, Starr gestured at a table in the far corner where a handful of men were seated.

'How are things going between you and DePard?'

'I see him whenever it can be arranged,' Starr replied, deliberately offhand. Long ago she had learned that Duke DePard didn't like his private affairs to become the subject of public discussion. 'He has become very fond of Rick.'

Vince squared around to face the bar, resting both elbows on it. 'A kid needs a man in his life. Someone he can look up to and admire. A role model. Not someone like my grandfather,' he inserted on a faintly bitter note. 'That man was a slave driver.' He glanced back at the corner table. 'You better grab DePard, if you can.'

'I intend to.'

He gave her an assessing look. 'You'll do it, too.' A smile briefly lifted the corners of his mouth, then he turned to study his beer. 'Does the kid ever ask about his father?'

'Not any more.'

Vince nodded, then straightened and flashed Starr one of his patented smiles, which had melted many a cynical heart. 'You say they're playing poker, huh?' He turned the charm up a notch. 'Would you mind staking me to fifty dollars in chips? I promise I'm good for it.'

'Don't worry. I'll make sure of that.'

'Hey, Starr!' someone yelled. 'Come deal us some blackjack.'

'Be right there,' she said and moved away from the bar.

Vince tracked her with his eyes, then let his glance drift to the back poker table, his smile fading when he picked Duke DePard from the others. He took another long sip of beer.

'You're slowing down.' Roy plunked down a third frosty mug.

'Not for long, Roy,' Vince said, with a grin. 'Not for long.'

He gathered up the third beer and carried both to a bar table. Hooking a toe under the rung of a chair, he pulled it out and sat down, pushing the mugs onto the table.

Rossiter's lathered horse gleamed wetly in the light that spilled from the Lucky Starr. It stood with its head hanging nearly to the ground, an ear swiveling in tired interest when Kincade reined the mustang alongside.

Stiff and sore, he lifted himself slowly out of the saddle. Once both feet were on the ground, Kincade flexed the muscles in his shoulder and back, feeling their screams of protest. Raising a stirrup, he loosened the cinch, then pulled the bandanna from around his neck and soaked it with water from his canteen. He wiped the dust from the buckskin's nostrils and washed its mouth, squeezing water into it.

Finished, he tied the reins to the post, then checked Rossiter's horse, running a testing hand down its chest and feeling the steamy heat beneath its wet coat. The canteen on Rossiter's saddle was empty.

'Something tells me you didn't get a drop of it,'

Kincade murmured to the horse, soaked his bandanna with water from his canteen and repeated the previous procedure.

He screwed the lid back on the canteen and hooked it on his saddle along with his wet neck scarf. Turning back to Rossiter's horse, he saw the cinch hadn't been loosened either. Kincade corrected that, then headed into the casino. The jukebox blared a Garth Brooks song and a cowboy by the slot machines whooped in triumph when lights flashed and bells jangled with a jackpot win. Kincade paused inside the door and scanned the boisterous throng. The noise was deafening after the silence of the desert night. He spotted Rossiter at a bar table, slicing into a huge steak. Kincade's stomach growled hungrily at the sight.

He started for the bar, then changed directions and crossed the length of the room to the narrow hall. A cowboy came out of the men's room, giving his zipper a final tug. Kincade stepped aside to let him pass, then went in the men's room to wash off some of the day's grime and sweat.

At the sink, he saw his reflection in the mirror above it. Dust caked his skin and the short stubble of a day's growth made the narrow angle of his features more pronounced and his cheeks gaunt. He smiled crookedly in silent commiseration with the man in the mirror, then reached down and turned both faucets on full force.

The sound of running water awakened his thirst. Kincade took off his hat and bent down, tipping his head under the faucet and letting the water rush into his parched mouth, drinking until his belly was full. Satisfied, he caught cups of water and wet his face, then worked a bar of soap into a lather and scrubbed his skin, feeling the cracking of the dust mask. He rinsed off the soap and drank a couple more swallows of water.

Dripping wet, he stepped over to the towel roll and

dried his face and hands. He felt almost human again. As he reached for his hat, the door to the men's room opened and Rusty came in. At least Kincade thought it was Rusty. His thatch of brick red hair was tucked in under a towering chef's hat that was canted to one side. The dark brown stubble that marked the beginnings of a beard covered the lower half of his freckled face and a long bibbed apron, stained with food and grease splatters, was tied around him.

'I saw you come back here and thought I'd duck in and say hi,' Rusty said.

'What are you doing in that getup?' Kincade frowned.

'I'm the new cook.' Rusty grinned. 'When I came in last night to eat, I ordered a steak and hash browns like always. But this time I told Roy to chop up some peppers and onions in my potatoes. He told me that if I didn't like the way he cooked, I could fix my own food. So I went in the kitchen and did just that. Next thing I knew, there was Starr offering me a job, cooking. It seemed better than sitting around doing nothing, so I took it.'

Kincade pushed his hat back on. 'There's a couple of horses tied out front. If you get a chance, take some water to them.'

A sandy brow shot up. 'You rode in?'

'Yeah.'

'You hungry?'

'Starved.'

'I'll throw a steak on for you,' Rusty said, and slipped out the door.

Kincade left the men's room. Rossiter was still busy with his food and never noticed Kincade when he crossed the room and took up residence at the end of the bar.

Finished with his meal, Vince leaned back in his chair and lingered over a beer, killing time by trading remarks with a foul-mouthed brunette at the next table. She looked twenty and acted forty, an attractive woman but a little too hard for his tastes.

Roy brought him a fresh beer. Rising, Vince took his beer, stroked a finger over the woman's cheek and made a promise he had no intention of keeping, then sauntered over to the blackjack table where Starr was dealing. She saw him and shoved a slip of paper at him.

'Let's keep it legal,' she said and resumed the game play with hardly a break in her rhythm.

Vince signed the IOU and pushed it back. She counted out a fifty-dollar stack of chips with one hand and flipped over her cards with the other, showing a queen of hearts and a nine of clubs. 'Pay twenty,' she told the player.

Smiling at the choice expletives that followed Starr's announcement, Vince moved off and drifted to the poker table in the corner. As always, Duke DePard sat with his back to the wall, facing the room. Vince stood to one side while the hand in progress was played out. He didn't bother to check out the three other players at the table. DePard was the only one who interested him. He was the one with the money.

DePard's expression was a study of grim concentration, his thick, bushy brows drawn together, hooding his eyes. His mouth was in its usual straight and stern line, half-hidden by the heavy mustache that covered most of his upper lip. As a poker player, he was cautious and conservative, looking at his cards once, memorizing them, then laying them down and never looking at them again until a hand was called and the bettors turned their cards over. The game always had his full attention. It never strayed until the pot was raked in by the winner.

Idly Vince clicked the chips together in his palm, liking the sound of them, the feel of them. Before this night was over, he planned to parlay this little stake into a lot more. A whole lot more, he thought and smiled.

The cowboss for the Bremmer outfit wrapped his hands around the pot and dragged it across the table to him. DePard tossed his hand onto the deck and tipped back in his chair, lifting his glance from the table to sweep the room. When it reached Vince, it stopped and centered sharply on him.

'Mind if I sit in for a few hands?' Vince pushed the empty chair back from the table without waiting for permission.

'The table stake's fifty,' DePard told him.

'I know the rules, Duke.' Vince let his chips clatter onto the table as he sat down. 'I have to warn you, boys, I feel lucky tonight.'

'We'll see.' DePard pointed a finger at one of the other players. 'It's your deal, Ernie.'

'The game's five card draw, jacks or better to open.' Ernie split the deck and began shuffling the cards together.

'Ante up, boys. Ante up.' Vince tossed a chip into the pot and pushed his hat to the back of his head, strands of dark wavy hair falling onto his forehead.

At the bar, Kincade saw Rossiter stroll over to the poker table, but it wasn't until Rossiter sat down that Kincade noticed Duke DePard. Curious that Rossiter would be playing poker with his sister's arch-enemy, Kincade finished the last of his steak and went over, taking his beer with him.

Two other cowboys were slumped against the wall, watching the game. Kincade joined them, the angle giving him a view of both Rossiter and DePard.

'You look like you've had a hard day, Rossiter,' DePard observed.

'You're looking at the sweat of honest toil.' An easy grin split his mouth as Vince fanned the hand dealt to him.

'Is that a fact?' DePard seemed unimpressed.

'Yep.' Vince discarded two cards from his hand, then sent DePard a sly look. 'We're gathering cattle out at Flat Rock.'

DePard's interest sharpened. 'What for?'

'To ship to market, of course.' He held up two fingers to the dealer and trapped the cards that sailed across the table.

'Right.' DePard sounded both amused and smug, though his expression never changed. 'And who do you figure will ship them?'

Vince took his time answering as he slipped the two cards in with the keepers in his hand and studied the result. 'An outfit out of Oregon.' He watched DePard's reaction out of the corner of an eye. The man had gone still, and silent. 'She's outfoxed you, Duke.'

'If it's true.' Recovering, DePard looked at the new cards he'd been dealt, then laid them down, and tossed some chips into the pot. 'Ten to you, Bill.'

'Oh, it's true.' Vince nodded. 'The trucks will be at the ranch Tuesday morning at nine to start loading.' The two players on his right both folded. Vince counted out a stack of chips and pushed them into the pot. 'There's your ten – and ten more.'

'Too rich for me.' The other player threw in his hand.

DePard pushed more chips into the pot. 'I call.'

Vince spread his cards on the table, face up. 'Three tens with an ace high. Read 'em and weep.'

He barely gave DePard a chance to say, 'Beats me,' and throw in his hand before Vince raked the pot to him.

Out of the next five hands, Vince won three of them. All were large pots. Kincade watched as Vince stacked the chips from his last win, then rapped the table. 'Come on, Murphy. It's your deal.'

'Deal me out.' DePard collected the small stack of chips in front of him and stood.

Startled, Vince looked up and frowned. 'You aren't quitting already?'

'Your luck's running too good for me.' The corners of DePard's mouth pulled into a smile that didn't reach his eyes; they remained hard.

With a swing of his big shoulders, DePard left the table and walked away with slow, measured strides. He never once glanced in Kincade's direction. If he had noticed him at all, it was obvious he hadn't recognized him.

Kincade watched as DePard crossed the room, speaking to no one until he came to a cowboy in a spotted cowhide vest sitting at a bar table. DePard said something to him, and the man turned, showing Kincade the large purple birthmark on his face. It was Sheehan, DePard's foreman, the one who had worked Kincade over.

Sheehan stood and followed DePard out of the lounge. Thoughtfully Kincade redirected his attention to the poker table. Vince lost the next hand. When he picked up his beer mug, he saw it was empty. He glanced at the cowboys along the wall.

'One of you guys tell Roy that I need another beer.'

'Tell him yourself.' The phrase, almost an echo of the one Kincade had used on Vince at the noon meal, brought Rossiter's glance slicing to him.

Displeasure, born of mutual dislike, immediately darkened his face. 'What are you doing here?'

'Having a beer.' Kincade raised the nearly empty mug.

'Have it somewhere else,' Vince snapped.

'I like it here.'

Vince made an effort to ignore him and concentrate on the next hand. He lost that one as well, and threw his cards down in disgust. He looked up and caught Kincade's gaze on him.

'Are you just gonna stand around all night, or are you going to sit in?'

Kincade shook his head. 'Poker isn't my game.'

'I'd like to know just what your game is.' Vince threw him a narrow glance and scooped up the first two cards dealt him.

'Maybe you'll find out someday.' A small smile touched the corners of Kincade's mouth as he lifted his mug and took a drink of half-warm beer.

Rossiter's only response was a contemptuous snort.

Over the next hour, the stack of chips in front of Vince went steadily down as he lost more games than he won. With each loss, he grew more flushed and irritable. A bet was made, and Vince called it, tossing all of his chips into the pot. He lost.

'Looks like you ran out of luck,' Kincade observed.

Rossiter placed both palms flat on the table and pushed his chair back, his eyes darkening with a sultry anger. 'When I want your opinion, I'll ask for it.' He stood up and swept a glance over the other players at the table, forcing a smile. 'Another time, boys.'

He walked away, heading for the bar. Kincade watched him for a minute, then ambled in the same direction. Vince ordered a fresh beer, drank a couple of swallows, then noticed Kincade leaning against the far end of the bar. Irritation flickered through his expression and he quickly drank down more beer. He set the mug down and slapped a hand on the counter in a gesture of finality, then swung away. As he headed for the door, he called cheerfully to Starr. She responded with a wave of her hand.

After the front door closed behind Rossiter, Kincade settled up his tab, collected his change and left. Outside the casino, he paused and cast a searching glance over the town's darkened buildings. Both horses were still tied to the post, dozing lightly, a plastic pail of water near their front feet.

Rossiter was nowhere around. Kincade listened, but heard no footsteps. He hesitated a second longer, then moved toward the horses, his boots making a heavy sound on the wooden sidewalk, accompanied by the *chink* of his spurs.

The mustang lifted its head, its ears pointing to Kincade. Then it swung its nose toward the corner of the building. Kincade wasn't surprised when Vince stepped out of the dark shadows a second later.

'Why do you keep following me?'

'I've heard that "suspicion always haunts the guilty mind,"' Kincade remarked, quoting Shakespeare again. 'Is that your problem, Rossiter? Do you have a guilty mind?'

'No.' The answer was quick. A little too quick. 'Why would you think that?'

'Hey, you're the one who's acting like you have something to hide.'

Rossiter frowned. 'I know you from somewhere, don't I?'

'Like I said before, we've never met.'

Confused and uncertain, Rossiter shook his head, then went to his horse and yanked the reins loose from the post. He pulled himself into the saddle, looked at Kincade one last time, then kicked the horse into a lope out of town. The mustang sent a ringing neigh after them.

'Are you heading back now?' Rusty stepped out of the shadows at the side of the building.

Kincade nodded. 'It's a long ride back to camp and it isn't going to get any shorter standing here.'

'It's a shame I don't have my horse trailer,' Rusty said. 'If I did, I could throw your buckskin in it and drive you both back.'

'A damn shame,' Kincade agreed and tightened the cinch before swinging into the saddle. 'Take care of yourself, Rusty.'

'You, too.'

Rusty remained standing there long after Kincade had disappeared listening to the sound of trotting hooves fading into the night. Finally he walked over, dumped the water from the plastic pail, and headed down the alley toward the kitchen back door swinging the empty bucket.

Somewhere after midnight Eden rolled over, for the hundredth time at least. Since turning in, she had slept in fitful snatches. Again she found herself half-awake, listening to the stirring of horses in the corral, the occasional snorts and soft whickers. Gradually the steady drum of hoofbeats began to register. Outside the tent, the old cowdog growled in its throat. There was a rider returning to camp.

Rising, Eden pulled on her boots and slipped out of the small canvas teepee. Like everyone else, she had gone to bed in the same dusty, sweaty clothes she'd worn all day. There were no such things as baths, pajamas, or clean clothes in a cow camp. She had washed her face and hands, and brushed the worst of the dirt from her hair before retiring, which was more than most had done.

Outside, she stood momentarily still, the outline of the surrounding hills lying blackly against the night. Facing the corral, Eden studied the dark shapes moving about. The hoofbeats had ceased, other sounds taking their place – the slap of leather, the jingle of bridle chains. At last she saw a figure walking toward camp.

'Which one is it, Cassius?' she murmured to the dog. 'Vince or Kincade?' The dog whined in answer and Eden moved to intercept the figure approaching the mess tent. Even with weariness tugging at him, Eden recognized the swagger in his walk before Vince reached her. She hooked her thumbs in the back pockets of her jeans and battled the sudden feeling of flatness.

'Sis,' he murmured in surprise when he saw her silhouetted against the tent's yellowing canvas. 'How come you're still up?'

'I couldn't sleep.' Which wasn't a lie.

'Not me.' He wrapped an arm around her shoulders and pulled her around to fall in step with him. 'I'm so beat I could sleep for a week and never wake up.'

She cast a glance over her shoulder toward the corral. 'Did Kincade come back with you?'

'No.' The cheerfulness went out of his voice.

'Did you see him in town?'

'Yeah. What of it?' Vince halted near the chuck wagon, his arm leaving her shoulders as he squared around.

'Nothing.' She gave a vague shake of her head. 'I just wondered whether he was coming back or not.'

'What do you care?'

'I care because I don't want to be short-handed.'

'You'd manage,' Vince told her.

'Probably, but that isn't the point.'

'You can lose sleep over him if you want, but I'm not. Good night.' He set off toward his tent.

Eden didn't follow him. She was too restless, too edgy, and sleep had been too elusive. She sagged against a chuck wagon tire and let her gaze wander over the dense shadows that gripped the desert. The day's heat was gone and the pungent breeze coming off the hills had a chilly nip to it.

Tilting her head back, Eden studied the stars strewn across the night sky like so many crushed crystals. A moon hung very low and very pale, accenting the brilliant black of the night. There was an air of lonely mystery about the night that brought a kind of ache, a sense of want for something Eden couldn't name.

She drew in a long breath and released it in a soft sigh,

lowering her head. Her hearing, sharpened by the quiet, began to pick up the blending murmurs of the night, the faint echoes, the sibilance of creatures abroad in the shadows, the rubbing sigh of the light wind over the canvas, and the approaching crunch of footfalls on the gritty soil. Eden looked up, expecting to see Vince, but the sound came from the opposite direction.

With a push upright, Eden swung around and saw Kincade. She felt a quick pull of attraction, something she had previously denied, and was instantly wary, both of him and the effect he had on her.

'You came back.'

'Did you think I wouldn't?' He stopped, a smile wrinkling the corners of his eyes.

'It wouldn't have surprised me.' Eden forced an even-ness into her voice, a note of indifference that she didn't feel at all. 'Men have gone off without handing in their notice before.'

'In my case, I merely went to town for a beer. I've had it and now I'm back.' Her long, dark hair was swept forward, spilling over one shoulder. Kincade reached out to finger a lock of it, drawn by the sheen of moon-beams on it. 'It was considerate of you to wait up for me, though.'

He was too close. Eden took a step back and came up against the tire again. 'I wasn't waiting up for you,' she denied as his hand fell back to his side. 'Vince woke me up when he rode in.'

'Yeah, I saw his horse in the corral.' His glance drifted in the direction of Vince's tent, then came back to study her face.

Moonlight sculpted her face and flowed down the full curves of her body. There was a hint of color in her cheeks and her eyes were dark with some inner dis-turbance. The sight pulled him, waking a recklessness. Reaching up, he cupped a hand to her face and stroked a thumb over her cheek. She stiffened and lifted her head, sending him conflicting signals.

'It's impossible for a man to look at you and not want you, Eden.'

'Don't.' She wasn't sure what she was protesting against – the caress of his hand, the remark he made, or her reaction to them. She only knew she didn't want to feel this way. His touch shouldn't snatch at her breath. It shouldn't heat the surface of her skin. She didn't want it. She had lived without it just fine.

'No, I shouldn't. And I shouldn't do this either,' he murmured as he brought his mouth down to hers.

As before, his mouth was warm and persuasive. She brought her hands up to push him away, but instead curled her fingers into his shirt to hold him there as he patiently rubbed his lips over hers, teasing and nibbling until there was no more resistance, no more stiffness. He smelled of leather, horses, and sweat – and a kind of rough masculinity that she would forever associate with him. She breathed it in as he dragged her closer and coaxed her lips apart.

Eden felt everything with impossible clarity: the hunger deep inside that was almost a physical ache; the hands that ran up her sides and over her back molding her to him; the hard male contours of his body and the intimate way she fit them.

He had expected to feel this degree of need. But not pain. He hadn't planned this. He didn't want it, but he couldn't stop. She filled his mind and crowded his senses with the silky feel of her hair, the fragrance of soap that clung to her skin, and the taste of her lips that left him hungry for more.

Kincade knew he had to stop, he had to back away. Yet he stayed for one more taste, one more stroke of her lush body, then dragged himself back and struggled to breathe evenly.

Because her knees felt shaky, Eden stood very straight. She waited until she was certain she could control her voice, then said with all the coolness she could muster, 'Are you quite through?'

'Yes.' His gaze was on her, unnerving her with his steadiness.

'Good,' she said in a voice hard with indifference. 'You have roughly four hours before you have to get up. I suggest you make use of it and get some sleep.' She turned and walked off.

DePard charged into the house at the Diamond D head-quarters, a black and angry look hardening his features. Sheehan was right behind him.

'That's the hell of it, Sheehan. I don't know which one,' DePard growled in irritation. 'Rossiter said she had hired an outfit from Oregon. That's all I know.'

'But where in Oregon?' Sheehan frowned. 'That can cover a lot of territory.'

'Do you think I don't know that?' DePard hit the wall switch in his office and flooded the room with light. 'That damned Rossiter woman. I could have sworn we had her choked off from everyone.'

'Are you sure Vince is telling the truth?'

'He has nothing to gain by lying about this.' DePard walked over to the bar.

Sheehan remained skeptical. 'I'm not so sure about that. The other day you agreed to pay him for any information he could get you. He could be telling you this just to get money from you.'

DePard shook his head. 'Vince Rossiter may be money hungry, but he's no fool. He knows how easy it would be to catch him lying. He wouldn't risk that. Not when he's so desperate to get his share out of the ranch.' DePard poured a measure of brandy into a glass, then lifted the decanter in Sheehan's direction in a silent question.

'Pour me one, too.' Sheehan walked over to the bar and slid onto a suede-covered stool, laying his hat aside.

'He's telling me the truth,' DePard stated. 'Vince knows that if she gets these cattle to market, she'll never agree to sell the ranch. And he knows I'm going to keep squeezing until she winds up in foreclosure or bankruptcy.'

'Would you let her sell?'

'That depends on what she might get out of it. If she walks away with nothing, then it becomes something to consider. But that isn't the problem now. It's this damned hauler.' DePard took a quick, impatient sip of his brandy.

'It has to be a one-man operation.' Sheehan frowned into his glass. 'None of the others would go against you.'

DePard jabbed a finger at him. 'You get on that phone tomorrow morning and start making calls to find out who it is.'

'Tomorrow is Sunday. I won't be able to reach anyone.'

'Call them at home. And the ones you can't track down tomorrow, you can call Monday.'

'That doesn't give us much time, Duke,' he replied, clearly troubled. 'You said the trucks are supposed to be there to start loading cattle Tuesday morning at nine o'clock. What will we do if we can't find out who it is before then?'

'Stop them.'

'How do you want me to do it?'

DePard looked at Sheehan, a cold smile pulling up one corner of his mouth. 'You're the one with a case full of marksmanship medals, Sheehan. Maybe you'd better get out your rifle and scope, and start practicing.'

11

From somewhere in the distance came the rumbling growl of diesel engines. Perched atop the fence-rail, the heels of his boots hooked on the middle board, Kincade lifted his head and spotted the long, billowing swirl of dust off to the west. His glance strayed to the loading chute where Eden stood with her brother, her head turned toward the telltale roil of dust. Cattle lowed uneasily in the pens behind Kincade, three hundred and fifty-odd head ready to ship.

The diesel roar grew louder, accompanied by the sound of grinding gears. Eden turned to her brother, a smile lighting her whole face.

'They're here.'

'Sounds like it,' Vince agreed, though with little of her jubilance.

The sight of Eden striding off to meet the trucks held Kincade's attention. With each swing of her leg, the faded denim fabric of her jeans was pulled tight across her bottom, revealing the roundness of each firm cheek. And the loose-fitting man's shirt almost, but not quite, concealed the bouncing sway of her breasts when she walked.

Alkali dust swirled like a thick fog around the

tractor-trailer rig as it rumbled into view. A second truck followed, nearly obscured by the gritty wake of the lead semi. The truck slowed to a stop, air brakes screeching, when it drew level with Eden.

The name *J J Trucking, Fields, Ore.* was stenciled in black on the driver's door. Blinking at the stinging dust, Eden walked over and climbed onto the cab's running board. The man behind the wheel was in his late forties with a muscular roll to his shoulders and a hard-used look about his face.

'Jerry Jones,' he said by way of introduction, the truck engine idling, vibrating the cab.

'Eden Rossiter.'

'Right. Sorry I'm late.' He spoke with the resignation of a man who had become used to Lady Luck frowning on him. 'These gravel roads – it took longer than I figured.'

'The cattle are over there.' Eden pointed to the holding pens. 'We're ready to start loading as soon as you're in position.'

'Won't take but a jiff,' he said and popped the clutch.

Eden hopped to the ground and stood back, waiting until both rigs had passed before following. True to his word, the man had his trailer backed up to the loading chute within minutes.

Bob Waters and Al Bender rode into the fenced alleyway between the pens. Leaving the mustang tied outside, Kincade swung off the rail and dropped to the ground. When both riders were in position, he unlatched the gate to the first pen of cattle and dragged the gate wide, blocking off one end of the alleyway while leaving the way clear to the chute. The pair walked their horses into the pen and began hazing the cattle out. Two more men were at the chute to keep the cattle moving once they started up the ramp to the stock trailer.

Kincade stayed by the gate, swinging an arm to wave the cattle toward the ramp. Pushed from behind by the hazing riders, red-coated hides soon filled the alleyway, bawling fretfully in confusion. With a clatter of hooves on the ramp's wooden floor, the first of them went up the chute. The lead cow balked at the opening to the trailer and tried to turn back.

Over the din of animal and man, a loud report rang out. Startled, Kincade looked at the chute to see if a cow had broken a board. At that instant another report sounded. This time there was no mistaking the explosive crack of a high-powered rifle.

'What the hell—' Al Bender's muttered oath was cut off by the echoing report of a third shot, followed by the nasty ping of a bullet ricocheting off the steel rim of a truck tire.

'Holy shit,' another rider yelled. 'Some fool's shooting at us.'

In the scramble for cover, both riders piled off their horses and the two men at the chute shot over the top, dropping into the pen with the cattle. There was another shot and the thwap of a bullet penetrating a rubber tire.

Crouching low, Kincade worked his way through the confused and milling cattle. He reached Bob Waters as another tire was punctured. Before Kincade could draw a breath, a bullet slammed into the truck body.

'That bastard's shooting holes in my cab,' the driver protested.

'Where is he? Have you spotted him?' Kincade took cover behind Waters's horse.

Waters pushed his glasses back on the bridge of his nose and squinted through the sweat stinging his eyes. 'Must be up that ridge. It's the only high ground around.' With a bob of his head, he indicated the boulder-strewn slope that began its rise a short distance from the holding pens.

Ducking down, Kincade peered under the horse's neck and thought he caught the flash of sunlight off a rifle barrel. Behind him, Vince shouted, 'Eden, for God's sake, get down!' Kincade turned and saw Eden near one of the saddled horses outside the corral. 'What the hell are you doing?' Vince yelled again when Eden jerked a rifle from its scabbard, yanked the reins loose, then grabbed the saddlehorn and swung herself into the saddle. 'Where are you going?'

Giving no answer, she wheeled the horse away from the pens and kicked it into a gallop. Kincade had a fairly good idea of where she was headed and why.

'The little fool,' he muttered and made a quick dash to the fence.

Vaulting it, he untied the mustang and climbed on. In one stride Kincade had the horse in a full run. He spotted Eden circling to the far side of the slope and gave her credit for having enough sense not to charge straight up the hill. Taking a direct line, he raced to intercept her.

Intent on the gunman somewhere on the hill crest, she never heard Kincade until he was almost on her. She tried to spur her horse faster, but it was too late. Bending low, Kincade grabbed her reins and pulled both horses to a plunging halt.

'What the hell are you doing?' The mustang sidled nervously under him as another shot rang out.

Eden flung up her head at the sound, then glared at Kincade. Behind all the anger was something wild and desperate. 'Let go of my horse.' She yanked on the reins, trying to pull them out of his grasp.

Despite the uneasy dancing of both horses, Kincade managed to keep his grip on her reins. 'Not until you start using your head. You can't go up there.' Suddenly he found himself staring into the barrel of her rifle. She levered a bullet into the chamber. The sight and the sound froze him.

'Get out of my way.' She sounded cool and steady and deadly.

Kincade almost let go of the reins, then considered the various things he had learned about her, and took a chance. 'Or what?' He held her gaze. 'You'll shoot me. That shouldn't be hard. You've killed a man before. The second one is always easier, I'm told.'

She went white and her eyes turned bright with pain. His taunting words had cut deeper than he'd expected. But they had given him the advantage he wanted. Kincade seized it, grabbing the rifle out of her loose grip.

With her reins now free, she whipped her horse around and sent it up the hill at a lunging gallop. Kincade gave chase.

He was out of the saddle before the rangy mustang came to a stop. But his raking glance found no one on the hill's bony ridge except Eden. She was on the ground making her own search. Extending his sweep, Kincade saw a man on horseback streaking toward the next hill. Eden spotted him at almost the same moment and grabbed up her reins to mount. 'He's getting away.'

'Unless you know something about tracking, he's gone.' Kincade caught sight of something black and white just before the man disappeared behind the hill. A vest maybe. DePard's foreman had worn a spotted vest last Saturday night at Starr's. A coincidence? Kincade doubted that.

Turning, he scanned the ridge top. A low boulder near the edge gave both concealment and a commanding view of the pens below. An area of grass around the base of it had been flattened and the few scuff marks in the dirt looked fresh.

'He might have crouched over there,' he said to Eden. 'I don't see any spent shells, but he could have taken them with him.'

When she made no response, Kincade turned back to her. Her rigid stance radiated anger. His only view of her face was in profile and that showed no expression. He glanced at the rifle in his hand – her rifle.

'Here.' He held it out to her. She took it without a word and jammed it back in the saddle boot. He suspected he knew the reason for her anger. 'That remark I made about killing a man,' he began. 'I only said what it took to stop you. I'm sorry.'

She whirled on him, her eyes like chips of hot black ice. 'You're fired.'

Shocked into anger, Kincade snapped back, 'Like hell I am!'

'You heard me – you're fired. Go pack your things and get out.'

'I'm not going anywhere,' he told her with the same harshness she used on him. 'I am staying right here on Spur.'

'No, you're not.' She erupted in a full blaze of temper. 'You're fired! Do you understand? I don't need you here. I don't want you here!'

'Why?' he shot back. 'Because you're a woman and I make you feel like one? Make you want like one?'

'No!'

'Liar.' He seized her shoulders and hauled her roughly against him, bringing his mouth down with bruising force.

She answered with a violence of her own, kicking, hitting, twisting to get free of him. But her struggles died when the anger in her changed to something else just as hot and just as volatile. Needs, longings sprang up fresh and terribly strong. She wanted to give way to them and feel – just feel.

Breaking away from the drugging heat of his mouth, Eden lowered her head, trembling, bracing herself to feel savage fingers tangling in her hair and jerking her head back up. When it didn't happen – when all she felt was the warm stroke of his hand down her back and the brush of his lips on her forehead as he murmured her name, she pulled free and walked quickly to her horse.

On legs that weren't quite steady, Eden climbed onto the saddle and reined the horse toward the slope, careful not to look at Kincade. By the time she reached the bottom of the hill, the raw achiness had subsided and she had pieced back together her scattered composure.

Another set of hooves clattered over the stony ground behind her. Eden ignored them and swung her horse toward the small group gathered around the second truck, parked a short distance from the one by the pens.

'Are you all right?' Vince came to meet her, grabbing the bridle and holding the horse's head while Eden dismounted.

'Of course.' She noticed the inordinate amount of attention being paid to the ground by the ranch hands, an interest accompanied by a lot of dirt-scuffing and spitting.

'What did you think you were going to accomplish by riding up there like that?' Vince demanded, angry now that he had determined she was unhurt.

'He stopped shooting, didn't he?' She made a visual examination of the tractor-trailer rig, trying to assess the extent of damage to it. The left front tire on the tractor was flat and a boy of about nineteen was walking around the stock trailer with a tire iron, checking the tires on it.

'Who was it? Did you see him?' Vince asked.

'Just a man riding away.' Saddle leather groaned under a shifting weight, the sound followed by the crunch of a booted foot on the gravelly soil. Kincade was behind her. Eden fixed her gaze on the grim-faced stock hauler striding toward her.

'I used your phone to call the sheriff.' He jerked a thumb toward the house. 'They're sending someone out right away.'

Knowing the sheriff, Eden doubted Lot Williams would be in any great hurry. He and Duke DePard were second cousins. He would suspect, the same as she did, that DePard was behind this. More than likely he was secretly applauding DePard's actions.

'What's the damage?' She pushed the shooting from her mind.

'It looks like about six tires flat on both rigs, and this one's out of commission with a bullet hole in the radiator.' He hurled a bitter look at the semi nearest them. 'I'll have to bring a flatbed down and haul it home.'

'What about the other one?'

'It's just a matter of switching tires from this one to it.'

'How long will it take?'

'Couple hours, I suppose.'

'I'll have my men give you a hand,' she said. 'The sooner we get it done, the sooner we can start loading cattle.'

'Not in my trailer, you're not,' the man told her. 'I don't want anyone taking potshots at me again.'

'The sniper is gone. I saw him ride off myself.'

'Yeah, and for all I know, he could be waiting somewhere along the road. I'm not about to risk my rig or my neck hauling your cattle out of here – not when some guy's out there with a rifle and a grudge against you.'

Panic rose, threatening to surface. Eden battled it back, struggling to maintain her composure. 'You agreed—' she began, outwardly calm, inwardly brittle.

'That was before I found out the kind of man you have for an enemy,' he cut her off, angry and resentful.

'You failed to mention that little piece of information, but your boys told me all about it when the shooting finally stopped.'

There was more toe-scuffing and spitting in the background. Eden wanted to plead with the hauler to reconsider, but pride wouldn't let her beg.

'I never guessed you could be so easily intimidated, Mr Jones,' she said, trying to shame him into changing his mind.

He reddened, but didn't budge. 'Say what you want, but that bullet could just as easily have punctured the fuel tank. I may not be too smart, but I'm smart enough to see that. Hire yourself someone else.'

'Very well.' Holding herself stiffly, Eden turned. 'Deke, Al, Bob, the rest of you, help Mr Jones get the tires switched so he can be on his way.'

With averted eyes and mumbled assents, they slowly scattered, some to the truck by the pens and the rest to the crippled rig nearest them.

Vince laid a comforting hand on her shoulder. 'I'm sorry, Sis.' The gentleness in his voice was almost her undoing. She had gone through too much, worked too long, and come too close to success for it not to affect her. For an instant tears blurred her eyes. 'I really thought you had a chance of beating DePard this time,' he said.

DePard. The mere mention of his name was enough to drive away the tears and bring back the anger. She swung around. 'No one knew I was shipping cattle this morning. How could he have found out?' Too late, she saw Kincade standing there.

'Maybe somebody told him,' Kincade suggested and deliberately looked at Vince, then turned and led his horse to the pens.

But it was the way Vince watched him, the tight and angry look on his face that made Eden suspicious. 'What did he mean by that?'

'The man's a troublemaker. Don't pay any attention to him.' But Vince failed to meet her eyes when he turned back.

'You went to town Saturday night,' she remembered. 'Was DePard there?'

'He might have been. What of it?'

She heard the testiness in his voice and ignored it. 'Did you talk to him? Did you tell anyone we were shipping cattle today?'

'All right, so maybe I did.' Vince became indignant. 'Maybe I was proud of the way you outmaneuvered DePard and wanted to rub his face in it.'

'You should have waited until *after* the fact to do your bragging,' she told him angrily.

'How was I supposed to know he would do something like this?' he argued, his voice lifting.

'You should have thought. You should have realized he would try to find some way to stop me,' Eden responded just as loudly, a thread of desperation entering her voice. 'My God, do you realize how hard it will be to find someone else, especially when word gets around about what happened today?'

'Do you think I don't know that? Do you think I'm not sorry? I've been kicking myself ever since that fool on the hill opened fire on us. Dammit, Eden.' He caught her shoulders, a pained look in his eyes. 'You scared the hell out of me when you went charging up that hill. If anything had happened to you, I could never have forgiven myself. This is all my fault and I know it.'

'Don't.' She couldn't deal with his feelings of guilt. Not now. Not when she had so many other problems.

Abruptly Vince dropped his hands and stalked off. She started to call him back, then checked the impulse. The old cowdog nuzzled her arm. She reached down and gave it an absent scratch behind the ears, then straightened. Gathering up the reins, Eden climbed into the saddle and rode back to the holding pens.

Close to an hour after the shooting, a sheriff's car rolled into the ranch yard. Eden was at the pens, watching while the last of the punctured tires was removed from the stock trailer. The marked vehicle stopped midway between the two rigs, but it was a full minute before the driver's door opened and a uniformed officer stepped out.

Eden recognized the tall, gaunt frame of Lot Williams, the local sheriff, but she made no move to approach him. He paused and hitched up his sharply creased trousers, his head turning as he made a leisurely sweep of the area. Finished, he started toward the pens, a relentless quality to his slow, measured stride. The neatly trimmed hair beneath his regulation hat was iron gray, and had been since he turned thirty. Lot Williams was somewhere in his late fifties now, with a face as narrow as his mind and etched with lines as deeply ingrained as his prejudices.

The stock hauler Jones went forward to meet him. Eden stayed where she was, watching the two converse. Jones did most of the talking, punctuating his remarks with a lot of arm-waving and hand-gesturing at his semi-trailer rigs, the holding pens, the punctured tires, and the ridge.

The sheriff listened with an expression of steely indifference, a contrast to the cold fury he had shown Eden that long ago night when he walked into the kitchen after seeing Jeff's body. She had been sitting at the table, scared and half-sick, haunted by the horrible images that wouldn't go away. At intervals, light from the ambulance and patrol cars flashed across the kitchen window, adding their own nightmarish quality to the moment.

Even though she had already told her story once, Lot Williams demanded that she tell it again. It wasn't easy the first time, and the second was worse. He interrupted her constantly, grilling her endlessly on every detail.

Eden no longer remembered how many times she had gone over it for him. She only remembered the way he twisted everything she said, taunted her, and insinuated things that weren't true. Her torn blouse, the scratches and bruises on her skin meant nothing to him. Finally she had broken down.

'Cut the act.' His voice had been harsh with contempt. 'Your tears don't have any effect on me.'

Her grandfather stood at the window, rigid and silent. Vince was in the living room. Seventeen and scared, she had faced Lot Williams alone.

Sometime after the ambulance took Jeff's body away, the sheriff had taken her in. Refusing to let her change out of her tattered blouse, he stood her up, wrenched her arms behind her back, and snapped the handcuffs on her wrists.

Eden rubbed her skin where the steel cuff had bitten into her wrist that long-ago night. The sensation was still fresh, like the hot shame she felt when Williams marched her outside, her hands behind her back, unable to clutch the torn front of her blouse together and cover herself from staring eyes. Thankfully Vince had run out and thrown his denim jacket around her, hurriedly fastening two of the buttons.

'It'll be okay, Sis,' he told her when the sheriff manhandled her into the backseat of the patrol car. 'They won't keep you in jail. You'll be out in no time.'

No time turned out to be almost forty-eight hours.

Every time she saw Lot Williams, she relived the events of that night. But she wasn't seventeen anymore.

She wasn't scared and confused. When Sheriff Lot Williams walked over to her, Eden met his piercing eyes without flinching.

'Jones tells me somebody used his trucks for target practice this morning,' he said.

'That's right.'

He lifted his glance to the hill. 'He did his shooting from up there, did he?'

'Yes.' Eden noticed that Lot didn't have a notebook with him. He had written nothing down.

His gaze came back to her. 'I understand you took a rifle and went up there after him.'

'I had the rifle.' Kincade came over to her side, using a handkerchief to wipe the grease from his hands. 'The lady was unarmed.'

His glance swung to Kincade, making a long and thorough study of him. 'And who are you?'

'Kincade.' He pushed his hat to the back of his head. 'I work for Miss Rossiter.'

'I haven't seen you around here.'

'Probably because I haven't been around here.'

'What happened when you got to the top of the hill?' He split his attention between them.

'We saw a man riding away,' Eden replied.

'What did he look like? Can you give me a description?'

'Average build,' Kincade began. 'He had on a dark hat, probably brown, a dark plaid shirt, a vest of some kind, and chinks. He was on a bay horse.'

Lot Williams studied him more closely. 'Could you recognize the man if you saw him again?'

Kincade shook his head. 'I never got a look at his face.'

The sheriff nodded and glanced at the ridge. 'Is there much up there in the way of tracks?'

'I saw some,' Kincade replied. 'But no shell casings.'

'I'd better go take a look,' Lot said without enthusiasm, then looked at Eden. 'I'll need to borrow a horse.'

'You can use that sorrel over there.' She pointed to a white-stockinged horse tied to a fence rail.

He nodded and crossed to the animal. He was only going through the motions of an investigation and Eden knew it.

'Something tells me the good sheriff isn't going to find one damned thing,' Kincade remarked idly.

Angry and frustrated, Eden turned on him. 'If you hadn't interfered, I would have made it to the top before Sheehan got away.'

His eyes narrowed on her. 'You know who it was?'

'I know who it had to be. So does the sheriff. But, thanks to you, I can't prove it.' She turned sharply on her heel and walked off.

The cowboss Bob Waters stood near the rear of the stock trailer, idly watching as the last tire was lifted into place. Joining him, Kincade took out a slim cigar and lit it.

'The sheriff doesn't appear to be very aggressive, does he?' Kincade studied the cigar he rolled between his thumb and forefinger.

'Nope.' Waters paused a beat, then added, 'I'm not surprised. The sheriff is DePard's cousin.'

Kincade's eyebrows went up. 'Talk about playing against a stacked deck.'

'Yeah.' But the curve of Waters's mouth held more grimness than humor.

It was almost noon when Jones climbed into the cab and revved up the tractor's diesel engine. Pulling away from the holding pens, the semi-trailer rolled past the scavenged rig and headed down the lane.

Over at the ranch kitchen, the cook banged on the triangle and kept up the racket to make sure the summons was heard above the diesel's roar. Kincade climbed onto the buckskin and scooped up the sorrel's reins leading it back to the barn while the other ranch hands drifted silently in the same direction. Eden stood next to the patrol car exchanging a few final words with the sheriff.

But Kincade took special notice of her brother, waiting on the porch. There was a tension in the way Rossiter held himself, and an impatience in the restless shifting of weight from one foot to the other. Eden stepped back, but didn't bother to wave as the sheriff's car accelerated slowly away from her. Once it was gone, she crossed to the porch.

'What did he have to say?' Vince asked, unable to read anything in her expression.

'That he would look into it.' Eden's tone made clear her lack of belief in that. 'He also told me to be sure and call if we had any more trouble.'

'That's it?'

'That's it.'

'But didn't you tell him DePard was behind this?'

She glanced after the departing patrol car, her mouth curving in a sardonic line. 'I didn't have to. He guessed that before he came out here. I imagine that's why he came himself instead of sending one of his deputies – just in case there was any evidence that might point a finger at DePard.'

'He's going to talk to DePard, isn't he?' Vince frowned, clearly upset.

'If he does, it will be to let him know there's nothing to link him to the shooting.'

'But he has to know DePard has gone too far this time,' Vince protested. 'One of those bullets could have ricocheted and hit someone. Maybe even killed somebody.'

'I'm sure the sheriff would have regarded that as a most unfortunate accident.' The bitterness came through, unchecked. Eden knew it came from the wretched sense of defeat she felt. She couldn't give in to it. She wouldn't. She crossed to the screen door. 'I thought I'd heat up some stew for lunch.' She opened the door and glanced back when she failed to hear his footsteps behind her. Vince still stood at the edge of the porch, scowling at the patrol car's dust. 'Is that okay, Vince?'

'What?' He half turned, then nodded absently. 'Yeah, sure. That's fine.'

Leaving him to brood alone, Eden went into the house. When she reached the kitchen, she swept off her hat and hooked it on the back of a chair. Pausing, she ran a hand wearily through her hair, letting her head and shoulders sag for a moment, then lifted both and took a deep breath.

Outside a pickup started up. Eden glanced out the kitchen window in time to see Vince's pickup peel away from the house, leaving a spray of gravel and dust behind him. Just for a moment, she envied his release of pent-up anger. But no problem was ever solved that way.

Sinking into a chair, Eden rested her elbows on the table and rubbed at the throbbing in her temples. Before the sound of Vince's pickup had a chance to fade, boots clunked on the wooden floor of the front porch. A knock rattled the screen door and Eden pushed out of the chair to answer the summons.

Kincade stopped at the bunkhouse long enough to wash up, then went straight to the ranch kitchen. Bob Waters and Al Bender were both seated at the long table chowing down when Kincade walked in. Stepping over the wooden bench seat, he sat next to Waters and spooned a large helping of spaghetti and greasy meat sauce onto his plate.

'Where are Hart and Connors?' He glanced at the two empty place settings.

'Probably at the house drawing their pay.' Bob Waters shoveled another forkful of spaghetti into his mouth and dabbed at the grease with a chunk of bread.

'They're quitting?' Kincade lifted his head in surprise.

'Yeah.' Al Bender grinned across the table at him. 'With all the bullets flying around this morning, they decided this work was hazardous to their health.'

A pickup charged out of the ranch yard. 'Sounds like Hart leaving,' Bob Waters observed and stabbed his fork into the mound of spaghetti again.

'I take it the two of you are staying on.' Kincade cast a bemused glance at the pair.

'Why not? The food's good.' Al Bender's eyes twinkled.

Bob Waters reached for his coffee cup. 'I come from a long line of people who fought for lost causes. It's in the blood.'

'What about you?' Bender asked.

Kincade recalled a line from Shakespeare and quoted it: ' "I am a kind of burr; I shall stick." '

12

Kincade rapped lightly on the screen door and waited. No footsteps approached and no voice called for him to enter. Puzzled, he knocked again and listened. But the only sound from inside was the faint rustle of pages being flipped.

He started to knock again, then changed his mind and walked in. A quick scan of the living room found it empty. A heavy sigh broke the quiet. It came from the kitchen. Kincade crossed to the doorway, making no attempt to silence his footsteps.

Eden sat at the table, poring over a trio of telephone books opened to the Yellow Pages. A pad of paper was next to them, with a list of three names and phone numbers scribbled at the top. A cold cheese sandwich sat on a napkin off to one side, half-eaten and forgotten. The glass of milk next to it hadn't been touched.

She was totally oblivious to his presence, too intent on her task to notice anything else. Something held him silent as his glance traveled from the tightly gripped pencil in her hand to her face. She looked upset, worried. It showed in her troubled eyes, and the tight, compressed line of her mouth.

This was an Eden Rossiter Kincade hadn't seen before.

Nowhere was there a trace of the volatile temper he had occasionally glimpsed. Instead she had the look of a woman struggling desperately to survive. And struggling alone.

In the short time he had known her, she had aroused both his curiosity and his interest, but, mainly, his lust. Seeing her now – like this – awakened all his protective instincts. It was a new feeling for him, and he wasn't too comfortable with it.

She dragged in a long breath and lifted her head, freezing when she saw Kincade. It was barely a second before she dropped the pencil and pushed back from the table, flipping the telephone books closed as she rose to her feet.

'What do you want?'

Kincade marveled at the quick way she donned her composure. Her pride was like tempered steel that she used both as a weapon to keep people at a distance and as a shield behind which she hid her feelings.

'I understand Connors and Hart quit.' He came the rest of the way into the kitchen and halted scant feet from her. 'Am I still fired?'

Because a pragmatic part of her wouldn't let her say what she wanted, Eden said instead, 'Are you certain you still want to stay?' Before he could reply, she continued, 'I can't guarantee the shooting this morning was an isolated incident. In fact, it's more likely that it will happen again. Somebody could get hurt the next time. That somebody could be you.'

'Would you nurse me back to health?' His eyes smiled at her.

She felt a sharp tug of attraction. Recognizing it, she fought it off, irritated with him and with herself. 'It isn't something to joke about.'

'What would you prefer I do?' he countered lazily. 'Cut and run the way Hart and Connors did?'

'I want to make sure you understand the situation here.'

'I think it was clear the first time we met,' Kincade replied with a touch of drollness. 'DePard is out to destroy you. How close is he getting?'

The question seemed to demand an honest response. 'If I can't get my cattle to market – very close.'

'You could always sell out and start over someplace else.'

The breath she released was heavy with disgust. 'That seems to be the universal answer to everything,' she declared, her look sardonic, the brightness of banked anger in her eyes. 'If people start harassing you and giving you trouble at work, just quit and get a job somewhere else. Your neighbors badger you, call you names, make you feel unwanted – why, of course, you sell and move away. Compromise, appease, give in, give up, that's the new American way. If a situation gets too hot, get out. Sorry, but that doesn't happen to be my way. I believe in fighting back.'

'I think DePard is counting on that,' Kincade said, slowly and thoughtfully. 'I think he would prefer to break your spirit.'

She gave him a long, considering look, then nodded. 'And that's exactly what he'll have to do. Because I won't give up.'

Kincade didn't want to see that either. He didn't want to see her on her knees, her pride stripped, her will broken. The mere thought of it filled him with a kind of anger.

The phone rang, shrill and sharp, startling both of them. Eden swung away to answer it. 'Spur Ranch.' She turned to look at Kincade. 'Yes—' A faintly puzzled look entered her expression. Once more she tried to speak, then looked at the phone and hung up. Curious and confused, she turned to Kincade. 'That was for you.'

'Me?'

'Yes. It was the cook at Starr's. He asked me to give you a message. He said that you lost something and that you'd better come get it because he wasn't sure how much longer it would be there. What was he talking about?' She eyed him curiously.

'Must be my pocket knife,' he lied, feeling the weight of it against his thigh. 'It has my name engraved on the handle, a present from my father. I noticed it was missing a couple days ago. I'd better go get it,' he said, already turning away.

Standing alone in the kitchen, Eden noticed how much emptier the room seemed without his disruptive presence, how much louder the silence was. It was a trick of the mind, of course. Nothing more.

'It's about damn time you got here, DePard.'

Hearing Vince Rossiter's voice, Rusty hurried to the pair of swinging doors that opened from the kitchen into the casino lounge. He swept his hat off and inched one of them open a crack. Pressing his face close, Rusty peered through the slit, adjusting his angle until Rossiter came into view.

DePard was with him. He said something to Rossiter but it was too low for Rusty to catch above the sound of Tanya Tucker's whiskey voice coming over the jukebox.

'Don't give me that bullshit.' Rossiter threw off the hand DePard placed on his shoulder. 'You know damned well why I'm upset.'

DePard nodded, made some appeasing comment, and gestured to the far side of the room. Rossiter briefly balked, then went with him. In the kitchen, Rusty shifted position to keep them in sight.

A second later, he felt the weight of a hand settle on his shoulder and nearly jumped out of his skin. Swinging around, he found Kincade behind him.

'You scared the bejesus out of me,' he accused in a hissing whisper.

'I saw Rossiter's truck outside,' Kincade said in a hushed tone, his glance flicking to the door. 'What's up?'

'Rossiter came barreling in here about an hour ago, told Starr to call DePard and get him over here. DePard just walked in.' Rusty took another peek out the door. 'They're sitting at the corner table now. Rossiter seems a mite testy.'

'With cause.' Kincade gave Rusty a capsulized account of the morning's sniper incident while he switched places so he could see the pair for himself.

The two were still talking, DePard calmly, and Rossiter with a lot of angry gestures. With the jukebox playing, Kincade caught only a word here and there, not enough to make any sense out of the conversation.

'What's happening?' Rusty strained for a glimpse, going up on his toes.

Kincade shook his head. 'I don't know.'

A few minutes later the jukebox went silent and Rossiter's voice came clearly. '. . . Go too far one of these times. I want you to back off.'

'The day it's sold, I will,' DePard replied.

'That will take time.'

'That isn't my problem.'

'Dammit, DePard, I'm warning you, if she gets hurt – if she gets so much as a scratch, you'll pay for it!'

Amused, DePard stood up and squared his big shoulders. 'A word of advice, Rossiter. Don't make threats you can't back up.'

Rossiter retreated quickly. 'You know how close Jeff and I were. He—'

DePard cut him off. 'You've used that line too many times. It's gotten old, Rossiter. Very old.'

Vince paled at the verbal slap and remained in his chair when DePard walked out. He sat there a long minute, his head bowed, looking half-sick, his hands clenched into fists. Finally he straightened and wiped a hand over his face. Kincade thought he saw the sheen of perspiration on his skin. The temperature in the air-conditioned casino had to be in the low seventies. Fear was the only thing that would make a man sweat in those conditions.

Kincade heard Vince order Roy to pour him a whiskey. Stepping back, he eased the swinging door shut.

'Doesn't sound like DePard has much use for him,' Rusty observed.

'DePard has a use for him, all right,' Kincade corrected. 'I suspect Rossiter has been feeding him information on his sister's plans. I know for a fact that he told DePard where and what time we would be loading cattle this morning.'

Rusty frowned in confusion. 'Rossiter told him that, and then comes in here and corners him, raving about how he doesn't want his sister hurt? That doesn't make a whole lot of sense. Is he for her or against her?'

'Maybe a little of both.' Kincade didn't understand it any better than Rusty. 'She told me once that her brother was trying to convince her to sell the ranch. His half would probably amount to a tidy sum.'

Rusty thought about that. 'I guess he could figure that if DePard started making things uncomfortable for her, she might be more easily talked into selling. Only DePard made it hotter than he figured.'

'That's possible.' Yet Kincade had the feeling that that wasn't the whole story. 'I think it's time I put in an appearance.' He dug in his pocket and pulled out the pocket knife. 'Here. I believe you found this in the men's room Saturday night. Lucky thing my name was engraved on it or you never would have tracked down the rightful owner.'

Rusty took it and grinned. 'You're gonna play the story out all the way, are you?'

'Might as well. I did get a message.'

'Am I going to get a reward?'

'First chance I get, I'll buy you a beer.'

'Yeah, when cows fly.'

Kincade chuckled and headed out the back door. The alley-way was empty. So were the streets. He circled around to the front entrance and walked in.

Vince stood slouched over the bar, nursing a beer chaser, the whiskey downed. He looked beaten, unsure, and bitter. He swung his head toward the door when Kincade walked in. He stiffened, coming erect.

'What are you doing here?' Vince demanded, showing the sullen edge of his temper.

'I could ask you the same question.' Kincade walked straight to the bar and said to Roy, 'I came to get my pocket knife.'

The bartender shrugged his skinny shoulders. 'Don't know anything about it.'

The bang and clatter of pots came from the kitchen. 'Your cook called the ranch and left a message that he had found it. Maybe you'd better check with him.'

'Never said anything to me about it,' Roy grumbled and headed for the swinging doors, as always taking his sweet time.

Kincade leaned an elbow on the scarred mahogany bar top and turned to face Vince, who was, again, hunched over his beer. 'I saw DePard leaving when I came in.' He hadn't, but Kincade doubted Rossiter would know that. 'Did you talk to him?'

'If I did, it's none of your business.' Vince took another gulp of beer.

'Have you decided to make yourself scarce, too?'

'I don't know what you're talking about.' Vince swirled the beer in his mug, watching the foam run up the sides of the glass.

'Connors and Hart quit. I guess they weren't comfortable with all the bullets flying around this morning. I thought you might be pulling out, too.'

'And leave my sister to face DePard alone?' Vince did a good job of looking angry and offended.

'It wouldn't be the first time, would it?' Kincade guessed and scored a bull's-eye when Rossiter paled, his glance dropping immediately to the beer mug.

Vince tried to bluff his way out of that. 'I don't know what kind of man you think I am—'

The door to the kitchen swung open and Roy came shuffling out. Vince threw him a quick glance and fell silent.

'This it?' Roy laid the pocket knife on the bar.

'That's it.' When Kincade reached for it, Roy closed his hand over it.

'There's a reward?'

Shaking his head in amusement, Kincade took out some bills and flipped them on the counter. 'Draw two beers and take one to the cook – while you're at it, remind him of what the Good Book says, "Virtue is its own reward."'

Roy snorted a laugh and shoved two mugs side by side under the tap. He filled one and pushed it at Kincade, then carried the second to the kitchen.

Vince eyed him coldly and briefly. 'There are plenty of empty tables in here. Take your beer and go find one.'

'No thanks.' With marked indifference, Kincade leaned on the bar and sipped at his drink.

'Why do you keep tailing me?' Vince glared in confusion. 'Just who the hell are you?'

Kincade smiled and lifted his frosty mug, never once looking at Rossiter. 'Your conscience, maybe.'

'Stop talking in riddles and come out with it. What did I ever do to you?'

'Nothing. Absolutely nothing.'

'Then get off my back. Better yet, take a page from Connors and Hart's book and pull out. We have enough problems without troublemakers like you working for us.' Vince spun away and strode, tight-jawed, to the front door.

Kincade watched the door slam behind him. He took a last swallow of beer, left the change on the bar, and walked out the door after him.

He drove in Rossiter's dust all the way back to the ranch. At the ranch, Kincade split away from the blue-and-white pickup and drove to the bunkhouse, parking near the ranch kitchen. He climbed out of the cab.

'Did you go to town?' The bandy-legged cook stood by a corner of the cook shack, a skillet of bacon grease in his hand.

'Yeah.'

His eyes narrowed hopefully on Kincade. 'Did you bring back any whiskey, maybe?'

'No. Sorry.'

Wild Jack grunted his displeasure. 'Damn fine shame,' he mumbled and dumped the grease on the ground.

DePard arrived back at the Diamond D headquarters at the same time that Sheehan drove up, with a horse trailer in tow. He honked the horn and yelled out the window to Sheehan, 'Come up to the house as soon as you get done here.'

Sheehan waved an acknowledgment.

He had a drink waiting for Sheehan when he walked into the study. 'To a job well done,' DePard told him and clinked his glass against Sheehan's tumbler of whiskey.

'I take it you've already heard how it went,' Sheehan guessed, lifting his glass.

'Lot Williams called,' he paused and checked his watch, 'well over an hour ago. Both trucks suffered some damage. One's out of commission and the hauler has now refused to ship her cattle. After today, she won't find anyone else willing to take the chance – no matter how much she might offer to pay them.'

'Rifle bullets tend to deliver a loud and clear message.' Sheehan downed his whiskey in one big gulp.

'They certainly do.' DePard smiled, taking pleasure in that fact. 'They shook Vince up. I just came from a meeting with him at Starr's.'

'What did he want?'

'Nothing, really. He made a lot of noise about being concerned for his sister's safety.' DePard shrugged it off.

'Then he'd better convince her to leave.'

'That's what I told him. Which reminds me – he's worried that she'll find out he's been feeding information to us. I've arranged for you to meet him Friday afternoon at Saddletree Creek along our west fence line.'

'I'll be there,' Sheehan promised.

13

The sun was a full, blistering blaze in the sky, scorching the land and everything on it. If there was a breeze, Kincade couldn't feel it and the matchstick thin strips of shade cast by the windmill's wooden tower offered little relief.

Stripped to the waist, Kincade labored to secure the new shaft in place, sweat streaming from every pore. A ruddy-faced Al Bender held it in place while Kincade tightened the last bolt.

It had been four days since the shooting. Four days spent at a myriad of tasks that were the province of the ordinary ranch hand, tasks that required him to be everything from welder and veterinarian to mechanic and common laborer.

Finished, Kincade rocked back on his heels and wiped at the sweat with the back of a gloved hand. 'That should do it.' He pushed to his feet, the heat sapping his energy.

'I just hope the damned thing works now.' Al mopped his face with a neck cloth, looking all of fifty, if not older.

Kincade's response was a soundless laugh. He dropped the wrench in the toolbox and peeled off his leather gloves, tossing them in as well. An insulated water jug sat in the sliver of shade next to the water tank. Kincade scooped it up, shook it to see how much was left, then tipped it up and guzzled down half before passing it to Al.

'Hell can't possibly be this hot,' Al declared and tipped the jug up, pouring most of the water into his mouth and letting the rest stream over his red face.

'Amen.' Kincade dragged his shirt off the wooden support.

Using it as a towel, he wiped the sweat from his face and neck, then ran it over his chest and stomach, making a couple of quick swipes under his arms before he tossed it back on the cross post. When he turned back, he saw Al staring at the long, raised scar that curved across the side of his rib cage.

'Nasty scar,' Al observed. 'How'd you get it?'

'A bull.' Kincade pushed his hat back on, its brim breaking the glare of the sun.

'Horn?' Al asked, guessing he had been gored.

'Hoof. I rolled about a second too late.' Kincade rubbed a hand over the six-year-old scar.

He didn't remember much about his short ride on the bull called Nine-One-One – how he had left the chute, whether the bull whipped left or right. But he remembered the bull had pitched him over its shoulder. He had landed hard on his back, dazed by the impact. But frozen in time, like a still photograph in his memory, was that instant when he had opened his eyes.

The image was still there, every detail in sharp focus – the Sunday afternoon throng in the stands, the dawning horror in their expressions, the cowboys hanging on the chute fences, the clowns in full stride coming to distract the bull, and the bull's gray, twisted body directly above him, a string of drool arcing from its tossed head, and the cloven front hooves taking dead aim on him.

Reflex had kicked in to move him out of the path. He had almost made it.

'It was a lot like getting cut open with a dull knife when he came down,' Kincade recalled. 'I had on a brand new shirt. Needless to say, it was ruined. I think I broke a couple ribs that time, too.'

'That time?' Al took a can of Red Man out of his pocket and studied Kincade with new interest. 'Sounds like you did a lot of rodeoing. Is that how you got those other scars?'

Kincade hesitated, then admitted, 'Most of them. After that spill, though, I stuck pretty much to bareback and saddle bronc events and left the bullriding to the ones with more guts than brains.'

Al settled a wad of tobacco between his cheek and gum. 'Did you ever compete at the big rodeo in Reno?' Al looked at him a little too closely. Kincade wanted to swear.

'A few times.'

'It's a real blow-out. I went a couple times myself,' he said thoughtfully. 'In fact I saw a guy win the barebronc event one time. From Texas he was, like you. As I recall, his name was K.C. . . . K.C. Harris. A tall, lanky guy with dark blond hair.'

'I can't say that I know him.' He held Al's gaze, aware he had been recognized. 'Can you?'

Al thought about that for a long minute, then turned and spit. 'No.' He rolled the chaw to the other cheek. 'I can't say that I do.'

Kincade relaxed a little. 'Thanks.'

'I guess you have your reasons.' Al waited to hear them, but Kincade had no intention of telling him.

Instead he ducked under the supporting struts and moved to the ladder. 'Let's see if we can get this working.'

'Watch your step,' Al advised when Kincade started

up the windmill's tower. 'Dry rot might have got to some of that wood.'

'I'm surprised this relic hasn't been replaced with galvanized metal.' He continued climbing. Except for the occasional creak of wood against nail, everything felt solid.

'Probably for the same reason most ranchers don't make many improvements. Lack of cash,' Al called up. 'The cattle market went to hell in the seventies, and nobody has made much money raising beef since.'

Fifty feet from the ground, Kincade swung onto the wooden platform that circled beneath the fan's eight-foot steel blades. The rugged desert landscape stretched out in a vibrating haze of heat. At this height a hot wind blew, tugging at Kincade's hat. He pushed the straw Resistol more snugly on his head, welcoming the stir of air.

The securing cables groaned with the strain of holding the blades motionless against the current of wind. Kincade released one, then the other, setting the blades free. The wind caught them and the blades turned, slowly picking up speed.

He called down to Al, 'She's loose.'

Al waved an acknowledgment, and Kincade sat on the platform, hanging his long legs over the edge, his glance traveling over the floor of the sage desert. The land ran for miles to the south with nothing to break it, its deceptive flatness creased with gullies and dry washes.

After a minute Al hollered back, 'Looks good so far.'

'Any water running into the tank yet?'

'A trickle.'

'Helluva view up here.' Kincade made another slow sweep of the vastness.

'And you can have it, too,' Al yelled from below. 'If

God wanted man to be that high, He would'a made his legs longer.'

Kincade's chuckle faded as his traveling gaze detected movement. He focused on the horse and rider in the near distance, approaching at a steady pace, the hooves of the trotting animal raising small puffs of dust.

'Got a good flow out of the pipe now,' Al announced. 'Looks like we got 'er fixed.'

'Rider coming from the west.' Kincade studied the rider's soldier-straight posture, a smile of recognition lifting the weary corners of his mouth.

On the ground, Al came to the same conclusion. 'Looks like the boss.'

'Yeah.' His answer was drowned out by the moan of the wind through the blades and the creaking of gears. Unhurried, Kincade got up and swung onto the ladder to make the long descent to the ground.

The sunlight bounced off the pickup's glass and chrome, throwing off brilliant flashes of light that, like the towering windmill, could be seen for miles. Drawing closer to both, Eden lifted the bay stallion into a canter. Part Thoroughbred, the stallion tried to take the bit, still eager to run despite the miles they had already covered. But the horse didn't fight Eden when she held him to a canter.

Short of the windmill, Eden reined in and let the stallion blow, her glance drawn to Kincade standing shirtless in the hot sun. A sheen of perspiration gave his tanned skin the look of highly polished bronze, hammered smooth over ropes of lean muscle. Involuntarily intrigued by the sight of his work-honed body, Eden let her gaze sweep over his chest, roughened by a triangle of thick, crisp hair that tangled its way downward past his navel and disappeared inside the waistband of his low-slung jeans.

Sensations began to stir within and Eden realized that for the first time in years she was noticing and reacting to a man's body. A response trickled slowly into her. She felt it and put a quick stop to it, her glance slicing abruptly to Al.

'How's the windmill running?' She swung out of the saddle. In her side vision, she caught the ripple of muscle as Kincade pulled his shirt off a wooden strut and slipped it on.

'Almost as good as new,' Al replied.

She led the stallion to the slowly filling water tank. Both men followed, Kincade more slowly. She felt his eyes on her, and avoided them, just as she had avoided him these last few days.

'On your way back to the ranch, swing by the Cinnabar section,' she said as the stallion nosed the water with disinterest. 'Some wire is down. I managed to fix the worst of it, but I'm not sure it will hold.'

'All right.' Al solemnly wiped his heat-reddened face with his kerchief.

Satisfied the stallion wasn't thirsty, Eden turned it away from the tank and prepared to mount. 'Keep your eye out for strays while you're there, too.' She stepped into the saddle and glanced down at Al, all too conscious of Kincade idly shoving his shirttail inside his jeans. 'I hazed a half-dozen yearlings back across the fence, but more might have gotten out.'

'We'll keep our eyes peeled,' Al promised.

At the moment Kincade was having trouble keeping his eyes off the high thrust of her breasts. Desire. As hot as he was, and as tired as he was, he felt it – a deep ache in his groin. Wondering if she felt it, too, he examined her face and saw awareness shimmering just below the surface.

He also saw a hint of tension and strain around her mouth and eyes, something he hadn't put there. He

wondered if Rossiter was pressuring her to sell again.
Probably.

She touched her heels to the stallion. It bounded
forward, its driving hooves throwing back bits of gravel
and dust.

Al watched her a moment, then spat tobacco juice at
the ground. 'Prowling's the best way I know to free up
a man's mind. A lot of problems have been solved just
riding and looking. And, Lord knows, DePard has given
her some heavy ones.'

'Her brother hasn't exactly made things easier for her.'
Kincade wiped at the sweat running down his neck.

Al made a sound of disgust in his throat. 'Vince is
like a pesky, damn horsefly. More a nuisance than a
problem.' He swung away from the tank. 'We'd better
get loaded up and on our way.'

Kincade had a lot of names for Rossiter; nuisance
wasn't one of them. But he kept that to himself and
went about filling the empty water jug while Al collected the toolbox and threw it in the back end of the
pickup.

As soon as Kincade climbed into the cab, they took
off, bouncing across the rough, trackless country with
Al at the wheel. When they came to a dry wash, Al
slowed and put the truck in four-wheel-drive.

'Yeah, DePard's got her boxed in tight this time,' he
remarked, almost idly. 'I don't see how she's going to
get out of this mess. Course,' he said with a wry turn
of his head, 'nobody figured she would get out of the
last one either.' He sent Kincade a sideways glance. 'By
now you're bound to have heard the story about her
shooting DePard's brother, Jeff.'

'Which story?' Kincade countered.

Al chortled briefly. 'Boy, you've got that right.' The
truck rocked its way down the embankment to the
gravel-strewn wash. 'Which story to believe? The one

where she kills him in a jealous rage? Or the one where she did it defending her virtue?'

'Which one do you believe?' Kincade watched him, mildly curious.

Al downshifted, gunning the engine to climb the opposite embankment. 'Back then, I leaned heavily toward the first. Everybody did. I mean, hell, I knew for a fact Jeff didn't put all those bruises on her,' he stated, then added in quick explanation, 'I was working for DePard at the time, but I had this drinking buddy Sam Clemens who was working here for old man Rossiter. He saw Jed slap the hell out of her when he found out that she shot the boy.'

For a long run of seconds there was only silence as they resumed their track across the rough sage land. 'The old man had a temper, and the way Sam saw it, he just lost it that night.'

'You worked for DePard back then. You must have known his brother. What was he like?'

'Jeff? He was a hard worker, never shirked. Tall and good-looking, kinda full of himself, but what kid of nineteen isn't? And he was smart, too. Smart as a whip. He was going places and everybody knew it. We all sorta took pride in that.'

'How was he with women?'

Al chuckled. 'He was like any young stud with all the juices flowing, eager to cover everything in sight.'

'Did he?'

Al was a long time answering him, his expression turning a little troubled. 'I guess that's what bothers me about the whole thing. I keep remembering how Jeff used to brag about the girls he'd laid, whose cherry he got. Bunkhouse talk can get pretty raunchy sometimes, but . . . I don't know.' He frowned and stared at the rolling flatness beyond the windshield. 'The way he talked, it just didn't seem like he had much respect for women.'

'Then it's possible he might have tried to rape her?'

It was plain that Al didn't like the point-blank question. 'Anything's possible,' he said irritably. 'Hell, they put a man on the moon, didn't they?'

His attitude said more clearly than his words that Al didn't want to believe Jeff DePard had sexually assaulted Eden. Not the bright young man who had seemed destined to make a name for himself.

Kincade thought about that, and he thought about Al, the contradiction between his beliefs and his actions. Finally he shook his head.

'What's wrong?' Al frowned at him.

'I was wondering why you're still working for her – considering all that's going on and the way you feel about what she did,' Kincade said, 'the reason has to be more than just the food is good.'

Al's brow creased in heavy concentration. 'Maybe what she did wasn't right. But what DePard's doing isn't right either,' he said finally. 'I mean, dammit all, she's a woman.'

It was a chauvinistic answer born out of the old western codes that died hard in this part of the country. Which was the very reason it was believable.

'Why are you staying?' Al turned the question on him.

'Like you, I was taught not to pick on girls.'

The Cinnabar section lay northwest of the ranch headquarters, separated from the rest by a barbed wire fence that ran arrow-straight into an area of rocky, juniper-clad hills. Al drove along the fence line until he came to the break.

Two cows with calves at their side trotted quickly away when the pickup rattled to a stop beside them. They were small-built with bony hips and heavy horns. Their coats were a brownish-tan color, not the rusty red shade of Hereford-cross cattle that Kincade had become used to seeing on the ranch.

Curious, he stepped out of the cab. A safe distance from the truck, the cows stopped and turned back to watch the vehicle and its occupants, giving Kincade a full side view of them. He recognized the Mexican breed of cattle immediately.

'Those are Corrientes.' He turned to Al, his surprise showing.

'Yeah.' Al threw a look at the cows and grabbed a pair of pliers out of the back of the truck. 'They use 'em a lot in rodeos for team roping and bulldogging and such . . . but I guess you know that.'

'I know it well. I just didn't expect to see any around here.'

'She started raising 'em about five or six years ago, bought a bull and ten cows. She's been building the herd ever since, keeping back the heifers and buying some more cows or another bull now and then. There's probably around a hundred cows now.' He walked over to the downed wire. 'Like I said before, the price for beef cattle has gone to hell, but these here rodeo cattle sell for a premium.'

'True.' It wasn't a statement of idle agreement but rather one of hard fact. Unlike bucking stock, the career of a calf or a steer used in rodeo events was invariably short. Calves grew too big and steers grew too heavy, or they became event-wise. Replacements were constantly sought by contractors who made it their business to supply stock for rodeos. It was a market with high demand and low supply. Knowing that, Kincade's estimation of Eden both as a businesswoman and a rancher went up several notches.

'Give her a couple more years to build the herd and this ranch will be turning a handy profit,' Al remarked, then shrugged. ''Course, that's supposing she makes it that long.'

That didn't seem too likely. Kincade told himself it

wasn't any of his business whether she lost the ranch or not. But he discovered he wasn't as indifferent as he wanted to be. That bothered him.

'Are you going to stand there all day, or are you gonna give me a hand with this fence?' Al challenged.

'Coming.' Kincade pulled on his gloves and headed over to help.

An hour later the downed wires were spliced together and they were back in the truck, traveling over a dim, rough track that led to the ranch house. The buildings were a low form in the distance when Kincade spotted a rider in a bright blue shirt cantering toward them. He sat up straighter.

'That looks like Rossiter.'

'Yeah.' Al then voiced the question that was going through Kincade's mind, 'I wonder where he's going?'

'Let's find out.' Kincade reached over and gave the horn two quick blasts.

Vince reined his horse off to the side and pulled in, waiting for the pickup to draw abreast of him. Al stuck his head out the driver's side window. 'Where you off to?'

'Thought I'd prowl around a bit.'

Vince leaned an arm on the saddlehorn and poked his hat back with a finger. 'Maybe check the east fence line. Why? Do you need something?'

When he glanced past Al and encountered Kincade's eyes, a wariness leapt into his expression. A wariness and something that looked suspiciously like guilt. He broke the eye contact with a quick turn of his head.

'Nope, don't need a thing,' Al told him. 'Just heading back to the ranch and saw you heading out.'

'In that case, I'll catch you later.' Vince backed his horse a few steps away from the pickup and turned it east. A sharp jab of his spurs sent the chestnut bounding forward, tail swishing.

Al watched him a minute, then shook his head. 'I never figured he'd still be here.' He released the brake and pushed his foot on the accelerator, easing the truck forward.

'What do you mean?' Kincade shot him a curious look, then glanced after the horse and rider loping away.

'He's been back at the ranch – must be close to two months now. Usually he gets a bad case of itchy foot and pulls out long before this. 'Course, I gotta admit the ranch hasn't been in this much trouble before. Usually it's the boss bailing him out of some jam.'

'What kind of jam?'

'The kind that jingles,' Al replied with a grin. 'Vinny-boy loves to gamble, and he's never learned to fold when he hits a bad streak. Some say he's got markers strewn all over the state under a dozen different names.'

'Does she know that?' Kincade thought of Eden.

Al snorted at the question. 'I should hope to shout. She's bought back enough of 'em, she ought to.'

'I wonder why he's hung around this long,' Kincade murmured.

'Beats me.' Al slowed the truck as they approached the ranch yard. 'You gotta give him credit, though. He really pitched in and took some of the slack after Connors and Hart walked out. Rossiter has never been one to turn his hand to ranch work since the old man died. And he sure as hell would never have volunteered to ride fence.'

Kincade was skeptical that Vince had turned over a new leaf.

Back at the ranch, Kincade grabbed a quick bite to eat, threw a saddle on a bay gelding, and rode back out, taking the same trail Vince had used.

Mid-afternoon, Kincade topped a ridge of low hills

and pulled up. The angling rays of the sun heated his back and sweat trickled down his face and neck. He scanned the silent, empty expanse of sage below, searching for a telltale lift of dust that would mark the passage of horse and rider.

Off to the east and south, he found it and the dark figure of the horse and rider making it. The sun caught the electric blue of the rider's shirt, confirming that the rider was Vince. Fixing in his mind Rossiter's direction and his own route to intercept him, Kincade put the bay down the slope.

A gully cut a path across the valley floor, its channel gouged out over time by the run-off of the rare rains that came to this dry land. Reaching it, Kincade rode the bay over the embankment and sat back as the horse slid on its haunches to the sand and gravel bottom.

Here, the air was still and close, little wind making the effort to dip down into the gully and stir it around. Kincade lifted the gelding into a strong trot and followed the course of the dry wash when it angled southeast.

After traveling some distance, he saw a fence swoop across the gully a good quarter mile ahead. Skeletons of sage brush clung to its wire strands, the detritus left by some torrential runoff. He searched and found a slight slope to the opposite bank. A moment later the bay scrambled over the top.

The instant he cleared the gully, Kincade spotted Vince. He was next to the boundary fence, barbed wire strands separating him from a second rider. At this distance Kincade couldn't see the second man clearly, but the spotted vest of black-and-white cowhide was unmistakable. Kincade aimed the bay toward the pair and lifted it into a trot.

*   *   *

Vince faced Matt Sheehan across the fence. 'You give DePard my message, Sheehan.' Vince tried to inject a note of authority in his voice and make it sound as if he was the one in control.

'I'll do that, all right,' Sheehan nodded.

'Dammit, she's called anyone who has a vehicle with more than four wheels, and struck out every time. He has her boxed.'

'It could be he'll think it's time to tighten the box.'

The words had an ominous sound. Vince felt a cold sweat break out. 'She is not to get hurt. One hand touches her and all bets are off. I swear it.'

Sheehan was unimpressed by the threat. 'Your money's already in the game, Rossiter. There's no pulling back just because you don't like the cards that are dealt.' His glance slid past Vince, his eyes narrowing abruptly. 'Who's that?'

Kincade was within fifty yards when Vince's head jerked around, his glance running to Kincade. He wheeled his horse and rode to meet Kincade. Unhurried, the second rider turned his horse parallel to the fence line and nudged it into an ambling trot.

Vince reined in and swung his horse to block Kincade's way. 'What are you doing here?' His voice was hot with anger.

Kincade glanced at the slow-departing rider. 'I could ask you the same question.'

There was something guilty in the quick look Vince shot over his shoulder, but he showed a righteous anger when he faced Kincade again. 'Riding fence. And when I say I'm going to do something, I don't like people checking up on me.'

Kincade deliberately let his gaze wander back to the rider. 'Who's your friend?'

'You mean him?' Rossiter cast another glance over his shoulder, a flicker of unease crossing his expression.

'He works for the Diamond D. He was checking fence, like me.'

'That's a fancy vest he's wearing. Looks like one of a kind.'

'Could be for all I know.' Vince was stiff and defensive.

The bay horse swung its nose at a fly nibbling on its sweaty wither. It buzzed away to find another likely place. 'Has your sister found someone to haul her cattle?'

The question appeared to startle Vince. 'No. Why?'

'Is that what you told DePard's man?'

Vince glared at him for a white-hot second. 'I've taken all I'm going to take from you, mister. If I turn around and catch you behind me one more time, you'll regret it. And that's a promise.' He jabbed a finger at Kincade in emphasis, then buried his spurs in the chestnut and took off.

Kincade reined the bay after him. All the way back to the ranch, he stayed within sight of Rossiter's dust.

The chestnut was in the corral, unsaddled, and nosing around for a good place to roll when Kincade arrived. Vince was nowhere in sight. Thinking he had beat a hasty retreat to the house, Kincade dismounted at the corral fence, pulled his saddle from the bay's wet back, then led the gelding into the corral and turned it loose.

Saddle and gear in hand, Kincade headed for the barn and its tack room. After the sun's bright glare, the shadows inside seemed deeper, blacker. Old hay rustled under foot. The chink of his spurs rang loud in the stillness.

Kincade had taken no more than a dozen steps when Rossiter's voice rang out in sharp challenge. 'You followed me for the last time.'

Kincade hesitated a step and searched the cloaking

darkness until he located Vince's shape. He stood
blocking the door to the tack room, his legs spread
and his hands on his hips.

'Now I'm going to find out what this is all about and
just who the hell you are, if I have to beat the answers
out of you,' Vince declared.

'You talk a lot, Rossiter.' Kincade resumed his even
pace, walking straight at the man, feeling the blood
heat in his veins and welcoming this unexpected confrontation.

'And you don't talk enough, but I'll change that,'
Vince snapped right back.

'Really?' Kincade taunted softly, nearly to him, his
eyes adjusting to the barn's shadowed gloom.

'You'll find out how much is talk,' Vince began, but
Kincade never let him finish the threat as he heaved the
heavy stock saddle at him.

It landed high, hitting Rossiter in the chest, drawing
a grunt of surprise and pain from him. He staggered
backward under the weight of it and came up against
the tack-room door. Kincade waded in after him with
cocked fists, blood humming in his ears, his vision
blurring at the edges.

Cursing savagely, Vince threw the saddle aside and
lunged at him, coming in low under Kincade's swing
and wrapping both arms around his middle, driving
them both to the hard floor. They grappled in the hay,
rolling in a tangle of elbows, knees and fists.

A right to the jaw knocked Kincade sideways. He
tumbled free and came to his feet, tasting blood from
a cut inside his mouth. Kicked-up chaff swirled in
the air. The smell of hay, manure, and saddle leather
was strong, but all of Kincade's senses were tuned to
Rossiter as he scrambled upright and met him, teeth
bared, arms swinging.

Kincade saw the movement and jabbed with his left.

Vince shifted and the punch missed. But Rossiter's right cross landed. Kincade never saw it coming, nor the left hook that followed it. Something slugged him on the jaw, powerful like the kick of a horse. He hit the floor hard and rolled, lights and thunder exploding in his brain.

Fighting to hold consciousness through the roaring in his skull, he knew he'd been hit. His head reeled with pain, but pain was an old companion. He had ridden with it, competed in the throes of it too many times to let mere pain stop him. Shaking his head to clear it, Kincade got his hands under him and pushed up, his hat gone, dislodged in the scuffle.

Vince's dark face loomed before him, lips curled back. He jabbed a quick fist at Kincade's stomach. Kincade tried to block it and failed. Vince, his eyes bitter with fury, moved in.

No longer punch-shy as a man often is before he's been hurt, Kincade was ready. When the punch came, he went inside of it, grabbed Vince with both arms, and tripped him with a backheel. They crashed to the floor, and he slugged Rossiter once as they rolled over.

Vince was slow getting up, and Kincade hit him twice before he could get his hands up. Vince took the blows and came back for more. In some distant part of his mind, Kincade gave the man credit for having more fight in him than he had thought. A second later Kincade was rocked by another hard right to the jaw that staggered him to his knees.

Instead of moving in to finish him, Vince hung back, breathing hard. 'Had enough?'

Kincade looked up through the sweat that stung his eyes, taking a moment to work his jaw and let his head clear. Something told him he had taken the best of Rossiter's punches, and they hadn't stopped him.

'Not hardly,' Kincade said in a voice that showed the extent of his own exertion.

A horse whinnied outside, but Kincade was deaf to the sound, blind to everything but the sight of Rossiter in front of him. Straightening, he bowed his head and waded in, delivering short, wicked jabs to Vince's stomach.

Weaving and smashing, he kept moving in. He feinted suddenly and lashed out with a right. Vince caught it coming in. Watching his face, Kincade knew the blow had hurt him. But there was no mercy in him, not for this man.

He bulled in close and slugged it out with him toe to toe, taking blows and delivering more. His face was a smear of blood from the cut above his eye. Maddened by a fighting lust, he pressed harder. Vince threw a quick left. Kincade ducked it and clipped Rossiter's jaw with an uppercut. With both hands, he slammed short wicked hooks to the head, then sliced Vince's cheek to the bone with an overhand right.

Vince went down, blood streaming. Winded and hurting himself, Kincade stood back, conscious of the sudden heaviness of his arms and the slogging of his lungs to drag in air.

Dazed and beaten, Vince sat on the floor, making no attempt to rise. He lifted a hand to the deep cut on his cheek and stared in disbelief at the blood on his fingers when he drew his hand away. Dumbly he looked at Kincade.

'What's going on here?' Eden's voice broke in between them.

14

Pivoting on a heel, Kincade saw Eden framed in the opening of the barn's double doors, silhouetted by the brilliance of the sunlight behind her. He knew the moment she saw Rossiter sitting on the barn floor, holding his cheek. Her whole body stiffened for a taut second; then she moved swiftly across the space.

'Vince, what happened?' She sank to her knees next to him. 'Dear God, you've been hurt.' She pulled a handkerchief from her pocket and pressed it against the gash in his cheek to staunch the flow of blood.

The fight went out of Kincade. He let his fists sag to his sides, fingers slowly uncurling. His left arm throbbed, and he reached over to massage it.

'I'm all right.' Half-irritated, Vince pushed her hand away and held the cloth himself, but she stayed, helping him up when he stood.

Her eyes were black and cold when she turned to Kincade. 'You did this.'

'You're damned right I did.' He felt no remorse, only regret that Eden knew he had injured her brother. He was aware she would hold it against him, and the only thing he wanted her to hold against him was her body. Desire was precisely what he felt when he looked at her. Maybe it was the freshness of battle that put it there. Or maybe he would always feel it every time he looked at her.

Her expression turned several degrees colder. 'You are fired.'

This time Kincade didn't try to argue with her.

'No.' Vince stunned them both by speaking up. 'He stays.'

'What?' she began.

He cut her off. 'I don't know why he's out to get me. But I want Kincade where I can keep an eye on him. I don't want to wonder where he is, or when he might turn up.'

Vince scooped up his hat and walked out. Eden stared after him, tiny lines creasing her forehead.

Instead of relief, Kincade felt tired and sore. Wearily he lifted an arm and wiped the trickle of blood from the cut above his eye onto the sleeve of his shirt. He saw his own hat lying among the hay rubble. Avoiding her eyes, he walked over and picked it up, slapping it against his leg, knocking the dust and wisps of hay from it.

He was close to her, close enough that when he started to walk away, she had only to reach out and catch his arm. The slight pressure stopped him in his tracks.

'What was the fight about?' Her voice was stiff, riddled with pride. 'He owes you money, doesn't he? How much?'

Kincade looked at the hand on his arm. It was tanned and strong, yet it still had the small shape of a woman's hand. 'He doesn't owe me any money. Not one cent.'

'Then what do you want with him?' she demanded.

He lifted his gaze to her face, centering his attention on her lips, soft and full, slightly parted. All the wanting and needing came back, stronger than before. If she didn't already hate him, Kincade knew she soon would.

The knowledge pushed him into taking what he could have now.

Abruptly he swung toward her and took a closing step. Startled by the suddenness of his movement, she backed up and came against the wooden partition of a stall. In one move, Kincade had her pinned against it, an arm on either side of her head, caging her in. Her heart increased its beat. From anticipation or fear, Eden wasn't sure which.

He stared down at her, things shifting inside, changing, altering. 'What makes you so certain it's your brother I want and not you?' he murmured. 'God knows, I can't seem to stay away from you.'

Eden noticed the change in his look. His eyes didn't darken with desire; their color intensified to a shade that took her breath away, hot and blue like a Nevada sky at the height of summer. A slow spreading warmth traveled through her.

'Don't.' But there was no conviction in her voice, and the word seemed to vaporize in the heated air between them, never reaching him.

There was no change in his expression or the intensity of his gaze. He had the look of a man caught in the grip of something powerful and primal. A male scenting a female. A mountain cat claiming a mate.

She made a sound in her throat that could have been another protest. Coming closer, he rubbed his lips over hers and felt them quiver in response. Her breath came out in a sigh. It was all the invitation he needed. He brought his mouth down, devouring hers. Wanting more, needing more, he pulled her closer, wrapping her tight to him.

But it wasn't enough. More than he wanted to taste her, he wanted to feel her. Her body was taut against him, holding back against the passion he could feel building. Her fingers dug into his shirt instead of pushing at him.

He could almost hear the thudding beat of her heart in her throat.

She told herself she didn't want this, that she didn't need this. It was a lie. The passion she tasted was no less volatile than the passion she felt. She wanted to touch him and feel the hard, flat muscles she had seen earlier at the windmill. She gave in to the urge, and discovered another kind of pleasure.

The way her hands reached, hesitated, caressed – the way her body tensed, then shuddered and relaxed – she was driving him crazy. He hadn't known he wanted her this badly. Restlessly, ruthlessly, he stroked his hands over her, molding her to his length, feeling her arch closer. He breathed in the heat rising from her skin, the musky, heady, womanly scent a man could drown in.

He tugged at the tail of her shirt, pulling it free from her jeans and pushing it up around her rib cage. He slid a hand under the white cotton and found a breast, soft and full, her heart pounding under his palm.

When she sank against him, Kincade went down with her and lowered her onto the bed of hay in the stall. Finesse and style were forgotten in an explosion of need.

It had never been like this. Month after month, year after year, Eden had convinced herself it could never be like this. Not for her. Not after what happened. Yet for the first time she wanted a man completely, as a woman. She wanted to use and be used.

As her body responded to his hard, pungent kiss and arched toward release, the fear came. Her mind flashed back. Other images, sounds, and sensations came flooding in – the roughness of his hands, the heaviness of his breathing, the weight of him crushing her, pinning her down. It was suddenly and revoltingly the same.

'No!' Eden struggled in panic. 'Don't touch me. Don't!'

She struck out with her fists, and Kincade grabbed her wrists in pure reflex. 'Goddammit, Eden.' He dragged her to him, but all the bitter accusations died on his tongue at the sight of her ashen face. The terror in her eyes was real, as were the tears and the panicked fury in them.

'Take it easy.' He relaxed his grip a little and she started to fight him again. 'Stop. I'm not going to hurt you.'

'Then let me go.' Her throat was tight, her voice hoarse with it. 'I don't want you to touch me.'

His temper rose and had to be fought down. 'I don't force myself on women. Not even ones who start out willing,' he stated but she looked unconvinced. 'I'm going to let you go. Okay?'

Silent, she watched him. The instant he released her wrists, she scooted backwards in the hay. He kept his hands in front of him, palms facing her, fingers spread as proof he meant her no harm. Moving slowly, he edged away and stood erect when he reached the stall entrance. He retreated another step and lowered his hands.

Still watching him, she scrambled to her feet and hastily tucked the tail of her shirt inside her jeans, trembling visibly. She pressed close to the wood partition and inched her way along it, her eyes never leaving him.

When she reached the end of the partition, her glance darted to a pitchfork propped against an inner wall, then raced back to him. He could almost see her mind working, trying to decide if she could reach the pitchfork before he could get to it. Kincade suddenly understood why a man's touch – a man's passion – evoked such fear in her.

'The story you told was true, wasn't it?' he said softly. 'DePard's brother tried to rape you.'

She reacted sharply to his words. Her head came up; pride surfacing with a rush that stiffened her spine and squared her shoulders.

'Am I supposed to care whether you believe me?' There was bitterness in her voice. 'I don't need pity from you or anyone else.'

'No,' he agreed. 'But you are entitled to respect.'

A flicker of surprise showed in her eyes, followed closely by confusion and lingering distrust. With an admirable display of control, she turned and walked swiftly toward the sunlight that streamed through the barn's tall opening.

Kincade never broke his stance until she was out of sight. Reaching down, he picked up his hat and brushed off the bits of chaff that clung to it. Anger rose up in him again, hot and bitter with loathing. And all of it directed at a dead man. Jeff DePard.

Eden crossed the porch and paused at the door to brush the hay from her jeans. Facing the door again, she dragged in a deep, steadying breath and fought to ignore the knotting in her stomach and the jangling of her nerves.

With as much composure as she could summon, she walked into the house and let the screen door swing shut behind her. It closed with a solid thud.

'Is that you, Sis?' Vince called.

'Yes.' Her voice sounded remarkably level. She was glad of that.

'Come give me a hand, will you?'

She heard water running in the bathroom and guessed he was there, tending his wounds. She had hoped for a few minutes to herself, and realized now that wasn't to be.

'Coming.'

His face was close to the mirrored door of the

medicine cabinet as he examined the deep cut on his cheek. When she paused in the doorway, he said without turning, 'It's about time you got here. I thought I'd never get this damned thing to stop bleeding.' He swung away from the mirror and showed her the inch-long gash. 'Do you think I'll need stitches?'

As ugly and painful as it looked, Eden didn't think so. 'A butterfly bandage should take care of it.' She quickly scanned the rest of his face. The flesh in several areas was already showing signs of swelling and discoloration, but outside of a small cut near his lip, there was no other injury that needed attention.

'What kept you? I thought you were right behind me.'

Turning, she collected the items she would need from the medicine cabinet, and answered him with a half-truth, 'I wanted to find out if you owed him money.'

'What did he say?'

'That you didn't owe him a cent. Sit down.' She pushed Vince onto the toilet seat. 'Hold still. This is going to hurt.'

'I told you the last time you bailed me out that I was through with gambling,' he reminded her, then winced, sucking in a loud breath when she applied antiseptic to the cut.

'I know what you told me.'

'You thought I was at it again.'

'You played poker with DePard the other night,' she reminded him and squeezed some antibiotic salve into the cut, then carefully dried the skin around it.

'It was just a couple of friendly hands. It wasn't a high stakes game.'

'Sometimes you don't know when to quit, Vince.'

'I gave you my word—' he began indignantly.

'I know. Hold still.' With the split flesh drawn

together, she pressed the bandage tightly in place. 'There you go.'

When Vince got up to look, Eden busied herself gathering up the salve, antiseptic, and extra bandages. Inside she was still churning, still confused and half-sick with the remembered fear.

'What's wrong, Sis? You look pale.'

She faltered for an instant, then insisted, 'Nothing.'

But she had a glimpse of her reflection in the mirrored door before she opened the cabinet. Her lie was obvious.

Kincade walked into the ranch kitchen, his throbbing left arm cradled in the crook of his right. There was a noticeable swelling in the hand and wrist, but all his fingers worked and he could rotate his wrist, which indicated he hadn't rebroken anything. The arm was only swollen – and sore as hell.

The cook had his back to the door as he guzzled from a bottle of vanilla extract.

'I need some ice.'

The cook pivoted with a guilty start and hurriedly hid the bottle under his left arm. He looked at Kincade's face. 'Whose fist did you walk into?'

Kincade sat down at the table and unfastened the cuff of his shirt. 'I'll need some towels and plastic bags, too.'

'No whiskey,' Wild Jack muttered as he went to the refrigerator to fetch the ice. 'Damn fine shame.'

Al and Bob Waters walked in, the screen door banging behind them. Al's eyes widened when he saw Kincade.

'What the hell happened to you?'

'Jammed my arm.' Kincade flexed fingers that were beginning to stiffen from the swelling, his expression grim and tight-lipped. At the refrigerator, ice cubes rattled into the metal dishpan the cook held.

'You jammed more than your arm. Who the hell did you tangle with anyhow?' Al eyed him curiously.

Kincade gave no sign that he'd heard him. 'I need to get this arm wrapped in ice. Give me a hand, will you?' he asked when Wild Jack set the pan of ice on the table and shuffled off to get plastic bags.

'I got some stuff in the bunkhouse for cuts and bruises.' Bob Waters turned on his heel and left at a quicker pace than he'd entered.

After studying the remnants of anger that continued to shine in Kincade's eyes, Al decided not to repeat his question. Something told him the other guy would probably look worse, which meant he would find out the answer soon enough.

The cook found two plastic bags. Still grumbling over the lack of whiskey, he held them open while Al filled them with ice. With one bag under his swelling arm and wrist, Kincade held the second on top of it. Al tore long strips from an old cotton dishcloth and fastened the bags in place. Wild Jack stood idly back and watched.

Al threw him a half-irritated look. 'If you aren't going to help, pour us some coffee.'

The cook grunted his disdain of the order. 'My grandfather sat at the fires of many great medicine men, watched them making healing poultices and powerful potions, listened to their chants. You are no medicine man,' he pronounced. 'You are a dumb cowboy.' But he ambled over to the coffee pot and came back carrying two mugs of hot, black brew.

Al looked at it and muttered, 'It looks black as sin. Must have been boiling all day.'

Wild Jack mumbled an unintelligible reply and walked back to the counter. Hinges creaked as Bob Waters elbowed his way through the door, his arms wrapped around an assortment of bottles, ointments, and bandages. He crossed to the table and began setting the items down, one by one.

'Got some special salve here that'll take the soreness right out of those bruises.' He shoved a jar toward Kincade. A translucent green cream oozed around the edges of its lid. 'Here's some liniment if your muscles start stiffening up. It smells like billy-blue-blazes, but it works. And some salve for that cut over your eye.' The bottle of home-made liniment was followed by a tube of antiseptic and a tumble of gauze rolls and adhesive tape. 'There's some spray stuff here, too,' he went on.

Al paid no attention to the remedies the cowboss set on the table. His gaze fastened on the square-shaped bottle in the crook of his arm. A bottle that looked suspiciously like a fifth of whiskey. He plucked it from Bob's arms and held it up.

'Here's what we need,' Al stated and unscrewed the cap. The liquor gurgled as he poured a double shot into Kincade's coffee, and splashed an equal amount in his own. 'Best painkiller made.'

Wild Jack spun on a dime, his glance racing to the whiskey bottle. He threw a glowering look at Bob Waters. 'Where did that whiskey come from?'

'I'm not about to tell you where I keep it stashed,' the Paiute replied.

Still glowering at him, Wild Jack stalked over to the table and snatched the bottle off it. 'Damn fine shame,' he declared, then proceeded to guzzle half the whiskey.

Through it all, Kincade remained silent, his mind focused on the aches, large and small, magnifying them until they blocked out all other thoughts. He downed a mouthful of coffee, welcoming both the whiskey-burn in his throat and the numbing cold from his ice-wrapped arm.

The makeshift ice bag did the trick. By suppertime,

the swelling was down and the pain had faded to a dull throb. Still stiff and sore in a dozen other places, Kincade headed for the ranch kitchen.

Halfway across the yard he spotted Vince, a shoulder propped against the corner of the adobe building. A criss-crossing Band-Aid closed the cut high on his left cheek. One eye was nearly swollen shut and a half-dozen places on his face showed the red-purpling of the bruises. He watched Kincade with cold care when he came toward him.

'Surprised to see me?' Vince murmured.

'A little.' Kincade studied the damage he had inflicted.

'I told you I would keep my eye on you from now on,' Vince reminded him. 'Get used to it.'

True to his word, Vince was still outside the ranch kitchen when Kincade came out after the evening meal. The other ranch hands threw a few questioning looks at both of them, but nothing was said.

The next morning Vince was a dark shape in the gray shadows of early dawn. Later, when Kincade rode out on his day's assignment, he looked back and saw Vince following a hundred yards behind him.

The second day was the same as the first, with Vince always somewhere in Kincade's vicinity. On the morning of the third day, Kincade decided it was time to change the routine.

He rode north and west from the ranch, watching the day's color sweep across the rough, dry land. There was always a swiftness and vigor to these morning changes. One minute stars glittered sharply in a dark sky. Then a crack appeared in the black eastern horizon and a pale violet fissure divided earth and sky. Suddenly, long waves of light rolled out of the east, sending even longer shadows spilling over the ground like water.

With the sun up, the day's heat came quickly, warming his back as Kincade lifted the sorrel horse into a lope,

putting distance between himself and the ranch buildings. A covert glance confirmed that Vince followed.

The ranch's western boundary reached deep into the
desert mountains. Forced to a slower pace by the rough
and broken country, Kincade used it to his advantage,
his glance constantly searching for a place that would
suit his purpose. Close to mid-morning he found it.

A tangle of boulders and fallen timber created an
impenetrable screen on the down slope of a saddleback.
Beyond it was a grassy bench, shaded by a scattering
of junipers. He walked his horse slowly past the screen,
then stopped and studied the approaches to it. There
were only two, and neither had a view of what lay
behind the screening deadfall.

Kincade swung the sorrel around to stand parallel
with it. Thus concealed from view, he waited for Vince
to ride past. For long minutes, the only sounds were
the stamp of his horse and the sibilant whisper of a
faint wind through the junipers.

The desert-bred sorrel caught the first rumor of
activity along their backtrail and signaled it to Kincade
with a lift of its head and an alert pricking of its ears.
A moment later Kincade heard the distant clatter of
iron-shod hooves on stony ground.

Kincade listened intently, at last able to discern that
Rossiter had chosen the other route over the ridge. A
small cascade of pebbles rolled down the slope ahead
of the horse. Kincade gathered up the sorrel's reins, his
own muscles bunching in anticipation.

A horse's nose bobbed into view. Kincade gigged
the sorrel with his spurs and charged out from behind
the natural blind. But it was Eden, not Vince, astride
the horse.

Startled, she hauled back on the reins. Simultaneously
Kincade did the same, swearing silently and viciously at
the glare of alarm in her eyes. It vanished the instant she

recognized him, her expression turning guarded and uncertain.

'Sorry. I didn't mean to surprise you like that.' He studied her face, drawn again by that unusual mingling of strength and vulnerability. These last three days he had done his damnedest not to think about her. Now he realized she had been on his mind the entire time.

'You're supposed to be checking the tank at Red Butte. That's almost a mile from here.' Her horse picked up her tension and sidestepped nervously.

'This section of the ranch is new to me. I thought I'd look around, familiarize myself with it while I was out here.' The explanation was plausible, but he wasn't sure she believed him. 'Where are you going?'

She hesitated before answering him. He watched the minute shift of expression on her face, the quick transition of light and dark in her eyes. Her lips parted and came together again. Her glance lifted and met his with a steadiness that ran an old shock through him, waking the hunger he had so carefully put away.

'I came to check on the brood mares.' Eden saw the compression of muscles along his cheeks, his attempt to conceal the heavy and hungry desire in his eyes.

She felt the heat of his glance, and the disturbance it created within. She waited for the fear to come, for the violent twist of revulsion she had felt the last time, in the barn. But all she felt was a shivery need and a funny, achy regret.

'Where are the mares?' He glanced in the direction she had been heading.

'There's a hanging valley about a half mile from here. I usually can find them there.'

At that moment her horse swung its head toward a distant point along the ridge and sent out a ringing neigh. Looking back, Eden saw a horse and rider posed on a high curve of the saddleback two hundred yards away. The rider wheeled his horse off the ridge and ducked out of sight, but not before Eden recognized Vince. She looked at Kincade, then at the deadfall with dawning understanding.

'You thought I was Vince.' A moment ago she had believed Kincade had sought her out deliberately, that he had wanted to see her. She used anger to cover her mistake. 'You were lying in wait for my brother, weren't you? Why? What has he done to you?'

Kincade ran his fingertips over his bruised right jaw. 'This isn't something I started.'

'But you'll finish it, won't you?' Bitterness mixed with her anger. 'Right or wrong, you'll strike back, and you'll keep swinging. You won't be satisfied until you've crushed him.'

'Are you talking about me – or DePard?'

Pride lifted her head and covered her like a hard finish. No emotion showed through, not even a lingering smolder of anger. A tap of the quirt and her horse moved out briskly. Kincade joined her, swinging his horse alongside.

Not a word was exchanged as they rode through the mottle of junipers. On the other side, the way narrowed and Kincade reined his horse in behind Eden's. Single-file they climbed the rocky defile, the silence between them lengthening and changing into something simple, more comfortable.

It was the land's influence, its absolute indifference to human emotions like anger. This vast Nevada land with its saw-toothed ranges and angular hills, its long sage-strewn valleys and purple canyons was passive and imperturbable. It bred silence into those who spent much time in it, took the hurry out of them and stretched their vision to take in its far distances.

Even during the short time Kincade had been in it, he had been affected by the land and its timeless rhythms.

Riding through it, surrounded by the wild emptiness of it, he felt its immensity. His gaze wandered over the craggy tops of its mountains and explored the wide sweep of its desert floor, then came to a stop on Eden.

Her shoulder made a straight line in front of him, her hips swaying slightly with the motion of the horse beneath her. Kincade watched her, unobserved. In many ways, she was like this land – strong and resolute. Like it, she could be hot one minute and cold the next. And like it, she had a fragility that wasn't readily apparent.

But there was more to her than that. She had a love of life that she couldn't entirely hide, and a hunger that her pride couldn't totally suppress. It was a hunger Kincade understood.

Nature had no use for the solitary thing; it served no function, no purpose. Therefore, nature had placed in humans a sense of incompleteness that made them drift toward others, that filled them with an ache, a need, and a want that only another human could satisfy.

When the trail widened, Kincade unconsciously moved up to ride alongside Eden. The morning sun sat high in the eastern sky, its light burning intensely. A dry wind carried the aromatic scent of the mountains' timbered reaches. Except for the jingle of bridle chain and the scrape of metal-clad hooves on stone, a quiet prevailed.

They rounded a shoulder of mountain and the valley spread out before them, a wide grassy meadow cupped high in the rocks. Cottonwoods and willows grew along the banks of a spring-fed stream that clucked and rippled its way through it.

The horses were there. Kincade counted nine mares, all with foals nearby, scattered over the short-grass meadow. A trumpeting snort came from the willows and Kincade saw two more mares, half hidden in the dappling shade.

Eden's horse nickered a greeting, and a young colt four months old charged out to meet them. At a midway point the colt stopped and reared up, its small hooves pawing the air, its ears laid back, and its head tossing with the mock ferocity of a herd stallion defending his band.

Amused by the display, Kincade glanced at Eden. 'I think we're being warned off.'

A smile edged the corners of her mouth, echoing the humor he found in the scene. 'I think you're right.'

A big pinto mare whickered to the colt. When it continued its challenging antics, the mare trotted out, the thud of heavy hooves loud in the stillness. As she neared the colt, her ears snaked back. The next minute she was on it, head low, teeth bared. The colt squealed with the first sharp nip and rushed for the safety of the other horses. The mare stayed at its heels, adding more well-placed nips to keep the colt moving. The colt came to a stop a respectful distance from the mare's teeth, looking very much like a sulky child.

The sight drew an exchange of glances and a laugh from both of them. Eden discovered a richness and a contentment in the morning that she hadn't known in years. The glow of the shared moment was in her eyes as she urged her horse forward to ride slowly through the scattered band of mares, Kincade ranging alongside.

The big pinto mare stood her ground and watched them. White with patches of brown on her rump and neck, the mare was stout and heavily muscled. She tossed her head and snorted, her ears going back, warning Kincade that he was getting too close. He started to rein his horse around her, then pulled up to stare at the mare's mismatched eyes, one blue and one brown. He knew that horse . . .

The big pinto stood in the bucking chute, ears swiveled

back and a brown eye rolling to catch the movement above and behind her. Clyde Hawkins had a solid grip on the halter to keep the horse standing square in the chute. The saddle was cinched tight, and the bucking strap was in place, pulled snug enough not to slip, yet loose enough to be a ticklish irritant that would increase the kicking action. All was in readiness.

Kincade climbed over the top rail and straddled the chute directly above the saddled pinto, adrenaline surging through his system, his attention focusing on the business at hand with an intensity that blocked out the sights and sounds around him, including the announcer's voice.

'In Chute Number Two, our next rider is K.C. Harris from Big Springs, Texas. K.C. is currently sitting in first place in the saddle bronc competition, but he's drawn the great bucking mare, Miss Fortune – twice nominated Bucking Horse of the Year. I have to tell you, folks, drawing this horse has been the *misfortune* of many a rider. We'll see what kind of luck K.C. has on her today.'

Tension hummed in the chute as Kincade lowered himself onto the mare, alert to the smallest muscle twitch. His weight touched the saddle and he felt the knotting of muscle that humped the pinto's back.

All concentration, Kincade toed his feet in the stirrups and double-checked his grip on the rope, making sure he had given the pinto the desired amount of rein. The mare swung her head to the side, showing him a blue eye and the patch of brown on her neck shaped exactly like a child's mitten.

The hard and heavy beat of his pulse drummed in his ears; the smell of rosin, horse, and sweat was strong around him. Every nerve had an edge to it. As always, an odd calm settled over him. He rocked back in the saddle and positioned his spurs above the horse's withers, his free arm aloft and his hat snug on his head. Time slowed down, seconds breaking into fractions. He knew the mare's reputation, and he knew in his gut that he could ride her. He also knew that failure could spell disaster. The thrill of rodeo was in that combination of challenge and danger.

Kincade gave a nod to open the gate.

The husky pinto shot into the air, exploding out of the chute like a rocket, a thousand pounds of compressed energy determined to rid itself of the man on her back. True to habit, the mare went straight for three high-kicking jumps and Kincade raked his blunted spurs over her shoulder with each leap. The horse came to a sudden stop, pitching Kincade forward against the pommel. Catlike, the pinto leaped sideways, twisting in midair.

His center of balance was lost. He stopped worrying about getting in his spurring licks; he was too busy fighting to stay in the saddle. The pinto ducked a shoulder and he lost a stirrup. With the next bone-jarring jump, Kincade sailed over the mare's neck. He threw out his arms to break the fall and landed wrong, catching his left hand underneath him. Something snapped and a white bolt of pain shot through him.

He came up, cradling his left arm, teeth clenched against the pain. He looked around for the big pinto mare. Free of her rider, the horse had relaxed into a gallop, lashing out with every other stride of her hind legs at the bucking strap around her flanks.

A pickup rider swung his horse alongside the mare and reached over to unfasten the strap. Immediately, the husky pinto slipped into a gliding run and made a big circle of the arena as if taking a victory lap. On the way to the pens behind the chutes, the mare went past Kincade. He caught the flash of a blue eye and swore there was a glint of laughter in it.

*   *   *

It was there now; so was the mitten-shaped patch of brown on the pinto's neck.

'What's wrong?'

Still caught up in the memory of that afternoon five years ago, Kincade answered without thinking, 'I know that mare. That is Gus Holt's top bucking mare, Miss Fortune. That wasn't what we called her though,' he remembered. 'To us, she was No Score because that's what you usually got when you drew her.'

'You rodeoed professionally?'

He hadn't intended to reveal his past to her, but it was done. 'All my life, practically.' Kincade continued to watch the mare. 'I was four when I rode in my first Little Britches Rodeo. After that it was all I wanted to do, and eventually all I did. It was always my dream to ride in the National Finals Rodeo. I almost made it a couple times.

'Five years ago I was one win away from it when I climbed aboard Miss Fortune here. She tossed me off as easy as you please. I broke my riding arm in the fall and lost any chance of qualifying that year.'

Looking back on those years when he had traveled the rodeo circuit, Kincade realized how very long ago those days seemed, almost as if they had happened in another life. The dream of becoming a national champion bronc rider had no allure for him anymore.

'What made you give up rodeoing?'

He was conscious of Eden watching him, a curiosity and an interest showing in her expression. 'I didn't have much choice. I broke my riding arm too many times.' He flexed his left hand and felt the twinges of lingering soreness in it from his fight with Rossiter. 'It can't take that kind of punishment anymore.'

'So you traded the rodeo circuit for the ranch circuit.' Eden didn't believe that even as she said it.

'Something like that.'

'You won't be satisfied with this kind of life for long.'

'Maybe not.' He shrugged off her comment.

Doubt surfaced again as she continued to study him. He had the look of a man with a purpose, a mission. Eden remembered the fight with her brother and the accusations Vince had made against him. Were they true? She was stunned to discover she didn't want them to be, that deep down she wanted to trust this man.

He turned, an eyebrow arching in question. 'I heard the mare was injured in a trailering accident and had to be destroyed. How did you end up with her?'

'Mr Holt contacted me after the accident. The mare's injuries were bad enough to end her career in the arena, but not serious enough to warrant destroying her. I paid the vet bill and Mr Holt wrote out a bill of sale.'

'How did he know you'd be interested in the mare?'

Eden hesitated before answering. 'I sent letters to several of the major rodeo stock contractors, letting them know I was starting a breeding program and asking them to contact me if they had any aged or injured mares they wanted to sell.'

'A breeding program.' He took another look at the horses scattered over the high valley. 'You mean all these brood mares are—'

'Former rodeo stock, bareback or saddle bronc,' Eden finished the sentence for him and relaxed a little when she saw the gleam of interest in his eyes. 'We all know a horse passes certain traits on to its get. For some horses, that trait is speed; in others, it might be endurance, agility, or cow sense.'

Kincade nodded and picked up the thread of her thought. 'And you believe that just as some horses are born to run, others are born to buck.' His mouth curved in a smile. 'Why not? Lord knows Jim Shoulders proved it could be done with bulls. I heard a few people were trying to develop a line of bucking stock. What kind of results have you had?'

'One four year old has turned out to be a good ranch gelding, and four three year olds we'll be trying out this winter.'

Eden reined her horse away from the mares and nudged it into a walk. Kincade did the same. But he wasn't ready to drop the subject.

'What stallion are you using on the mares?'

'My ranch stallion. I'd like to get a stallion that's a proven bucker. I heard about one in Oklahoma this past spring. Vince checked it out for me, but the stallion was part draft horse. If the colts he sired didn't buck, they would be too big and clumsy for ranch work.'

'You must be talking about Rod Bucher's stud Loco Louey. He's a Belgian cross.'

'You know the horse?' She glanced at him in surprise.

'Just about every cowboy and stock contractor on the circuit knows Bucher and his stud. Truthfully, I don't know which one is crazier – Bucher or his horse. That stallion is vicious, the closest I've ever seen to a true mankiller. I went to Bucher's place to see the horse once. It took four men twenty minutes just to get the stallion into the steel chute Bucher had built to hold him. And another hour to saddle him. He had to be ridden with a special-made muzzle to keep him from reaching back and biting the rider. The animal is too dangerous. No contractor wants a horse like that in his bucking string. Rodeo is a competitive sport. It was never intended to be a life and death struggle, and that is exactly what that stallion would turn it into, both in the arena and out of it.'

'Vince never mentioned any of that to me,' Eden murmured.

'Maybe he had other things on his mind.'

Eden gazed at the sweep of land before them. Rodeo had been a part of him, just as this land was part of her. To be torn from it, to be forced to leave it, permitted only to view it from a distance would be a torture too horrible to imagine.

Kincade pulled up. 'What lake is that?'

She looked in the direction he indicated, and smiled at the ghostly shimmer of water to the north. 'It's a mirage. That's the southern edge of Black Rock Desert, a playa, really. It's a dry lake bed that once was part of prehistoric Lake Lahontan, which covered much of the Great Basin fifty thousand years ago. It's big and barren, and strangely beautiful, virtually impassable during the rainy season and hard as cement the rest of the year.'

'Black Rock Desert.' He frowned. 'Isn't that where they set a land speed record not too long ago?'

Eden nodded. 'A British racing team did a few years back.'

'I remember reading something about it.'

'It's awesome country when you're out in the middle of it. Nothing for miles in any direction but hard, white ground with almost no vegetation. Fremont was afraid to cross it when he discovered it during his expedition, yet hundreds of emigrants did just that on their way west.'

'How big is it?'

'Roughly seventy miles long and as much as twenty miles wide. Nearly a million acres in all.'

'And on the other side of it?' Kincade asked curiously.

'Another mountain range, and beyond that, the plains of western Oregon. Imagine crossing that desert in a wagon pulled by oxen, then facing the mountains and the struggle it must have been to cross them and reach to the Oregon plains. To travel that same one hundred miles today by car would take maybe two hours. By oxen, it must have taken—' She stopped, silenced by the thought that suddenly flashed in her mind. She stared at the desert mirage and the far-off mountains that were little more than vague shadows on the horizon. The Oregon border lay just beyond those mountains.

'What is it? Is something wrong?'

It took a moment for his questions to register. Eden turned. 'No,' she said. 'Nothing is wrong. You'd better go check that tank at Red Butte. I have some checking of my own to do.'

She swung her horse away and headed back to the ranch.

15

The sun was well below the horizon. Only a knife-edged ridge of amethyst remained in the western sky to mark its passing as the deep purpling of dusk spread over the land. Eden had switched on the truck's headlights a mile back. Light beams sliced through the gathering shadows illuminating the rutted track that led to the ranch house.

Braced against the bouncing of the truck, Eden kept a firm grip on the steering wheel. She was hot and tired after the long drive cross-country, yet exhilarated.

The lights from the ranch buildings shone out of the darkness. Eden drove straight to the house and climbed out of the truck. Despite the tired ache in her muscles and the stiffness in her joints, there was a lift to her step when she crossed the porch. She caught a whiff of fried onions and hunger pangs struck, forcibly reminding her that she had eaten nothing since breakfast.

Her nose followed the delicious scent to the kitchen. There, she was greeted by the sound of potatoes and onions sizzling in the skillet and the sight of Vince standing at the stove, a metal spatula in his hand dishing a hamburger steak smothered in onions onto a plate.

'I'll forgive you anything if you tell me you fixed enough for two.' She swept off her hat and shook her hair loose.

He threw her a glaring look. 'Do you realize how late it is? Where the hell have you been?'

Eden wanted to tell him. She wanted to tell Vince the whole plan. But she couldn't take the chance he might let something slip the way he had before. 'Is that your way of telling me you didn't cook enough for me?'

'I already have a plate of food put aside for you. Satisfied?' In irritation, Vince lifted a skillet lid to show her the food it covered.

'I should be late more often.' She went to the sink to wash up.

'You could have left a note saying where you were going. If anything had happened to you, at least I would have known where to start looking.' He carried both plates to the table.

'You're right. I should have.' Her hands were still slightly damp when she slid onto her chair. 'Now, can we save the rest of your brotherly lecture until after dinner? I'm starved.'

Her request was met with silence, an answer in itself. Ravenous, Eden dug in.

'That was good.' Finished, Eden pushed her plate back and reached for the rest of her milk.

'You never said where you were.' Vince leaned back in his chair, fastening his dark gaze on her.

'Everywhere.' She faked a slight grimace. 'And if you know where we can hire a couple more men, let me know.'

'You'll find somebody.'

'I can't afford to wait any longer. I've decided to start the fall roundup tomorrow.' She gathered the dirty plates and silverware into a stack and carried them to the sink.

'It's early.'

'And we're short of help. It could take us twice as long.' If they did a normal, thorough job of it, which Eden didn't intend for them to do. She wanted to make one fast and dirty sweep of the ranch, gathering up everything in sight, and be done in two weeks. DePard would expect her to be tied up a month or more with roundup, and that's what she wanted him to think.

'What will you do with the cattle after you round them up? You can't ship them anywhere. DePard has you boxed in.'

'I'll cross that bridge when I come to it.' She set the dirty dishes in the sink and went back to clear the table.

'There won't be any bridge. DePard has torn them all down. You're doing all this for nothing.'

'That's your opinion.'

'That's the truth,' he said in exasperation. 'Why won't you accept that?'

'Because that would mean DePard wins. And I'm not going to let him. It wouldn't be fair. You, of all people, know that.'

Stopped by her forceful response, Vince looked away. 'I know.'

'Then help me. Don't fight me.'

He came out of the chair and squared around to face her, stiff and indignant. 'In my own way, that's exactly what I'm doing.'

She believed him. She let out a long sigh. 'I know. So why are we arguing?'

'Because you won't listen to me. This time I'm right.'

Rather than argue the point, she glanced at the bandage on his cheek. 'As soon as I'm done with the dishes, remind me to change that bandage.'

'I put a fresh one on this morning.' Automatically he reached up to touch the bandaged cut on his cheek.

'How's it healing?' Eden opened the refrigerator and put the condiments away.

'Fine.' Vince trailed after her when she crossed to the sink. 'I saw you with him this morning. You looked pretty chummy.'

'Not really.' She was instantly on guard against both her feelings toward Kincade and Vince's subtle prying. 'We just rode out to check the brood mares.'

'You seemed to find an awful lot to talk about. Did he say anything about me?'

'No.' Eden realized just how hard she tried not to think about Kincade, how she fought to block any thought of him from her mind. 'Mostly he talked about himself. He used to compete on the professional rodeo circuit until he was forced out by injuries. You remember that big pinto mare I bought, Miss Fortune? He rode her once.'

'He was a rodeo rider?'

Eden felt the hard probe of Vince's gaze and kept her face averted. 'That's right. As a matter of fact, he knows that stallion you checked out for me in Oklahoma this spring.'

She went on, detailing the things he had told her about the horse. But Vince had stopped listening, a sick feeling spreading from the pit of his stomach. He moved away from the sink, his mind racing, rejecting, yet always returning to the same chilling possibility. The one that made sense of so many things. A fine sweat broke across his brow, the seeds of panic sprouting.

'Vince?'

He turned with a start. 'Sorry. What did you say?' His palms felt clammy. He rubbed them over his thighs.

'Just that he didn't think much of the stallion either.' She gave him a puzzled look.

'The stallion, right.' Vince nodded, nervous now. 'Like I told you, I knew he wasn't what you wanted.'

He edged toward the door. 'It's hot in here. I need some air.'

He left before she could ask more questions.

Outside, he paused on the front porch and dragged in a shaky breath. The chrome on his pickup reflected the glow of the house lights.

As he dug into his pocket for the keys, a voice came out of the shadows. 'Are you going somewhere, Rossiter?'

He froze, fear – like any strong emotion – heightening his senses. He caught the aroma of cigar smoke and saw the burning tip glowing from the shadows like a red eye. Kincade, alias K.C. Harris, moved out of the shadows and into the pooling light from the house.

Vince stared at his face, the high cheekbones, the sharp jaw. It was there, the resemblance to Marcie. He had the same faded blue eyes and tawny blond hair. Why hadn't he seen it before?

'What do you want?' He had to force the question through the constricted muscles in his throat.

Kincade idly flicked the ash from his cigar. 'I thought it was time to remind you who was following whom.'

Vince didn't wait to hear more. He turned on his heel and went back inside the house, straight into the darkened living room. He made his way to the window by the gun cabinet and peered out. Kincade was a solid black shape in the shadowy darkness. Vince pulled back from the window and pressed a hand to his mouth, chewing at the inside of his lip.

Pushed by restlessness and worry, he swung from the window and raked his fingers through his hair. He propped a hand against the locked gun cabinet. For long minutes Vince stared at the rifles inside without seeing them. Slowly his eyes focused on the one Eden had taken when she went after DePard's man, shooting from the ridgetop. For more long minutes, he stared at it, his expression slowly clearing. Straightening, he turned and left the room.

'I'm going to Starr's for a beer,' he called to Eden on his way to the front door.

'If you run into anyone looking for work, bring them back with you.'

'Will do.'

With keys in hand, Vince went out the door. He never once glanced in the direction of the cigar's smoldering eye, but went straight to the pickup and climbed into the driver's seat. A turn of the key and the motor roared to life. He reversed away from the house and took off down the lane.

A mile down the track, the reflection of headlight beams flashed in his rearview mirror. Vince smiled when he saw them.

'That's right,' he murmured softly. 'You just keep following me.'

A half-dozen customers, all locals, were in the Lucky Starr when Vince walked in. The raucous notes of a honky-tonk piano came from the jukebox as Mickey Gilley sang about girls getting prettier at closing time.

At the bar, Roy spotted him and said something to Starr. She turned, the movement setting the acres of fringe on her green shirt to swaying. 'Well, if it isn't Mr High, Wide, and Handsome himself,' she declared, coming to greet him. 'It's a surprise to see you tonight.'

'I thought this place probably needed some livening up.' Vince pushed down his impatience and smiled.

'It certainly could, but what else is new?' Starr said, then paused and ran a glance over his face, a curious frown forming. 'What happened to you?'

Vince hesitated, then lied masterfully. 'Same old story, Starr. A jealous husband and no back door.'

Her laugh was short and husky. 'You always were an excellent liar, Vince. I'm not sure you would recognize the truth if it hit you in the face. Or, is that what happened?'

'It doesn't matter.' He threw a quick glance over his shoulder, impatience surfacing again. Kincade would be walking through that door any minute. He didn't have much time. 'I need you to do a favor for me, Starr.' He put an arm around her shoulders and steered her toward the bar.

'What kind of favor?' she asked with her usual caution.

'Get a message to DePard for me. Tell him I need to have Sheehan meet me the day after tomorrow at Eagle Gulch crossing. He needs to be there in the morning by ten o'clock sharp. It won't be easy for me to slip away, and I won't have time to wait for him. Have you got that?'

'I've got it.' Starr nodded, her curiosity deepening. 'But what's stopping you from calling DePard yourself?'

'I don't have time to explain. Will you do it? It's important.'

'I'll do it.'

'I knew I could count on you.' Vince winked and gave her shoulders a squeeze, then pointed her toward the stairs and her office on the second floor. 'You'd better go call him now.'

The front door opened and Kincade walked in. Starr's sharp eyes spotted the matching bruises on Kincade's face and shot Vince a quick, telling glance. 'It looks like you landed a few punches of your own.'

'One or two.' He smiled.

She headed for the stairs, issuing a greeting to Kincade when she passed him on the way. Relaxed and confident, Vince signaled Roy for a beer. He was still smiling when

Kincade walked up and leaned on the mahogany bartop some three feet from him.

'Pour the man a beer, Roy, and put it on my tab.' Vince motioned to Kincade as the swinging doors to the kitchen opened a crack and Rusty peered out. When he saw Kincade at the bar with Rossiter, he let them swing shut.

'I prefer to buy my own,' Kincade stated.

'Suit yourself.' Vince lifted his mug, hefting it toward Kincade in a mock salute, a smile lurking around the corners of his mouth. 'Better drink up. It'll be six weeks or more before you taste another one.'

'Oh? Why's that?' Kincade shoved some money at Roy when the bartender set a mug of draft in front of him.

'We'll be heading out on fall roundup tomorrow.'

Roy overheard and frowned in surprise. 'So early?'

'We're short of help so it's likely to take us longer,' was the explanation Vince offered. 'If you hear of anyone looking for work, send them out our way.'

Roy grunted and shuffled off.

Vince turned at an angle, leaning an elbow on the bar to face Kincade. 'You know, I honestly think I'm getting used to your company. It doesn't even bother me now when you turn up.'

'You seemed a bit bothered earlier tonight.'

'Who wouldn't? You startled the hell out of me.' Vince smiled easily. It threw Kincade.

'Really? Is that why you bolted for the house?'

'Forgot my keys. I had to go get them.' Vince paused a beat. 'I have to be honest. Eden gave me quite a lecture tonight about the way I've been acting. As she pointed out, DePard is giving us enough grief without me making an enemy out of you. She's right, you know.' He touched the bandaged cut on his cheek. 'Maybe I had this coming. Anyway, if it's all the same to you, I would just as soon forget the whole thing.'

'And if it isn't?' Kincade challenged, not entirely certain he believed any of this.

'There's not much I can do about it.' Vince lifted a shoulder in a light, uncaring shrug. 'I learned long ago that there's no reasoning with a man bent on vengeance. If you don't believe me, talk to DePard. Myself – I'm not holding any grudges. It's a waste of energy.'

'A lot of satisfaction can be gained from it.'

'Couldn't prove it by me.' Vince looked past him and straightened from the bar. 'Did you get your phone call made, Starr?'

'I did.'

A look passed between the pair that made Kincade suspect the exchange of some hidden message. The suspicion grew stronger when he noticed Rossiter's smile smooth out in satisfaction.

Vince turned toward a group of men sitting at a bar table. 'Hey, Hoague, what do you say we get us a poker game going? I feel lucky tonight.'

The barrel-round gas station owner pulled his heavy bulk out of the chair. 'If you're as lucky as you were Saturday night, it'll be money in my pocket.' He poked the shoulder of another man. 'Come on, Murphy – cast a little of your bread on the waters.'

Minutes later a four-handed game of poker was in progress. Kincade remained at the bar, idly nursing his beer. His attention strayed to Starr when she walked by carrying a tray of empty drink glasses. She handed the tray to Roy, then turned, her glance seeking Kincade.

'Slow night,' he remarked.

'I've seen it worse.' She wandered over to where he stood, approaching with that slow, catlike walk of hers. 'You hired on at Spur, didn't you?'

'It seemed the thing to do.'

'It was a mistake,' she said on a warning note.

'I don't think so.' Kincade turned to face the poker table and leaned back against the bar to sip his beer.

'She won't be able to keep the ranch. DePard will see to that.'

'He'll try.'

'He'll succeed.'

'Maybe.' He swirled the beer in his mug. 'I know her brother has been feeding DePard information to make sure DePard's plans are successful. Is Vinny-boy using you as a conduit?'

'You're a clever man, Kincade. You figure it out.' A long lazy smile curved her lips. 'Now, if you'll excuse me, I have work to do.' She was still wearing that same superior smile when she left the casino-lounge and headed upstairs to her second-floor office.

Two hours later, Vince gathered up his winnings and sauntered over to the bar where Kincade stood. 'I'm ready to leave,' he said, then winked. 'Are you?'

Chuckling softly, he slapped Kincade on the back and headed for the door on legs that weren't too steady. In no hurry, Kincade reached in his pocket and paid for his last beer, then pushed away.

Braced for trouble, Kincade went out the door and immediately stepped to the side. But Vince wasn't lying in wait for him. Still cautious, Kincade edged toward the corner, keeping close to the building.

A truck motor turned over and caught, the steady rumble of it filling the night's quiet. Kincade rounded the corner in time to see Vince's pickup pull away from Starr's and head north out of town. He stared after the red taillights.

Rusty came out of the deep shadows of the alleyway, the white of his food-stained bibbed apron standing out

sharply in the darkness. Like Kincade, he glanced after
the departing truck. 'How's it going?'

'I'm not sure.' Kincade took out a cigar and lit it.

Rusty skimmed his face with a glance. 'Looks like you
two went a couple of rounds.'

'A couple.'

'Then, did I hear right? Did he offer to buy you a
drink?'

'Yep.'

Rusty shook his head. 'Doesn't make sense.'

Privately Kincade agreed. 'He wants to forgive and
forget.'

'Maybe you should try it, Kincade,' Rusty suggested,
dead serious.

'I can't.'

'Marcie wouldn't like this. You know that.'

'Marcie was too tender-hearted.'

'Yeah, but don't forget – what goes around, comes
around, Kincade,' Rusty warned.

'In that case, Rossiter has a lot of grief coming
to him.'

'And you're going to see that he gets it.'

'That's right.'

'How? Have you figured that out?'

'Not yet,' Kincade admitted. 'But there's something
he wants – or something he dreads – something that
will make him suffer more than anything else. When I
find out what that is, he'll pay.'

'When you set out to cause somebody pain, you could
be the one doing all the grieving when it's over.'

'It will be worth it.'

'Will it?' Rusty challenged. 'Are you sure?'

'You aren't going to change my mind, Rusty, so stop
trying,' Kincade stated. 'If you don't want to help, go
back to Oklahoma.'

'I wouldn't be much of a friend if I turned and

walked away just because I think you're wrong. And you are wrong, Kincade. You're about as wrong as a man can get.'

'We'll see.'

'You make it damned hard to be your friend, Kincade. I'm going to tell you this – and I'm only going to say it once – whether you're right or wrong, I'm going to be here if you need me. And by God, you'd better call me if you do – or you'll find out what this red hair on my head is all about. You hear me?'

'Loud and clear.' Kincade nodded, the smallest smile playing at the corners of his mouth.

'Good.' Rusty stalked off, disappearing into the alleyway.

16

The dawn stillness was broken by the swelling sounds of activity in the ranchyard – the slide of boots in stirrups, the groan of saddle leather taking a rider's weight, the clump of hooves over hard-packed ground, and the rumble and clatter of wagons rolling out.

Eden stood off to one side and watched, impatient for the crew to be gone, and careful not to let it show. The bed wagon lumbered closer, with Vince at the reins. The instant he saw her, he halted the team and motioned for her. With her nerves screaming at yet another delay, Eden went over to him, the folded maps in her hip pocket brushing higher against her back with each hurried stride.

'What do you want? You're holding up the others.' She sent a quick glance at the riders halted behind the bed wagon. Kincade was one of them, something she tried not to notice.

'Why aren't you coming with us?' Vince frowned.

'You have a short memory.' Eden struggled to conceal her irritation with it. 'I told you last night that I had to pick up some extra supplies.'

'You did? When?'

'After you got home from Starr's, where you had too

many beers. I'll catch up with you tomorrow at Big Timber Canyon.' She backed away from the wagon and lifted a hand in farewell.

The wagon lurched forward. As Eden turned to walk away, Kincade saw a packet of papers slip out of her hip pocket and fall to the ground. When she continued toward the house, he spurred his horse over to retrieve them.

'Eden, wait up.' He swung out of the saddle, stepping to the ground. 'You dropped something.'

When he picked them up, Kincade saw they were maps of Nevada. One was a state highway map and the other a more detailed map of county and secondary roads. Both were folded open to the same section and both had a series of Xs in various places, one with a circle around it and two others with larger Xs crossing them out.

'What's this? A treasure map?' he joked when Eden came back.

'Of course not.' In a rare show of agitation, she yanked them out of his hand. 'They're ordinary road maps.'

'And you carry them with you.' They might be road maps, but her attitude suggested the marks on them had a significance that she didn't want him to discover. 'I suppose you need them to find your way to town.' Kincade kept his voice light and teasing, but his curiosity was aroused.

'Don't be ridiculous.' There was impatience and the beginnings of anger in her eyes. She gripped the maps a little tighter. 'I suggest you stop standing around wasting time. You have work to do.'

Kincade hesitated a moment, then gathered up the reins and stepped onto the bay. He checked the gelding's restive stirrings and glanced back at Eden. 'If you have something you don't want DePard to know, I hope you haven't told your brother.'

'I don't know what you're talking about.' But there was a betraying flicker of unease in her eyes.

'Have it your way.' Kincade reined his horse away, lifting it into a lope.

Shortly after seven they arrived at Big Timber, a box canyon formed by the curling finger slopes of a low mountain. The horse cavvy was pushed through the canyon's entrance and turned loose to graze on its treeless floor. Kincade searched, but saw nothing taller than sagebrush, not even a scattering of old tree stumps along the banks of a summer-shallow creek that meandered through the canyon.

He frowned at Al. 'They call this Big Timber Canyon, but where are the trees?'

'As near as anybody can remember, there never were any.'

'Then how did it get the name?'

'A little Nevada humor, I expect. There isn't much to laugh about in this country.' Al sent a traveling glance over the vast landscape of rocks, sage, and sand. 'Most of the time you have to make up your own jokes.'

'And they're usually on the dry side, like the land,' Kincade observed with a wry smile.

Al chuckled. 'Yup.'

They set up camp outside the mouth of the canyon. As soon as his tent was pitched and his gear stowed inside, Kincade went to the mess tent. Wild Jack had a pot of coffee boiled. Kincade helped himself to a cup. The coffee was weaker than the cook's usual brew, but it was scalding hot. Kincade blew on it to cool it and took a seat on the wagon tongue to wait for the rest of the crew to finish.

Vince was the last to arrive. 'Never knew anybody could take so long stowing their gear away,' Al remarked. 'What were you doing all that time in your tent, anyways? Catching a little morning shut-eye?'

'Just making sure there weren't any rocks under my bedroll.' Vince grinned. 'You boys know me. I like my comfort.'

The cowboss Bob Waters walked up. 'It's time we got the day's work lined out.' He crouched down and proceeded to draw a crude map of the area in the dirt, using his finger. 'We'll break this into sections and concentrate on areas where there is good graze no more than half a day's walk from water. That's where we'll find most of the cattle anyway. You'll work in pairs—'

Kincade spoke up. 'I'll go with Rossiter.'

'My thought, exactly.' Vince gave him a nod and a thin smile.

Sunlight flashed on the lenses of the Paiute's round glasses as he glanced from one to the other. 'Just remember what you're out there for,' he said.

'I'll remember.' Kincade nodded.

'Good. You'll have this east section here, all the way to Butler's Draw.' He marked out the area on his ground map. 'It's a lot of territory to cover but it's mostly all flat country. Al, you and Deke take Tabletop. I'll cover the Windy Springs area. Any questions?' Meeting only silence, he stood up. 'Then let's get in the saddle.'

As one, they all moved toward their horses. Vince lagged behind to match strides with Kincade. 'I've heard of sore losers before, but this is the first time I've ever met a sore winner. In case you haven't noticed, I got the worst end of that fight.' He tapped the bandage on his cheek.

'I noticed.' Kincade looped the reins over the bay's neck and slipped a toe in the stirrup.

'Glad to hear it.' Vince pulled his cinch stirrups snug, gave his horse a hard slap in the belly, and gave the strap another pull. 'You'd better tighten that cinch up another notch,' he advised Kincade.

'It's fine.' He swung into the saddle.

'It's your neck.' Vince shrugged his indifference and mounted up.

The sun was in their eyes when they rode east out of camp, traveling at an easy, rocking lope. Half a mile from camp, they spotted a dozen head of cattle grazing on the next rise, a mixed group of cows and hefty, late-winter calves weighing six hundred pounds and better. The instant the cattle saw the approaching riders, they turned tail and took off for open country.

Vince swore and yelled, 'They'll run for miles if we don't turn them.'

Kincade had already guessed that and spurred his horse into a run. Vince's mount was only half a length behind as they tore after the fleeing cattle. The morning came alive with the pound of hooves, the clink of spurs, the snap of sagebrush, and the steady, rhythmic belly-grunts of horses on a hard run.

The ground was rocky and uneven, spotted with clumps of sage, some standing up to four feet tall. The low ones Kincade's horse popped over; the tall clumps he weaved around.

They were gaining on the cattle. Barely twenty yards separated them. Whipping the romal over and under, Kincade asked his horse for another burst of speed.

They topped a rise and a towering clump of brush loomed directly in his path. The bay swerved to avoid it and the saddle slipped, pitching Kincade headlong into the brush. Instinctively he twisted to take the brunt of the fall on his right side and protect his weakened left arm. He crashed into the brush, branches snapping and popping, breaking his fall.

He lay there for a stunned instant, conscious of sharp broken stems poking him in a dozen different places. Nothing throbbed; there was no searing of pain anywhere, just the vague overall ache that comes from a hard landing.

In a kind of scrambling roll, Kincade disentangled himself from the sagebrush and got to his feet. His shirt was torn in a couple of places, but other than minor scratches, he was unhurt. He looked around for his horse. The gelding stood a few yards off, the saddle tipped far down on its side.

Vince galloped back and pulled his horse to a plunging stop. He made a quick visual inspection of Kincade, a smile forming on his face.

'I came back to see if you were still alive. A man could break his neck in a fall like that.'

'You aren't going to be rid of me that easily, Rossiter.' Kincade caught up the gelding's reins. 'You haven't got that kind of luck.'

'We'll see.' Grinning, Vince swung his horse around and whipped it after the cattle.

Kincade watched him a moment, then pushed the saddle back in place and straightened the blanket under it. He hooked the stirrup on the horn and this time made certain he had the cinch snugged tight before he climbed aboard.

After a mile's run, Vince got in front of the cattle and turned them. He was holding them when Kincade finally joined up with him. Together they herded the bunch back to the canyon.

That night in the mess tent, Vince wasted no time telling the others about Kincade's spill.

'Too bad you couldn't have stayed on,' Deke remarked. 'You might have invented a new way to ride sidesaddle.'

'Or a new version of the Indian trick of hanging off the side of his horse,' Bob Waters suggested, straight-faced.

'Aww hell,' Al proclaimed, waving his hand in a dismissive gesture. 'These Texas boys never did know how to cinch up their saddles tight. That's why they talk so funny. It's from landing on their heads too many times.'

The good-natured ribbing continued right up to the moment when Kincade crawled into his tent for the night. 'Are you going to sleep in your bedroll tonight, Kincade?' Al called over to him. 'I thought after you found out how soft that sagebrush was, you might curl up in it.'

Kincade joined the short round of laughter the comment evoked. But it wasn't as easy to ignore the bruises when he climbed into his bed. Tired and sore, he closed his eyes, but sleep was a long time coming.

In the pitch-black hour of predawn, the first stirrings of activity traveled through the camp as Wild Jack fired up the cook-stove and put coffee on to boil. The aroma of it scented the cool air when Bob Waters made his rounds, rousting the crew from their tents.

As usual, Vince was the last to arrive at the mess tent. With coffee in hand, he joined the others and Bob Waters immediately started to line out the day's assignments.

'Kincade and I will take the Eagle Gulch section,' Vince volunteered. 'I know every place a cow can hide in that area – and probably a few they haven't found yet.'

'You've got it,' Waters told him.

'Better make sure your cinch is tight today, Kincade,' Vince grinned.

'You can count on it.'

The first rose flush of dawn tinted the eastern horizon when the crew made its way to the horses. Kincade smoothed the blanket on his horse's back and swung the saddle onto it. He had taken a couple extra pulls on the cinch when, off to his right, he heard Vince swearing.

'Got a problem?'

Vince walked over, leading his horse, the clatter of a loose shoe giving an uneven cadence to the clop of its hooves. 'My damned horse is fixing to throw a shoe,' he grumbled. 'You might as well head out without me.'

'You were supposed to check the shoes last night,'
Deke reminded him.

'I did. It wasn't loose last night,' Vince snapped, then
checked his temper and turned to Kincade. 'Make your
initial sweep along Eagle Gulch and I'll swing to the
north and hook up with you below Temple Butte.'

'Fine with me. Just don't be long getting there,'
Kincade told him. 'I'd hate to have to come looking
for you.'

'Don't worry. I'll be there. You can count on it,' he
replied, a hint of cockiness in his smile.

When Kincade rode out a few minutes later, Vince
was at the bed wagon, pounding the first nail to reset
his horse's shoe.

The morning air was brisk and crystal clear. Raw and
untamed, the land rolled before him, an undulating
expanse of dips and swells, curry-combed with shallow ravine and studded with squatty knolls. Kincade
cantered over it, buoyed by the freedom of its openness
and the winelike quality of the air. Temple Butte hung
in the distance. Kincade aimed for the maroon wall of
its sheer scarp and kept riding until he reached the wide
arroyo of Eagle Gulch. With his boundary defined, he
began scouring the area for cattle. It had once formed
the bed of a river, but the mountain spring that fed it
had dried up centuries ago.

Vince concealed his lathered horse in some brush behind
the knoll, dug his binoculars out of his saddlebag, and
scrambled up the slope. At the top he settled himself
in a dish-shaped hollow scooped out by an eroding
wind. Clumps of small and spindly sagebrush clung
to the top and side of the sandy bowl, thick enough to
obscure his presence yet thin enough to keep his view
unobstructed.

He took off his hat and laid it on the ground beside

him, tugged his bright yellow neckcloth loose and stuffed it in his hip pocket, then loaded the rifle and levered a cartridge in the chamber. Only then did he pick up the binoculars and begin to glass the rolling sage flats on both sides of the gulch.

Sweat rolled down his face and stung his eyes. Vince wiped it away on his sleeve then again raised the binoculars to his eyes, making another sweep of the area. He had almost completed the arc when a horse and rider pushing three cows came into view. He zeroed in on Kincade, then lowered the glasses to look with a naked eye. Less than a mile away and traveling slowly.

With glasses raised, he rechecked Kincade's location, then scoped out the route he was likely to take. Vince watched him a few minutes more. Soon Kincade was close enough to make the binoculars unnecessary. Vince tucked them back in their leather case and licked lips that had suddenly gone dry. He picked up the rifle, nerves leaping, twisting, coiling, and tightening. Sweat ran freely now as he brought the rifle up.

By nine that morning Kincade had scared up three cows. He drove the red-coated trio ahead of him, the bank of the deep gulch hemming them on the right. A rocky knoll crowned with sagebrush partially blocked his view of Temple Butte, where he was to meet up with Rossiter. Kincade cast another glance to the north, searching for a telltale lift of dust that would indicate Rossiter's presence. He saw none and grew uneasy.

A cow trail curved around the foot of the knoll, following the narrow ledge of land that separated the gulch from the base of the low hill. Kincade swung his horse out to the left, crowding the cows onto the trail.

A long-eared rabbit leaped from beneath the brush at his horse's feet. Startled, the gelding shied and spun to the right. At the same instant, Kincade heard the crack of a rifle and felt a puff of wind against his cheek.

Instinct – that primal will to survive – kicked in. Kincade flung up his head, a dozen things registering at once. The loudness of the report meant that it had come from close range, and the knoll's brushy top provided both concealment and a field of fire. Looking up, Kincade caught the metal glint of a rifle barrel coming to bear on him. Caught in the open, with no cover nearby, Kincade clamped his spurs into his horse and wheeled it toward the rocky slope, whipping it into a hard gallop as a second shot tugged at his shirt sleeve. Taking an angle that made him a difficult target, Kincade charged straight for the top.

A man rose from the brush and stepped forward, trying to get a better shot. Kincade saw at once that it wasn't one of DePard's men. It was Vince. No longer was it strictly a survival instinct that drove him, but rage as well.

Vince got off one more shot before Kincade crested the knoll, but he fired too quickly and the bullet missed by a wide margin. Frantically he backed away from the onrushing horse and rider and worked to lever another round into the rifle chamber.

Kincade hadn't done any bulldogging since his college rodeo days, but he hadn't forgotten the moves or the timing. As his horse was nearly abreast of Rossiter, Kincade dove out of the saddle, striking Vince in the chest and driving him to the ground. Vince landed with a heavy grunt and the rifle went sailing. Carried by his own momentum, Kincade rolled off.

Recovering quickly, Vince lunged at him, but Kincade managed to get a knee up and throw him off. As Kincade scrambled to his feet, his hand touched the smooth metal of the rifle. He grabbed it up and lifted it no higher than hip-level before pointing it at Vince. Vince saw it and froze in a half-crouch, his eyes glued to the rifle. At some point, he had lost his hat, and a cowlick of dark hair curled onto his forehead.

'Forgive and forget – isn't that what you said?' Kincade jeered in barely controlled rage.

'What did you expect me to do, Harris? Stand around and wait for you to make your move?'

Harris. The significance of it leaped at Kincade. 'You know who I am.' The rifle was suddenly a satisfying weight in his hands, lethal and tempting.

'Did you really think I wouldn't figure out who you are?' Vince challenged, then dropped his air of bravado to rush desperately to his own defense. 'Dammit, I had nothing to do with your sister dying. She was alive when I left that motel room.'

'And you took every dime she had when you left, didn't you?' Kincade tightened his grip on the rifle, the hatred building. 'It was always the money you wanted, wasn't it? It was never Marcie.'

'She gave it to me,' Vince insisted. 'I didn't take it. Marcie gave it to me. It was her idea. She wanted me to have it.' His glance darted again to the rifle. 'Look, I'd give you back the money if I could. But I don't have it. Eden needed it and I gave it to her. You just give me some time and I'll pay it back. I swear.'

The sound of Marcie's name coming from his lips, the false protestations of innocence, the big promises, and the sight of Vince standing there alive while Marcie was dead combined to break through the last of his restraints. Kincade snapped the rifle to his shoulder and squeezed the trigger. The roar of the rifle blast drowned out Vince's sharp cry as he stumbled backwards and fell.

In a blind fury, Kincade levered another cartridge into the chamber and fired again and again and again, only dimly aware each time of the way Rossiter's body jerked with each shot. He kept up the barrage until the hammer finally clicked on an empty chamber, once, twice.

Kincade lowered the rifle, trembling with the violence that was still within him, and half-sickened by it. The smell of cordite hung in the air, sharp and pungent. Kincade dragged in a deep breath of it, conscious of an ache in his throat and chest that wouldn't go away.

For a long minute he stared at the small furrows the bullets had plowed into the ground all around Rossiter's tightly curled body. Only when Vince stirred, lowering the hands he had used to cover his face, did Kincade look at the man cowering there, completely unscathed. The old loathing surged back.

A little dazed yet, Vince glanced first at the rifle, then at Kincade. 'You dirty rotten son-of-a-bitchin' bastard.' His voice shook with a mixture of fear and anger.

'Go on. Get out of here before I change my mind and bash your head in with this rifle,' Kincade warned, half-raising it in threat.

Warily, Vince backed up a few steps, then turned and scrambled down the slope amid a clatter of dislodged stones. Kincade listened to the snap and rustle of brush at the bottom of the knoll, the sounds marking Rossiter's hasty passage through it.

Lost, confused, and angry, Kincade looked at the spent shells scattered over the ground near his feet. Deep down, he had secretly wanted Rossiter to die. An eye for an eye, a life for a life – the ideal revenge. He'd had his chance. He could have killed Vince and made a good case of self-defense. But when the moment had come, he hadn't been able to do it.

Why?

A horse snorted somewhere at the base of the rocky knoll, the sound followed by the clink of bridle chain and the slap of a rider hitting the saddle. Gripping the rifle with a kind of controlled savagery, Kincade turned in time to see Vince whip his horse into a gallop and race off across the flats.

He watched him for a taut, angry second, then swung away and snatched his hat off the ground, jamming it on his head. Scanning the area, Kincade located his own mount some twenty yards from the bottom of the slope, its trailing reins tangled in some brush. He started down the knoll after it, then stopped when he heard the drum of hoofbeats approaching from the opposite direction. A rider in a black-and-white cowhide vest halted his horse on the other side of the gully. Kincade recognized the rider even before he saw the purple splotch the birthmark made on the man's face.

'What was all that shooting I heard?' Sheehan called over to Kincade.

'I saw a snake.'

The Diamond D foreman frowned his skepticism. 'It took that many shots to kill it?'

'I guess I'm just a lousy shot.' Kincade suddenly understood Rossiter's plan – prearrange a meeting with DePard's foreman, kill Kincade from ambush, and lay the blame on Sheehan. With the cattle-loading incident to support his claim, it probably would have worked.

'Rossiter won't be keeping his meeting with you, Sheehan,' Kincade told him. 'This time you can be glad he didn't.'

'I don't know what you're talking about.' Sheehan put his spurs to his horse, cantering off.

At the bottom of the knoll, Kincade caught his horse and mounted. The cattle were long gone. He turned and started back to camp. Then he saw the dust cloud Vince had raised. Its direction didn't lead to camp. Vince was traveling on a line that would take him straight to the ranch house.

He was running again.

A part of Kincade said, let him go. But he had

trailed him too far and too long; he couldn't quit now.

Kincade set out after him, driven by the need to finish what he had started and grimly aware his heart wasn't in it, not with the same intensity as before. But he couldn't give it up. Not yet.

17

With barely four hours sleep after a day that had been physically and mentally demanding, Eden felt the heaviness of fatigue dragging at every muscle when she pulled into the deserted ranchyard. A thick film of dust coated the pickup, obscuring its faded red color. More clung to her clothes, giving them, and her skin, a gritty feel. Eden climbed out of the cab, visions of a long hot shower filling her head. The old cowdog stood in the shade of the porch, wagging his tail in welcome.

Smiling, Eden went to the back of the truck and lifted out the spare bedroll and sleeping tent. Clutching the bulky pair in front of her, she started for the porch. Vince burst out of the cottonwood grove, striding rapidly toward the house. Stunned to find him at the ranch, Eden hurriedly dumped the tent and bedroll back in the truck.

'Vince. What are you doing here?'

He threw her a look, but never slowed up. His face was pinched and pale, something angry and almost frightening in the set of his features.

'What is it? What's wrong?' She immediately jumped to the most obvious conclusion. 'Someone's hurt. Who? How bad is it?'

'No one's been hurt . . . unfortunately,' he muttered the last, almost under his breath and hit the porch steps ahead of her. In one stride he was at the front door, yanking it open.

Eden caught up with him inside the house. She grabbed his arm, catching him off balance and spinning him back to face her. 'If nothing is wrong, what are you doing here?'

'I'm clearing out, that's what.' He jerked his arm free and broke for the stairs.

Eden had guessed what he was going to say, but actually hearing it was like a body blow. She saw all her carefully laid plans dissolving before her eyes. She ran up the stairs after him.

Vince was jamming clothes from his closet into the open suitcase on his bed when Eden walked into his room.

'You can't leave yet, Vince. We're in the middle of roundup. Dammit, I need you.'

'You'll get along just fine without me.' He emptied his dresser drawers and stuffed his underwear into the suitcase along with the rest of his clothes.

'Not this time. You—' Eden stopped and fought to hold her temper in check.

'Sell the damned ranch!'

'No!' Her reply was equally sharp and explosive.

'Goddammit, Eden, can't you see we will be cursed by the past until you do!'

'I can't quit now. I won't!'

'That is exactly what I expected you to say.'

As he threw the last of his things into the suitcase, Eden saw how adroitly Vince had shifted the focus from his actions to hers. He was a master at that.

'Dammit, Vince, I'm not asking you to spend the rest of your life on Spur. Just two more weeks. That's all.'

'That's two weeks too long.' He closed the suitcase with a snap and dragged it off the bed.

'Why are you suddenly in such a hurry to leave?' Eden followed him to the head of the stairs.

'I don't have time to explain, and you wouldn't understand if I did.' His spurs clanked with each thud of his boots as he went quickly down the steps.

'What does that mean?' She went down the stairs after him, convinced now that Vince was in some kind of trouble again. It did absolutely no good to tell herself she had enough problems of her own without taking on his. Even with all their differences, the bond between them was too strong.

'Don't ask questions, Eden.' He was impatient with her, which only made her all the more certain he was guilty of something.

'Vince, what have you done this time?' She was right behind him when he pushed out the door.

'Nothing. Not a damned thing.' The bitterness and frustration in his voice gave a ring of sincerity to his denial. He crossed the porch, his long strides eating up the ground between the front steps and his pickup. He yanked open the door on the driver's side, threw his suitcase into the cab, and climbed in after it.

'I don't understand.' Eden stopped next to the door.

'You don't need to.'

'Just tell me where you're going.' She ran alongside the truck as he reversed away from the house.

Vince looked unsure. 'I'll go to Reno and lose myself there. After that . . . I don't know.' He shifted out of reverse gear. 'If you need me, just leave a message with Axel like always.' He started to pull away, then leaned out the window and called back to her, 'And for God's sake, don't tell Harris a thing.'

'Harris?' She knew no one by that name, but her

bewildered response was lost by the accelerating roar of the pickup's engine.

Kincade rode into the ranchyard at a gallop. He pulled up at the corral and wasted no time stripping the gear from his lathered horse and turning it loose in the corral already occupied by Rossiter's mount. He took a step toward the bunkhouse, then heard a vehicle start up over by the house.

Vince. It had to be, he thought, and broke into a run. He reached the clearing in time to see Rossiter's blue-and-white pickup before it disappeared down the ranch lane. Eden stood in the yard, her face turned to escape the brunt of the dust cloud. Kincade hesitated, then took a chance and walked over to where she stood.

'Where is Vince off to this time?' He had to work to make the question sound casual.

'Reno, he said,' she replied in an absent murmur, then stiffened and threw him a sharp look. 'What are you doing here?'

But Kincade already had more information than he had hoped to get from her. He headed for the bunkhouse, determined not to give Vince a bigger head-start than he already had.

Moving quickly, Eden stepped in front of him, blocking his path. 'You're supposed to be out with the crew rounding up cattle.'

He looked at her coolly, a hard and relentless cast to his features. Whiskers darkened the hollows of his cheeks and intensified the arctic blue of his eyes. 'The plans got changed.'

'By whose order?' She knew she had lost control and fought to regain it.

'Mine,' he said and walked around her.

Turning, Eden watched him cross the yard with reaching, restless strides, his spurs kicking up little snake heads of dust. She threw a glance over her shoulder at the slowly dissipating cloud left by Vince's truck. The connection was easy to make. Too much had gone before that foreshadowed this. Too much that she hadn't wanted to accept.

The reason wasn't clear yet. But now she had to find out.

When she reached the bunkhouse, Kincade was on his way out, his duffel bag in hand. 'You're going after Vince, aren't you, Mr Harris?' Because she already knew the answer to that, Eden went on. 'That's your real name, isn't it? Harris?'

'It is.' He shifted his grip on the bag and took a stride, angling away from her toward his truck.

'What do you want with Vince?' Eden demanded. 'What has he done to you?' Again she tried to block him, but barely slowed him down.

'That's my business.' He swung the duffel bag into the back end of the truck and dug in his pocket for the keys.

'Vince is my brother. That makes it my business.'

'Not this time, Eden.' He pinned her with a look that was harsh and unyielding. 'You may have bailed him out of trouble in the past, but this time you can't help him.' He opened the driver's door and climbed behind the wheel of the truck.

The finality of his words was chilling. It momentarily stopped her. The truck started up with a rumbling growl and reversed away from the bunkhouse. Pushed by the sudden and strong alarm she felt for her brother, Eden ran to the other side of the truck. She didn't know what was between Vince and Kincade, but it didn't matter. She had to help Vince, protect him if she could. And she couldn't do that here at the ranch. She had to go with Kincade, prevent him from hurting Vince.

As the pickup rolled forward, she caught hold of

the door handle and ran a few steps alongside the moving vehicle before she could pull the passenger door open. She jumped onto the running board and scrambled inside.

Kincade saw her and slammed on the brakes. 'What are you doing? Get out!' His glaring look threatened to bodily throw her out.

'No.' Undaunted, Eden smoothly engaged the passenger door lock and settled back in the seat. 'You're going after Vince. And if you find him, you'll have to go through *me* first because I'm going with you.'

'Like hell you are!' Kincade jammed the gear shift lever into park and shot across the seat.

Eden turned to meet his attack, her hands coming up to fend him off. Ignoring the resistance she threw at him, he hooked an arm around her and dragged her against him, pinning her arms between them. She continued to struggle while he fumbled for the door handle. She heard the snap of the lock popping up and the metallic click of the door unlatching. Recognizing the futility of it, she gave up the fight and altered her tactics.

'Even if you push me out of the truck, you won't be rid of me,' she told him. 'I'll just climb in the back end.'

His face was inches from hers. Awareness flared, ignited by his nearness and the memory of other times when she had felt the heady pressure of his mouth on hers. Recognition of it was in his eyes, too, and he wasn't any happier about it than she was.

'The only way you can stop me is to tie me up, and I'll fight you every minute if you try. Think how much time that will take,' she reasoned. 'Vince will be halfway to Reno by then. Of course, that may not matter to you.'

'You know it does.' A grimness settled over his expression. 'But if you think coming with me will change anything, you're wrong.'

His glance flicked to her mouth in that instant before he abruptly released her and slid back behind the wheel. He yanked the gear lever into drive and tromped on the accelerator. The pickup leaped forward, tires spinning, the partially latched passenger door rattling in its frame. Eden grabbed the handle and managed to get the door closed while the vehicle continued to gather speed. She sagged back in the seat, trembling inside, her mind racing.

'You're a fool, Eden.' His attention never left the rough track before them, his eyes intense like his long-boned and narrow face. 'Haven't you got enough trouble with DePard without borrowing more from your brother?'

'DePard will wait until I get back.' A few days delay wasn't critical, but the threat to Vince was immediate. It was a difference Eden recognized, just as she recognized she couldn't let Vince face it alone.

'He wouldn't risk everything to help you. You know that.' Kincade drove at a speed Eden wouldn't have risked, and she knew every rut in the lane.

'I know my brother better than you do,' she stated with unshakable certainty.

'Do you?' he taunted. 'Then you must know he has been conspiring with DePard to force you to sell the ranch?'

'If he has, then it's because he believes it would be the best thing.'

'Your loyalty to him is admirable but badly misplaced. The man is a taker who thinks only of himself and what he wants. He doesn't give a damn about who he hurts in the process. Not even you.'

'That's your opinion.'

'No, that's the truth,' Kincade fired back. 'And you'd better face it. Your brother doesn't have the scruples of a snake.'

Her control snapped. 'Why? Because you say so?' Eden challenged in full temper. 'Am I supposed to believe *you*? A total stranger who comes to the ranch looking for work and gives me a phony name? Who lies?'

'I did it for a reason. And for your information my name is Kincade. Kincade Harris.'

'Is that supposed to justify everything?'

'No.' His mouth tightened briefly, its line turning even grimmer. 'No, I guess not.'

'Why do you hate him so much? What has he done?' Eden demanded.

'I'll let Vince tell you that when we catch up with him.' He slowed the truck to make the turn on the gravel road, then increased its speed again.

Catching something ominous in his words, Eden fell silent and anxiously scanned the road ahead. But there was no dust cloud in the distance. Vince was still well ahead of them, but she doubted that he would be driving as recklessly as Kincade. They had to be gaining on him.

In record time she saw the gray and weathered buildings of Friendly rise out of the sage flats. The truck never slowed until they reached the outskirts of town. Then, unexpectedly, Kincade applied the brakes and the pickup fishtailed to a stop.

'This is your last chance, Eden,' Kincade told her and switched off the engine. He jerked the keys from the ignition. 'There is nothing you can do to help him this time. If you're smart, you won't be here when I come back.'

Not waiting for a response, he climbed out of the truck and headed for the rear entrance to Starr's. A pair of hamburgers were sizzling on the grill when Kincade pushed open the backdoor to the kitchen.

He took one step inside and called out, 'Rusty!'

'Yo!' Rusty answered as he plunged a basket of French fries into the deep-fat fryer, grease bubbling and splattering.

'Rossiter's on the run. Headed for Reno.' Before he finished, Rusty was tugging off his apron. 'We'll use the desk at Harrah's for messages.'

Rusty nodded his understanding. 'I'll be right behind you.'

That was all Kincade needed to hear.

Eden saw Kincade disappear into the alleyway behind the Lucky Starr. Where was he going? Why? Confused, she sat in the truck, listening to the snap and pop of the slowly cooling engine.

The engine! She scrambled out of the truck and raced around to the hood. Unfamiliar with the truck model, she wasted precious seconds searching for the latch. She finally located it and the hood popped loose. When she raised it up, the trapped heat rushed out. She retreated a step, then went back and began unscrewing the distributor cap. It was a delaying tactic, aimed at giving Vince more time to get away. She had no hope of stopping Kincade.

Absorbed in her task, Eden didn't hear the warning chink of spurs that signaled Kincade's return. She released a strangled cry of surprise when a hand seized her elbow in a numbing grip and pulled her out from under the hood. The distributor cap sat at a drunken angle, still in place. One more turn and she would have had it off.

'Nice try,' Kincade murmured and screwed the cap back on.

'A few more seconds and I would have had it.' Eden rubbed at her arm, the nerves still tingling from the bite of his grip.

'But you didn't have a few more seconds, did you?'

He slammed the hood down and checked to make sure it was securely latched, then headed for the driver's side. Eden was quicker, climbing into the cab ahead of him while he stopped to unbuckle his spurs and the short leather chaps. He tossed them onto the seat between them and started up the truck.

As they pulled away, Eden glanced back at the alley. 'What were you doing? Where did you go?'

He seemed to hesitate, as if debating whether to answer her. 'To let my partner know Rossiter had skipped.'

'Your partner?' The phrase had a connotation that had Eden holding her breath. 'Are you with the police?'

Deep grooves bracketed the corners of his mouth. 'Not hardly.'

She should have been relieved that Vince wasn't wanted by the authorities, but the knowledge that Kincade was acting outside the law made it impossible.

The town was behind them and the long gravel road stretched ahead of them, the strong light of the sun bouncing off the hood of the pickup into the cab. Kincade reached for the pair of sunglasses lying atop the dash and slipped them on. A silence fell between them, thick with tension.

Better than an hour out of Friendly, they reached the Lovelock interchange and turned onto the interstate, heading southwest. Reno was still another ninety miles away. Eden watched the speedometer needle creep up to hover at the outside edge of the speed limit.

'How well do you know Reno?' Kincade turned his head toward her, the mirroring lenses of his sunglasses throwing back her own image.

'I don't.' The whine of the tires on the pavement

seemed to echo the inner screaming of her own nerves as Eden fought to maintain an outward show of calm. 'I went there a couple of times to see my lawyer.'

'You mean back when you were charged in the death of DePard's brother?'

'Yes.'

'That was quite a while ago.'

'It's been eleven – almost twelve years since the trial.'

'Reno has changed a lot since then.'

'You've been there?' She shot him a quick, stiff look. It was a possibility that hadn't occurred to her.

Kincade lifted a shoulder in an idle shrug. 'Name any city that has a major rodeo and I've been there. Many times.' Which meant he wouldn't be a stranger to the city, but she told herself that he still couldn't know it as well as Vince did. 'Any idea about where your brother might go?'

Anger flashed through her that he would even think she might tell him. 'Why should I answer that when you won't tell me what it is Vince has done?'

'Like I said before, ask him.'

'I'm asking you. I want to hear your side of the story.'

'This isn't about sides, Eden; it's about cold, hard facts.'

'What are the facts? What did Vince do? Did he take somebody's life savings?' she guessed. 'It has to be about money. With Vince, it's always money.'

'Not this time.' Again, the tone of his voice was chilling.

Just for a moment, she doubted, then she shook her head. 'No, there's money involved somewhere.'

'Where's he going, Eden?'

'I'm not about to tell you.'

'I'll find him, Eden,' he said when she failed to reply.

'You can make it hard, or you can make it easy. The choice is yours.'

'Then it will have to be hard. Even if I knew, I wouldn't tell you.' But she had a good idea where Vince would go first, dressed as he was in range clothes. To Axel Gray's apartment in Sparks to shower and clean up.

A blackjack dealer at the Nugget, Axel Gray was only a voice on the phone to Eden. Vince had met him seven years ago, shortly after their grandfather died. Since then Axel's place had been their message center whenever Vince went on one of his extended trips. Vince called Axel his good luck charm, insisting nothing bad would happen as long as he stayed in touch with Axel. It was almost a superstition with him.

'It doesn't matter. I have a general idea where he'll go first,' Kincade told her. 'Your brother is a vain man. He'll want to clean up and change into better clothes.' Eden felt a chill, thinking Kincade had somehow managed to read her mind. 'He'll stay away from the smaller motels. His truck would be too easy to spot. He'll pick one of the big hotel-casinos. That's more his style anyway.'

'You still don't know which one.' She managed to keep her voice level, not wanting Kincade to guess how close he had come to the truth.

'We'll check every single one out until we find him.'

18

Reno sprawled across the valley floor, the footslopes of the rugged Sierra Nevada range rising beyond it. Traffic jammed its thoroughfares while glittering showgirls in elaborate costumes smiled from billboards that boasted such names as Harrah's, Bally's, and The Flamingo. More vehicles choked the parking lots of the opulent hotel casinos, towering monoliths of concrete and glass that vied for attention with sparkling fountains, flashy neon, and showy flowers.

Kincade cruised slowly through another lot, scanning the multitude of cars, trucks, and vans, trying to locate Vince's pickup. Eden had lost track of the number of parking lots they had already searched with no success. With the circuit completed, Kincade turned back onto the street.

The sun slipped behind the Sierras and the first street light winked on when Kincade drove into a service station and pulled up next to a self-service pump. Without a word, he climbed out, unlocked the gas cap, and stuck the pump nozzle into the tank to fill it. Eden spotted the ladies' restroom along the outside of the building and stepped out of the truck.

She made it as far as the second island before Kincade caught her by the arm. 'Where are you going?'

'To the restroom, if it's any of your business.'

He held onto her arm and called to an attendant, 'Are there telephones in the restrooms?'

'Nope. We got one inside, though.'

'Thanks,' he said and released her arm.

'You thought I was going to call Vince and let him know where we are, didn't you?'

'It occurred to me.'

'I don't know where he is. I already told you that.'

'And I also know you would lie to protect him. He isn't worth it, Eden.'

'I don't agree. But wherever Vince was, you can be sure he isn't there now.'

He frowned, then looked up at the deep bluing of the sky and sighed. 'You're right. He would be gone by now.' He turned and walked back to the gasoline pump.

She went to the restroom. When she came out, Kincade was inside talking to the service station attendant. She waited for him in the truck, a weariness pulling at her. Lack of sleep, long hours, and a tension-filled afternoon all combined to drain her reserves.

'What now?' she asked when Kincade slid behind the wheel.

He took his time answering her. 'The way I see it your brother has two choices – either lie low and spend the night in front of a television set or lose himself in a crowd. I'm betting on the latter.'

'He has a third choice; he could leave town.' Eden hoped that Vince had.

'He could.' Kincade slipped the key in the ignition and gave it a turn. The engine responded with an answering growl that grew to a steady rumble. 'But he's been away from the neon and the nightlife for a while. He'll want to sample some of it before he leaves.'

When Eden saw the dazzling display of lights along the Strip, she had to agree. There were miles of long neon tubing in brilliant pinks, blues, reds, and white, and acres of light bulbs. None of them were static. They were all moving, flickering, twitching, flashing, blinking on and off, racing up, down, and across, shooting into space and exploding in a cavalcade of more lights. Crowning it all was the celebrated arch that spanned Virginia Street, spelling out in lights the town's famous slogan: RENO – THE BIGGEST LITTLE CITY IN THE WORLD.

Kincade glanced at her and wagged a finger at the blaze of lights. 'What do you think of these "blessed candles of the night"?'

'I think Shakespeare was referring to stars when he wrote that.'

'Only because he hadn't seen Reno's Glitter Gulch.' His mouth curved in a slanting smile. Eden smiled back and glanced out the window again. Kincade pulled the truck into a lot and left it there. Together they set out on foot.

The sidewalks were crowded with people wandering from one brightly lit casino to another. Kincade steered Eden into one of them. She stopped to avoid walking into a tall blonde in a frothy dress, high heels, and a mink stole who was on her way out.

'Ooops, sorry.' The woman executed a graceful side-step to avoid Eden.

Eden stiffened under the blonde's brief but assessing glance, painfully conscious of her scruffy cowboy boots, faded jeans, and man's shirt – and two days worth of dust and grit ground into them. She tugged her hat lower on her head and tilted her chin higher as she responded to the guiding pressure of Kincade's hand on her waist and entered the casino.

The noise assaulted her first. The incessant clatter of

slot machines, dinging bells, voices chattering nonstop, punctuated by the squeals and whooping shouts of winners. From a nearby lounge came the tinkling notes of a piano, the casino's din drowning out all but fragments of the melody.

As they moved deeper into the casino, people claimed Eden's attention. They filled the aisles between the rows of slots. A group of cowboys in flashy pearl-snapped shirts, crisp new jeans, and snakeskin boots hooted at a buddy who was swearing at a machine. A young Japanese couple played the slot next to them, whispering and pointing in puzzlement at the winning combinations posted.

Sequins and ragged jeans, sweats and satins, suits and Bermuda shorts, pearls and turquoise bolos, the dress was as extreme and varied as the clientele. Short hair, gray hair, long hair, blonde hair, no hair, wigs, mustaches, ponytails, beards, toupees – it was all there beneath the glare of lights that were as bright as daylight.

When Kincade halted at the edge of the gaming area, Eden paused as well and surveyed the money-green tables. Chandeliers dripped crystal from coffered ceilings lined with mirrors. Only they weren't mirrors; they were an eye-in-the-sky, one-way glass-and-catwalk system staffed by the gaming establishment, a sophisticated safeguard against cheating on either side of the table. Vince had told her about it once.

'I know your brother likes poker.' Kincade turned his head toward her, his glance probing, measuring. 'What else does he like to play?'

Eden looked at the blackjack table, the roulette wheels, the secluded baccarat areas, and the craps tables. 'Any of it and all of it, I guess,' she answered truthfully.

At the craps table a man in a yellow golf shirt rubbed a pair of dice between his hands and murmured softly.

He tossed the dice and talked to them all the way as they rolled across the table, bounced off the side, and chattered to a stop.

Exultant, the man shouted, 'Eight the hard way, yes!' Another man, two players down, swore in disgust and walked away from the table.

An old woman with two scarves tied on her head brushed past Eden, smelling rankly of an unwashed body. She clutched a plastic tub with a scattering of quarters in the bottom and looked as if she were wearing every article of clothing she owned. The old woman walked up to a quarter slot, carefully put one coin in, and pulled the handle. The reels whirled, then, one by one, clunked to a stop. Nothing. Expressionless, the woman slowly and deliberately selected another coin, dropped it in the slot and took another chance.

Chance. It was all a game of chance, played under different guise, different odds, different rules, but it was still chance – a kind of electricity in the air, a subtle tingle. A fever that got in the blood. Eden saw it glowing in the eye of nearly every player, whether cool or intense, desperate or confident.

She felt the contagion of it, the pull of excitement, the temptation to test her luck. One more roll of the dice. One more pull of the handle. A silver ball clattered over the raised spokes of a roulette wheel to finally lodge on a black number and thousands changed hands.

This was where Vince would be, in a casino like this. She understood at last the lure of it. Vince had stayed in Reno; he would be drawn to it.

With a new feeling of urgency Eden scanned the crowd, trying to spot Vince before Kincade did.

They searched casino after casino, going from one to another until they all blurred together. The bright lights that turned night into day, the absence of clocks, and the continual whirl and clink of slots created a perpetual timelessness that was disorienting.

Kincade pushed his way back into Harrah's and automatically checked to make sure Eden was behind him, then cursed himself for it. She was proving to be a distraction. He spent too much time keeping track of her and not enough watching out for Rossiter.

But there she was one step behind him, the brim of her hat tipped forward shadowing her face, dark hair spilling about the shoulders of the shapeless man's shirt that couldn't completely conceal the curves underneath it. Something he had noticed a few too many times.

Tired and frustrated, Kincade bit back a sigh and stopped a few feet inside the entrance to make a cursory, visual sweep of the casino floor. When he didn't immediately spot Vince, he turned and headed toward the hotel desk.

'Where are you going?' Eden asked.

'To see if there's a message from Rusty.'

'Rusty. Who's Rusty?'

'My partner.'

'Is he here in Reno, too?'

'Somewhere.' He nodded.

Eden made no comment to that, but he knew it worried her that someone else was looking for her brother – just as he knew that she hoped to somehow interfere with him when he finally came upon Vince.

At the registration desk, Kincade recognized a familiar face behind the counter and walked past the clerks straight to a middle-aged man wearing glasses and a preoccupied frown. 'Hello, Kirk. It's good to see you again.'

The man regarded him with a blank look, then broke into a smile. 'Mr. Harris. I didn't realize it was you. You look like you've had a long, hard drive. I expect you'll want your usual suite.' He started to signal one of the clerks.

'No. Not right now at least,' Kincade stopped him. 'Have any messages been left for me?'

'I don't believe so. Let me check.' He stepped into the back offices.

Kincade turned sideways, resting an elbow on the counter while he watched the people wandering by. Out of the corner of his eye, he saw Eden adopt a similar stance, propping herself against the counter.

'You must stay here often,' she remarked.

'Whenever I'm in Reno.'

'I imagine a lot of people do. I wonder if the clerk remembers them.' She didn't ask why he remembered Kincade.

'He has a nine-year-old boy who wants to be a cowboy when he grows up. One year I arranged for his family to have front row seats for the entire run of the rodeo.'

'That was nice.'

'That was easy.' Kincade turned back to the counter when he heard the night manager returning.

'Sorry, Mr Harris. No messages.'

'Thanks.' He backed away from the counter to leave. 'Tell Matt I said hello.'

'I will,' the man promised, then added with a smile, 'You should see the way he gets around in his new wheelchair. He calls it Dandy, says it's his cutting horse.'

The man laughed and lifted a hand in parting as Kincade moved to shortcut to the casino floor. Eden fell in beside him.

'A wheelchair,' she murmured. 'You didn't mention the boy was crippled.'

'It didn't seem important.'

'You have a soft heart after all.'

'Not where your brother is concerned,' he stated flatly. He slowed to descend the short flight of steps to the casino floor.

Eden stumbled on the second tread, pitching forward. Kincade caught her before she fell. For an instant she sagged against him and he felt the soft give of her body. She smelled of sage, dust, and woman, and his hold tightened. She immediately pulled back.

A change lady stopped. 'Are you all right, miss?'

'I'm fine. Just . . . just tired.' Eden pushed his hands away, denying the need for their support. But he saw the exhaustion in her face, the dullness of fatigue in her eyes even as she tried to shake off the effects of it. 'What time is it, anyway?'

The woman glanced at her watch. 'A few minutes past two.'

'In the morning?' Eden gave her an incredulous look.

'It's hard to tell in here, isn't it?' The woman smiled in understanding and moved off in response to a summons from one of the players at the slots.

Eden pressed a hand to her stomach. 'No wonder I'm so hungry.'

It was said more as an observation than a complaint, but Kincade grimly recalled the faint tremor of her muscles when he had held her, a tremor caused by hunger, not a reaction to him. With an impatient lift of his head, he surveyed the crowded casino. He needed to be out looking for Rossiter. That's why he was here.

Instead he took her arm and propelled her toward the restaurant. 'Come on. We'll grab something to eat at the coffee shop.'

The hostess showed them to a booth. Sliding in, Eden took off her hat and dropped it on the seat beside her, a tired sigh breaking from her. With both hands, she pushed the hair back from her face, then flipped open the menu.

'Everything looks good,' she murmured.

Kincade glanced up from his own menu. At that

moment her expression revealed little of the tension and stress she was under. But it showed itself in other little ways like the tight curl of her fingers on the menu, the taut muscles in her neck, and the stiffness in her shoulders. He thought of all the grief DePard was causing her, and now her brother. He wondered how much more Eden could take before she broke under it.

A waitress came by. 'Can I bring you something to drink while you look over the menu?'

'Two beers,' Kincade said.

'I'd rather have coffee,' Eden said, but the waitress had already walked off.

'You're wound tighter than a spring. Caffeine is the last thing you need right now,' Kincade told her. 'The beer will relax you. After you've eaten something, you can have coffee.'

'I don't need to relax.' But that was the only argument she offered.

The waitress came back with the beers, took their order, and left. Thirsty, Kincade took a long drink of his beer. Eden did the same, then set the glass down, clasping both hands around it.

She looked at him, her gaze level and direct. 'What happens when you catch up with Vince?'

He glanced at the fingers she laced tightly around the beer glass. 'That remains to be seen.' Kincade lifted his own glass, downing another swallow. It didn't taste as good as the first.

'You won't—' Eden stopped, as if unable to finish the thought.

He raised an eyebrow, a dryness pulling at the corners of his mouth. 'Kill him? That's against the law.' He couldn't tell her that he'd had his chance to do that and blown it. 'There are other ways and means.'

'Don't.' That was all she said, her chin lifted, her

shoulders squared, ready to resist any attempt to hurt Vince.

Silently Kincade admired the loyalty she showed for her brother. She had a steadfast quality, a stubborn pride and iron will that Vince lacked.

Unable to give Eden the assurance she wanted, Kincade made no comment. The waitress came with their food and they ate in silence. Finished, Kincade pushed his plate back and watched Eden eat the last few bites of her meal. When she was through, he noticed her beer glass was empty as well.

'Feel better?' he asked.

'I think I'm too full to move.' And too tired, Eden could have added, a lethargy setting in now that she'd eaten.

'How about some dessert?' The waitress gathered up their empty dishes.

'Just coffee for me,' Eden said.

'Make it two.' Kincade took a cigar from his pocket.

'Two cups coming up,' the waitress said cheerily and left, dodging a party of three the hostess ushered to the table opposite their booth.

Eden glanced up as chairs were shifted and rearranged to accommodate a cowboy in a wheelchair, his hat in his lap, his right leg in a cast that went from hip to toe. His glance strayed to the booth and stopped on Kincade, a frown forming.

'K.C.?' he said none too certainly. Then a smile broke across his face. 'K.C., you old son-of-a-gun, it is you. How the hell are you?'

Excusing himself, Kincade slid out of the booth and went over to the table. 'I'm fine, Hawks. Too bad you can't say the same. What happened?' He gestured to the cast.

'Damned horse fell on me and busted it to hell.' He rubbed a hand on the injured leg. 'Hugh Hazlett has this young stud that's a dandy cutting horse prospect. He'll be working good for a while, then blow up for no reason. After that, it's like riding a Kansas twister. That's why he hired me to train him, I guess. Probably figured an old bronc rider like me could stay on him. He sure figured wrong. I got the hospital bills to prove it,' the man called Hawks declared, then paused. 'What have you been up to? Last I heard, you got thrown in San Antonio and landed in a hospital. Your riding arm, again?'

Kincade nodded. 'The doctor managed to piece it back together.' He flexed the fingers in his left hand as if to show it still worked.

'Take my word, you're gonna know whenever there's a change in the weather.' The man chuckled. 'Say, did you hear about Bud Tyler?'

'No.'

When the conversation at the table turned to people she didn't know, Eden stopped listening. The waitress set a cup of coffee in front of her. She took a sip, but it was too hot to drink. Leaving it to cool, Eden sagged back against the corner of the booth, letting the softly cushioned sides support her. Her eyes felt dry and gritty from lack of sleep. She decided to close them – just for a little while.

After chatting a few more minutes, Kincade headed back to the booth and met the waitress, a coffee pot in her hand. 'Poor girl,' the woman murmured, throwing a glance over her shoulder at Eden. 'She's sound asleep.'

One look confirmed the waitress's statement. Eden sat curled in the corner of the booth, her face soft and slack in sleep, her head tipped at an angle that guaranteed her neck would be stiff when she woke up. She looked small and vulnerable, claimed by the exhaustion he had noticed in her earlier. The sight pulled at him with a strength he couldn't ignore.

'Tell her I'll be back if she wakes up,' he told the waitress.

'Sure.'

But she was still asleep when he returned. 'Eden. Eden, come on.' He had to shake her awake.

'Wha—' Groggy, she tried to fight through the layers to the surface, but it took too much effort. Her neck hurt. She lifted a hand to rub at the soreness, but it was too heavy. She felt hands pulling and lifting her upright. Even though she was half asleep, Eden still somehow knew they belonged to Kincade. She tried to help him. 'Where are we going?'

'We're calling it a night.' His voice seemed to come from a great distance. She struggled to hear it, but missed a few words. 'Registered for both of us.'

'Good.'

They were in the coffee shop. She knew that, but it was all blurred. Her eyelids were too heavy. She couldn't keep them open. It was the beer. She shouldn't have drunk it on an empty stomach. It was the last clear thought she had as she took a few weaving steps toward the exit before Kincade scooped her up.

'I can walk,' she mumbled in a voice thick with sleep.

'Sure you can,' he agreed dryly.

By the time he reached the elevator, she was asleep, her head resting in the crook of his neck. He felt a nameless, tender feeling as he carried her into the suite. Defenseless wasn't a word he had ever associated with Eden. But that's what she was, with no mask to cover the softness in her face.

Kincade crossed the sitting room and went unerringly to the second of two bedrooms the suite contained. Using the point of his elbow, he flipped on a light. A king-sized bed filled the room, its covers turned back in precise folds. A double row of plump pillows lined the headboard. He carried Eden to the bed and sat her on the edge of it. His hands caught her before she tipped back onto the mattress.

'Come on, sit up, Eden, so I can get your boots off.'

She mumbled a vague acknowledgement and spread both arms to prop herself upright. Kincade knelt down and began pulling off her boots and socks. She had small feet, as smooth and delicately boned as the rest of her. He tugged off a sock and lowered her foot to the floor, his fingers trailing over its high arch.

As he started to rise, he saw she had her shirt unbuttoned. He froze for an instant, staring at the plain white bra she wore under it, the material stretched taut to hold her full breasts. He felt his blood heating up and a strangling tightness grip his throat. He wanted to swear bitterly and viciously when her hands moved automatically to the snap of her jeans, but he didn't trust the sound that would come out. It didn't matter that her eyes were still closed, or that she was more asleep than awake. Desire was a hot, knotting ache inside him.

'I don't remember ever being this tired, Vince,' she mumbled, the snap and the zipper giving way at the same moment.

Christ, she thought he was her brother. Kincade was dangerously close to correcting that impression. Instead he grabbed her pant legs and gave them a yank, tipping her over backward onto the mattress, a murmur of contentment coming from her.

Two quick tugs and her dusty jeans were on the floor next to her boots and socks. He gathered her up, stripping the shirt from her limp arms and tucking her under the covers, but not before he had a glimpse of white cotton panties and slim, shapely legs sculpted with lean muscle. She immediately rolled onto her side and snuggled into a pillow.

Careful not to look at her, Kincade walked over to the

long, plate-glass window and closed the heavy drapes, blacking out the extravagant neon glitter of the Strip. Long, restless strides took him across the room, his glance running to the pile of dirty clothes on the floor. He flipped off the light when he walked out the door.

Dawn was breaking along the eastern rim of mountains when Kincade returned from prowling the casinos. He unlocked the door to the suite and walked in, his duffel bag under one arm and a shopping bag in the other hand. Hesitating, he glanced at the door to Eden's room, then left the shopping bag in a chair in the sitting room and walked directly to the suite's larger bedroom, his footsteps heavy with fatigue.

He dropped his duffel bag on the thick pewter-gray carpet. It landed with a dull *thump* that he ignored as he turned on the lamp by the bed. Working to keep his mind blank, Kincade went to the adjoining bath, turned on the shower, and peeled off his dust-and-sweat-caked clothes, checked the temperature of the water, then stepped beneath its pulsating spray.

From habit, he soaped himself down, then stood beneath the stinging jets, letting the water sluice the lather from his skin and the tension from his muscles. Steam rose in a thick, billowing mist around him, closing him in and blocking out everything for a time.

Out of the shower, Kincade went through the motions of drying himself off, then wrapped the towel around his middle and stepped up to the sink. A disposable razor lay on the marble counter. He picked it up and began shaving off the two-day-old beard while the whiskers were still wet, ignoring the tired and bloodshot eyes that stared back at him from the steamy mirror. Finished, he splashed water on his face and patted on some after-shave lotion, compliments of the hotel. But none of it, not the shower nor the shave, had the reviving effect he sought.

He returned to the bedroom and dug a clean set of clothes out of the duffel bag. He held them a moment and stared at the shimmer of satin sheets, touched by the pool of light from the bedside lamp. A few hours sleep was what he really needed. Recognizing that, Kincade laid the clothes aside and climbed into bed.

The satin felt cool against his skin when he slipped between the sheets and stretched out. He closed his eyes and tried to forget that Eden was only a room away.

But as he drifted off, he imagined she was there, in bed with him, his hand gliding over her skin, slipping that plain white bra from her, and cupping the weight of her breasts in his palms, his mouth grazing down her stomach, breathing in the musky, heated smell of her, her fingers curling into his hair, her body arching, the small, stifled gasp she gave at the invasion of his tongue, her body stiffening with the pain of impossible pleasure, then shuddering with it before he plunged into her and found release for his own, not letting her go even then, but sleeping in a warm tangle of arms and limbs.

19

His eyes snapped open, then came part way together again to shut out the glare of the sun, which was streaming through the window, framed by the heavy black-out drapes he had deliberately not closed. He rolled over and peered at the digital clock on the nightstand. It was a few minutes before ten in the morning.

Wide awake, Kincade sat up and swung his legs out of bed. Then he heard it. A muffled cry, a kind of sobbing, coming from Eden's room.

Frowning, he quickly pulled on a pair of Levi's and went to investigate. When he entered the darkened room, Kincade saw the vague shape of her threshing about in the bed, strange guttural sounds coming from her throat.

'Eden?' When she failed to answer, he moved to the bed and turned on the lamp.

She flung her head away from him, her arms outstretched and rigid, her fingers digging into the tangled covers, her body twisting. The lamplight glistened on the wet track of tears on her cheeks, trailing from eyes that were tightly closed.

'Eden, wake up.' The instant he laid a hand on her shoulder, she lashed out at him.

He barely managed to dodge her raking nails before she came at him again. Trapping both arms, he pinned her to the mattress. Her eyes were open now, and filled with fear. She looked straight at him, but something told Kincade she wasn't seeing him; she was still caught in the throes of her nightmare.

'It's a dream, Eden. Wake up,' he ordered a bit more forcefully. The words penetrated. He watched the awareness slowly enter her eyes, replacing that sightless stare of panic and dread. In that moment, her expression was poignantly childlike, vulnerable and frightened. Some instinct kept him from gathering her close and soothing her fears as he wanted to do. Instead, he relaxed his hold on her arms and straightened, standing next to the bed and giving her room.

'That must have been a nasty dream,' he murmured. She turned her face away from the light and lifted a hand to her damp cheek. He saw the tremor in the movement and the unconscious moistening of dry lips. Without a word, he turned and walked into the adjoining bath.

Soundlessly Eden pushed herself into a sitting position, dragging the bedcovers with her and bundling them close as a kind of protection. Inside she was still quivering from the after-effects of the nightmare. She struggled to control it and block out the images that flashed at the edges of her consciousness. Water ran in the bathroom sink. Then it stopped and she heard the soft pad of bare feet approaching the bed.

'You looked like you could use this.' He offered her a glass of water.

The sight of it made Eden aware of her parched mouth. She downed a quick swallow of it, washing away that cottony sensation, then lowered the glass and stared into it, unable to look at Kincade. Not now. Not yet.

'Thanks,' she said, hating the thready sound of her voice. 'You were right. I was thirsty.'

'What were you dreaming about?'

She stiffened instinctively, her guard coming up. 'Who are you trying to be? A father confessor now?' She tried to inject a note of lightness, but the edginess crept in to betray her.

'Are you Catholic?'

'No, I'm not.' She shoved the water glass onto the night table by the bed. 'Look, I'm fully awake now. The nightmare's over. I'll be fine.'

'You don't sound like it.'

'It doesn't matter how I sound,' she insisted. 'It will pass. It always does.'

'Then you've had this dream before.'

'If you must know, yes!' she flashed impatiently and dragged the covers more tightly around her, irritated that he continued to stand there, his hands tucked in the pockets of his jeans.

'Obviously you weren't dreaming about Vince then,' he guessed. 'Which means the nightmare must have been about DePard's brother, the one who was killed.'

Her glance shot to him, her eyes wide with apprehension before she jerked their focus from him. *Bingo*, he thought as a new curiosity rose.

'Maybe it's time you talked about that night,' he suggested, interested in hearing her version of it. More interested than he cared to admit.

'I have talked about it. Over and over and over.' She pushed out the words through jaws tightly clenched. 'First to my grandfather, then the police and my lawyer, then again at the trial. That's enough for anybody.'

'But the nightmares haven't stopped,' Kincade reminded her. 'What happened that night?'

'When?' Eden challenged hotly, resorting to anger for protection. 'What gory detail do you want to know? How it felt when he was mauling me? Or the way he looked when the gun went off? How about the blood that was all over me?'

'Why don't you start at the beginning?' He strolled over to the bed and sat down on the edge of it near the foot, signaling his intention to stay there until she did as he suggested.

'The beginning. Now, that's original,' Eden struggled to sound caustic, flippant. 'I was seventeen. Jeff was older. Vince's age. They were friends, as a matter of fact. After graduation, Jeff went off to college. I saw him a few times when he was home. Vince would pick me up after school and Jeff would be with him.' The words flowed out; this part had been easy. 'I never really knew Jeff. I mean, I was just Vince's kid sister. Jeff never paid much attention to me until . . . that spring. He would say things to me, put his arm around my shoulders, and look at me in a way that was kind of scary and exciting, too.' Just talking about it, Eden felt seventeen again, naive and uncertain. 'All the girls were envious that he had noticed me. He was good-looking, a star athlete in college. On top of that, he was a DePard.'

Kincade made a wry face. 'I wouldn't call being a DePard any recommendation.'

Eden saw the smile that lurked at the corners of his mouth. There wasn't anything else he could have said that would have made her feel better than that.

'Back then, it was,' she told him, holding back a smile of her own, then sobered with the memory of that night. 'Anyway, one Thursday after school, Vince told me that Jeff wanted me to go out with him Saturday night. I wasn't allowed to date. In a way, I was relieved to remind Vince that Jed wouldn't let me go out on dates. Vince said he could sneak me out, that it would be easy. He guessed that I was nervous at the idea of going out with Jeff. He suggested that if I was worried about anything, we could double date and he would bring Rebecca Saunders. Finally I agreed.'

'In other words, Vince set you up with DePard.' It was one more thing Kincade held against him, but he was careful to keep it out of his voice.

Suddenly Eden needed to move. A restlessness caught her up and pushed her to the opposite side of the bed. She dragged the sheet with her, pulling it loose from the foot of the bed and wrapping it around her Indian-style as she stood. 'It was still my decision to sneak out of the house and meet Jeff. Vince didn't talk me into it. If anything did, it was the idea that someone as handsome and popular as Jeff DePard wanted to go out with me.'

'Where did you go?'

Eden walked to the window, freed a hand from the entwining sheet, and lifted the drape open a crack to look out. The morning sun was high and bright, bleaching the blue from the sky. There were cars on the street and people on the sidewalks, but fewer than last night.

'Seven miles south of the ranch, going toward town, there is a series of rock pools fed by a hot spring. It's had a dozen names over the years, but everybody just refers to it as the Springs.' She took a long breath and continued, little emotion coming through. 'It was arranged for Jeff to pick up Vince's date and meet us at the Springs at nine o'clock.' She stared blindly into the sunlight, unwilling to turn back to the room's thick shadows. Darkness made the memory much too real. 'Jeff and Rebecca were already there when Vince and I arrived. I remember it was a beautiful night, quiet and not too cool. The stars were out, thousands of them . . .'

Without the headlight beams on Vince's truck to dim their brilliance, the stars glittered overhead like so many diamond fragments strewn across the velvet arch of the sky. Excited and tense, Eden waited for Vince to join her before she approached the pair waiting by the small fire. The smallest sounds registered in the desert stillness: the faint, gurgling bubble of water in the spring-fed pools beyond, the soft crackle of wood burning, and the heavy thudding of her own heart.

'Ready?' Vince flashed her a smile.

She nodded once and ran exploring fingers over one side of her hair to make sure no tendrils had escaped. 'Do I look all right?'

She had pulled her hair back from her face and anchored its heavy weight with combs in an effort to appear older and more experienced. She didn't want Jeff to suspect she had never been on a date before.

'You'll knock him dead, Sis,' Vince promised with a wink.

Taking her arm, Vince guided her over the rocky ground to the ledge of smooth stone that extended out to form the upper rock pool. Yellow flames blazed cheerily near the center of the ledge, the area immediately around it blackened by the char of previous fires. Its flickering light revealed two blankets that had been spread over the flat stone. A red-and-white insulated cooler sat between them, a portable radio and tape deck stood on top of it, surrounded by a collection of cassettes.

Eden saw it all, looking anywhere but at the tall, broadshouldered man, backlit by the fire. She could feel Jeff's gaze, like a pair of invisible hands moving over her as she moved steadily toward him. It was unnerving and a little scary, but exciting, too.

She glanced at the woman next to him, her sun-streaked hair tousled in the deliberate disarray favoured by so many models in magazine ads. Older than Eden by two years, Rebecca Saunders had worked in Reno for nearly a year before her father became ill, after which she returned home to look after him and her younger brothers and sisters.

The black jeans Rebecca had on were so snug Eden knew she would never be able to climb on a horse in them. Her T-shirt was equally tight and the baggy vest she wore over it did little to conceal the lack of a bra.

'Hi. We finally made it,' Vince declared. 'Hope you haven't been waiting long.'

'Just long enough to get the fire started,' Jeff replied, the low and lazy pitch of his voice turning Eden's nerves all jittery again. She was glad Vince was there to keep the conversation going. She suddenly had no idea what to say, how to act, or what to do.

'That's right,' Rebecca chimed in. 'Jeff picked me up early and we stopped to eat. We were having such a good time, we were almost late ourselves.'

'Yeah, Duke invited a bunch of his political friends over to the house for dinner tonight. I decided to clear out and leave them to all their talk on hot issues and campaign strategy,' Jeff explained. 'So I called Rebecca and arranged to pick her up sooner than planned.' Then his glance went to Eden. 'Hello, Eden.'

'Jeff.' She sounded a little breathless; she was a little breathless.

'Yes, hello, Eden,' Rebecca echoed his greeting and sent her a smile that was pure poison.

Confused, Eden wondered what she had done to make Rebecca dislike her. But she had no time to dwell on it as Jeff claimed her attention again.

'You look wonderful tonight,' he murmured.

'Thank you.' She touched a hand, a little proudly, to the wide eyelet collar of her white blouse. It lay in soft ripples, creating a ruffle effect around the blouse's v-neckline.

It was her best blouse, plain enough to satisfy her grandfather, yet feminine enough to suit her.

She had agonized over what to wear tonight. Her wardrobe was a meager one, consisting of school clothes and ranch clothes. Vince had told her to wear jeans, but she wore jeans every day of her life. She wasn't about to wear them on her first date. Finally she had decided on this blouse, a flared skirt in a flowered print, and sandals.

Jeff held out his hand. Eden hesitated, then placed hers in it. He glanced at it briefly, then back at her. 'Your hand is cold.'

'Yes.' She knew it was nerves that had turned her fingers to ice – and tied up her tongue as well, it seemed.

'I guess I'll have to hold on to them to keep them warm.'

'Or I can stand by the fire and warm them over the flames.'

He chuckled. Had she said something clever? She had made the comment out of sheer desperation, wanting to give more than a one-word response.

Still holding her hand, he turned, drawing her closer to the fire. 'There's beer in the cooler, Vince. Help yourself,' he said, then glanced at Eden. 'Want one?'

She shook her head. 'Not right now, thanks.'

'You don't mind if I have one.' He was already moving toward the cooler.

'Of course not.' Eden sank onto the blanket, curling her legs to one side and adjusting her skirt over them.

Rebecca was at the cooler, lifting the lid off when Jeff reached it. She handed a can to Vince. 'You're in luck. There's enough left for you to have one. Jeff and I dipped into it on our way here. Didn't we?' She flashed him a sexy and secretive smile and took out another beer, presenting it to him.

'A man has to satisfy his thirsts.'

'A woman, too.'

There seemed to be some sort of hidden meaning in the exchange, but Eden couldn't puzzle it out. She listened to the snap and fizz of beer tops popping, feeling left out.

Jeff came back and sat on the blanket next to her. She tried to think of something to say. 'When do you go back to college?'

'Tuesday, maybe.' He took a swig of beer. 'It depends.'

'On what?'

'On whether I decide to cut a couple classes or not.'

'Let's have some music.' Rebecca popped a cassette in the tape player. 'I feel like dancing.'

The music came on and she turned the volume up, filling the night with a driving disco beat. She looked pointedly at Jeff. When he didn't move, Rebecca grabbed Vince's hand and pulled him up to dance with her.

The loud music made any further attempt at conversation impossible. Eden would have had to shout to make herself heard. Instead she watched the couple dancing in the outer arc of the firelight, her eyes drawn again and again to Rebecca as she moved to the beat with a writhing, twisting motion that was somehow sinuous. Wanton and shameful, her grandfather would have called it. Eden conceded there was something wanton to it, but it had a kind of beauty as well.

She glanced at Jeff and saw that he was watching Rebecca as well. She didn't blame him. At the same time, it hurt.

The song ended. In the brief break before the next one started, Eden smiled bravely. 'She's good, isn't she?'

Jeff lifted a muscled shoulder, feigning indifference. 'If you like that kind of dancing.'

Eden decided he did. He never took his eyes off Rebecca while she danced to the next song until the very end. Then he leaned over, close to Eden's ear. 'Want to dance?'

She shook her head a little vigorously. 'I can't dance like that.'

He grinned and leaned even closer. 'That wasn't what I had in mind.' He went over to the cassette player and switched tapes. A slow, sentimental ballad came over the twin speakers. He came back to Eden and reached down for her hand. Self-consciously she let him pull her to her feet.

'I warn you I'm not a very good dancer,' she said as his hand moved onto her waist.

'Not enough practice, I'll bet.'

'With school, homework, and chores, there isn't much time left.'

'I don't imagine old Jed cuts you much slack either.'

'No.'

'There's nothing to it, really.' His hand slid a little further around her waist, drawing her closer. 'Just relax and let your body sway with the music.'

Her foot bumped against his. 'You forgot to mention what to do with my feet.'

'Ah, now, that's the secret. You just stand in one place, shuffle them around and pretend to move them.'

'Is that right?' Amused, Eden looked at him, flirting a little, something she hadn't had much practice at.

'It is.'

After several bars Eden had to agree the method worked quite well. She had just begun to relax a little, gain some confidence, when he released her hand and fingered the ruffle of her blouse.

'I like your blouse.' He ran his fingers down it, the fabric slipping loosely between them, the back of his hand brushing over her breast. 'What do you call this material?'

He continued to slide his fingers up and down it, his hand rubbing against her breasts each time, setting her nerve ends pleasantly a-tingle. She was afraid to say anything, afraid he would discover what he was doing and stop.

'Eyelet.' She somehow managed to get the word out.

'Eyelet.' He explored the embroidery around one of the holes. 'I like it. Especially on you.' His glance lifted from its inspection of the fabric to her face, a pleased look in his eyes.

'I'm glad.'

Releasing the collar, he curled his fingers around her hand again, turning it and drawing it to rest against him while the hand at her back pressed her closer until there was no more space between them.

'Your hand is warm now,' he murmured.

It was the heat traveling through her. She felt herself color and lowered her chin to conceal any blush. Almost immediately Eden felt his cheek against her hair.

'You smell good.'

'It's the perfume I'm wearing. Vince gave it to me for Christmas.'

'Did you put some behind your ears?' His head dipped down to discover the answer for himself, the warmth of his breath feathering over her ear and neck. Delicious little shivers danced over her skin and radiated through her whole body. She closed her eyes, trying to hold off the weakness that attacked her limbs.

'What's the name of it?' His lips repeatedly touched her neck as he formed the words, the contact intensifying the sensation.

Eden could barely breathe, let alone think. 'Emeraude,' she whispered, finally remembering the name on the bottle.

'It does things to a man.' He rubbed his mouth along her cheek.

'Does it?' She hoped so because he was doing things to her.

'Hmmm. It makes him want to find out if you taste as good as you smell.'

His mouth was at the corner of her lips. Aroused

yet unsure, Eden turned her head just that fraction necessary to make contact. He wasted no time claiming her lips.

It wasn't her first kiss. When she was fifteen, Buddy D'Angelo used to walk her from class to class. One time he stopped her in an empty stairwell and kissed her. Actually it had felt more like he simply pushed his mouth on hers. It hadn't been like this, all hot and moist, scary and thrilling at the same time. She tried to emulate the rolling and rubbing action of his mouth, her breath quickening.

Again and again Jeff kissed her, retreating a breath and coming back, devouring her lips with a greediness that was contagious and addictive. Eden suddenly realized the music had stopped and they had long ago abandoned any pretense of dancing.

Embarrassed, she pulled away and darted an anxious glance in Vince's direction. Jeff caught her chin and turned it back to him. 'Don't worry about him. Your brother is too busy to notice us.'

It was true. In the one glimpse she'd had, Rebecca had been wrapped all over Vince and he had been nuzzling at her neck. But Eden was too self-conscious to respond to Jeff's next kiss with the same ardor. When the pressure of his mouth became insistent, she twisted away from it.

Another slow, dreamy ballad swelled into the night and Jeff resumed the swaying pretense of dancing to it, transferring his attentions to her face, trailing kisses over her eyes, nose, and temple. Eden tried to stop him. The sensations were all too new and felt too good.

The song ended, and another took its place, propelled by a fierce, driving beat. Jeff gave an angry mutter and pulled away, striding quickly to the cassette player and switching it off. Rebecca laughed, soft and musky.

'Lord, nothing destroys a mood quicker than the

wrong music,' she declared in a voice still rich with amusement. 'Grab another beer out of the cooler while you're there, Jeff.'

Without the heat of Jeff's body against hers, Eden felt the coolness of the night air. She shivered once and hugged her arms together, partly in reaction to the temperature and partly to ease their empty feeling.

Vince glanced at her. 'Cold?'

'A little.'

'Better come over by the fire and warm up.' He reached down and picked up a dead branch, using it to stir the embers.

Eden moved back to the fire and held her hands high above the flames. When Jeff joined her, she felt more nervous than she had earlier in the evening, and she didn't understand why.

'It's gotten cooler, I think,' she said, feeling compelled to explain her actions.

'I know another sure way to warm up.'

She was almost afraid to ask. 'What's that?'

'Take a long, leisurely dip in the hot pools.'

'What a great idea, Jeff.' Rebecca's eyes lit up. 'Let's do it.'

'Not me. I didn't bring a swimsuit.' Eden couldn't bring herself to admit she didn't own one.

'Don't be a goose,' Rebecca chided mockingly. 'You don't need a suit. Not to go skinny-dipping,' she said as she shrugged out of her vest and gave it a playful toss. It landed at Jeff's feet. 'Are you coming, Jeff? Last one in is a fool.'

She was already heading for the pool, peeling off her T-shirt as she went, the firelight reaching far enough to show a golden and totally bare back.

Vince grinned at Jeff. 'I think I'll keep her company.' He started after Rebecca.

Frozen, Eden stared after them until she saw Rebecca

wiggling out of her jeans. She abruptly turned from the sight, looking anywhere but at Jeff. She tried to shut out the sound of water splashing, the murmur of Vince's voice and Rebecca's throaty laugh.

'You don't know what you're missing, Jeff,' Rebecca called back.

Eden bounced a glance off his face. 'You can join them if you like,' she said stiffly.

'But I don't like,' he said and took her hand, leading her away from the fire. 'Come on over here and sit with me.'

He pulled her down beside him on the blanket and leaned back against the cooler, turning her sideways to recline in his arms. She tried to relax and enjoy the closeness, but couldn't. She glanced hesitantly at the pool.

'They can't see us if that's what you're wondering,' Jeff said.

'It wasn't.'

'It was.' He smoothed a hand over her hair. Before she realized his intention, he pulled out a comb. She reached up to stop him. 'No. I like your hair better loose around your face.' He removed the other comb and tossed both aside. 'There, that's better.' He ran his fingers through it. With a thumb and a forefinger he traced the curve of her jaw, circling the point of her chin, then up to her mouth.

Her lips parted with the pressure of his finger. Eden felt the tip of it against her teeth and gently nipped at it, raking her teeth over his skin. She didn't understand the sudden darkening of eyes or the near groan that came from his throat. He moved his hand away and brought his mouth down, grinding it against her lips.

There was pain in the kiss and a crude kind of pleasure that she wasn't sure she liked. She was relieved when his mouth rolled off hers and buried itself in the hollow of her neck, touching off those exciting little shudders again.

On and on it went, his lips devouring her with wet, open-mouthed kisses, then racing to her neck to nip and nibble. His hands ran over her back and shoulders, down her waist and hips, rough and demanding sometimes, soft and stimulating at others. Each time that she tried to discover her part, he leaped to another.

It didn't matter. Eden loved kissing him. She could keep doing it all night and still want more. That was how greedy she felt, greedy and frustrated that she didn't know what to do, or how to do it.

'Give me your tongue,' Jeff muttered against her lips. When she hesitated, he repeated the demand. 'Give it to me.'

Tentative, she let it slide out. When she felt the wet lick of his, she broke off the contact and hid her face in his shirt. He nipped her ear and slid his tongue inside it, drawing another shudder from her. The hand that had been on her waist traveled to the front, gliding up her ribcage to the underside of her breast.

'Don't.' She pushed it down as a laugh came from the rock pool.

'Forget about them,' he muttered.

'I can't.'

He swore and pulled at her hair, forcing her head up and bruising her lips with another punishing kiss, easing up only when she showed resistance.

Within minutes Eden heard the murmur of voices and the slap of wet feet on stone. She pulled out of his arms, whispering, 'I think they're coming back now.'

Sitting up, she hurriedly tucked her loosened blouse back inside the waistband of her skirt, and tried to smooth out the wrinkles that had been crushed into her skirt. With the sounds coming closer, she pushed ineffectually at her hair, trying to arrange it in some semblance of order.

Rebecca was the first to approach the fire, her T-shirt plastered to her still-damp skin. She sat down close to the fire's warmth to put on her shoes.

'God, that was fabulous.' She gave her head a toss, sending droplets of water arcing through the air. 'You two missed out on a lot of fun.' But her taunting look faded as her eyes narrowed on Eden. 'Or maybe you didn't,' she murmured, a bitterness and an anger creeping in.

Vince trotted up to the fire, fully clothed. 'It gets a bit chilly once you're out of the water. Come here, Rebecca, and warm me up. Did you drink all that beer, Jeff?'

'There's still some in the cooler.'

'None for me.' Her shoes on, Rebecca grabbed her vest and stood up. 'It's late. I need to get home and make sure Dad's all right. Ready, Jeff?' She faced him, her stance challenging, the vest slung over one shoulder.

'Hey, what is this?' Vince frowned. 'If you have to go, I'll take you home.'

'You don't need to. Our place is only a couple miles from the Diamond D. It's right on Jeff's way.'

Vince stepped up behind her and rubbed his hands over her shoulders. 'Honey, I'd go out of my way for you anytime.'

'Vince can take you,' Jeff spoke up. 'Eden and I will stay and load things up, put out the fire,' he added, sliding a lazy look at her before glancing back at Vince. 'I'll take Eden back to the ranch. She can show me where to drop her off.'

'It's all settled. Let's go.' Vince turned Rebecca toward the truck. She hurled an angry look at both Jeff and Eden, then moved stiffly off.

After the pickup had disappeared down the rough track that led to the road, Jeff rose and walked over to the cooler. 'Are you sure you don't want to change your mind and have a beer? Your brother's gone now.'

'No, I really don't want one.' Thinking they were about to leave, Eden started to rise, but Jeff popped the top on a can and strolled back to the blanket, stretching out to rest on one elbow.

She felt his eyes on her, unnerving in their steadiness. The silence stretched to an uncomfortable length. 'Rebecca didn't seem too happy when she left.'

'That shouldn't surprise you,' Jeff mocked. 'She had hoped the evening would turn out differently. She was wrong.'

'She wanted you to take her home, didn't she?'

'Among other things,' he said, but didn't elaborate. There was no response to make to that, and Eden couldn't think of anything else to talk about. She stared at the lights from Vince's truck, watching them for a long time before they became lost in the glow of the town lights some twenty miles distant.

'You're awfully quiet,' she ventured, unable to endure the silence any longer. 'What are you thinking about?'

'You.' He reached out and trailed his fingertips down her arm.

'How boring.' She gave him a nervous smile. 'I'm surprised you didn't fall asleep.'

'Sleep isn't what I had in mind, but it's close.'

She was suddenly very uncomfortable. She wished Vince hadn't left. She had felt safer when he was there. Which was ridiculous, Eden told herself. She was perfectly safe now.

Just the same she stood up. 'I'll fold up the other blanket while you finish your beer.'

She made slow work of folding the blanket, conscious of his eyes on her the whole time. When she had it in a neat, smooth square, she carried it over to the cooler and laid it on top. Aware that Jeff hadn't budged from his spot, she started picking up the empty beer cans scattered about.

'Do you have a sack or something I can put these in?' she asked, juggling half a dozen empty cans in her arms.

'Bring them over here.' He rolled to his feet.

Eden went over to him. He took two from her and pitched them down the slope. Before she could stop him, he hurled the rest away.

'Why did you do that?'

'I got rid of them, didn't I?'

She turned from him in disgust. 'I'll take the blanket and the tape deck to your truck.'

'Why?'

She swung back to frown. 'I thought you wanted to load up before you took me home.'

'What's the hurry? You can bet your brother isn't going to be in any rush to get back.' When she failed to respond, he curled a finger under her chin and tilted it up. 'What's the matter? Are you still upset about those beer cans? You aren't going to let that spoil things, are you?'

When he put it like that, she decided she had made too much out of it. This was a special evening, too special to be ruined just because she was annoyed by some thoughtless action of his.

'Of course not,' she relented, offering a small smile of apology.

'Good.' His mouth curved but his eyes never lost their unnerving intensity as he continued to study her. 'I'll put on some music so we can dance.'

He took her agreement for granted and sifted through the cassettes until he found the one he wanted. He slipped it into the tape player. Within seconds a slow song drifted from the speakers, the volume down.

With an odd reluctance Eden let him draw her all the

way into his arms, bodies touching. His mouth traveled over her hair to her cheek. She could smell the beer on his breath. She had noticed it when they danced before, but this time it bothered her. She kept her face averted, closing her eyes when he proceeded to nibble on her neck, finding pleasure in the sensation, but not as much as she had earlier.

A dozen times and more, his demanding mouth sought hers. She accepted his heated, forceful kisses that he never gave her a chance to return. It was good, and yet, it wasn't. She wanted this, and yet she didn't. What was wrong with her? She pressed closer to him, conscious of one song fading into another and another.

He drew back, cupping her face in his hand and lifting it to give her a heavy-lidded look. 'What do you say we put out the fire?' he suggested and Eden glanced at the dwindling flames of the small bonfire. 'Don't be cute,' he said with impatience. 'You know that's not the fire I'm talking about.'

He took two short steps and pulled her down onto the blanket with him. She wanted to object, but the words wouldn't come. She was out of her depth and knew it. At the same time she didn't know what to do about it.

When his mouth closed on hers, Eden tried to push him away, but his weight was already pressing her down. He was too heavy, too strong, and the first seeds of fear took root.

'Jeff—' she began a choked protest, but the minute she opened her mouth, he plunged his tongue inside.

Revulsion shuddered through her. She tried to repel the invasion, but her resistance seemed to only inflame him further, driving his tongue to stroke deeper. His breathing grew louder, rougher, the weight of his body heavier, crushing the air from her lungs. She was going to suffocate.

Then his mouth rolled off hers, and he shifted

slightly, giving her space. She gulped in a quick breath, swallowing back a sob, tremors taking the strength from her body.

His hand closed over her breast. 'You've got great tits,' he murmured, tipping his head down to gaze at them. 'Your nipples get hard as rocks.' He caught one between his thumb and forefinger and she felt the pinch of his grip through the twin layers of her blouse and bra.

'Don't.' Eden grabbed at his forearm and tried to pull his hand away. The muscles in his arm tightened, easily resisting her attempt.

'Stop worrying.' His face was over hers again, a gleam in his dark and lusting eyes. 'No one can see. There isn't anyone for miles.'

His words sent a cold chill through her. He was right. There was no one. No one at all to help. Galvanized by fresh fear, Eden gave him a quick, hard shove and rolled sideways to get out from beneath him.

The suddenness of it took him by surprise. She almost made it. But the hand that had been on her breast caught hold of her blouse, fingers grasping the material. When she tried to wrench loose, she heard the fabric rip. Crazily she turned back to rescue it from his snaring fingers.

'My blouse.' Anger trembled in her voice. 'You tore it.' It was her favorite, the nicest one she owned.

'You don't need it anyway.' Too late she discovered his fingers at the buttons. 'Take it off.' The first two were already free and he was at work on the third when she brought her hands up to interfere.

'No!' The refusal was quick and hot.

In reply he grabbed the front flaps of her blouse and pulled them apart, snapping off buttons and tearing more cloth. Deaf to her strangled cry of shock and alarm, he shoved his hands inside and slid his fingers under the band of her bra. As he pushed it up and over her breasts,

Eden strained backwards, recoiling. He used her action to drive her back flat on the blanket again, hooking a leg over her to hold her there while he fastened his mouth on her left breast.

Frantic, she pushed at his face, trying to force him off. When that failed, she grabbed his hair and tugged. He came up sweating.

'You little bitch.' He caught her arms and forced them high above her head, snagging her wrists and trapping them in the vice-grip of one hand. 'Don't pretend you don't want it.' He pushed his face closer to hers, an ugliness in his expression as he roughly kneaded her breast with his free hand, then drove it lower, onto her stomach. 'I remember the way you pushed against me. You've got the hottest pants in four counties, don't you?'

His hand sought the junction between her legs, his fingers curving to cup it through the folds of her skirt even as Eden squeezed her legs tightly together to prevent it. Using the heel of his hand, he rubbed her bone while she cringed from the contact. But there was no give to the smooth ledge rock beneath her. Once more his mouth and teeth took possession of her breast, the noisy suckling sounds he made as revolting to her as the sensations of it.

'No, no, no.' It was the word Eden repeated over and over again in an attempt to deny this violation as she twisted and writhed under him, her body arching and bucking, trying to throw him off.

Blood pounded in her ears and her breath came in swift, panic-shallow sobs. She rocked her head from side to side, fear now coupled with a wild desperation.

Through a veil of hot tears, she saw his arm, the one that held her wrists pinned above her head. Raising her head up, she twisted to reach it, the muscles in her neck straining with the effort. The instant she felt it, Eden sank her teeth into the fleshy part and bit down hard.

There was a yowl of pain from him, and her arms were loose. 'You bit me, you little bitch.'

She heard his snarled words as an exploding agony spread across her jaw, the force of Jeff's backhanded blow splitting her lip and snapping her head to the side, banging it on the covered rock. Her ears rang and she tasted blood on her tongue. Her own blood. While she was still too stunned to react, he hit her again and again, brutal in his intent to subdue, his voice filtering through, calling her names and hurling obscenities.

One moment he was hitting her, and in the next his hand was tugging at her skirt, pulling it up. She felt the cool of the night against her skin, then his fingers were clawing at her panties, his nails scraping her flesh.

'No!' The word came out in a throaty shriek of fear. Eden struck out at this degradation, this awful helplessness.

Her first blows landed harmlessly on his shoulders. Swearing, Jeff tried to capture her wildly swinging fists, but one got through and slammed into his nose. He grabbed it, his eyes closing against the sharply smarting pain. With added strength coming with a surge of adrenaline, Eden tumbled him off her and almost scrambled clear. But he caught her blouse and tried to yank her back. This time Eden ignored the sound of tearing cloth and jerked free.

She struggled to her feet, the blanket slipping and sliding beneath her. She chanced a look back and saw Jeff rising up, blood gushing from his nose.

'You little bitch, when I get my hands on you, I'll kill you.'

She believed him. Holding back a sob, Eden broke into a run. She had to get away; it was the one clear thought. The truck. If she could make it to Jeff's pickup, she had a chance.

20

Kincade remained on the edge of the bed, his body angled toward Eden. She stood at the window, her staring eyes fixed on some distant point outside. There was little expression in her face, and even less in her low voice. Yet, beneath the swaddling folds of sheet, her body was stiff, almost rigid, and her fingers whitely gripped the heavy drapery fabric.

'It was like a nightmare,' Eden murmured. 'Jeff was gaining on me. Yet the harder I ran, the slower my legs seemed to move and the pickup didn't seem any closer. When I did reach it, I was so scared and shaky, I fumbled with the handle and just barely got in and locked the door before Jeff grabbed the handle. I heard him yanking on it and scooted over to lock the passenger side, then started looking for the key – behind the visor, under the floor mat, in the ash tray. Suddenly Jeff tapped on the window. I looked out and saw him laughing and dangling the keys. It was a horribly evil laugh.'

Kincade saw the faint, involuntary shudder that quivered through her. He felt a stir of anger rising again and fought it down.

'When I saw him put the key in the door lock, I panicked and threw myself at the passenger door. I knew if I could get out the other side before he got the door open – but he grabbed my leg. I kept kicking at him, but he wouldn't let go. He dragged me across the seat, telling me all the vile and filthy things he was going to do to me. That's when . . .' Her voice wavered and she stopped and closed her eyes as if to shut out the memory of what happened next. Her digging fingers balled more of the heavy drape into her hand.

Kincade waited, giving her time to collect herself before she resumed. But even after she opened her eyes, the silence continued. Kincade quietly prompted her with a question. 'Jeff had a gun in his truck, didn't he? Was it a rifle or a handgun?'

The sound of his voice brought her head up. Eden looked at him for a moment, then turned back to the window.

'A rifle,' she replied at last. 'He had two hanging on the rack in his back window.'

She released the drape, letting it fall as she swung away from the window. The room's shadows thickened again, further concealing her face. When she spoke again there was a rehearsed quality to her words. Kincade suspected they were words she'd had to repeat endless times.

'I don't remember grabbing it. I don't remember pulling the trigger. I only remember the way Jeff laughed when he saw it – then the explosion and the look of shock on Jeff's face.'

'You had no choice, Eden.'

'No, there wasn't a choice,' she agreed with a small, troubled shake of her head. 'The bullet struck him in the chest. He wasn't dead, but – he needed help and he needed it quick. I tried to stop the bleeding.'

Eden looked down at her hands, remembering the warm, wet feel of his blood on them, the distinctive odor of it, and that overwhelming sense that his life was flowing out of him, defying her every effort to keep it in. She dragged in a long breath.

'Somehow I managed to get Jeff in the truck. Which proves, I suppose, that when you are very afraid, you can do things you wouldn't normally have the strength to do. It was too far to town, but Spur was only seven miles away. It was the longest seven miles I ever drove . . .'

The ranch buildings loomed as solid black shapes just beyond the stab of the headlight beams. The house was dark, not a single light showing. Gulping back a sob of relief, Eden lay on the horn, sending out one long blast, then punched it again and again in a series of short, staccato cries for help.

Lights blinked on in the house as she slowed the truck and came to a careful stop near the front porch. She honked the horn one more time and switched off the motor, leaving the headlights on. She cast an anxious glance at Jeff, lying so still on the seat, then pushed out of the truck, and ran for the house.

Just as she reached the porch steps, her grandfather came out of the house, hurriedly pulling his suspenders over his undershirt, his grizzled hair going every which way.

'What the hell's going on out here?' He frowned when he saw Eden. 'What are you doing out here? I thought you were in your room asleep.'

She shook off his questions. 'You've got to get a doctor, an ambulance. He's been shot—'

'Who's been shot? Vince?' He bulled his way past her and headed straight for the truck.

'It isn't Vince.' Eden ran after him, reaching him as he opened the passenger door and peered in, the dome light clearly illuminating Jeff's deathly pale face and the darkening blood stains all over the front of his shirt. 'It's—'

'The DePard boy. Duke's little brother.' He shot Eden a quick look, the thick brush of his heavy eyebrows drawing together to form a solid line. Then he bent his long frame and climbed halfway in the cab.

'He's bleeding bad,' Eden said when he bent over him. 'I tried to stop it, but . . .'

Jed backed out of the truck and turned, a stunned and hopeless look on his face. 'He's dead.'

'No.' Numbly, Eden shook her head, needing to deny it. 'You're wrong. You've got to be wrong. He's alive. I tell you, he's alive!'

Frantic, she tried to push past him into the cab, but her grandfather caught her back and turned her away from it.

'He's dead, Eden,' he repeated.

'No.' Her voice broke into a sob.

'I went a little crazy then,' Eden admitted. 'I started crying and screaming. Jed, my grandfather, slapped me a couple times. I was hysterical,' she said in defense of her grandfather's actions.

'And someone saw your grandfather strike you.' Kincade shook his head, seeing how something so innocent had gotten twisted into something sinister. 'That's where the idea came that your grandfather had roughed you up to make it look like Jeff had assaulted you.'

'Yes,' Eden nodded. 'As soon as I settled down, Jed asked me what happened, and I told him that Jeff had tried to rape me. He wanted to know how I'd come to be with Jeff . . . That's when Vince came out of the house. Jed told him to take me inside.'

'Then Vince was already home.'

She hesitated an instant, then nodded. 'Yes, Vince got

there a few minutes before I did. He and Rebecca had quarreled so he had taken her straight home and come back. Later the sheriff and his deputies arrived – and the ambulance. Lot started questioning me—'

'Lot Williams was sheriff then?'

'Yes. He made me tell him what happened over and over and over.' Eden shook her head, recalling the way he had tried to twist things, make them into something different, make them sound like it was all her fault, that she had led Jeff on, let him think it was what she wanted.

'You didn't have an attorney present? Did he read you your rights?'

'He did, yes. But I didn't think I needed a lawyer, so when Jed told me to answer his questions, I did. It wasn't murder, and I didn't know how he could say that it was.'

'But he did.'

'Everyone did. Duke DePard made sure of that.'

'Not everyone. The jury believed you.'

'True.' Her smile was long and full of irony.

'It's over, Eden.'

'No.' She sighed. 'DePard won't let it be over. He wants me to pay and pay and pay.' She rubbed a hand over her sheeted arm, her skin crawling with the memory of Jeff's hands on her. She felt dirty and unclean again, just as she had that night. And just as that night, she wanted nothing more than to scrub away the sensation. 'Excuse me.' She walked to the adjoining bath.

Kincade watched the door close behind her. He heard the snap of the lock and stood a moment longer. He sensed there was more to the story than Eden had told him, but it could wait. He went to the window and threw open the drapes, letting the morning sunlight flood the room.

He stared at the traffic below. Vince was out there

somewhere, but for the first time in a long, long while, Vince didn't dominate his thoughts. Eden did. He told himself he shouldn't care what happened to her, but it was too late. He already did.

The bathroom door muffled the sudden rush of water in the shower, reducing the sound to a low but distinctive murmur. Hearing it, Kincade had an instant image of Eden standing beneath the spray, hands lifted, her face turned up to it, and the water streaming down her.

His mouth came together in a hard, taut line, a muscle flexing in his jaw and cheek. With a restless swing, he turned from the window and headed for the door, pausing long enough to pick up the dirty clothes on the floor.

Ten minutes later there was no more sound of water gushing from the showerhead. Fully clothed now with a clean shirt tucked into his jeans, Kincade rolled a cigar between his lips. A ravel of blue smoke curled from its tip. The plush carpet absorbed the tread of his boots as he made a slow circle of the suite's sitting room.

The jingling of the telephone pulled him around. In two strides he was at the writing desk, the receiver in his hand.

'Hey, Kincade, it's me.' Rusty's voice came over the line. 'Any luck?'

'None. You?'

'In a way. I started asking questions. I figured if our boy was a regular in this town, somebody had to know him. Sure enough, I was right.'

Kincade searched for some sense of elation. It wasn't there. 'Who is it? Where can we find him?'

'He's a blackjack dealer at the Nugget, works the evening shift. His first name is Max, or something like that. He's close to six foot, slender – about one hundred sixty-seventy pounds or so. His hair is dark, parted in the middle, and slicked back. He has a long handlebar mustache. The cocktail waitress said we can't miss him. Just look for a guy who resembles Snidely Whiplash, and that's our man.'

'Sounds easy. Maybe too easy.' Kincade laid his cigar in an ashtray and jotted down the description on a hotel notepad.

'Yeah, I know. But there's no guarantee Vince has touched base with this guy since he got in town. Hell, there's no guarantee Vince is still in Reno.'

'Something tells me he is.'

'We'll see. I know I've called every hotel, motel, and two-bit inn in town, so save your quarters. He isn't registered at any of them, at least not under his own name.'

'That doesn't surprise me.'

'Me either,' Rusty replied. 'Anyway, I plan to be at the Nugget when the evening shift comes on duty just in case Vince shows up with this Max guy.'

'I'll meet you there.'

'I wouldn't if I were you. Vince will be watching for you, but he won't be looking for me. The way I figure it, if he doesn't show up at the Nugget, maybe I can get his friend to give me a line on where he might be. Hopefully, without arousing his suspicion.'

Kincade was forced to concede, 'That's probably the best way to handle it.'

'I think so. Just stick close to the hotel so I can get word to you in a hurry if I turn up something.'

'All right.'

'I'm going to catch me a couple hours of sleep,' Rusty said and gave Kincade the number of his motel. 'Talk to you later. Take care.'

'You, too.' Kincade hung up.

'That was your partner, wasn't it?'

He turned. Eden stood in the doorway to her room,

her hair still wet from the shower, a terry cloth robe provided by the hotel tied around her, and a scrubbed-clean glow to her face.

'It was Rusty.' Kincade tore off the sheet with his notes, folded it and slipped it into the breast pocket of his shirt.

'Did he find Vince?' She was motionless, a tension in every line. Which told Kincade that she also believed her brother was still in Reno.

'Not yet.' He gave her a long, considering look. 'Does the name Max mean anything to you?'

'Max?' she repeated as if it were important that she had understood him correctly.

'That's right. Max.'

'No, it doesn't mean anything to me. Is Vince supposed to know him?' She tipped her head to one side.

Kincade smiled. 'I would hate to play poker with you, Eden. Sometimes you don't let your expression give anything away.' But the very fact that she had not let any reaction show in her face made him wonder. If she didn't know this Max, why conceal it?

'I don't know what you're talking about.'

'No?' He lifted an eyebrow, amused.

'No, I—' She was interrupted by a knock at the door.

'Room Service,' came the muffled announcement.

'I ordered breakfast. I thought you might be hungry.' Kincade crossed to the door.

A white-jacketed waiter wheeled the serving cart into the suite. 'Afternoon, Mr Harris. Good to have you back with us. Got a gorgeous day out there for you.' He saw Eden in the doorway and flashed her a smile. 'Afternoon, ma'am.' She nodded in response and slid a hand up the front of her robe, clutching it together near her throat. 'Where would you like me to set this up for you, Mr Harris?'

'Over there will be fine.' Kincade indicated a clear area near the writing desk.

'Right.' He nodded and pushed the cart into place. With practiced efficiency, the waiter snapped the table leaves up, arranged the place settings, and retrieved the hot food from the warming ovens below. Delicious aromas of crisp bacon, freshly brewed coffee, and yeasty breads filled the sitting room. 'Want me to pour the coffee, Mr Harris?'

'We'll take care of it.' Kincade signed the check and handed it back. 'Thanks.'

'No problem. Just call when you're through and we'll clear all this out for you.' He headed for the door. 'Enjoy your breakfast.'

Kincade locked the door behind him and turned back. Eden still stood in the bedroom doorway. 'Better come eat before it gets cold.' He pulled a chair out for himself and sat down.

Eden walked over and took a seat, her glance running over the table appointments, taking note of the white tablecloth, the glass stemware, the individual salt and pepper shakers, and the crystal bud vase with a single pink rose and a spray of baby's breath.

'Do they usually do all this when you order a meal in your room?' She touched a velvety rose petal.

'At the better hotels they do.' Idly he looked over the table, trying to see it through her eyes. He had spent too many years living out of hotels. He had long ago ceased being impressed by such amenities.

'It's nice.' She unfolded a mauve napkin and laid it across her lap.

'It is.' With his fork, Kincade cut into the poached eggs, mixing them into the bed of corned beef hash. 'How's your breakfast?' he asked after she had taken a bite.

'Very good. And you were right – I am hungry.'

'I figured you would be. I knew I was.' When she made no reply other than a nod, Kincade let the silence stretch for a time and concentrated on his breakfast, taking the edge off his hunger. 'Want to tell me the rest of what happened?'

'The rest?' Startled by his question, Eden looked up.

'Yes, the rest. Given what you told me, there wasn't sufficient evidence to charge you with murder. Suspicion isn't enough. There had to be something more.' Kincade buttered a slice of toasted sourdough bread while continuing to keep one eye on her.

'Rebecca Saunders,' she said, then explained. 'One of the deputies had seen Jeff with her that night. It turned out Rebecca had led everyone, including her father, to believe that she had a date with Jeff that night, not Vince. And that's what she told the sheriff when he questioned her. After she found out Jeff was dead, she made up this whole story about how Vince and I had barged in on them – and how upset and jealous I was because Jeff was with her. She claimed that Jeff had insisted she let Vince take her home so he could cool me down.'

'And when Vince said differently, the sheriff decided he was lying to protect you,' Kincade guessed.

'Rebecca was very convincing.' Eden broke off a piece of toast and held it. 'I think people wanted to believe her anyway.'

'So, what happened? Did Rebecca eventually change her story?'

'Are you kidding?' Eden showed the first trace of real bitterness. 'She found out how beneficial it was to stick to her story.'

Kincade frowned. 'What do you mean by that?'

'I mean that within a month after Jeff died, Rebecca's father had the bypass operation he had been needing, paid for by DePard. A little later their house was painted and fixed up, the children had new clothes for school, and Rebecca had a big, new car to drive her father back and forth to the doctor for his checkups and therapy – all of it thanks to DePard. She had discovered her own silver lode and she mined it for every dime she could get.' Eden poked at her eggs with a fork. 'Even if she wanted to, she couldn't have told the truth. It had gone too far.' She shook her head at the memory and suppressed a little shudder. 'If she had testified against me at the trial, I would probably be in prison now.'

'She didn't?'

'No. She was killed in a car accident two months before my case went to court.'

'What happened when you met privately with DePard?'

Her fork slipped from her fingers and clattered onto the plate. 'How did you know about that?'

'It just stands to reason.' Kincade lifted the insulated carafe of coffee and poured coffee for both of them. 'I know if I were DePard and you were accused of killing my brother and the sheriff was a cousin of mine, I would demand to meet you face-to-face.'

'He did,' Eden admitted. 'That morning right after Jeff died, while I was still in jail . . .'

A single, bare light bulb enclosed by a wire cage cast a stark glare over the small cell. Eden had prowled its narrow confines endlessly since she had been locked into it . . . and prowled dangerously close to the outer limits of her sanity in the process. She sat now, cross-legged in the middle of the cot, her arms clasped tightly around her waist.

The woman in the next cell moaned loudly, as she had done for most of the night – when she wasn't vomiting or shouting obscenities at the deputy on duty, that is.

The woman hadn't been sick for several hours, but the smell of it still lingered in the air.

Between the strangeness of the jail, the noises of it, and the nightmare of events that had led up to it, sleep had almost been impossible. Eden was exhausted and scared, her nerves stretched thin. Now for the first time, tears welled in her eyes. She blinked them away.

Bolts clanged, springing open with a sharp sound that raced through Eden like a high voltage electrical charge. Half hopeful and half fearful, she looked toward the barred door that separated the cells from the rest of the jail's facilities. The heavy metal door swung open. Lot Williams walked through and approached her cell, an ominous echo to his footsteps. Without a word, he inserted a key in the lock to her cell.

Instantly she scrambled off the cot. 'Am I being released? Can I go home now?'

'Stay back.' He snapped the order and Eden halted instantly, brought up short by the harshness of his voice. Satisfied, he opened her cell door and motioned her forward. 'You have a visitor.'

A smile of relief broke across her face. 'It's my grandfather, isn't it? He's come to take me home.'

He gave her a cold, silencing look. 'Come with me.' He gripped her arm just above the elbow and propelled her ahead of him.

Beyond the locked inner door, he steered her down a succession of corridors, then jerked her to a stop in front of an unmarked door. Still keeping a tight grip on her arm, he reached around, turned the knob and gave the door a push inward.

'In here,' he said and thrust her inside.

Sunlight flooded the room, and the brightness of it hurt her eyes after the hours she had spent in the dim cell. She flinched from it and threw up a hand to block its blinding glare, catching a brief glimpse of a big wooden desk and an empty office chair behind it.

'I'll be waiting outside. Let me know when you're through,' the sheriff said.

Eden looked back as he pulled the door closed, thinking he was talking to her. Then she caught the fragrance of an expensive masculine cologne and swung back to face the room. She stared in shock at Duke DePard.

He stared back. Pain was etched in every rugged line of Duke DePard's face; his eyes were dark and stormy with it. He stood rigid near a corner of the desk. Eden could feel the animosity pouring from him in waves.

'Have a seat, Miss Rossiter.' He extended a hand, palm upward, to indicate a vacant straight-backed wooden chair.

She didn't want to see him; she wanted to turn and run. Instead, Eden walked numbly to the chair and sat down, tightly lacing her fingers together on her lap.

Conscious of the grief DePard had to be feeling at Jeff's death, Eden felt she had to say something. 'I'm . . . I'm so sorry—' she began.

'Not as sorry as you're going to be. Not by half!' Duke snapped. A grief-born fury rumbled up from somewhere deep inside him. With an effort, he directed her attention to a sheaf of papers on the desk.

'Sheriff Williams has given me your rather sensationalized account of last night's events.' He glanced at the notes in his hand, then back at Eden.

She wished she were smaller, small enough to curl up and hide in some corner until all this went away. Please, God, she didn't want to have to answer these questions.

DePard lifted the notes, indicating them. 'All this must have been very traumatic for you. It's easy to see how you might become frightened and panic, feel compelled to twist things around. You see, Miss

Rossiter, I have already learned that you are not telling the truth.'

Panic clawed at her throat. 'What do you mean? Who told you that?'

'The sheriff spoke with Rebecca Saunders. She was the one who had a date with Jeff last night – not you.'

'No. She was my brother's date. It's true Jeff picked her up, but—'

'Please. She has no reason to lie, while you most certainly do. That's why you made up this lurid story claiming my brother attempted to force himself on you.'

'But he did,' Eden insisted. 'He hit me and held me down and tried to—'

'That's a goddamned lie.' Duke vibrated with anger, his big hands doubled into clenched fists at his side. 'Jeff would never harm a woman. Everybody knows that.' He struggled again to control his temper. 'To put it quite crudely, any number of women would have been more than willing to spread their legs for him, and Jeff knew it. He would never resort to rape.'

'But he did.' Eden felt totally defenseless, and battled to hold back the sobs rising in her throat. 'Can't you understand? I never wanted him to die. I tried to save him. I tried to get help.'

'But you failed. Jeff is dead,' DePard stated, blunt and hard. 'All the remorse and regret in the world will not bring him back. But if you are truly sorry for what you've done, you will not destroy his name with these lies.'

'They aren't lies!'

'They are, and I can prove it. If you persist with this vicious story you will be the one who will be ruined. Do you understand me?'

Eden was stunned into silence, not by DePard's threat, but by the malevolence in his expression, the venom in his voice.

'Fortunately,' DePard continued, adopting a more reasonable tone, 'no one other than Sheriff Williams and myself knows anything about this damaging account of yours. There is still time for you to retract it.'

'Retract it?' Eden wiped at the wet tear-tracks on her face, accidentally rubbing the bruised and swollen flesh where Jeff had hit her.

'Exactly.' DePard tossed the notes on the desk and sat back on his chair. 'Everyone knows Jeff was a gun buff. He loved to hunt and target shoot. It would be very likely that last night he showed you the new rifle he received this past Christmas. Perhaps he even set up a few beer cans and used them for targets to show how proficient he was. Maybe he let you try it and at some point something went wrong. Perhaps you thought the rifle wasn't loaded or that the safety was on when the gun *accidentally* discharged.'

Eden looked at him. 'You want me to say the shooting was an accident?'

DePard nodded. 'A terrible, tragic mishap of the sort that happens much too often, even to someone experienced in the use of guns. After Sheriff Williams completes his investigation, I'm quite sure Jeff's death will be ruled accidental and no charges will be filed against you. First, of course, you must tell the sheriff the *correct* story.'

'What about Rebecca and the things she said?'

'I am confident Rebecca Saunders can be persuaded to cooperate,' DePard stated. 'Are you going to change your story or not?'

'I . . . I don't know.' Tired and confused, Eden wanted to talk to her grandfather, to Vince, to someone who could advise her what to do. 'I need to think.'

'You don't have time to think.' DePard came out of his chair, impatient and annoyed, and showing it. 'I must have your decision immediately. There are already reporters outside from every newspaper and television station in the state, clamoring for details, demanding to know the circumstances surrounding the death of Nevada's star quarterback. I can't keep quiet about this much longer. So make up your mind, and make it up now!'

When she hesitated, DePard warned, 'You will gain nothing by waiting. I swear, the instant any word leaks to them of your claim that Jeff assaulted you, the deal is off.' His hand slashed through the air in a gesture of absolute finality. As it completed its upward stroke, DePard pointed an accusing finger at her. 'Or is that your plan? To sell your story to one of them?'

Eden was shocked into a denial. 'No!'

'Don't play games with us.' DePard took an angry step closer to Eden's chair. 'How much do you want? Ten thousand? Twenty?'

'I don't want any money from you,' Eden protested, indignant that he would even think that.

Suddenly he towered over her. 'Fifty thousand and that is my final offer,' DePard threatened. 'You take it, and you change your story, or I swear by everything that's holy, you'll regret it. You'll find yourself without a single friend in this county. And before I'm through, you'll be tried for sure and spend the rest of your life in prison!'

Eden broke off her sightless stare into the past and looked at Kincade, then immediately dropped her glance. 'His voice kept getting louder and his face got angrier. The accusations, the insults, the threats – after all I'd already been through, they became too much. I started yelling back, telling him that just because he was wealthy and powerful, that didn't mean he could buy me off or threaten me into silence. I said a lot of other things along that same line,' Eden admitted. 'I was seventeen and scared – and horribly idealistic, I suppose. I thought the truth would vindicate me.'

'In an ideal world, it would have,' Kincade said over the rim of his coffee cup.

'But this isn't an ideal world, is it?' Eden countered sardonically, then sighed. 'Anyway, after the sheriff took me back to my cell, I was in such a state that I ended up crying myself to sleep. When I woke up a few hours later, the story was out.'

'And, needless to say, DePard had withdrawn his offer.'

'Yes. Looking back, I know I should have accepted the deal. If I had, I would have escaped all the name-calling and notoriety of the trial. I would have been free to live my life without being constantly harried at every turn by DePard. As it is . . .' She let the words trail off.

'I have the feeling that, deep down, you aren't really sorry you didn't take it.'

'I suppose not. Lies aren't easy to live with either.' She placed her napkin on the table. 'Breakfast was good. If you'll excuse me, I need to dry my hair and get dressed.'

Kincade rose when she did. He remained standing while she crossed the room. When she disappeared inside her bedroom, he walked over to a chair and picked up the shopping bag he had left there, then headed for her door.

She opened it just as he got there. 'Where are my clothes?'

'They were dirty so I sent them out to be cleaned. They'll be back by six tonight. In the meantime you can wear these.' He handed her the shopping bag. 'I had to guess at some of the sizes, but I think they'll all work. If something doesn't fit, I can exchange it.'

'You bought me clothes?' She looked surprised.

'I didn't think you would want to sit around all

afternoon in that robe,' he replied with a teasing smile. 'Go ahead. Try them on, see if they fit.'

Fifteen minutes later, Eden emerged from the bed-room, all woman and looking it. The dress Kincade had chosen was a simple cotton knit, dyed a vibrant royal blue and belted at the waist, with push-up sleeves and a wide flaring skirt.

'How does it look?' She stood before him.

Kincade ran an admiring eye over the result. 'The dress looks fine and *you* look beautiful. How does it feel?'

'Different.' Eden felt feminine in it, vulnerable. She didn't think she liked that. 'Actually, I haven't worn heels and a dress since—' She deliberately didn't finish the thought.

'Since the trial, right?' Kincade guessed.

'Yes.' She smoothed a hand down the front of it in a self-conscious gesture. 'Why did you buy a dress? Why didn't you get jeans or slacks and a top?'

'Three reasons. With a dress, I didn't have to worry about length, the belt would cover up any minor mistake in size, and the last reason is purely selfish,' he told her. 'When a woman has legs as beautiful as yours, it's a sin to hide them in jeans.'

If Eden had been the type to blush, Kincade suspected her cheeks would have been flaming now. As it was, she looked uncomfortable and wary.

Kincade gathered up his hat. 'Ready to go?'

In answer, Eden walked over to join him. 'I take it we're off to tour the casinos again looking for Vince.'

'Rusty's handling that. Your brother will be watching for me, not him,' he explained. 'I thought we'd go get some fresh air.'

21

Side by side, they left the hotel and walked straight into a swirling wind. It whipped at the hem of Eden's dress and tunneled under it, lifting the material and threatening to send it flying up about her face. Hurriedly Eden battled the billowing skirt down. The wind swept on down the street, its playfulness thwarted.

Eden shot a glance at Kincade and saw the lazy, wicked gleam in his eyes. 'Things like that don't happen when I wear jeans,' she said in criticism of his clothes choice.

'More's the pity,' he drawled and opened the pickup's passenger-side door for her.

She laughed in response, startling herself. Her guard was down. Probably because she had told him so much, even some things she had never confided to Vince. Maybe it was wrong, even unwise, but at the moment she didn't care. Selfishly she wanted to enjoy herself, fully aware it was likely to last.

Kincade drove to a city park a short distance from downtown Reno and went straight to an area on the park grounds that had kiddie rides. With tickets in hand, he guided Eden to the carousel.

Hampered by the dress's skirt, Eden raised no

objection when he lifted her onto the back of a prancing steed, sitting her sidesaddle on it. Round and round they went, taped calliope music filling the air with its happy sound.

Afterward they ate cotton candy and laughed at the stickiness the pink clouds of spun sugar left on their hands and faces. They watched the antics of the children and of one round-eyed youngster in particular as he took his first ride on the miniature roller coaster. Later, armed with bags of popcorn, they wandered to the pond to feed the ducks.

Kincade spent most of his time watching Eden. The ducks swarmed around her, flapping their wings and quacking their hungry demands. Laughing at their greediness, Eden tossed popcorn to them, making sure the more timid ones in the back received their share of bounty, and crouching down to feed the bolder ones from her hand.

He studied the smile on her lips and the carefree look she wore. He put those there. A whole host of feelings swelled inside him. Pride, tenderness, and desire among them.

When Eden scooped the last of the popcorn from the bottom of her sack, Kincade made certain his own bag was empty. 'Sorry, guys, but it's all gone.' She straightened from her crouched position and wadded up the empty sack. 'You'll have to find some other generous soul to feed you.' The ducks immediately fell to inspecting the ground, searching for any tidbit they might have overlooked. Eden turned to Kincade, sunlight flashing on the pond's smooth surface behind her. 'Greedy little devils, aren't they?'

'Noisy, too,' Kincade observed when the flock of ducks took off in a quacking waddle straight for a little blond-haired four year old with a bag of popcorn.

'Very,' Eden agreed. 'But it was still fun.'

'It was.' But Kincade knew he hadn't enjoyed it for the same reason she had. As they started away from the pond, the heel of her sandaled pump sank into the soft ground, tipping her off balance. Before she could recover on her own, his hands had caught her and pulled her to him.

Gripping his shoulders for support, Eden glanced up and the laughing comment died on her lips at the look in his eyes. She could feel the sudden and heavy thump of her heart in her chest. His hands settled more comfortably on her waist, strong and warm, without demand. Slowly he lowered his lips toward hers, giving Eden the opportunity to avoid the contact. When she felt the moist heat of his breath, she almost did.

'Do you know your lips are still sticky?' he murmured against them, his mouth curving.

Remembering that moment of shared laughter over the cotton candy's messiness, Eden smiled as well. 'I'm not surprised,' she whispered back, conscious of her voice being swallowed by him.

'I like it.' He grinned and she was lost, desperate to believe this was all innocent and carefree – the romantically harmless kind she had been denied in her life. She wanted to be young and trusting again, the way she had been before that night with Jeff. Just for a moment. Only a moment.

When his mouth increased its pressure, slanting across hers, she responded to it. Desire fluttered, tremulous and uncertain. She was afraid of it, more than him. Afraid of where it would lead, and what it might destroy.

The response took Kincade by surprise, because he hadn't forced it from her; she had given it freely. It was all he could do to keep from going back for more. But even if she wasn't, he was conscious of the people around them. He drew back, his hands tightening on her waist to hold her away.

'Ready to go?'

She gave him a blank look. 'What?'

His mouth crooked in an understanding smile. 'I wondered if you were ready to leave – head somewhere else.'

It took a second for his words to register. Her thoughts were still full of the kiss. She had enjoyed it. Perhaps too much. 'I'm ready whenever you are,' she said with a shrug.

'Let's go.' Releasing her, he reached for her hand and lightly gripped it to lead her back to the truck.

With the sun slowly sliding toward Peavine Mountain, Kincade followed a back road that curled into the foothills. The radio was on, tuned to a country station, making conversation unnecessary. There was a comfortable silence between them. Kincade didn't question it, just as he didn't question how completely he had blocked Vince Rossiter from his mind.

The route eventually brought them to another park on the outskirts of town with a stunning overview of the city. Leaving the pickup in a parking lot, they walked a few feet down a slope. Kincade shook out an old Indian blanket he kept behind his truck seat. He helped her onto the blanket, then stretched out beside her, plucking a seed stalk and chewing on the end of it.

'What a view.' Eden gazed at the city-sprawl of high-rises and homes.

'Reno at your feet.'

For a moment Eden took advantage of the silence to study him. He sat propped on an elbow, his long legs sprawled in front of him. Against the bronze of his skin, the pale track of an old scar stood out whitely on his temple.

He gazed at the city below with that same quiet intensity she had seen in him before. At times she had the feeling he was two different men. One moment he was gentle and almost teasing, and the next, he could be cold and iron-hard. She found herself wanting to know more about him. It was a dangerous curiosity, but she couldn't pull back from it.

'Where are you from, Kincade?'

'Texas.' He rolled the grass stem to a corner of his mouth.

She smiled at his noninformative answer. 'Where in Texas?'

'A half-dozen different places. Probably more than that if I took the time to count.' His mouth curved slightly. 'I was born in Waco, went to kindergarten in Amarillo. I think we moved outside Sweetwater after that. My dad worked for various ranchers, sometimes as a hired hand, sometimes as foreman or stock manager. He'd leave one job to get better pay, then leave it to have better hours, or better benefits. Don't get me wrong,' he said with a quick glance. 'I never minded the moving. In fact I liked having new horses to ride, new territory to explore, new friends to meet. Once we hit high school Dad made sure he didn't take a job that would mean moving out of that school district. It was mostly for Marcie's sake, though.'

'Marcie was your sister,' Eden guessed. 'I'll bet she was a barrel-racer. Did she go out on the rodeo circuit with you?'

'Marcie never liked horses.' Kincade pulled the seed stalk from his mouth and sat up, bending his knees and resting his arms on them while he started plucking at the stalk, tearing off bits and discarding them. 'She was always afraid of horses even when she was little. Given a choice she always walked or rode her bike. She didn't like to go near a horse especially after—' He clamped his mouth shut, grimness pulling at the corners.

'After what?'

He threw her a hard look, then turned and tossed the grass stem away. 'She took a bad fall when she was eight and wound up with a crippled left leg. It was my fault.'

'What happened?'

He was a long time answering. 'We were living outside of Big Springs in an old house on the Bar Six, where my dad worked. It was one of those hot September days in Texas. After school, Marcie and I went to the creek about two miles from the house to splash around and cool off. She rode her bike and I took the bay gelding the foreman had said I could ride. His name was Rocky. Anyway, we got to playing and fooling around and lost track of time. Suddenly there was the sun going down. We were supposed to be home before dark. That was one rule our parents strictly enforced. Marcie and I both knew we would be in big trouble if we didn't make it. You never saw two kids move as fast as we did, pulling on our shoes, grabbing up our clothes. That's when we discovered her bike had a flat tire. She wanted to push it home and I wanted her to ride double with me. We started arguing. I called her a scaredy cat and a chicken for being afraid of horses, which didn't help at all. She tried to convince me to go home without her, but I knew I'd be in bigger trouble if I left her out there alone with night coming. I finally talked Marcie into riding back with me, but she said I had to promise not to go fast.'

'Promise not to go fast,' Kincade repeated the phrase in a voice bitter with regret. 'Those words were like a dare.' His mouth twisted in a humorless line. 'What do you suppose it is about older kids that make them delight in tormenting their younger sisters and brothers?'

'I don't know, but they do.' Eden spoke from experience. As an older brother, Vince had been far from an angel at times. 'It's almost like a game to them. They aren't intentionally cruel – just playing at it.'

Kincade nodded. 'I only wanted to scare Marcie a little – that's all. When she started screaming for me to stop, I just made Rocky go faster. I never thought Marcie would have the guts to let go of the saddlehorn and grab at the reins. Unfortunately she only got hold of one, but she pulled that horse's head around so fast and so hard that we were going down almost before I realized what she'd done. I bailed off before we hit the ground, but Marcie went down with the horse.'

'That's when she hurt her leg.'

'Smashed it to pieces. Literally.' He reached over and scooped up a handful of coarse sand near the blanket's edge. 'Most of the soil on the ranch was like this. It would have given under the impact, cushioned her fall. But we went down in one of the few rocky stretches. Her leg was crushed between half a ton of horse and solid rock.'

His hand closed into a fist around the sand as he looked up at the sky, a sheen of moisture in his eyes. 'Before that day, I didn't know what it was to be scared – not deep-down, sick-in-the-gut, shaking-all-over scared. By the time I shook off the effects of the tumble, I went back to make sure she was all right, too. The horse was already up, but Marcie was lying there, not moving. I took one look at her leg and threw up. Some tough guy, huh?' he said in self scorn.

'Kincade.' She laid a hand on his arm, wanting to comfort, to take some of the pain.

'I knew she needed help, but I couldn't leave her. I was scratched and skinned up in a couple places. So I took my handkerchief and smeared blood over it, then tied it to the saddle horn and gave the horse a slap for home.'

'That was clever.'

Kincade dismissed it with an impatient, half-irritated shrug. 'It was dark before they found us. I don't know how much longer it was before the ambulance came. Or how many operations Marcie ended up having. She was in and out of hospitals for the next three years. They said she was lucky to come out of it with only a bad limp.'

'You were a boy.'

'Right, and that excuses everything.' Kincade dumped the sand on the ground and brushed his hands off, then rolled to his feet and held out a hand to her. 'What do you say we go have dinner? That cotton candy wasn't exactly filling.'

'Sure.'

The unspoken message was clear: His sister was a closed subject, not to be reopened. Now or later.

In an atmosphere redolent of Old San Francisco, with heavy woods, gleaming chandeliers, and secluded tables, Eden and Kincade dined on steaks while a harpist played songs of love and longing. They talked about everything and nothing – and stayed clear of more serious and potentially touchy topics like Vince.

The plates were cleared and the waiter returned, picking up the nearly empty wine bottle and turning to Eden. 'No more for me, thank you.' She placed her fingers over her wine glass, still half full of ruby-red wine.

He topped off Kincade's glass, emptying the bottle. 'Anything else, sir? A cognac, perhaps?'

Kincade shook his head. 'Just the check.'

'Right away.' With a slight bow, the waiter retreated, taking the empty wine bottle with him.

Kincade took a cigar from his pocket, then hesitated, glancing at Eden. 'Do you mind?'

'Not at all.' She smiled a permission and lifted her glass.

He placed the cigar between his lips, struck a match, and held the flame close to the tip, drawing the fire to it. Smoke trailed fragrantly into the still air as he looked at Eden, aware of the building silence.

The candlelight flickered over her face, accenting the

faint hollows of her cheeks. She held the wine glass in both hands, staring into it in a preoccupied fashion.

'You've grown very quiet all of a sudden,' Kincade observed. 'Something wrong?'

She looked up with a slight start and shook her head, forcing a smile. 'Just thinking.'

'About what?'

'I was supposed to join the crew at Big Timber Canyon yesterday. They'll be wondering what happened to me.' Not to mention Vince and Kincade, but Eden deliberately didn't mention that. 'I was wishing there was a way to get word to them that everything is fine.'

Kincade started to remind her that she shouldn't have come with him, but he didn't want to refer to Vince even indirectly. 'You figured out a way to get around DePard, didn't you?' he said instead.

'I don't know what you mean.' But she stiffened a little.

He smiled. 'I think you do.'

'Well, you're wrong. I haven't a clue what you're talking about.'

'The maps. You weren't carrying them in your back pocket for no reason. Come on, what's your idea?' When she hesitated, he guessed the reason for her wariness. 'You don't have to worry about me saying anything to DePard, Eden. It's your brother who doesn't want you to get those cattle to market, not me. He thinks if you don't, you'll be forced to sell the ranch. And if that's what Vince wants, I intend to make damned sure he doesn't get it.'

'I see.' She hesitated a moment longer, then admitted, 'I *had* a plan.' She stressed the past tense. 'But with you and Vince both gone, I'm not going to be able to pull it off. Not unless I can hire more help.'

'What was the plan?' He was curious now.

She ran a finger around the rim of her wine glass, a

smile playing at the edge of her mouth. 'Take the cattle to market myself.'

'Where would you rent the trucks to haul them?'

'I wasn't going to use trucks.' She leaned forward and the candlelight caught in her eyes. 'I was going to drive them to the sale pens across the border in Oregon.'

'Drive them.' Kincade lowered his cigar, understanding dawning. 'The maps. You were checking the route.'

'Water was the critical factor. I had to make certain it would be available at the end of each day's drive. It is.'

'Why Oregon? Winnemucca is closer.'

'But that would mean crossing the Diamond D. DePard would never let me get by with that. I eliminated Lovelock, Reno, and auction barns in California for similar reasons – too much risk that word would get back to DePard and he would do something to stop me. But the route north is empty country, practically uninhabited, no towns, only two ranches, and we wouldn't come within ten miles of either one of their headquarters on the trail I plotted. There's only one highway to cross a few miles from the border, and there's hardly any traffic on it. I hung around there an hour and saw only one pickup go by. It would be a sheer accident if anyone spotted us.'

Kincade nodded. 'It could work.'

'I think it can, too.' Eden sighed and made a slight face. 'It would have been a job with six riders. Now, with only four – counting myself – I won't be able to pull it off.'

'It shouldn't be that hard to hire extra men.'

'Hopefully.'

'How long will the drive take?' Kincade asked when the waiter returned with the check.

'Ten days, give or take.'

'DePard might get suspicious when neither you or any of your crew are around for that long.' He checked the total and slipped some bills into the leather folder with the dinner tab.

'He shouldn't. That's the beauty of the plan. During fall roundup we're usually out for six weeks,' Eden explained. 'This time I planned to make it a more hit-and-miss operation – scour the areas where the water and graze are good and the highest concentration of cattle will be, and skip the rest. We may miss a hundred or more cattle that way, but we should be done in three weeks. If we use Sayer Wells on the edge of Black Rock Desert as the final gather point, then we can rest a day and throw the cattle across Black Rock Desert that night. That way no one will see our dust trail when we pull out and make the first move north.'

'You've spent some time thinking this through.' Kincade tapped his cigar out and rose, coming around the table to pull out her chair.

'I've tried.' She stood and accepted the guiding pressure of Kincade's hand at her back to steer her toward the exit. 'If it would all go the way I planned, we'd be back before DePard even knew we left. I only wish I would be able to see the look on his face when he found out what I did.'

'Revenge is sweet, right?' Kincade smiled down at her.

Eden shook her head. 'How can revenge be sweet when it turns to stone the heart of the man who commits it?'

He arched her a questioning look. 'Shakespeare?'

'No. Eden Rossiter.' She expected a smile or some amused comment. Instead she was met with silence. There was only one explanation for that. Vince.

22

Eden was relaxed again when Kincade unlocked the door to the hotel suite and stepped back to admit her. Walking in, she felt regret that this innocent time with him was winding to an end. She knew that too soon they would be at odds again over Vince.

A pair of wire hangers holding her freshly laundered shirt and sharply creased blue jeans hung on the door knob to her bedroom. Seeing them, Eden fingered the soft knit of the dress he had bought her. She turned back when he closed the door.

'I enjoyed dinner, and the afternoon.' She smiled her pleasure in it, savoring it all the more because she knew how short-lived it would be.

'I'm glad, because I did, too.' Facing her, he brought a hand up to her cheek, cupping it and stroking a thumb over the curve of it.

Eden felt the quickening inside her. She knew it was wrong, futile. Yet, she didn't move away from it. 'Should you check with the desk for messages?'

'There's no need. The telephone message light isn't on. There haven't been any calls.'

'Maybe the light isn't working,' she said, fighting a breathlessness.

'It is. I checked.' He took a step closer, his head tipping and lowering toward hers.

'No.' Eden wasn't sure what she was saying no to – herself or him.

'No what?' When his mouth whispered over hers, her heart leaped into her throat. Eden knew it was no good and turned from it.

'This is a mistake, Kincade.'

'Why?' His thumb continuing its light stroke of her cheek.

'Because.' But she knew she had to give a better reason than that. 'I don't like being touched by men.'

'Only because those touches in the past weren't loving ones.' He drew his head back, his glance softly teasing. 'And as I recall, you didn't seem to have any problem when I kissed you this afternoon.'

'That was different,' she insisted.

'Oh?' he mocked gently. 'Different, how?'

Eden turned accusing eyes on him. 'This afternoon you were satisfied with just a kiss. You want more than that now.'

'You're right. I want more,' he admitted, his expression turning serious. 'But I won't *take* more, Eden. I'm not Jeff.'

No, he wasn't Jeff. That, in itself, scared her, because she wanted to believe him. 'Is that supposed to make me trust you?' she scoffed.

'Believe it or not, you can,' he told her, his gaze steady, unwavering. 'You were thrown, Eden. Hurt in a nasty spill. Are you going to shy away from encounters with other horses? Even tame ones?'

'You aren't tame.' Inexperienced with men, she might be, but Eden knew that much about Kincade.

'But I'm broke to ride, Eden. And I respond to slightest pressure on the reins. Try me,' he urged, a small smile showing. When she hesitated, he added,

'You've got to master this sooner or later. It might as well be now.'

'I don't know if I can,' she admitted with rare candor.

'Neither one of us will ever know if you don't try.' He made it a matter of courage, a challenge that pride insisted she rise to meet.

This time Eden didn't avoid his lips when they brushed hers, then came back to cover them, warm and persuasive. His encircling arm drew her closer. She half-waited for that trapped feeling, but his hold was loose, light. A second later she forgot about it, her attention claimed by the coaxing pressure of his mouth.

He lifted his head a fraction of an inch, breaking the contact, his moist breath caressing her skin. 'This was inevitable from the first moment I saw you on the street.'

Maybe it had been inevitable from the beginning. For years Eden had managed to deny that she was missing anything, there was anything she wanted from a man. Until Kincade came along and awakened all those feelings again.

When his mouth came back onto hers again, the stirrings of hunger escaped her restraint and became part of her response. On her own, she leaned closer to him. Through the soft knit of her dress, she felt the brushing contact with his muscled thighs.

She wavered, wanting to draw back from the edge of this unexpected precipice, but Kincade chose that moment to deepen the kiss, take it to the next level. Her indecision dissolved under this heat of new longings. She rested her hands against his chest, fingers spreading across its muscled solidness as she drank in the taste, feel and smell of him.

His hand came between them, his fingers tugging

at the buttons of his shirt, popping them loose. A second later, he was shrugging out of it, giving it a toss and carrying her hands back to his naked chest an instant before his mouth claimed hers in another hot, drugging kiss.

Within seconds, she was lost in a mindless blur of sensation that swept her deeper and deeper into his embrace. Her restless hands became fascinated with the hard sinew and bone of his shoulders, his flesh warm and vital to her touch. The smell of his skin and the taste of his tongue were new and exciting, potentially addictive.

When his hand glided down her back, following the track of her spine, it sent little waves of heat lightning flashing through her nerves, recharging their sensitivity. Cool air touched her skin where her dress zipper gaped open. There was a wild fluttering in the pit of her stomach, a little bit from fear and a lot from desire.

'Kincade—' The instinct of self-preservation insisted she make some form of protest, however weak and ill-formed.

'It's my turn.' His teeth gently tugged at the lobe of her ear, but his hands had stilled their movement. 'Is that okay?'

Permission feathered from her in a whisper. 'Yes.'

She held her breath as his hands gently pushed the dress from her shoulders. The rustle of it falling to the floor added to the roar of blood in her ears.

Without giving her a chance to become conscious of her semi-nudity, Kincade lifted her into the cradle of his arms. He didn't carry Eden to her bedroom, where she had recounted the trauma of that night so many years ago. He took her to his room, a place free from the nightmare of those events. He laid her on the bed, tugged off the rest of his clothes and joined her.

Sensing her tension and uncertainty, he rolled her on

top of him, giving her the position that implied domi-
nance and control. He worked to keep his touch casual,
nonthreatening as he combed his fingers through her
hair, pushing it back from her face.

'If I do something you don't like, tell me and I'll stop,'
he murmured. 'But if there's something you want me to
do, tell me that, too. Promise?'

'Promise.' But she searched his face, trying to decide
whether she could believe him.

'For a change, why don't you kiss me,' Kincade
suggested.

Cautiously, wary of instigating something she wasn't
sure she could finish, Eden lowered her mouth to
his. Kincade took it from there, burning away any
lingering tentativeness on her part. There was none of
the roughness, just the velvet caress of his hands and
the easy intimacy of his mouth, pulling her under.

How and when her undergarments were discarded,
Eden couldn't have said. She was too busy reveling in the
sensation of flesh against flesh. His warm lips nuzzled
the valley between her breasts. When they mounted a
slope to encircle its pointed peak, her pulse skyrocketed.
In some distant corner of her mind, she realized that
Kincade was conquering her body one area at a time.

She felt helpless, something she had sworn never to
feel again, not at the hands of a man. Yet it was a battle
she wanted to lose as the heat gathered and knotted,
becoming a pressure deep within. The sweet intensity
of it bordered on pain.

At his initial thrust, she stiffened, then gasped at
the shafting pleasure. She strained for more, wrapping herself around him. Then it was all greed, on
both sides, greed that ended in a moment of explosive need.

Eden lay quiet in his arms, her body still tingling

from their love-making. She felt warm and good all over, with a new lightness of spirit.

Even as she acknowledged the welling tenderness inside, Eden sternly reminded herself it would be a mistake to let it mean too much, to think this changed anything. She would be a fool if she did.

Kincade wondered if Eden knew how she looked. Naked with one leg hooked over him, her skin warmed by that afterglow of good sex, her hair spreading over the pillow.

He wondered what she was thinking, what she was feeling. But he asked instead, 'Are you okay?'

'I'm fine.' The very quickness of her answer revealed an uneasiness with the moment.

He sensed her growing embarrassment. He wasn't about to let her become uncomfortable with the situation, or with him. He turned toward her. Immediately she started to shift away from him.

'No, you don't.' Kincade gathered her back to him and pressed a kiss on her hair. 'This is where a man and woman lay in bed all wrapped together in utter contentment, and she tells him what a wonderful lover he is.' When she remained silent, he twisted his head to look at her. 'Well?' he prompted with humor, not arrogance.

She saw the teasing light in his eyes and recognized his attempt to ease any awkwardness she might be feeling. Pride had gotten her through worse situations. She called on it now.

'You were a wonderful lover,' she replied, deliberately injecting a dutiful tone and hoping it covered some of her stiffness.

Kincade chuckled and rolled sideways to face her. 'That's what I call being damned by faint praise.' Smiling, he lifted a strand of hair and tucked it behind her ear, then traced the angle of her jaw with his fingertips.

He stopped at her chin and rubbed the pad of his thumb over her lower lip. His smile faded and the light in his eyes changed in intensity. 'You were a wonderful lover, Eden,' he murmured, and she felt a sudden tightness in her chest at the discovery of how desperately she wanted to believe him. 'Exciting, bold, greedy, and beautiful. Incredibly beautiful.'

Funny, she had felt more comfortable when he had teased her. She wanted it back. 'Am I supposed to stroke your ego now?'

'Not my ego.' He grinned and stretched closer, rubbing his mouth over hers. 'Impossible, isn't it?' he said against it. 'To want again so quickly.'

'Yes,' she whispered, feeling all the eager stirrings again.

'Love isn't always gentle, Eden.'

Even with his warning, she wasn't prepared for the assault of his kiss. It wasn't rough, it wasn't demanding. It was hot. Searing hot. Blatantly sexual. The heat flowed over her, followed by Kincade's hands. She abandoned herself to it, and to him.

Much later, as they lay in a sated tangle of arms and legs, Kincade felt a completeness holding her close to him. A feeling that was solid and profound, one that warmed him like the golden glow of a lamp in the window on a stormy night. He hadn't been looking for it. He hadn't been aware that he even wanted it.

But he knew he didn't want it to end tonight. He also didn't see how it could go on.

'I've been with more than my share of women, Eden.' He stroked her hair. 'But you need to know it was never like this for me. Not with any of them.'

'You don't have to say that.' She was still. Very still in his arms.

'I know I don't have to, sweetheart. I want to. Can you

understand that?' He rubbed his chin over the top of her head. 'I don't want you to think this was just another good time in a whole string of good times for me.'

'Is this what's known as letting a girl down gently?' Eden mocked, hurting and wishing he hadn't said anything. It would have been easier if he hadn't brought feelings into it.

In the next breath, she was flipped on her back, her arms pinned to the mattress, and Kincade loomed above her, anger and impatience darkening his face. 'Dammit, I'm serious!'

The telephone rang, and he swore again, softer but with more bitterness. Releasing her, he rolled away, swinging his legs out of bed and sitting up. Even before he picked up the phone, Kincade knew this was the call he had been subconsciously dreading.

So did Eden. She stared at his back and the roping of strong, lean muscles. Part of her wanted to smooth her hands up them and across his wide shoulders, to press against him and hold on.

'Wait a minute.' Kincade said into the phone and flipped on the bed lamp. 'Let me find something to write on.' Eden slipped off the other side of the bed and padded to the bathroom. 'Okay. Go ahead.'

After a quick wash, she donned the bathrobe hanging on the door hook and walked out. 'Slow down, Rusty. You're going too fast.'

She felt his eyes on her when she left the room to return to her own. Her head carried a little higher than normal; that was pride. Her heart ached for things that couldn't be; that was foolish.

Collecting her clothes, Eden dressed quickly. As she tugged on her boots, she heard Kincade moving about in the other bedroom. Standing, she pushed her tousled hair into some semblance of order before she jammed her hat over it.

She walked back into the suite's sitting room, conscious of the rub of starched denim against her skin. After only one afternoon in a dress, the sensation of blue jeans on her legs felt strange. Fighting the urge to pace, she waited with growing tension for Kincade to emerge from his room.

He came out, giving his shirt a final tuck inside the waistband of his Levi's. He stopped when he saw her, his glance traveling over her white shirt and creased jeans with a thoroughness that reminded Eden he had touched every inch of skin they covered.

'You know where Vince is, don't you?' She held his gaze, daring him to deny it.

His features were hard; there was no gentleness, no warmth anywhere in his face. 'Yes.' He gave her a long, measuring look. 'Does the name Axel Gray mean anything to you?'

'Yes.' Inside she railed at Vince, furious that he had hung around in Reno. He should have left. He should have pulled out long before now.

'Dammit, Eden,' Kincade exploded. 'Why the hell didn't you tell me about him? You could have saved us both a—' He broke off and swung away from her.

Saved what? Eden thought. A lot of heartache? But she agreed those words were better left unsaid.

'Vince is my brother, Kincade.'

He shot her another glaring look. 'Do you think I'm not sorry about that?' He snatched up his hat and pushed it on his head, then started for the door, digging the ignition keys from his pocket.

Eden caught him before he reached it, a hand pulling at his arm to stop him. 'Don't go after him, Kincade.' She made it a request; she wouldn't beg.

'I have to.' He steeled himself against the silent appeal in her eyes. Just as she had a loyalty to her brother, he had one to his sister. He owed this to Marcie. It was the last thing he could do for her.

'No, you don't,' Eden argued. 'You can let him be. Just forget whatever it is that he's done to you. Pretend it never happened and walk away.'

'No.'

The one-word answer stung more than all his angry shouting and swearing. 'If what we just shared really meant something to you – if you cared at all – you wouldn't do this. You'd let him go.'

'Is that why you did it?' he challenged hotly. 'Is that why you went to bed with me? So you would have something to hold over my head?'

She slapped him, and the crack of her hand across his face rang through the room like a verbal declaration of war. Seething, her eyes smarting with tears, Eden wheeled away.

'No.' Kincade grabbed her arm and spun her back, yanking her close and banding his arms around her to hold her there. She struggled but succeeded only in knocking her hat off. Kincade immediately grabbed a handful of hair and pushed her head against his shoulder.

'What happened between us was special, Eden,' he said in a voice still thickened with vibrations of anger. 'Nothing is going to destroy that. Not you, and not me.'

'By all means, let's not spoil a good time.' The sarcasm was there, mixed in with the hurt and anger.

His fingers dug into her shoulders when he set her back to arm's length. 'We made love tonight. You can't call it anything else.' He saw her hesitation and the pain in her eyes. 'Neither one of us is ready for that word. But that doesn't change it, Eden.'

'It doesn't change anything else either.'

'No, it doesn't.' Kincade relaxed his grip. 'I have to

find your brother, Eden. And you feel you have to protect him. Don't try to stop me, and I won't try to stop you, okay?' He released her and held out his hand. 'Deal?'

Eden hesitated. 'I'm coming with you.'

'I won't stop you.'

'Deal.' She shook his hand, but she didn't return his smile.

When Kincade turned to leave, she retrieved her hat, then followed him out the door. The bargain wouldn't last. Eden was convinced of that. A clash was inevitable, and when it came, all of Kincade's high words and allusions to love would go up in smoke.

Smoke. That's all it was. An attempt to blind her, to bend her to his will. While she might care about him more than she had any man, she didn't love him. She wouldn't love him.

Men were selfish. It was always their wants, their needs, their ambitions. They expected a woman to do all the compromising, all the adjusting, all the giving. As long as her wants and needs coincided with his, everything was fine. When they didn't, they fought. A woman never won those fights, not in the long run.

Eden reminded herself of all of that, and ignored the achiness in her throat as Kincade drove along the Reno streets, his profile filling her side vision. They passed into the city limits of Sparks and Kincade checked the directions he had hastily written on a slip of hotel note paper. Two blocks farther, he turned on a side street and followed it to an apartment complex.

A single lamp post threw a wide pool of light over the building's parking lot. Kincade spotted Vince's truck. Rusty's pickup was parked next to it. Kincade pulled into an empty space beside it and climbed out of the cab.

Rusty moved out of the shadows to meet him, his

face clean shaven once again, showing the multitude of freckles he had attempted to conceal beneath a beard. 'The apartment's on the top floor, third window from the left. He's up there. I saw him at the window a few minutes ago.'

Eden came around the back of the truck in time to hear the last. Rusty gave her a startled look of recognition, then turned to Kincade for an explanation. Kincade offered none.

'Eden, this is Rusty Walker, a friend of mine. Eden Rossiter.' Kincade identified her with a lift of his hand.

'Ma'am.' Rusty briefly gripped the point of his hat brim. Eden simply nodded. After a moment, Rusty turned to Kincade. 'What do you want to do? Go knock on the door?'

'Is there another way out of the building?'

'A couple of them. But even if he slips by us, he won't be able to go anywhere . . . I tinkered with his truck.'

'Good man.' Kincade grinned, then lifted his head with sharpening interest when the apartment light went out. 'Looks like Rossiter is coming to us.' He studied the openness of the parking lot and the yards beyond it, then inspected the shrubbery by the entrance closest to the parking lot. 'Considering that neither one of us has on running shoes, maybe we should meet him by the door.'

'I think you're right.'

Kincade looked at Eden. 'Are you coming?'

'Of course.' She fell in step with him, her attention focused on the building's side door and her mind searching for some way to warn Vince in time.

A pair of lantern-style lights were mounted on the brick wall flanking the door, illuminating the area immediately in front of it. The paved walkway between the entrance and the lighted parking lot lay in shadows.

When they reached it, Eden had a clear view of the lighted hallway beyond the glass door. Vince was coming toward them. She immediately made a break for the door, but Kincade caught her and pulled her off the walk into the shadows. At the same time he called to Rusty to take the other side.

'I thought you weren't going to stop me.' Eden twisted her arm, trying to break his hold on her wrist.

'From protecting him, no. But I'm not about to let you warn him.'

'How can I protect him if I can't warn him?' she shot back, her eyes spitting at him.

'That's your problem.' He watched the door.

Raging, Eden turned back as Vince came sauntering out, whistling a tuneless air. 'Vince, look out!' she shouted.

He stopped with a jerk, his glance flying to Kincade.

'Going somewhere, Rossiter?' Kincade stepped out of the shadows, drawing Eden with him and distracting Vince as Rusty slipped from behind a tall shrub and stepped between Vince and the apartment entrance.

Vince wheeled back for the door, saw the way blocked, and spun around to glare at Eden. 'You told him where to find me? How could you do that?'

'I didn't—'

Kincade broke in, 'Save your breath, Rossiter. She didn't tell us anything. She didn't have to. You aren't that hard to find. Haven't you learned that yet?'

Vince went on the attack. 'What are you doing with my sister? I swear to God, if you hurt her, I'll kill you—'

'You tried that once, remember?'

'What do you mean?' Eden saw at once she wasn't going to get an answer from Kincade. 'Vince, what is he talking about?'

'Nothing. He's just trying to act big and tough,' Vince

jeered, then put on an act of his own. 'All right, you've found me. Now what, big man?'

'Now – we're going for a little ride.'

'Where?'

'Why, to your favorite place, of course.' Kincade's smile was thin and cold.

'My favorite?' Vince frowned warily, then shook his head. 'I'm not budging one inch until I find out where you're taking me.'

'You'll go where I tell you to go.' Kincade never raised his voice, which gave his words a more ominous ring.

'Oh, yeah?' Sweat beads formed along Vince's upper lip.

'Yeah. Not that it's a great secret where you're going. I know how much you love it back at the ranch.' Kincade ignored Eden's surprised look.

'The ranch?' Vince scoffed. 'You're kidding. I despise that hellhole – Ahh, that's your game, is it?' He nodded slowly. 'You plan on making my life miserable?'

'I haven't begun to make your life miserable, Rossiter. Believe me, you're not going to get off easy. Your sister is determined to keep the ranch and you're going to work until you sweat blood to help her keep it. You got me?'

'I got you,' Vince grumbled.

'Rusty.' Kincade never took his eyes off Vince.

'Yo.'

'I could use another pair of eyes to keep track of Slippery Sam here. I already know Eden could use an extra hand. Feel like working some cattle?'

'Why not? I haven't got anything better to do.'

'Any objections to hiring Rusty?' Kincade spared Eden one quick glance.

'No.' But she still wasn't sure what to make of any of this.

'Good.' Kincade dug in his pocket. 'Do you think you can find your way back to the hotel?'

'I think so.' Eden frowned, 'Why?'

'Take my truck and go get our things.' He handed her the keys. 'Kirk will check me out.'

'What are you going to do?'

'Rusty and I are going to help your brother get his things packed.' When she still made no move toward the pickup, Kincade added, 'Don't worry. There won't be any rough stuff unless your brother gets cute. And with two of us, I don't think that will happen.'

'How can I be sure you'll be here when I get back?'

'You've got my truck.' Moving forward Kincade took Rossiter's arm and turned him back to the door. 'Let's go pack your bags, Vinny-boy. We've got a long drive ahead of us.'

'Keep your hands off me.' Vince jerked his arm away, but not before Kincade had pushed him forward. Rusty pulled the door open. With a mocking bow and a sweep of his hand, he invited Vince to enter first.

Eden watched them go down the apartment hall, then looked at the keys in her hand. After another second's hesitation, she turned and went to Kincade's pickup.

The upstairs apartment was the typical bachelor's digs of mismatched furniture and cheap framed prints on otherwise bare walls. An empty pizza carton and beer cans cluttered the coffee table in front of the television, and dust balls lurked under the chairs and in the corners. Kincade looked at none of it as his gaze swept the room and came to light on a telephone half-hidden under a copy of *Sports Illustrated*.

'My clothes and things are in the guestroom down here.' Vince headed for the hallway that led off the small living room.

'They can wait. You have a phone call to make

first.' Kincade walked over and tossed aside the swim-suit issue.

'A phone call?' Vince swung back, frowning. 'To who?'

'DePard. You didn't keep your rendezvous with Sheehan, remember? By now DePard will be wondering why you haven't gotten in touch with him.' Kincade picked up the receiver and held it out to him.

'He'll be asleep at this hour,' Vince protested.

'Wake him up.'

'And tell him what?'

'Tell him the truth. Tell him your sister still hasn't found anyone to haul her cattle to market, and with the roundup going on, it's going to be impossible for you to keep in touch with him on a regular basis, but if anything new comes up, you'll find a way to get word to him. You tell him that and nothing else.'

'What if he asks why I didn't meet Sheehan the other day?'

'Make up a lie. You're good at that.' Kincade pushed the phone at him. 'Now, make that call.'

Reluctantly Vince took the receiver and dialed the number.

Duke DePard sat on the edge of his bed dressed, as always, only in his skivvies. His hand still rested on the black phone on his bedside table. His head was bowed in deep thought, his gray chest-hairs silvering in the lamplight.

He hated phone calls in the middle of the night. They always resurrected the memory of the night Jeff was killed.

After a moment, Duke picked up the phone again and punched out the numbers to Sheehan's quarters. The foreman answered on the third ring, his voice thick with sleep.

'It's DePard,' Duke identified himself. 'I just got a phone call from Vince Rossiter.'

'Rossiter?' There was a stunned pause, followed by, 'My God, how come he's calling at this hour? It's the middle of the night.'

'I know—'

'What did he want?'

'He claimed it was the first chance he'd had to slip away. He said that Kincade guy is keeping close tabs on him, that he suspects Vince is feeding us information about his sister's activities. Vince is worried he'll say something to her, and she'll clam up and quit confiding her plans to him.'

'That sounds like something she'd do.'

'Vince wants to play it cautious for a while. So we aren't to worry if we don't hear from him. He said he'll only contact us if he finds out something important.' Duke combed his fingers through his hair, smoothing the coarse gray strands tousled from sleep.

'Do you believe him?' Sheehan asked.

'What he says makes sense,' Duke admitted with a touch of grimness. 'But something doesn't smell right.'

'What?'

'I don't know. It's just a feeling – I can't put my finger on it.'

'What do you think we should do?'

'Sit tight and wait – and keep our eyes and ears open. Make some calls tomorrow and see what you can find out, if anything.'

'Consider it done,' Sheehan told him, and DePard rang off.

Kincade and Vince were at the rear of Vince's pickup when Eden drove into the parking lot. The hood of Vince's truck was up, and Rusty Walker had his head stuck under it, fiddling with something under the motor. Eden parked beside it, switched off the engine and stepped out.

'Your things are in the back,' she told Kincade.

'Good.'

Rusty slammed the hood down, bounced his hands on it once to make sure it was latched, then sauntered back to join them, wiping his greasy hands on a rag. 'It should run now.'

Kincade nodded, then looked at Vince. 'You'll follow me, but don't get any ideas. Rusty will be on your tail all the way back to the ranch.'

'Do you think that rattletrap of his can keep up?' Vince cast a disparaging look at Rusty's pickup.

'You shouldn't judge by appearances, Rossiter,' Kincade advised. 'That truck has a modified three-fifty-four under the hood. He can run circles around you without half trying.' He waved Eden into his truck. 'Go ahead and get in.'

'Wait a minute,' Vince protested. 'How come she's riding with you?'

'Because I said so.'

Twenty minutes later the trio of pickups were on the interstate headed east, the lights of the Reno metroplex a glow in the sky behind them. Eden hadn't exchanged a word with Kincade since they left the apartment.

'Why are you doing this?' she finally asked.

'Doing what?'

'Taking Vince back to the ranch,' she replied.

'You heard him – he hates the place. It's a prison sentence to him.'

'Is that all?' She struggled to keep the regret out of her voice.

'I wish to God that was all,' Kincade muttered in self-directed anger. 'I wish I could say you didn't enter into it. But you did. I can't let your brother get away with what he did, but I don't want to hurt you either.'

That was the problem. He couldn't summon up that fierce hate anymore. He had lost the edge it had given him, the hardness. Now when he looked at Vince, he thought of Eden, not Marcie. A fact that weighted him with guilt.

'It's a hell of a mess, isn't it?' he sighed. 'I'm damned if I do – and damned if I don't.'

Without thinking, he reached over and took her hand, linking their fingers. The headlight beams rushed ahead into the night, merging into one, the only light showing in the miles and miles of darkness around them.

23

Shortly before noon the next day, the four of them rode into the camp at Big Timber Canyon. Wild Jack trotted out to meet them on his bandy legs, long gray hair bouncing against his shoulders with each step.

'It's about damned time you got here.' He scowled at Eden and held the reins to her horse while she swung out of the saddle. 'Everybody think this time you weren't coming back, that maybe DePard had run you off.'

'That will happen when cows fly.' She hooked the stirrup over the saddlehorn and loosened the cinch a notch to give her horse a blow.

'I've seen cows fly. Four of them,' Wild Jack stated. 'I saw it with my own two eyes.'

'Yeah, and how drunk were you?' Vince mocked.

The cook puffed up indignantly. 'I wasn't drunk. That day, I was sober as a Baptist preacher the day they load four prize heifers in airplane. I saw the plane take off with those four cows inside. They flew.'

'He's got you there, Rossiter.' Rusty grinned.

'The hell he does. It was the plane that flew, not those cows.'

'What did the cows do?' Wild Jack argued. 'They

weren't on the ground. The plane flew. The cows were in plane. The cows flew.' Finished, he gave a big wide grin, confident his logic was irrefutable. Then he looked at Rusty and frowned. 'Who are you?'

'This is Rusty Walker, a new man. He just signed on.' Eden took back the reins. 'This is our cook. Everybody calls him Wild Jack.'

'Hello.' Rusty touched his hat to him.

The cook grunted in his best savage-Indian imitation and inspected the thick freckling of Rusty's face. 'Your Indian name must be Many Spots.'

'Can't rightly say. I don't have an Indian name.' Rusty returned the cook's inspection of him with eyebrows raised, skeptical of what he was seeing and hearing.

'You do now,' the cook declared. Abruptly he turned on Eden with a dark glower. 'Did you bring supplies?'

'They're on the packhorse.' She jerked a thumb at the horse Kincade led.

The cook snatched the lead rope from his hand and gave it a tug, chirruping encouragement to the animal. The horse stretched its neck in initial resistance, then plodded forward. The cook led it up to Eden, then stopped and ran a feeling hand over the canvas-wrapped bundle.

'Did you bring vanilla?' He shot her a quick look. 'We don't have much.'

She smiled. 'Don't worry. You have plenty now.'

'It's damn good thing,' he declared, then treated her to one of his narrow-eyed scrutinies. 'You look different.'

'I look tired, you mean.'

'Not tired. Different. You were gone a long time. You've changed.'

She flashed a half-irritated look at the cook, then glanced at Kincade. The smile left her mouth, her lips coming together in a firm line. 'There's something wrong with your eyes, old man.' She turned and headed for the chuckwagon, leading her horse.

'These eyes are like an eagle's. See far. See close. See much.' He toddled after her, dragging the pack horse with him. 'These eyes saw your dust when you were still on other side of valley.'

'Enough!' Eden rounded on him. 'Take those supplies up to the chuckwagon and unpack them.'

The cook set off, grumbling. 'No respect for elders. It's a damn fine shame.'

Vince trailed after him. 'Have you got any of that black, bitter water you call coffee? I could use some.'

Kincade walked up with his horse and paused next to her, his gaze traveling after the cook. 'You know he drinks that vanilla extract.'

'We've never had a cook that didn't drink. At least with the vanilla, he drinks it and keeps right on cooking. But if he doesn't have vanilla, he goes off on a whiskey binge that can last for weeks.'

Bob Waters rode in. 'Where have you been? We've been wondering what happened to you. I never guessed that you hooked up with Kincade and Vince. What took you so long to get here?'

'Sorry, but there wasn't any way to get word to you that we would be delayed. I hired a new man. His name's Rusty Walker.' She indicated Rusty with a nod of her head. 'This is my cowboss Bob Waters. You'll take your orders from him.'

'Does he know the situation with DePard?' Bob asked.

Eden replied with a nod. 'We were about to grab a quick cup of coffee before we hit the saddle again. You might as well join us and fill us in on the areas that still need to be covered. I'll be riding out with you. We have some things we need to go over.'

She was back to being the boss again, in capital letters.

All business, Kincade noticed. The woman who had laughed at his antics, ridden the carousel horse, licked sticky cotton candy from her fingers, delighted in the ducks, and made wild love with him was locked back inside again.

In less than thirty minutes, they were in the saddle and out scouring the hills for cattle. The unvarying pattern of their days was established. Rousted from their beds while the sky was still black and glittering with stars, they trudged to the chuckwagon for a quick wash – and a shave, if they had the energy – and that all-important first cup of coffee.

Fortified with a hearty breakfast, they saddled their horses by predawn's pearly light and rode out before the sun broke the horizon. All day they searched for cattle, combing them out of the hills, rooting them from canyons, chasing them across sage flats, and herding their catch back to camp by late afternoon. There, the day's gather was sorted and separated, the slick calves tagged and branded, the bull calves castrated, the injured doctored, and the aged cows palpated to determine whether they were pregnant or not.

Then it was to the remuda to select the next day's mount, check it over for soreness or injury and re-shoe it if necessary. After the physical demands of a sixteen-hour day, they were dragging by the time they reached the chuckwagon's mess tent. Most nights, if there hadn't been a hot meal waiting for them, they would have been too tired to fix their own. The only change in the routine came when they moved camp every three or four days.

The only complaints were from Vince, and he kept his grumbling to a minimum, especially around Kincade. But the resentment was there with each bitter look he gave Kincade. He offered no trouble though, not with both Kincade and Rusty watching him. Not that Kincade particularly cared.

As the days wore on, he found he was thinking less and less about Vince, and more and more about Eden. She had assumed the role of boss and never dropped it, not even for a moment. She did more than give orders, she led by example.

And as hard as she pushed them to complete the roundup in record time, she pushed herself harder. She was the first one up every morning, the first at the mess tent, the first at the horses, the first in the saddle, and the last to return to camp, the last to dismount for the day, the last to select her horse, the last to the supper table, and the last to turn in at night.

Kincade had seen Eden stumble in exhaustion, catch herself, shake off the effects, and push on to the next task – which made it impossible for any of the crew to do less.

Kincade might have admired that if he hadn't been growing steadily more irritated with the way she acted toward him. There was nothing in her glances, her attitude, or the remarks she made to him that suggested he was – or had ever been – anything other than a ranch hand. She treated him exactly as she treated everyone else. No friendlier and no colder.

He told himself that was fine. Under the circumstances, it was probably best. Yet the longer it went on, the more it grated. After the second week, he'd had enough.

With dawn's flush chasing back the darkness, Kincade swung his saddle onto the sorrel's back. Farther down the line came the groan of saddle leather taking the initial weight of a rider. Kincade glanced down the way and saw Eden backing her horse away from the picket rope.

Reaching under the sorrel, he grabbed the belly strap and straightened to thread it through the cinch ring. While his hands automatically went through the necessary motions to snug the cinch tight, Kincade watched as Eden rode over to confer again with Bob Waters, the old cowdog trotting beside her horse.

She wore a short denim jacket against the lingering chill in the air. Edges of dark hair showed beneath her hat brim, the length of it caught at the nape to hang down her back. She sat slim and straight and poised in the saddle, a lithe strength and authority apparent in her carriage.

But Kincade knew the spirited woman behind that businesslike facade, one who laughed and loved and raged with equal abandon. He knew the full, rounded curves beneath those shapeless men's clothes, and he wasn't about to let her forget any of that. He dropped the stirrup in place and grabbed the reins, preparing to mount.

Next to him, Al Bender hauled his tired body into the saddle and reined his horse away to join Eden. The sorrel moved out as Kincade swung aboard and promptly intercepted Al.

'I'll be riding out with Eden this morning,' he told him.

Al glanced at him, baggy-eyed with missed sleep. 'Is that what she said?' he asked, not trusting his own memory.

'No, it's what I said.'

Al shrugged. 'Suits me. I could use some slack and she doesn't cut you any when you ride with her.'

Eden saw the exchange between the two men. When Kincade walked his horse over to her, she noticed the determined set of his jaw and the way his gaze bored into her. He had a nick on his cheek where he had cut himself shaving this morning. She could almost smell the soap on his skin, skin that she remembered only too well the way it felt beneath her hands. Unsettled by the disturbing memory, she firmly closed a mental door on it.

'I'll be riding with you today,' he told her. 'Al's going out with Rusty and Vince.'

He appeared to be primed for an argument, but she wasn't about to give him one. 'All right. If you're ready, let's go.'

She wheeled her horse toward the open country and nudged it into a shuffling trot. The dog loped alongside her. The creaking of saddle leather confirmed that Kincade was there as well. They rode out of camp straight into the golden fire of a Nevada sunrise.

'There's a natural tank in the wide canyon at the base of Cobbler's Peak. It's been known to have water in it this late in the year. There were quite a few tracks heading that direction yesterday,' she said after they'd traveled some distance. 'We'll check that area first.'

'Fine by me,' Kincade replied and let the silence build again. 'So, what are you going to do about it?'

'About what?'

'Us.'

'There is no *us*.' She sounded amazingly calm.

'Really?' He mocked, a caustic edge to his voice. 'I suppose the time we spent together in Reno – the bed we shared – never happened.'

'Of course, it happened,' Eden said, striving for lightness. 'It was a very pleasant interlude. Now it's over.'

'An interlude. Is that what you've decided to call it?'

'That's what it was. That's all it was.' She gave him a look of mild reproval, and silently congratulated herself for handling the discussion so well. 'Or are you disappointed that I'm not mooning over you and casting lovesick glances in your direction? Would it help if I apologized?'

'For what? Losing your nerve?'

He swung his horse around and rode back to her.

When he pulled up, their knees brushed and his hand closed on her saddlehorn, catching up her rein in his grip.

'The horse still has you scared.'

Stung by his jibe, Eden glared at him hotly. 'Nice try, Kincade, but that ploy won't work a second time. I rode that horse, put him through his paces. Now that I've had time to think about it, I've decided I don't want him in my string.'

'Why?' he challenged, leaning closer, making her aware of him, his nearness and his anger. 'Are you afraid you might start to like him too much?'

With an effort she ignored the mad flutterings of her pulse and held his diamond-hard gaze without flinching. 'Why don't you just admit it, Kincade, your ego can't take the thought of being rejected.'

'My ego wouldn't have a problem with that if I believed it was really the way you felt. But you are lying through your teeth.'

'I'm sure that's much easier for you to believe than the truth.' She wanted to gather up the reins, preparatory to moving out, but one was still caught in his grip on her saddle horn. And Eden wasn't about to get into some childish tug-of-war game over possession of it. 'As far as I'm concerned, you can think whatever you like. This discussion is over. We have cattle to gather. It's time to get to work. And *that* is an order.'

'This discussion is far from over.' He was out of the saddle and jerking her from her horse before she could mount a defense. The old cowdog sat down to watch.

Both horses shied away from the struggling pair as Eden fought to pull free of his crushing hold, using her hands, elbows, knees, and feet. The point of her boot connected with his shin, drawing a curse from him. In the next second they were both tumbling to the ground. Before she could roll free, he was on top of her, trapping her beneath the weight of his body and pinning her arms to the side. She was breathing hard, her heart was pounding, from both the exertion of the brief fight and the solid, male imprint of his body pressed against hers.

'We're having this out, and we're having it out now. To hell with the cattle,' he growled, his breathing almost as labored as her own.

'Let me go,' she commanded, holding herself iron-stiff in an attempt to deny the awareness of him that had sharpened all her senses.

'So you can run again. No way, sweetheart.'

'I'm not afraid of you, Kincade.'

'Oh, you're afraid alright. But not of me. You're afraid for yourself.'

'I don't have to listen to this.' She turned her head far to the side, scraping her cheek against the sandy soil beneath them.

'You're going to listen alright.' Capturing her chin, he forced her to look at him. 'You've been running ever since I mentioned the word "love" back in Reno. The thought of falling in love with me terrifies you, doesn't it?'

'I'm not in love with you,' she flashed.

'No, and you're not going to take the risk that you might. That's why you've made sure to keep your distance from me since we've been back.'

'There's work to do. We're in the middle of round-up,' Eden tersely reminded him.

'That proved to be very convenient for you, didn't it? I wonder what excuse you would have used otherwise,' he taunted.

'It isn't an excuse; it's a fact.'

'Here's another fact for you – you're afraid of getting emotionally involved with anyone, because love involves trust. And that's something you can't bring yourself to do – although, God knows, the men you've known haven't exactly inspired it.'

'I am not going to talk about Jeff again.' She made the mistake of trying to wriggle free, but only succeeded in increasing the contact.

'It isn't just Jeff. It's everyone from a father who dumped you off and never came back to a worthless brother who only shows up when he needs money and a bunch of cowhands who work for a few months then drift on to greener pastures.'

'Now you're going to tell me that you aren't like them,' she said cynically.

'I'm not.' Inches away, his eyes glittered with a disturbing intensity.

'I agree,' she said with false coolness. 'You are more like DePard.'

Kincade went grim. 'Vince. That's your out, isn't it? You decided there was no need to try to make things work between us because my quarrel with Vince would eventually kill it anyway.'

'Well, won't it?' Eden challenged, battling back tears.

'Only if we let it.'

'You're a fool.' And she would be an even bigger fool if she believed him.

'And you're a coward. You're so afraid of getting hurt that you won't find out whether I'm right or not.'

'That's not true.'

'Prove it.' His face dipped toward her. She turned at the last second and his mouth grazed her cheek. Undeterred, he nibbled his way down her jaw line to that sensitive spot in her neck, igniting a series of sensual shudders.

She had trouble getting air in her lungs. 'I don't have to prove anything to you.'

'Not to me.' He nuzzled the hollow behind her ear, his voice a low seductive rumble. 'Prove it to youself.

Do you want to feel like this? Be touched like this?' A caressing hand ceased its roamings and shaped itself to her breast with familiar intimacy. 'Kissed like this?'

His mouth rolled onto her lips, parting them with persuasive force, awakening again all her sleeping needs. Against her will, her lips moved in response against his before she managed to regain her senses and twist away from his kiss.

'This isn't love,' she insisted, denying the fierce ache in her heart.

'Maybe not.' He rubbed his mouth near a corner of her lips. 'But I'm not as sure of that as you are. I don't know about you, but what I'm feeling is more than just desire.'

'Really?' Eden strained to find skepticism.

'Love isn't like a switch that can be turned on and off. It's more like the wind – something you can't see, but you can feel it. Sometimes, it's nothing more than vague stirrings. Other times it's a soft and gentle breeze. Or it can be a fierce gale with all the fury of a thousand tempests.'

When his mouth claimed hers a second time, it was a whirlwind, and Eden was caught in its vortex, the world spinning around them. She could hear the roaring of it in her ears, taste the wildness on her tongue and feel the power of it, the agonizing pressure of it that had only one release.

In its aftermath, she lay exhausted and spent atop the bed of their clothes. Kincade gathered her into his arms and held her. His hand wandered with absent-minded intimacy over her waist and thigh while he waited for his heart to resume its normal beat.

She stirred against him and his arm automatically tightened to keep her beside him, but Eden made no move to get away. Her fingers curled into the springy hairs on his chest, gleaming golden in the sunlight.

'I think I'm on to your game,' she murmured, breaking the silence between them.

'Oh? And what's that?'

'You like to "commit the oldest sins in the newest kind of ways."'

Kincade chuckled at the quote. 'I've used that line from *Henry IV* before.'

'You have?' She tilted her head back.

'Yes. You would be surprised how far a guy can get with a woman simply by quoting some titillating line from Shakespeare,' he advised with a knowing look. 'That one always worked. But there was another one I used a lot, too.'

'Which one was that?'

'"Let me take you a button-hole lower."' He waggled his eyebrows in mock lechery.

Eden laughed, delighting in the line. 'Which play is that from?'

'You aren't going to believe me,' he warned.

She propped herself up on an elbow, scooping her hair back to fall in a single curtain over one shoulder. 'Which one is it?'

'*Love's Labour Lost.*'

'You're kidding,' she said and laughed again, then sank back to lie in the crook of his shoulder.

'I've missed that.' He idly rubbed his hand up and down her arm.

'What?'

'Hearing you laugh.'

Eden sobered at the comment, reality stealing in. 'If we lay here much longer in this sun, we're going to get burned.' She sat up and tugged at the shirt trapped beneath him. 'Let me have my clothes so I can get dressed.'

'A sunburn could be awkward to explain.' He sat up, releasing her shirt and reaching for his own.

As they dressed, Kincade was conscious of her silence. He zipped up his jeans and watched as she tucked her shirt inside her Levi's and turned to glance at the horses grazing a few yards away, guarded by the dog. An innocent action on the surface, but he knew Eden was building up the wall he had just battered down. He picked up her neckcloth and carried it over to her.

'Thanks.' Her glance bounced off him as she took it from him and wrapped it around her neck, knotting it loosely.

'Eden,' he began.

'Don't.' She shook her head and took a long breath before she looked at him, squarely meeting his gaze. There was pain in her eyes, but there was also determination. 'I don't need this kind of complication in my life right now.'

'That's progress of sorts, I suppose. At least now you regard me as a complication.'

'Don't make jokes. I'm serious. I can't afford to get involved with you or any man. I have enough problems on my hands with this roundup and getting the cattle to market. I have to concentrate all my energies on that. A distraction right now is the last thing I need.'

'Now I'm a distraction. Keep going and I may raise a couple more notches.' He was sated enough to be amused rather than angry.

'Stop it, Kincade. It isn't funny.'

'I agree.'

'Good. Then try to understand this – I've got a fight on my hands with DePard. If I'm going to win, it's going to take everything I've got. I can't afford to make any mistakes.'

'You don't have to wage the fight alone, Eden.'

'It's my ranch, and it's my problem.'

'Problems never seem as bad when you share them with someone.'

She shook her head in disagreement. 'It's better not to count on anyone but myself.'

'And damn lonely, too. Life is lonely enough without compounding the loneliness.'

'You don't understand.' Eden sighed in irritation and regret.

'I understand better than you think. The key word here is trust,' Kincade said.

'It isn't easy.' She tipped her chin a little higher.

'Nothing worthwhile ever is.'

'Have you forgotten Vince?' She couldn't keep that touch of bitterness out of her voice.

'No, and I'm not about to,' he replied. 'Why don't we take this as it comes? A day at a time, a step at a time.'

'You aren't giving me any choice.' She scooped her hat off the ground and batted the dust from it, releasing some of her frustrations. 'It's my life. I should be able to say whether I want you in it.'

'It's too late.' He hooked a finger under her chin and nuzzled the corner of her lips, teasing her into kissing him back. 'I'm already in your life. Even with your brother, I'm still here.'

She felt the warm heat of his lips, the softness of them and the gentleness. She still felt it when he drew back. 'You're just going to keep pushing this, aren't you? You aren't going to let up until I agree. I don't have time to fight with you.' And she couldn't tell him to leave because she needed his help if she expected her plan to succeed. Kincade knew that, too. 'We'll try it your way for a while.'

'That's my girl.' Kincade smiled as she turned toward the horses.

She spun back, furious. 'I am not your girl. And let's get something else straight while we're at it. I won't have you bragging to the crew about this. I won't have them making sly comments and snickering behind my back. Do you hear?'

All the anger was to disguise her fear of embarrassment – and worse, loss of respect. Kincade understood that. 'I've never been the kind to kiss and tell, Eden.'

'You'd better not. Or I swear, I'll hog-tie and castrate you so fast, you won't know what happened.'

'I think I might.' The grooves around his mouth deepened with his effort to hold back a smile.

'Around the crew, you aren't to touch me, you aren't to come near me,' Eden warned.

Kincade pulled a straight face. 'You mean I can't visit your tent?'

'No!'

'We can't go for moonlight strolls?'

'No.'

'I can't blow you kisses across the campfire?'

'Oh, God.' Pivoting, she threw up her hands and stalked after the horses.

Chuckling, Kincade followed.

As much as Eden hated to admit it, she soon discovered how much easier the work seemed and how much faster the time went with Kincade to share it. When they finally made the turn for camp late that afternoon, pushing a couple dozen head of cattle, her muscles aching with exhaustion, she discovered she had enjoyed every minute of it.

It was something she had never experienced with anyone else, not even her brother. Unlike Vince, Kincade had worked without complaint, never grumbling about the drudgery of the job or cursing the heat and the dust. Once Kincade had taken off on a wild chase after a yearling steer. When he came back nearly half an hour later, driving the steer ahead of him, his horse all lathered and blowing, he was all tired smiles, his eyes glowing with satisfaction over this tiny victory.

He didn't say a word, just pushed the steer into the gather and fell back to ride beside her.

Another time he pulled up on the crest of a hill to admire the view, then looked at her and remarked, 'This is some country.' It was the tone of his voice rather than his words that told Eden that he, too, saw the prodigal beauty of this land. To Vince, it had always been a hellish wasteland; he never saw the richness of it, the vastness, the wildness.

The camp was in sight, and the sun was in their faces. Eden tipped her chin down and watched the bobbing of her horse's head. She had enjoyed the time with him too much, and that was a mistake.

'This can't become a habit,' she told him.

'No, I suppose not.' His ready agreement surprised her. Eden had expected an argument. His sideways glance teased, proving he had other ways of making his point. 'Someone might get the idea there was something going on between us, and we couldn't have that, could we?'

'No.'

Kincade grinned. 'As Wild Jack would say, it's a damned fine shame.' He kicked his horse into a lope and pushed a straggler back into the herd.

A ghost of that smile still haunted the corners of his mouth when they threw the day's gather in with the rest of the cattle being held at the camp. Eden immediately peeled off to find her cowboss. Kincade watched her as Rusty rode up and swung alongside him.

Kincade glanced at him, then made a quick scan of the other riders. 'Where's Vince?'

'Answering nature's call.' Rusty nodded to some bushes some distance from the tents.

'Did he give you any trouble?'

'He's too tired to even think about it. Can't say the same about you, though,' Rusty said, looking him over.

'Truth to tell, I don't feel too bad.'

Rusty continued to study him. 'My eyes may not be as good as the cook's, but you look different. In fact, you look downright pleased with yourself.'

'Do I?' Kincade smiled and glanced at Eden.

Rusty followed the direction of his look. His eyes widened briefly in surprise. 'So that's the way the wind blows.'

'That's the way it blows,' Kincade admitted.

'I knew something has been rubbing you crosswise these last couple weeks, turning you all broody and grim, but I thought it was Vince.' Rusty took off his hat and scratched his head, then pushed it back on with a grin. 'Well, what d'ya know? Kincade Harris is in love.' Rusty recognized all the signs now, having gone through it all himself. Then he saw the problem. 'What are you going to do about Vince?'

'Exactly what I set out to do.'

'You'll lose her.'

'Not if I can help it,' Kincade stated, but his smile left him.

24

Years ago Sayer's Well had been the site of a prospector's cabin. No trace of it remained, only the free-flowing well that had been dug to provide a water supply. The grass grew thick around it, and the summer heat had seared it a tawny yellow, locking in the richness of its nutrients.

It was here at Sayer's Well, with Black Rock Desert stretching just beyond the rocky finger of a mountain, that the final sort was made and the cattle bound for market were bedded down for the night.

With the evening meal finished, Eden helped herself to a last cup of coffee and wandered over to the crackling fire where the weary crew had gathered. An old stump sat on the outer edge of the circle. Eden sat on it and took off her hat, shaking her hair loose in a tired gesture.

Kincade sat across the fire from her, propped up on an elbow, his long legs stretched, one knee raised. She felt his glance touch her and move away, just a simple glance and nothing more, but she had learned in the last week how much could be communicated by a look.

Al Bender swirled the coffee in his cup. 'It's gonna be good to get back to the ranch, take a long shower, and put on some clean clothes. I feel like I'm carrying around thirty pounds of Nevada dirt.'

'You smell like it, too,' Deke joked.

Kincade's glance came back to her, expectantly. But Eden wasn't ready to inform the crew they wouldn't be returning to the ranch in the morning.

Bob Waters poked at the burning logs with a stick, the firelight reflecting on the round lenses of his glasses. 'It took us just two days over three weeks to complete the roundup. That's pretty fast time.'

'I should shout it is,' Al declared. 'And we covered a helluva lot of territory in those three weeks, too.'

'We missed a lot, too.' Bob looked at Eden, feeling obligated to remind her of it.

'I don't think we would have found much stock in the areas we skipped,' she repeated her previous reasons for bypassing them. 'We'll hit them in the spring.'

'Fall, spring, I don't see what difference it makes,' Vince stated. 'All this work has just been a big waste of time. I mean, what good is it to gather up these cattle when you haven't any way in hell of getting them to market? We worked like a bunch of dogs for nothing.'

Eden offered no defense of her actions and the silence around the fire grew loud. Finally Bob Waters stood up and tossed the dregs from his cup into the fire. There was a sizzle and a hiss as he shot a stony look at Vince.

'Kincade had you pegged right, Rossiter. You talk too damned much.' He headed toward the chuckwagon, his spurs jingling with each step. 'Got any more of that coffee?'

'Yeah, I think I'll get me another cup, too.' Al Bender rolled to his feet to follow him.

'A beer is what would taste good right now,' Vince declared a little loudly to show his indifference to the cowboss's remark. 'A frosty cold beer is just what this little celebration needs. Better yet, a couple cases of them.'

'No.' Kincade slowly rose to his feet. 'What this celebration needs is a little music.'

'If you're thinking of Wild Jack's transistor radio, forget it,' Vince told him. 'Out in these hills, all you're going to pick up is static.'

'I wasn't thinking of the radio,' Kincade replied and glanced down at his friend. 'You still carry that harmonica with you, Rusty?'

'It's like my bank card.' He grinned. 'I never leave home without it.'

'Well, warm it up. I feel like doing a little two-stepping.' Kincade walked around the fire to the area Bob and Al had just vacated. 'Better move back, Deke. You're sitting in the middle of the dance floor.'

'Pardon me.' The lanky cowboy promptly got up and shifted over to a place near Rusty.

When Kincade turned to Eden, she sighed. 'I suppose I'm in the way, too.'

'Nope.' He reached down, took the mug from her hands and pulled her to her feet before she even guessed his intention. 'You can be my partner. I don't like to two-step alone.'

'Too bad. I don't know how,' she stated when he set her coffee mug on the stump.

'Do you know how to walk?' he asked while Rusty played a few experimental notes in the background.

'Of course, but—'

'Then you can learn to two-step. It's simple.'

'I don't think so.' She pulled back.

'Come on, Boss, you can do it,' Bob Waters chimed in, returning with a steaming cup of coffee. Al was right behind him. 'Kincade's right. It's real easy.'

'Yeah, Boss, you can do it.' Deke clapped his encouragement.

'I—' Eden shook her head.

'Just try it,' Kincade coaxed. 'All you have to do is take two slow steps and two quick ones. I'll show you while Rusty tries to find the tune he lost.'

More calls of encouragement followed, and Eden sensed it wasn't authority the crew wanted her to show now, but some humanness. If she refused, she would lose some of their respect.

'All right. I'll try.'

'Stand beside me.' Kincade maneuvered her into position, draping his arm along her shoulders and gripping her right hand. 'Starting with the right foot, we'll take one slow step, then another slow one, then two quick ones. Got it?'

'I think so.'

'Okay, here we go.' After a half-dozen times with no mistakes, Kincade stopped her. 'Now, let's try it with music. Ready, Rusty?'

In answer, the harmonica's lively notes filled the air. Kincade bounced her hand to the beat of the music, establishing the tempo, then started forward.

Around and around the miniature dance floor they went – to the whistles and hoots of the crew. Gradually the slow-slow, quick-quick pattern came naturally to Eden and she stopped concentrating on her feet and gave herself over to the enjoyment of the moment.

Kincade's arm was a comfortable and familiar weight on her shoulder. Tucked firmly to his side, she felt the warm heat of his body, her arm rubbing his rib cage, her hip brushing his muscled thigh with each step. Here was a closeness, a simple intimacy that she had missed all week.

'I've got it, haven't I?' She looked up and basked in the beam of approval and something else in his eyes.

'You've got it. Want to try a circle turn?'

'Why not?' At that moment, she was game for anything.

'Atta girl.' He grinned. 'All right, when we come to the
quick-quick part, you'll do the turn,' he explained, then
added, 'Don't worry, I'll push you through it.'

In her side vision, Eden was conscious of hands clap-
ping and dusty boots tapping in time with the sprightly
music. The dancing firelight threw its wavering glow
over masculine faces, and above the mountains a big
moon was rising.

'Ready?' Kincade prompted. At her uncertain nod, he
smiled. 'Okay, here we go. Slow, slow – pivot.'

His hand pushed her into the start of a turn, but
she was half a beat slow in responding. Suddenly
everything was off, the timing, the pattern, the music.
In her haste to catch up, Eden got her feet tangled and
yelped in dismay when she stumbled into Kincade. Both
of them staggered sideways. When he started laughing,
Eden joined him.

She looked up, and their eyes locked with an almost
audible click. His face was close, achingly close. And his
mouth . . . she dug her fingers into his shirt, wanting
him, needing him. His head dipped a fraction of an inch
closer – and someone coughed.

The silence hit her. There was no music, only the snap
of burning logs. Self-consciously, Eden pulled back and
snatched a quick glance at the grinning faces around
the campfire. All except Vince. He glowered at them,
his hands clenched into fists at his side.

'That's enough for me, I think.' She forced a lightness
into her voice, trying to pretend nothing had happened,
fully aware she wasn't fooling anyone. Pride insisted
she go through with it. 'After working all day, I don't
really have the energy for this. In fact, I think I'll call
it a night.'

Her cheeks were hot. She needed to escape their

knowing looks. Eden hadn't taken two steps toward her tent before Vince was at her side, gripping her elbow. 'I'll walk with you.'

She didn't want him to, but she wanted a scene even less. And Vince was in the mood to make one. She could feel the barely restrained fury in the grip of his fingers.

Short of her tent, but well away from the others, Vince stopped her. 'Stay away from that guy.' It wasn't a warning or even some well-intentioned brotherly advice. It was an order.

'What?'

'Don't play innocent with me. He was making a move on you and you were going for it. I saw the way you looked at him like you were ready to jump his bones. Everybody did.'

'No.' The simple protest came out half-strangled.

Vince looked at her, his face twisted with anger and regret. 'He's been working on you all along, hasn't he? Dammit, I should have guessed he would do that.'

'What are you talking about?'

'Christ, he doesn't care about you, Sis. He's just using you. He wants you to fall for him so he can get back at me.'

'What?' She felt a squeezing in her chest, intense and painful.

'He's been sympathetic, hasn't he?' Vince challenged. 'Pretended to believe your story, made noises that you got a raw deal. Subtly, of course. He'd never come right out and say it. He's too smooth for that.' His gaze narrowed on her. 'How did he handle the situation with me? What kind of tack did he take? Did he say that his problem with me had nothing to do with you? That you aren't to worry, he'll make it work out?' She couldn't answer, she didn't need to. Her wordless look told Vince what he needed to know. 'Damn him. Damn him to hell.'

'Why are you saying this? What's going on? Why would he do that?'

'Don't you see? As far as he's concerned, it's poetic justice.'

'Why? What did you do, Vince?'

'Nothing. I told you that.'

But she wasn't satisfied with his non-answer. 'You had to do something or he wouldn't be so determined to get even with you. Now, what was it?' She demanded to have the truth. 'Tell me, Vince.'

'I didn't do anything. You've got to believe me. This time I'm totally innocent of anything.' He started to move away.

Eden caught his arm. 'That isn't good enough, Vince. I can't just take your word for it. I have to know what happened. Why would hurting me be poetic justice?'

'Because his sister killed herself, okay?' he snapped.

Her hand fell away from his arm as she stepped back, reeling inwardly from his answer. 'Marcie,' she whispered, feeling suddenly sick and empty inside. Recovering a little, she looked at Vince. 'Why? Why did she commit suicide? It had something to do with you, didn't it?' He looked away, but not before Eden caught the flicker of guilt in his eyes. 'Oh, God.' Her breath caught on a sob. She pivoted, turning her back on him.

'Sis. Sis, it isn't what you think. I just dated her a few times when I was in Oklahoma.'

His hands curved onto her shoulders. Eden shrugged them off. 'Don't lie, Vince.'

'All right, I went out with her a lot.'

'Why?' She spun around. 'She was a cripple. Hardly your style.' Pain made her harsh.

'How did you know that?' He looked at her in surprise, suddenly uneasy.

'Never mind that. Just answer my question. Why?'

He looked anywhere but directly at her. 'The horses were racing at Remington Park. I had some hot tips that didn't pan out, and I got in deep with a couple of bookies. One of them got a little testy when I didn't pay up and threatened to get rough. She was there when it happened.'

'She gave you the money to pay him, didn't she?'

'I couldn't ask you for the money, Eden, not after I swore I wouldn't gamble anymore. Look, I never asked her for the money.'

'No, you never do. You just hint around until it's volunteered.' Eden hated to remember how many times he had used the same ploy on her.

'But even when she offered it, I didn't take it. I thought we could just skip town. I didn't know the guy had a tail on me. Suddenly there were these two thugs pounding on the motel room door. She had the money with her and gave it to them.'

'If you were trying to skip town, why did you take her with you? Why didn't you just leave?' She saw him struggling to come up with an answer.

'She wanted to come. I never made her any promises.'

'And that makes it all right?' Eden mocked, trembling and on the verge of crying. 'Oh, God, Vince, don't you see she wanted you to love her? She thought if she paid the money you would really care about her.'

'Dammit, everything was fine when I left. She said she understood. She was alive. How was I supposed to know she was going to take those pills?' he demanded angrily.

'No, you couldn't know. But it doesn't change anything, does it? She's still dead.' Numbly Eden turned away and moved toward her tent.

'Sis . . .' He took a step after her.

'Good night, Vince.'

Eden crawled into her tent and stretched out on the blankets, letting the tears come. She cried silently, but no less deeply. She cried for Marcie, for Kincade, for Vince – and for herself.

With the roundup over, everyone slept until first light. Eden waited for all of the crew to gather for breakfast, then announced they would be driving the cattle to market.

'We'll rest up today, check over the equipment, and make any necessary repairs,' she stated, ignoring the stunned looks on every face except Kincade's. 'Tonight, we'll pull out and cross Black Rock Desert. The moon will be full, so we should have plenty of light to see by. With a little luck, we'll be in Oregon the first of next week. After breakfast, Bob, you and I will get together and go over the route we'll be taking.'

Her decision wasn't open to discussion. To make that point, Eden took her coffee and walked away from them, telling herself that her action had nothing to do with the fact that she wasn't ready to face Kincade yet. Not with what she knew now. It was all too fresh, the ache still too raw.

It was Vince who came after her, catching up with her and stopping her. 'You aren't serious about this, are you?' he demanded, incredulous and half-angry.

'I'm dead serious.'

'But you can't go taking off cross-country with a bunch of cattle, traipsing across other people's property, not to mention government land,' he protested. 'It's illegal. You need permits to do something like this.'

'Probably. I didn't bother to check,' she admitted. 'This way I can honestly say that I didn't know I was breaking the law, if it turns out we are.'

'That's stupid.'

'No. It's desperate. DePard has too many friends. One question to someone in authority would tip my hand. I can't afford to have him figure out my plans. If I end up getting slapped with a penalty or a fine, I'll pay it. But first, I have to get the cattle to market.'

'Don't be a fool. He's going to find out what you're doing.'

'Not from you.' Kincade joined them. 'This time you won't have a chance to tell him what's going on.'

Vince reddened briefly, then stiffened and turned an accusing look on Eden. 'He knew about the drive before this morning, didn't he? You had already told him your plans.' He glared at Kincade. 'That's why you insisted I call DePard, isn't it?'

Kincade's smile was cool and sardonic. 'I didn't want DePard to get curious and come over to investigate when he didn't hear from you. As it stands, he'll simply think you're still tied up with the roundup.' His smile lengthened. 'I told you that you were going to help Eden keep the ranch.'

Vince clamped his mouth shut and stalked off, fuming at the way he had been manipulated and leaving Eden alone with Kincade. Something she didn't want.

She searched for something to say. 'I suppose the others think this is a crazy stunt, too.'

'A little.' His smile took on a warmer look. 'Although I think the idea appeals to their sense of adventure. You aren't going to have any problems with them.'

'Good. That's the last thing I need.' She shifted away from him. 'You'll have to excuse me. I've got a lot to do.'

She ducked inside her tent and rummaged through her things, pretending to search for the maps. She heard Kincade moving away and sagged back on her heels, drawing in a deep breath to calm her shaky nerves.

*　　　*　　　*

The moon stood full and high in the eastern sky, dimming the glitter of the surrounding stars. The barren expanse of Black Rock Desert stretched away into the darkness, a vast white shimmer under the moon's spotlight.

Summer's heat had sucked all the moisture from the broad mud plain, drawn its salts and alkalines to the top, and baked it until it had cracked and hardened into a tessellated and pale marblelike surface. The night rang with the clatter of hooves on the hardpan, the din of it accompanied by the confused lowing of cattle and the creaking of saddle leather.

Eden rode alongside the herd, strung out now in a dark-red stream of beef. The mix of yearling calves and aged cows had settled down from an initial, anxious trot into a strong walk. She kept them moving. Now and then the cowdog darted close when a head turned toward the open desert with a notion of bolting.

A short distance behind her, a cow made a break for its home range. Eden swung her horse around to chase it, but the dog raced after it, turning the cow back to rejoin the others. By the time she reined her horse around, Kincade was beside her.

'It's begun,' he said. 'Nervous?'

'A little.' But the tension she was feeling at the moment was a different sort, one that had nothing to do with the start of the drive. Eden fixed her gaze on a point ahead of them and said bluntly, 'I know about Marcie.'

After long seconds of silence, Kincade said skeptically, 'Do you really?'

'She committed suicide. She gave Vince the money to pay off his gambling debts. When he left her anyway, she couldn't stand it and took her own life. And you blame Vince for that.'

'He took more than her money. He took her will

to live.' The words were pushed through clenched teeth.

She heard the anger that he used to cover his pain. It was in his face, too. 'Now you're using me to punish Vince for what he did to your sister.'

His head jerked around at the accusation. An instant later, his hand closed around her reins, pulling her horse to a halt. 'I told you not to judge me by the men you've known. I'm not your brother. I don't use women.'

'That's very convincing.' Because it hurt, she lifted her chin higher. 'But you don't really expect me to believe you, do you?'

'Dammit, it's the truth!'

'It doesn't matter. That's what's sad.' She breathed in, trying to ease the tightness in her chest. 'What Vince did was wrong, but that doesn't make him responsible for your sister's death. It was her decision, her act. You can't blame him for it.'

'The hell I can't.'

She released a sad and silent laugh. 'I honestly thought you might be different. But you're just like DePard. He holds me responsible for Jeff's death, as if I'm somehow to blame for the fact that Jeff assaulted me, that I somehow invited it, encouraged it. Vince never gave your sister those pills; he never put them in her hand. She acted on her own. But you can't accept that. You have to hurt someone. You think it will somehow wipe out what she did.'

'You don't know what the hell you're talking about,' he snapped, almost savagely.

'Don't I?' Eden flared. 'Maybe you need to ask yourself just who you are trying to punish. Vince? Or yourself? Isn't it your own guilt you can't live with? But you can't accept that so you shove all the blame on someone else. That way you can feel noble.'

'That's not true.'

'Isn't it? She was crippled in an accident. She probably forgave you for your part in it long ago. But you never forgave yourself. Now you're going to make Vince pay for it. That isn't noble. That's twisted.' She kicked her horse into a lope, bringing the quirt down sharply on its rump, and riding away from Kincade. Tears burned the back of her eyes.

By daybreak, the ghostly expanse of Black Rock Desert was behind them and the cattle were loosely bunched around a grassy seep, their noses to the ground, idly tearing off mouthfuls of the seared yellow grass. The smell of bacon, flapjacks, and strong coffee drifted from the chuckwagon. Kincade filled his plate and went over to a shady area to eat by himself, apart from the others. Rusty wandered over and sat down next to him. Kincade never acknowledged his presence with a word or a look.

Rusty scraped the last bit of food from his plate, then set it aside and took a couple idle sips of his coffee. 'It's amazing how far sound carries in this desert country,' he remarked and stared off across the sage-dotted hills. 'It's like being out in a boat in the middle of the lake and hearing people talking on shore, as plain as if they were right beside you.'

Kincade took a drink of his coffee and said nothing.

Rusty smiled. 'She gave you a real tongue-lashing.'

'She doesn't know what she's talking about.' Kincade's response was curt and irritated.

'I don't know.' Rusty tipped his head to one side and gathered up his plate, then pushed to his feet. 'I don't think Marcie could have said it better.'

He walked off, leaving Kincade to chew on that. It wasn't something Rusty expected his friend to swallow easily or readily. The truth was rarely palatable.

They let the cattle rest and graze all morning. In early

afternoon, they drove them a few more miles to better water and bedded them down for the night.

The next day they established the routine they would follow for the rest of the trek: rising before dawn and in the saddle before the sun was above the horizon, lining the herd out to make the morning's march. At noon they stopped for a two-hour respite to let the cattle graze and keep their weight on. Then it was on the trail again until almost sundown.

The second night out Kincade cornered Eden as she approached camp lugging her saddle. He faced her, his hard features set in cold, uncompromising lines. 'I'll see your cattle all the way to market,' he told her. 'After that all bets are off.'

'As far as I'm concerned, they were never on,' Eden replied, just as cold and hard as he was.

25

After six days on the trail, they were almost a full day ahead of schedule. Shortly after one o'clock, they pulled out of their noon camp, as always leaving Wild Jack behind to follow after he had stowed the last of the gear in the chuckwagon and hitched the team.

Kincade rode drag with Rusty, an easy task since the cattle stepped out as if eager to be on the move again. The terrain was a gently rolling plain capped by acres of blue sky. A dozen pronghorn antelopes observed the passage of the herd from the crest of a hill, showing their usual curiosity, tails flicking in jerky little slaps.

Better than an hour from the noon camp, Bob Waters galloped back from his position near the point. He pulled up and swung in alongside Kincade.

'The boss wondered if you had seen any sign of Wild Jack yet?' he asked, turning in the saddle to scan their back-trail.

'No.' Kincade looked back as well. 'He should have caught up with us by now.'

'That's what I thought. I'd better ride back and see what's keeping him. He might need some help.'

'I'll go with you,' Kincade said and called over to

Rusty. 'We're going back to look for the chuckwagon. Keep an eye on Rossiter.'

Rusty signaled his understanding with a wave. Together Kincade and the cowboss peeled away from the herd and galloped back over the trail. They were nearly to the noon camp when they saw the chuckwagon with only one horse hitched to it. The other was gone. So was the cook, they discovered.

Kincade dismounted and first checked the horse to see if it had gone lame, then walked around the wagon to see if there was a problem with it. Bob Waters studied the tracks Wild Jack had left.

'I don't profess to be a great tracker,' Bob straightened and looked to the west with a thoughtful frown, 'but it looks like he unhitched the horse and rode off, heading west.'

'I think I've found the reason.' Kincade stared at the broken bottles of vanilla extract scattered over the ground behind the wagon. When the cowboss joined him, Kincade examined the small cupboard door hanging open in the back of the wagon. 'It looks like the latch broke and his supply of vanilla spilled out when he was coming up this incline.'

'Ten to one he's headed for the bar in Gerlach or else the lodge outside the reservation.' Bob Waters swore softly and succinctly. 'He took off with the damned harness still on the horse and we don't have a spare along. Old Dandy is strong,' he waved a hand at the horse still standing in the traces, 'but he isn't strong enough to pull this wagon by himself. We'll have to leave it and take what food we can carry.'

'The pack saddle is still in back,' Kincade remembered. 'In two days we'll be in Oregon. Three days at the outside. We can load the horse down with enough supplies to get us by until we get there.'

'We'd better get started,' the cowboss said, then

sighed in disgust. 'That damned cook better have a couple whiskeys for me.'

When they finally caught up with the herd, Bob Waters explained the situation to Eden and concluded with, 'I left a note pinned in the chuckwagon saying who it belonged to and that we'd pick it up on our way back through. I didn't want some rancher to come across it and think it had been abandoned.'

'If we're lucky, no one will spot it.' Privately Eden hoped that would be the case. She didn't want anyone's curiosity being aroused, not when they were so close to their destination.

That night Rusty was assigned to the cooking duties. But he didn't have the luxury of the chuckwagon's propane stove. He had to use an open fire.

'What the hell do you call this?' Vince held up a biscuit in disgust, showing the charred bottom on it and the doughy center. 'This food isn't even fit to eat.'

A beleaguered Rusty instantly bristled. 'If you think you can do better, go ahead.'

Tired and irritable, Eden snapped, 'Vince, just shut up and eat. None of us could do any better and complaining won't change it.'

Grumbling to himself, Vince scooped up a spoonful of beans. Like the biscuits, they tasted scorched and half-cooked. No one went back for second helpings.

Late the next morning, they reached the highway on the northern edge of the state. Scouting ahead, Eden looked in both directions, but there wasn't a vehicle to be seen for miles. The only thing visible was the canopied roof of a combination gas station and convenience store nearly a mile down the road.

Bob Waters rode up, the herd strung out behind him. When he reined in next to her, Eden wasted no time issuing instructions. 'It's all clear. We'll station two riders on the highway, one on each side of the herd, just in case a car comes. I want the cattle taken across in a hurry. About a mile north there's a big hollow. We'll noon there.'

'Done.' Bob Waters immediately rode back to issue more specific instructions of his own. 'We're taking them across now. The boss has the point. She'll lead them over. Al, Kincade, I want you two to push the leaders. As soon as they're across, peel off and take up a position on the highway. The rest of us will bring up the rear. No dawdling. Keep them moving at a trot.' He paused. 'Any questions?' When none were offered, he nodded. 'Okay, let's move out.'

The lead yearlings eyed the pavement suspiciously, then trotted across it without a fuss. Kincade reined his mount in a big half-circle and took up his post several yards from the herd, watching as the cattle streamed across, pushed by the following riders.

The sun came straight down, setting up a heat fog that deepened out on the flat. Refracting layers of hot air trembled up from the baking pavement, distorting Al's shape on the other side of the herd.

Whistling shrilly between his teeth, Vince rode his horse onto the highway and swung wide to come close to Al. 'Al, have you got some cash on you?'

'Some. Why?' Al eyed him warily.

'That convenience store down the road – they make pizza. I don't know about you, but after eating those leather weights Walker called flapjacks this morning, I want something decent to eat at noon. I only have enough cash on me to buy two pizzas. If everybody is as hungry as I am, it's going to take more. You want to chip in or not?'

Al dug deep in his pocket and came up with a couple of wadded bills. He handed them over to Vince. 'No damned peppers. They give me gas.'

'Thanks.' Vince swung his horse off the highway and spurred it into a run.

On the opposite side of the herd, Kincade stood up in his stirrups when he spied Vince taking off. 'Where's Rossiter going?' he shouted the question across to Al.

'After pizza,' Al yelled back.

Kincade swore and checked the impulse to go after him when he heard a vehicle behind him. He glanced back as a camper slowly crawled to a stop.

A ten-year-old boy stuck his head out the side window. 'Look, Dad! It's a real cattle drive with cowboys and everything.'

Impatient, Kincade scanned the trailing riders and finally spotted Rusty. He shouted and waved his arm until Rusty lifted a hand in response. 'Rossiter,' he yelled and pointed to the rider galloping toward the distant convenience store. 'Go after him!'

Rusty immediately swung away and hurried his horse across the highway, then shipped it into a run after Rossiter. The last of the yearlings trotted across the highway and Kincade swung in behind them, trusting that Rusty wouldn't let Rossiter get away.

At the noon camp, the mixed herd spilled into the grassy basin and the crew came together in a loose group. Kincade watched the lip of the hollow, tension bunching his muscles with each passing minute. Then he heard the drum of hooves. An instant later Vince crested the rise, holding aloft four cartons of pizza tied together with a string. Rusty came behind him, balancing a Styrofoam cooler on the saddle in front of him.

'Pizza and cold beer.' Vince stepped out of the saddle. 'This is what I call good eating.'

Deke came up to take the cooler of beer from Rusty and wasted no time in removing the lid and hauling out a six-pack from its bed of ice cubes.

'Any problems?' Kincade asked the first chance he had to see Rusty alone.

'None. He was right inside the store when I rode up.'

Kincade lifted his hat and ran a hand through his hair, his glance straying to Rossiter. Instinct said not to trust the man, not to take his actions at face value. Eden was with Vince, her hat tipped back, laughing as she tried to scoop up a strand of stringy cheese that stretched from her mouth to the pizza slice in her hand.

'Do you think he made any phone calls?'

Rusty thought about that. 'He already had the pizzas ordered when I got there. He might have had time to make a call, but it would have been a fast one.' He looked at Kincade. 'You're thinking he could have phoned DePard and told him where we are?'

'It's the way his mind works,' he concluded grimly. 'He'd do it now just to spite me.'

'What do you think we should do?'

'Just keep our eyes peeled for DePard. Not much else we can do.' He slapped a hand on Rusty's shoulder. 'Come on. Let's get some of that pizza and beer before it's all gone.'

A gold Cadillac sped across the sage flats, throwing back clouds of dust to trail like a banner behind it. DePard was bent over the wheel, his gaze fixed on the catch-pens directly ahead of him. He slowed as he neared them and laid a hand on the horn, the loud, intermittent blast of it carrying above the din of bawling cattle and barked orders.

Sheehan sat atop his big bay horse, one leg hooked over the saddle as he watched the work in the pens. When he heard the honking of the car's horn, his head came up alertly. He recognized the Cadillac and instantly straddled the saddle, walking the gelding forward to meet the car when it stopped.

DePard rolled down the window. Heat and dust poured in. 'Starr just called the house.' Frustration and anger edged his voice. 'Eden Rossiter is driving her cattle to market. She's nearly to the Oregon border now.'

Sheehan stiffened, then swung out of the saddle. 'Frazier,' he called to one of the workers in the pen, 'take care of my horse,' he ordered, then climbed into the car and slammed the door.

In short order, DePard passed on the message Starr had given him. 'We should have anticipated a daring stunt like this from her.'

'A cattle drive,' Sheehan repeated, still trying to take it in. 'How close is she to the border?'

'Close, that's all Starr said. Which could mean two miles or twenty.' DePard reversed the car and pointed it back toward the Diamond D headquarters, accelerating. 'Get Pete on the radio,' he said crisply. 'Tell him to get the plane out, have it fueled and the engine running. We'll be there in,' he checked his watch, 'twenty minutes.'

The shadow of the twin-engine Beechcraft swept over the dull white playa of Black Rock Desert and climbed the granite-toothed range of mountains beyond it, then raced up the long, broad valley. At the controls, Duke DePard brought the plane down to a lower altitude, his gaze always moving, searching, combing the land below for the moving herd and its attendant riders. Darkly tinted aviator lenses protected his eyes from the glare of the afternoon sun.

Sheehan occupied the right seat, making his own visual sweep from his side of the aircraft.

'We're coming up to the highway.'

'I see it,' was DePard's clipped response.

'Do you see anything yet?'

'We'll find them. You can't hide that many cattle in

open country like this,' DePard said as they flew over the highway and left it quickly behind them.

'We might be in the wrong area,' Sheehan suggested.

'We'll make this run. If we don't find them, we'll swing wider, hit more of the mountain areas,' DePard stated. 'But I still think she'll take this route. She can make better time and her idea is to strike fast. She planned to be there and back before I ever found out she was gone.' He leaned forward, his attention focusing on the long dark stripe against the tawny yellow of the high plains grass. 'Wait a minute. What's that?'

'Where?' Sheehan stretched his neck, trying to see.

'At ten, nearly eleven o'clock,' DePard identified the position. 'I'm going down a little lower.' He pushed the plane's nose down in a shallow descent.

'I see it.' Sheehan pressed close to the windscreen, his voice quickening in discovery. 'It's them.'

'Let's make sure it isn't some other rancher with his cattle.' DePard dipped a wing for a better view as they flew by the herd at a scant thousand feet off the ground. Sheehan trained his binoculars on the riders.

'It's Rossiter, all right. That's Al Bender down there,' Sheehan confirmed. 'I know for a fact he's still riding for her.'

'Now we know where she is, but where is she going? The way I see it, she has two choices, the Eastern Plains sale barn or—'

'I vote for Ike Bedford's,' Sheehan said and pointed. 'It's on the other side of that ridge of mountains. If she takes the pass, she can be there by late tomorrow.'

Climbing to a higher altitude, DePard flew over the spiny mountain ridge and on to the cluster of buildings surrounded by matchstick-size pens seven miles beyond it. Circling the site, DePard studied it from the air and agreed, 'You're right. She'll go to Bedford's.'

'You've got her now, Mr DePard.' Sheehan settled

back in his seat with a satisfied look. 'Bedford can be persuaded to refuse delivery of her cattle. She'll be stuck out here. And no one is going to let her cattle eat their grass for long. You can deal her fits.'

'I know.' DePard completed another circle and headed back over the route Eden Rossiter would take. Nearing the mountain range, he flew lower and inspected the gap in its bony ridge and the easy slope leading to it from both sides. 'She'll lose a day going around this range. She'll take them through the pass,' he confirmed for himself Sheehan's earlier assertion.

Again the herd showed up as a long dark splotch in the near distance. DePard took aim on it, then swooped low to buzz the herd.

'What are you doing?' Sheehan protested as he stared at the upturned faces of the riders below. 'They'll know it's us.'

'I want her to know,' DePard smiled, putting the plane into another climb and setting a course for the Diamond D. 'You know what she'll do now, don't you?'

'What?'

'She'll push the cattle through the pass tonight and try to make it to Bedford's by morning.'

'It won't do her any good. You'll have Bedford in your pocket by that time.'

'I know.' DePard leveled the plane out at ten thousand and adjusted the trim tab. 'Do we still have some of that dynamite left?'

Spooked by the low-flying aircraft, the herd threatened to scatter. It took better than twenty minutes to get them bunched and settled down again. Eden joined the knot of riders on the near side of the herd and reined in to give her hard-breathing horse a rest. Too late she saw Kincade on the other side of Rusty Walker and her brother.

'Looks like they've quieted down pretty good,' Bob Waters observed.

'Just the same, we'll give them a few more minutes before we move out again.' She spied Al Bender slowly walking his horse around the herd.

'That was DePard in the plane.' Vince gave her a hard, you-should-have-listened-to-me look.

'I know.' The Diamond D insignia on the plane's tail had been impossible to miss.

'I wonder how he knew where to find us,' Kincade mused, sliding a look at Vince. 'It couldn't be that you made a quick phone call to him back at that convenience store.'

Indignant, Vince straightened from his slouched position in the saddle. 'I never called DePard.'

'Are we splitting hairs now?' Kincade taunted.

'What makes you so sure it was me? Why couldn't it have been Wild Jack? Or the note Waters left on the chuckwagon?'

Eden broke up the argument before it went further. 'It doesn't matter how DePard found out. It's spilled milk. He knows and now we have to deal with that.'

'How?' Vince scoffed.

Eden had thought about that. In truth, she had thought of little else since she recognized the twin-engine plane. 'If we keep moving, go through the pass tonight, we might make the sale pens before DePard gets to Bedford.'

Vince stared at her. 'You're crazy.'

'The way I see it, it's the only chance.' Eden saw Vince was prepared to argue that point, and she wasn't in the mood for it. 'You and Kincade give Deke a hand with the cavvy.' She nodded to the horse remuda still stirring restlessly a quarter mile from the herd.

'You heard the boss,' Kincade prompted when Vince showed reluctance. Vince threw him a glare and reined his horse away from the group, lifting it into a trot. Kincade followed.

'I think I'll take a turn around the herd.' Bob Waters walked his horse away taking a parallel line to the cattle.

Rusty angled his freckled face toward Eden, a near smile deepening the corners of his mouth. 'You got rid of everybody else. I guess that makes me next.'

His observation was a little too accurate. Uncomfortable with it, she tried to pretend it wasn't true. 'I don't know what gave you that idea.'

'Kincade tells me I get crazy notions now and then.' He watched the line of her mouth tighten. 'You don't like me mentioning him, do you?' Before she could deny that, Rusty went on. 'I was hoping you might have squared things between you.'

'I don't know what you're talking about.'

'Oh, I think you do.' He smiled. 'You've been good for him, you know. When Marcie died, it was like her death had killed all the warm and good feelings inside him. But I've seen them back in his eyes when he looks at you.'

That wasn't something she could safely talk about. Yet, she didn't want to ride off and end the conversation. 'You knew his sister?'

'I was in love with Marcie since high school. But she never looked at me that way. To her, I was like another brother.'

Eden listened for bitterness, but heard only regret. 'Then you must hate Vince, too. As much as Kincade does.'

'No. I tried to for a while. I almost made it a time or two,' Rusty admitted. 'But you would have had to have seen how happy Marcie was with him. How can you hate a man who can make a woman that happy? You would have thought she owned the world.' He smiled at the memory, and his smile had nothing but fondness in it.

'But . . .' Eden was confused. 'Look how much he hurt her when he left.'

'I know.' Rusty nodded. 'I also know if Marcie were alive, she wouldn't hate him for that. She'd be hurting bad, but she wouldn't hate him.'

'You seem very sure of that.'

'I am. I know Marcie, and I know Kincade. You told him some things that are hard for him to swallow. Right now it's got his back up. But after he chews on it awhile, it'll go down.'

'I only want Kincade to leave my brother alone. I'm not interested in anything else from him.' She didn't want his friend to get the wrong impression.

'If you say so.' Rusty looked off into the distance. 'It's funny all the things that go through your mind when someone you care about dies. All the things you're sorry about, all the things you regret. You're always wondering if there was something you should have said, something else you should have done, that might have made a difference,' he mused. 'Marcie was always a quiet and timid girl. She didn't make friends easily even before she got her leg hurt. Then afterward . . . the limp made her even more self-conscious around people she didn't know well. I guess Kincade and I were both guilty of protecting her a little too much.'

'That's understandable.'

'When she met your brother, she blossomed like a rose in the full sun. Love took her too high. Losing pushed her too low. I would have been there for her.' He looked at Eden, his voice tight, his eyes bleak with grief. 'If she only had reached out, I would have been there. I guess that's what I'm most sorry about. That she couldn't bring herself to reach out. She was afraid, you know. She'd been hurt, so hurt that she was afraid to reach out to someone else. And that's when you need to do it the most. Remember that, Miss Rossiter. Marcie didn't.'

He bent his head down and reined his horse away to slowly circle the herd. Hurting inside, Eden watched him.

The cattle were a moving tide of black traveling up the barren mountain slope. The dull thud of their hooves was occasionally punctuated by the scrape of a hoof on stone. With only a quarter moon hanging in the sky, the night was dark, and the breeze tunneling through the pass ahead of them had the nip of winter's breath in it, a warning that the season wasn't far off.

Eden rode near the front of the herd. Farther ahead, at the point, Bob Waters was a dark figure silhouetted against the wash of stars. Her tiredness lifted a little at the sight of him skylined ahead of her. The leaders were nearly to the summit of the pass.

The ground began to level out beneath her horse, and the cattle nearest her broke into a trot, as if knowing the long climb was nearly over. Her horse tugged at the bit, eager as well. Smiling, Eden glanced ahead again and saw a shooting star arc across the sky and disappear from view, blocked by the curve of the mountain pass.

Suddenly Bob Waters wheeled his horse around and threw up an arm, shouting, 'Look out!'

Startled, Eden checked her horse. At almost the same instant, there was a deafening *boom* that shook the ground. The side of the pass erupted in a black shower of flying rock and dirt.

Her horse reared straight up, twisting from the blast. The air and ground vibrated with another series of explosions that hurled more debris into the air. Frantic, Eden clung to the horse's back, fighting to keep her balance when it wheeled and lunged into the air again.

Fleeing cattle blocked its path of flight. More slammed into its side. Somewhere, the cowdog barked.

On the other side of the herd, Kincade had a glimpse of Eden's pale face as her horse skyed again, then came down and vanished behind a swarm of black shapes. Her horse was down. Eden was down. Fear leaped into his throat and lodged there.

He barely had control of his own mount as he whipped it into the maelstrom of frightened cattle, his eyes glued to the spot where Eden had disappeared. Some separate part of him kept waiting, convinced he would soon see her standing there against the onrush, swinging her quirt, carving out an island of safety in the midst of a black sea. With each passing second that it didn't happen, his fear grew.

Desperate to reach her, he drove his horse through the thinning tide, whipping, spurring, and cursing. Halfway across, he saw her horse trot off riderless. He never noticed the explosions had stopped, that the only sound was the loud and eerie rumble of hooves and rubbing hides. Farther down the slope came the barking of the dog, the shouts and shrill whistles from the trailing riders trying to turn the herd and check its blind flight.

A rider streaked into Kincade's view, taking a high path along the curving wall of the pass. He plunged his horse down it and bailed out of the saddle before the horse came to a full stop. Eden lay motionless on the ground, her face ashen in the darkness. Kincade reached her a full second after the other rider knelt beside her.

He piled out of the saddle at a run, his heart pounding with dread. 'Eden.'

Before Kincade could drop to his knees beside her, Vince stopped him with a savage glare. 'Stay away! Don't you come near her.' He gathered her up, carefully cradling her upper body in his arms.

'Is she—' Kincade couldn't say the words. He refused to even consider the answer.

'Dead?' Vince hurled it at him. 'No.' The answer came out in an ugly snarl. Then Vince looked down at her face, his expression and his voice softening. 'No, she's just . . . unconscious.' He glanced at the blood on the hand cupping the back of her head. 'She hit her head when she fell. Her pulse is still strong.' He lifted his head and looked at Kincade again. 'She's alive – no thanks to *you*.'

Kincade stood there, needing to touch her, to hold her, to see for himself that she was all right.

'You did this to her,' Vince accused bitterly. 'You encouraged her to make this drive. If you hadn't been around, I could have talked her out of it. I could have protected her. Dammit, I knew DePard would never let her get away with it. That was him up there.' He jerked his head toward the summit of the pass. 'Him and his men. Throwing dynamite. That's how crazy he is. Why the hell do you think I've been trying to get her away from here? One of these times he won't be satisfied with just scaring her. He'll deliberately harm her. That's how twisted up with hate he is.'

Bob Waters rode up, saw Eden, and immediately swung out of the saddle. 'The boss, is she okay?'

'She will be.' Vince scooped her legs up and stood. 'I need to get her to a doctor. Catch my horse.'

'Take mine.' Bob Waters led his horse to Vince and helped Vince lift Eden onto the saddle.

'Let me—' Kincade took a half step toward them.

'No,' Vince snapped, warning him off again. 'I don't need anyone to come with me. You stay with the cattle, deliver them to the pens – if you can.'

Kincade watched him ride off with Eden in his arms.

'Come on.' Bob Waters laid a hand on his shoulder, then drew it away. 'Let's get these cattle pointed back in the right direction.'

26

Morning sunlight bounced off the glass doors to the emergency medical clinic, throwing its blinding glare back into Kincade's face as he approached the entrance. Tense and steeled against this moment, Kincade pushed through the doors. Rusty followed a step behind him.

The plump, rosy-cheeked nurse behind the counter glanced up when he walked in. 'May I help you?' She greeted him in a warm, slightly officious voice that didn't match her image as everybody's mother.

'I'm Kincade Harris. I came to see Eden Rossiter. I understand she's here.'

'You're the mysterious Kincade,' she said with a bright twinkle in her eyes. 'She mumbled your name a few times when she was coming around. Her brother didn't seem to know who you were.'

'Then she's still here?'

'Yes, the doctor's with her now.'

Alarm flickered through him. 'Is she all right?'

'Oh my, yes.' The nurse laughed softly. 'Other than a nasty bump on the head, a mild concussion, and some bruises. The doctor's just checking her over prior to releasing her. Not that he has much choice in that. She's determined to leave. She keeps going on about her cattle. Why don't you come with me? I'll take you back. I'm sure the doctor won't mind.'

She came out from behind the counter and walked briskly down a wide corridor to one of the rooms at the end. She pushed the door ajar and peered in. Over the top of her head, Kincade could see the headboard of a hospital bed and a doctor in a white lab coat with a stethoscope for a necklace, but he couldn't see Eden.

'. . . have a dandy headache for a few days,' the doctor was saying. 'The prescription I've given you will help that. Just try to take it easy. Otherwise you're fine.'

'Thank you,' Eden spoke. Her voice sounded strong. Something trembled through him, but Kincade knew better than to analyze it. 'Now may I leave?'

The doctor chuckled. 'We just can't keep you down, can we?'

'Excuse me, doctor,' the nurse interrupted. 'Your patient has visitors.'

He pivoted to face the door, smiling. 'She's not my patient anymore. She's on her own now.'

The nurse pushed the door open wider, and Kincade walked into the room as the doctor walked out. Eden was sitting on the edge of the bed, and the sight of her was like a wild wind spinning through him, lifting him, filling him, stirring up a multitude of needs and wants. She looked strong and vital despite the smudges of fatigue under her eyes.

Unsteadied by the rip of longings, Kincade halted. His glance flicked briefly at Vince. Exhaustion had made hollows of Rossiter's eyes. He was haggard and drawn, going on nerve alone.

'Did you get the cattle penned?' Eden broke the silence when Kincade didn't.

'No. DePard got to the owner first.'

'I told you,' Vince jeered.

Kincade ignored him. 'Bedford refuses to let any cattle

owned by you to pass through his sale barn.' He reached inside his denim jacket and pulled a set of papers from his shirt pocket. 'I'm buying your cattle. Here's a check and a bill of sale for you to sign.'

Eden took the paper from him, glanced at the check, then at the sale document. 'You aren't going to be stupid enough to sign that, are you?' Vince demanded. 'How do you know his check is good?'

'She can call the bank. They'll verify I have the funds to cover it.' Kincade watched her, holding her gaze when she finally looked up. 'I came away from the rodeo with more than broken bones to show for my time.'

'I'll need a pen,' she said.

'Right here.' Rusty stepped forward with one, his smile beaming with approval.

'You aren't really going to sign that,' Vince protested.

'There comes a time, Vince, when you simply have to take some things on trust.' She clicked the pen and wrote her name in the signature blank, then handed the bill of sale back to Kincade.

Hesitant to read too much into her words, Kincade slipped the document back in his pocket. There were a hundred things he wanted to say to her, but he couldn't seem to put any of them into words.

'This isn't going to work, you know,' Vince challenged.

'It will work. Eden doesn't own the cattle anymore. I do. Bedford no longer has a reason to refuse. Even DePard would agree to that.'

'DePard.' Distracted by the mention of his name, Vince turned away and pushed a hand through dark hair that showed the furrows of many such harried finger-combings. 'Every time I think about that dynamite going off and your horse going down – he should be arrested. He could have killed you.'

'But he didn't,' Eden reminded him. 'I'm fine, Vince.'

'This time,' he said grimly and started for the door.

'Where are you going?'

He stopped at the door and looked back, his eyes haunted with pain and guilt. 'I've got to talk to him, make him understand he can't keep doing this. He's not God.'

'He won't listen, Vince.'

'Then I'll make him listen.' He charged out the door.

'No—' Eden stood up too quickly. Pain slammed through her head and the room swayed. When she grabbed for the end of the bed, her fingers closed around Kincade's arm.

'Take it easy.' His hands were at her waist, steadying her and trying to ease her back onto the bed.

She resisted their efforts. 'No. I have to go after Vince. I have to stop him.'

'He's a grown man, Eden. He knows what he's doing.'

'You don't understand.' Eden pushed at his hands, her glance racing to the door, then just as swiftly to Kincade's face. 'How did you get to the clinic?'

'I borrowed a pickup from Bedford. Why?'

'Let me have the keys.' She held out a hand, snapping her fingers in impatient demand.

'No.'

'I have to go after Vince.'

'You're in no shape to drive.'

'Then you drive me. I don't care.'

'Look, you're upset.' Kincade tried to calm her.

'Yes, I'm upset. You can't reason with DePard. Vince knows that. I'm afraid—' Eden cut off the thought. 'If you won't take me, let me have the truck.'

'What is there to be afraid of? DePard isn't after your brother. And Vince certainly doesn't need you to protect him.'

'He's my brother. If you won't help me, then get out of my way.'

Kincade's temper was on a short fuse, and she just lit it. 'Dammit, Eden, you've been hurt. You can't go tearing off by yourself. You may not have the sense to recognize that, but I do.' She started to argue and Kincade shouted her down. 'Your brother, your brother, that's all I hear. He's twisted us both up in knots. Me, with the way he used Marcie. And you, with his gambling debts and his lies and his petty deceits. Yes, he loves you in his own peculiar way, but that doesn't change what he is.'

'And it doesn't change the fact that he is my brother. I can't let him go off like that. I can't take the risk that he might—' She stopped again, breaking off the sentence.

'He might what? Get hurt? Let him. It's time he got hurt after the way he's hurt so many others. Are you so blind that—' This time it was Kincade who stopped, memories flashing, pieces suddenly fitting together, changing the entire picture. 'Or has everyone else been blind? Including me.'

'I don't know what you mean,' Eden murmured, all caution and wariness.

'Just what is it you're afraid your brother might do? Try to kill DePard, maybe? Why would you think he might do that?' Kincade watched her, measuring every guilty shift and change in her expression.

'He wouldn't.'

'Wouldn't he?' Kincade remembered too well Vince's attempted ambush of him. Taking Eden by the shoulders, he shoved her into Rusty's keeping and pulled the bill of sale from his pocket. 'Take care of this.' He handed it to him, then pointed to Eden. 'And keep her here.'

He was out of the room and striding down the corridor by the time Eden managed to recover and pull away from Rusty. He shifted to block her path to the door.

'I'm going after them,' she told Rusty. 'Either with you or without you.'

'I already figured that out, so calm down. I'll do the driving, but first we've got to find ourselves some wheels.'

Dust churned up by Vince's vehicle hung in the air when Kincade drove into the town of Friendly. He spotted a gold Cadillac El Dorado parked next to a Diamond D Ranch pickup and slammed on the brakes. The old truck fishtailed at the abuse, then jerked to a stop. A station wagon with Oregon license plates sat next to the Cadillac. Kincade swung in beside it and climbed out.

Even before he opened the door to Starr's, Kincade recognized Rossiter's voice raised in anger. He stepped inside and made a quick survey of the scene. Roy was behind the bar, managing to look less bored than usual. Starr stood close to the action.

DePard sat at a center table. Sheehan stood to his right, his chair pushed back from the table. DePard tipped his head back, regarding the angry man facing him with untroubled ease.

'You said yourself she'll be all right, Vince,' DePard said calmly. 'I don't understand what you're upset about.'

'Goddammit, she's my sister,' Vince raged, leaning both fists on the table. 'I won't let you go on hurting her.' He had his back to the door. He didn't see Kincade walk in.

'If you really want to protect Eden, why don't you tell DePard who really shot Jeff?' Kincade challenged.

Vince whirled, his face going as white as the shirt DePard wore. His reaction confirmed Kincade's suspicions.

'I don't know what you're talking about,' he insisted. 'I wasn't even there.'

'Is that why you look sick? Why don't you turn around so DePard can see your face, Vince?'

Vince's tongue flicked out, wetting dry lips. He threw a quick glance at DePard and tried to laugh. 'This is ridiculous. The man doesn't know what he's talking about.'

'Don't I? You've got guilt written all over you,' Kincade said.

'That's a goddamned lie!'

'Is it? What happened that night, Vince? Did you get scared when you found out Jeff had died? Did you decide that Eden would have a better chance of getting off if she had been the one defending her honor instead of you? Were you afraid a jury might not be quite as sympathetic? That you might serve some jail time?'

'Shut up. Dammit, shut up.' Vince swung a fist.

Kincade saw it coming and dodged it. The blow glanced harmlessly off his shoulder. Kincade threw a quick jab to the ribs. Vince staggered sideways, recovered his balance and came back at Kincade like a wild man.

Intent on the brawling pair, no one noticed when Rusty and Eden walked in. A hard right to the jaw sent Vince crashing against the mahogany bar. His hat flew off, landing at Starr's feet. Eden gave a little cry and started forward. Rusty stopped her.

'It's all but over now,' he told her as Vince sagged, holding himself with an arm hooked over the bar top, his legs rubbery beneath him.

Kincade grabbed him by the shirt front and half hauled and half dragged Vince from the bar, then pushed him into a chair. He leaned down, a hand gripping each armrest as he brought his face close to Vince's.

'You ready to talk, Vince?' Kincade breathed hard from the brief but violent fight.

Eden stole a glance at DePard. DePard had backed up to give the fighters room. His expression was one of impatience and sharp interest.

'Come on, Vince.' Blood trickled from a corner of Kincade's mouth. He wiped at it with the back of his hand. 'Talk.'

'Damn you,' Vince murmured, his face crumpling.

'I've been damned for a long time. Now, talk. It was you that night, wasn't it? You went back to the Spring after you dropped Rebecca off, didn't you?'

'Yes.' It was barely more than a whimper.

'Louder, Vince,' Kincade ordered. 'DePard can't hear you.'

'Yes, dammit. Yes!' Vince shouted the words in belated defiance. Kincade pushed back from the chair and straightened to stand erect. 'Jeff dragged Eden out of his truck.' Vince hurried to explain. 'Her blouse was torn open. She was . . . she was trying to get away from Jeff. He was mauling her, forcing her back to the blanket. I yelled at him, told him to let her go. But . . . he just laughed. That's when I saw the rifles in his truck. I only meant to scare him,' Vince insisted. 'I thought when he saw I had a rifle, he'd let Eden go. Instead he started coming toward me, taunting, laughing.'

Kincade turned away and Vince saw DePard. He leaned forward, lifting a hand in a beseeching gesture. 'It isn't what you think, DePard. I never meant to shoot Jeff. One minute he was jeering. Then – he lunged for the barrel. I don't even remember squeezing the trigger. The rifle went off. It just went off. You've got to believe me. It was an accident.'

'You bastard.' DePard took a step toward him.

Kincade held up a hand, checking the movement. 'When did you decide Eden should take the blame?'

'I never even thought about it until the old man – Jed – took it for granted that she had shot Jeff. That's when I got the idea.' Vince looked up, and immediately looked down at the floor. 'I didn't want to go to prison.'

'So you sentenced your sister to one,' Kincade said in

disgust. 'With DePard for a warden, and the ranch for an isolation cell.'

Vince hung his head lower. 'I knew it would be hard for her at first, but I thought it would all blow over after a while.'

'It didn't though, did it? It only got worse.'

Vince nodded, then looked up. 'How did you know about Jeff? No one else ever guessed.'

Kincade sighed a humorless laugh. 'Maybe I recognized the signs of a guilty conscience. I don't know.'

'What will happen now?' Vince glanced around uncertainly.

'That's up to DePard. Not me.' Kincade turned and saw Eden. He walked over to slide a hand on her shoulder and draw her forward. 'I guess it depends on whether DePard has a conscience or not. Eden was never anything but a victim.' He looked straight at DePard, demanding that he acknowledge that. 'First a victim of your brother, then of you and everyone around here. It's always hard to admit when you're wrong. But if Vince hadn't shown up that night, if your brother had lived, he would have been guilty of rape. To me, that would have been a lot harder to live with. That's why you've been doing your damnedest to cover it up, isn't it? But the louder you shouted his innocence, the guiltier you were.'

'You have no right to talk to him like that.' Sheehan stepped up.

'Let him be,' DePard ordered.

Kincade studied him. 'I have a feeling you won't be doing anything about this, will you? You'll let Vince walk rather than see this whole thing splashed across the headlines again.'

DePard glared at him, then looked away, recognizing there was nothing to be gained.

Vince rose cautiously from the chair, then hesitated, his glance darting around the group as if he wasn't entirely sure he would be allowed to leave unharmed. He took a step, then another. As he headed toward the door, Starr picked up his hat and moved to intercept him.

'You're not coming back this time, are you?' she guessed, her voice pitched low, intended for his hearing only.

'No.' He took the hat from her. 'The kid needs a father he can be proud of. I'm a loser, Starr. I always have been.'

He turned and walked swiftly toward the door, his head down. When he reached Eden, Vince paused uncertainly. 'I'm sorry, Sis, I've got to go.'

'I know.' She realized he couldn't bring himself to face the stares, the talk, the censure that would follow this.

'You'll be okay,' he said to assure himself.

'Of course.'

He threw one last hurried glance over his shoulder and walked out the door. With his departure, there was a small stirring in the lounge. The attention shifted to DePard. Feeling it, DePard flexed his big shoulders and cast a challenging glance at the watching faces. His mouth tightened beneath his heavy mustache.

'Let's get the hell out of here,' he muttered and strode stiffly toward the door, certain Sheehan would follow him. He did.

But DePard's steps slowed when he drew level with Eden. He stopped, his chin lifting a fraction, his expression cool and harshly proud. 'It seems a mistake was made.' It was clear from his tone how difficult it was for him to say those words, how much he resented the necessity of them.

'It was,' Eden agreed with an equal amount of pride in her carriage. 'But don't bother to apologize, I wouldn't want you to choke on it.'

DePard stiffened at the invisible slap. 'That attitude is unnecessary.'

'Probably. Right now you want to offer an apology only for appearance's sake. If you are ever truly sorry, I'll accept your apology.'

Resentment darkened DePard's eyes. He stared at Eden and trembled on the verge of temper, then walked out.

'A lot of people will find it awkward for a while,' Kincade warned.

'I know.' Eden sighed, her shoulders slumping a little. She lifted a hand and pressed her fingers against the throbbing in her temple.

Rusty immediately led her to a chair. 'You better sit down a minute.'

Her lack of an argument proved the need for it. All three of them took a seat around a bar table. Starr came over.

'How about something to drink? Beer? Coffee? It's on me.'

'Coffee,' Kincade said, and the others nodded in agreement.

Starr moved away, leaving the three of them alone. Rusty stretched back in his chair and eyed Kincade.

'Vince left,' he reminded Kincade. 'Do you want me to follow him?'

Kincade shook his head. 'Let him go. It's over.' He glanced at Eden. 'I had to do it. The lie had lived too long.'

'It's probably best that the truth came out,' she agreed.

'Why did you do it, Eden? Why did you say you were the one who shot Jeff?' Kincade had his own thoughts on that, but he wanted to hear her reason.

'I don't know.' She lifted her shoulders in a light shrug. 'Vince had killed a man to protect me. Taking the blame seemed a small thing to do for him. Neither one of us thought any of this would happen.'

'No, I suppose not.' A run of silence followed his

words. Kincade studied Eden, watching for some sign that would give him an insight to her feelings, but she avoided his eyes. 'With Vince gone, there isn't any reason for me to stay – except you.'

She lifted her head, her expression guarded. 'What am I supposed to say to that?'

'You could say you want me to stay, if you mean it.'

'We still have the remuda to drive back and the chuckwagon to pick up. And there's always plenty of work at the ranch.'

'That isn't what I meant and you know it. If I stay, I'll look at you whenever I want. Put my arms around you, steal a kiss, and I won't care who's watching. There won't be any "Yes, Boss," "No, Boss."'

Eden wrapped her hands together, trying to keep control over that sudden surge of joy inside. 'I'm not used to someone fighting my battles for me.'

'Like today, you mean,' Kincade guessed. 'I wasn't fighting that battle *for* you. I was fighting it *with* you. There's a difference. Do you want me to stay?'

She looked at him. 'I don't want you to go.'

'That's good enough for now.' Kincade smiled, watching the pleasure come into her eyes and feeling his own chest swell with the fierceness of it.

Rusty hooked an arm over his chair back and beamed at the two of them. 'Wasn't it Shakespeare that said, "All's well that ends well"?'

Eden looked at Kincade, mirth sparkling in her eyes, and they both started laughing. Rusty glanced from one to the other and frowned in bewilderment as they laughed some more.

'What did I say that was so funny? Come on, what'd I say?'

They just laughed.